# The Trouble With Panthers

William Culyer Hall

*The Trouble With Panthers*

Author copyright 2010, William Culyer Hall

ISBN 10:  1-886104-42-5
ISBN 13:  978-1-886104-42-6

The Florida Historical Society Press
435 Brevard Avenue
Cocoa, FL 32922
www.myfloridahistory.org/fhspress

P•R•E•S•S

For my Father

# Publisher's Note

The primary mission of the Florida Historical Society Press is to preserve Florida's past through the publication of books on a wide variety of topics relating to our state's diverse history and culture. Our non-fiction books include *Florida's Big Dig: The Atlantic Intracoastal Waterway From Jacksonville to Miami, 1881 to 1935* by William G. Crawford; *Jacob Summerlin: King of the Crackers* by Joe A. Akerman, Jr. and J. Mark Akerman; and *Henry Plant: Pioneer Empire Builder* by Kelly Reynolds. Our latest non-fiction titles include an updated reprint of the classic book *Palmetto Country* by Stetson Kennedy; *Conservation in Florida: Its History and Heroes* by Gary White; and *Florida's Freedom Struggle: The Black Experience from Colonial Time Through the New Millennium* edited by Irvin D.S. Winsboro.

Our goal of disseminating Florida history to the widest possible audience is also well served by the publication of novels firmly based upon scholarly research. Teachers and students alike find that our high quality fictionalized accounts of Florida history bring the past to life and make historic events, people and places more accessible and "real." Our critically acclaimed novels include *DeLuna: Founder of North America's First Colony* by John Appleyard; *Saving Home* by Judy Lindquist; and *Hollow Victory: A Novel of the Second Seminole War* by John and Mary Lou Missall. Some of our other popular titles include *Canaveral Light* by Don David Argo; *Florida's Frontier: The Way Hit Wuz* by Mary Ida Bass Barber Shearhart; and *A Trip to Florida for Health and Sport: The Lost 1855 Novel of Cyrus Parkhurst Condit* edited by Maurice O'Sullivan and Wenxian Zhang.

This novel, *The Trouble With Panthers* by William Culyer Hall, is a bit of a departure for the Florida Historical Society Press. Set in 2004, it can not be properly called an historical novel. The fictional family depicted in the novel, though, has been in Florida's cattle industry for several generations. Their struggles with contemporary change very accurately reflect what many pioneer families are going through as they attempt to adapt from Florida's past to an inevitable future. As the wise old Native American Solomon tells the earnest young cattleman Bodie Rawlerson: "What has been will be again. What has been done will be done again; there is nothing new under the sun." We believe that this book will promote thoughtful discussion about our state's pioneer history and its relevance to contemporary society, which is why we proudly present it to you.

Dr. Ben Brotemarkle
Executive Director
Florida Historical Society
September 2010

# Author's Note
# And Acknowledgements

The Trouble With Panthers is entirely a work of fiction. Certain historical names are used for the sake of realism, but no character is based on or intended to depict an actual person. All episodes and dialogues between characters are products of the author's imagination.

The author would like to thank Mr. Gilbert A. Tucker, and his sons Andy, Fred and Burt, for the insight they graciously offered on cattle ranching in Florida. Thanks also to Gilbert's grandson, Drew Tucker, who made the cover of this novel possible.

*No man knows when his hour will come:*
*As fish are caught in a cruel net,*
*or birds are trapped in a snare,*
*so men are trapped by evil times*
*that fall unexpectedly upon them.*

*Ecclesiastes 9:12*

**When** *suddenly cast in shadow, the boat builder looked up from his labor and turned and squinted over his spectacles to see what could so thoroughly dim an August sun. A dark figure stood in his shop's doorway, a featureless silhouette tall and unmoving. "Can I hep ya?" the boat builder said, and, though having no inkling why, immediately regretted having said anything.*

*"I've come to purchase the black airboat you have parked out front," said the stranger, stepping forward and striding to within an arm's length of the stooped old craftsman.*

*Upon seeing the stranger's unblinking blue eyes and pleasant countenance, the old man visibly relaxed. He wagged his head from side to side. "That black one ain't for sale," he said. "A feller done bought and paid for that one."*

*The stranger stood stone-faced. "I'm willing to pay a high price," he said, "very high indeed."*

*The old man again shook his head. "Don't make no difference. I cain't sell what ain't mine."*

*At this the stranger nodded and casually revealed the blade palmed in his right hand. "No," he said. "I suppose you can't."*

**In the hour before dawn** Seth Rawlerson leaned against the barn directly below the Curlew Cattle Company's sole nightlight. A still, amber figure, he stood one-legged with a boot jacked back against the concrete wall, a lit cigarette wedged in the fingers of his right hand. He waited, gazing at the outlying darkness, listening to the mercury-vapor lamp hum above his head. When the boy led a saddled horse from the open barn bay to his left, Seth drew on the cigarette and turned sufficient to address his son.

"You run across any trespassers out there," he said, "don't go tryin to be no hero. You come get help."

The boy halted the Appaloosa and turned and grasped the pommel horn and swung effortlessly into the saddle. He looked down at his father, the horse stepping and standing and tossing its head. "Yessir," he said. "I ain't feelin one bit heroic. It's all I can do to keep my eyes open."

Seth Rawlerson exhaled twin streams of blue-gray smoke from his nose. "Well see that you don't let old Sol talk you into nappin when he peeks over the trees. We got to be in Daddy's office at eleven sharp." Rocking forward, the cowman then pushed away from the barn wall. He dropped the cigarette to the ground and snuffed it with his boot. "Just check the north fence and come on back. You find any breaks, don't try to patch 'em. We'll take care of it after the meetin. You got that?"

Casting his father a sideways look, the boy squared his hat and shifted the reins to his right hand. "Yessir. It's a lot to remember, but I reckon I got it." That said, he nudged the horse's flanks with his heels, and the animal stepped into the surrounding night.

Seth momentarily stood mum, staring at the dark void now before him, listening to the waning clop of hooves. Then he smiled and shook his head and muttered: "smartass."

*

The near-full moon already set, the boy rode blindly at first, trusting the horse and memory while waiting for his pupils to dilate. He headed due north, negotiating two cross fences in rapid succession, opening and closing the galvanized metal gates without dismounting, with scarcely a rattle of steel or break in forward momentum. Once beyond the encumbrances, he urged the horse to a brisk walk, following a trail etched in each of their minds by simple repetition. It was early November and the Florida morning pleasantly cool, the promise of a new day slowly thinning the eastern edge of night, a fine, peaceful beginning, and in it, no warning of any sort.

He rode the fire-stunted flatwoods northward for more than a mile, sitting the horse with a poverty of movement, the beast but an extension of him, himself, merely an augmentation of horse. They passed through low palmettos, wiregrass and solitary pines, the steady chop of the horse's hooves muffled by sandy soil, its great head sawing slowly from side to side, its ears scissoring to the sounds of a day surely eminent: whistling flights of wooduck and merganser; the single-noted covey calls of quail; phantom deer snorting their disdain for his human intrusion; the woof of a startled boar hog flushed from the trail. He rode and the darkness thinned and the raspy cry of thrush birds formally announced the dawn. When he crossed a sandy, deep-rutted tram—a woods road known to his people as "the cemetery reach"—the open flatwoods gave way to wind-wrecked forest, to mature yellow pines evidencing the storms of August and September, the Hurricanes Charlie, Frances and Jeanne. Here, he sawed the horse through many felled trees, through those still standing but bending to a wind long gone. He rode, and soon the pines abruptly ended at a wall of bone-gray cypress, a dense swamp where night still lingered.

The boy entered the swamp following a faint trace, a century old log-drag hold-

2

ing water tea-brown and mirroring the early morning sky. As he advanced, the water rose to the horse's brisket and the Appaloosa began to lunge, whereupon the boy kicked out of the stirrups and hooked his bootheels over the saddle's bow. He rode thusly for almost a minute, the horse plowing ahead with him rocked back in the saddle. Then the water began to recede. The ground rose up, and he rode from the swamp and its attending darkness with his horse all sleek and steaming, tossing its head jauntily. Without pausing he guided the animal up a cattle trail girded by thick palmettos, up a slight incline and on to the northern boundary of his family's property. There, at the four-stranded, barbed wire fence, he stopped the horse in a plowed firebreak and allowed the Appaloosa to shake. He sat for a moment, looking and listening.

Beyond the running fence a mixed stand of liveoaks and pines bustled with activity, a circus of squirrels in the oaks, a roiling swarm of crows blacking the crowns of the taller pines. The boy watched the crows with great interest, marveling at their number. Seeing the birds now, so soon after three powerful hurricanes, he pondered how they had survived such wind. And in his pondering, he ultimately concluded they had not, that the raucous birds were surely tourists, snowbirds timing their invasion to avoid the suffering side of Florida. "Them's Yankee crows," he said aloud. Then he bumped back his weathered Stetson and reined the horse westward.

He followed the fence at a leisurely pace, occasionally listing in the saddle to examine some particularly interesting sign in the plowed ground, but mostly just daydreaming and reveling in the beauty of the morning, the sun warming his back, his new shadow stretching long and thin over the ground ahead. He rode, and in an hour he'd seen plenty of sign but no breaks in the fence, no storm-leaned trees having succumbed to gravity, none affecting the fence anyway. And a few minutes on there were no longer trees to evaluate, those populating each side of the fence suddenly ending and the single-filed posts of the fence left to march westward through a treeless plain, through waist-high switchgrass and a few squatty wax myrtles. And beyond the tall waving grass lay seemingly nothing, a great void where sky and earth blended seamlessly together.

The boy stopped the horse and sat looking and listening. He squinted against the haze of distance in studying a horizon completely unreadable, a mirage, a ragged formation of dark clouds. He smelled fish and decaying vegetation. He heard an osprey's shrill racking cry. Then he twisted in the saddle to locate the sun. Nine

3

o'clock, he judged, no later than nine thirty. He turned back and reached and stroked the horse's neck. "Let's take a peek at the lake," he said, and the horse shook its head and emitted a low whicker. "We got time—long as you don't let me get distracted." Then he clucked the horse forward, veering from the fence, quitting the firebreak and angling southwest through the stirrup-deep switchgrass. Shortly, he saw the shimmering water of Lake Kissimmee, and something else that instantly quickened his pulse.

The unnatural arc of an airboat cage was just visible above the switchgrass. He stopped the horse and stood in the stirrups. Definitely an airboat. He settled back in the saddle. Shifting the reins to his left hand, he reached back with his right and slid his grandfather's rifle from its boot scabbard. He looked at the model 1873 Winchester, a lever action forty-four-forty in his family's possession for more than a century. He felt the weight of it in his hand. Then he stood the weapon on his thigh and put the horse forward at a walk.

He rode directly toward the beached craft, his eyes panning the lakeshore, the switchgrass sawing peacefully in the wind, the woodline behind and to his left. A common egret stalking the shallows near the boat. Redwing blackbirds flitting among cattails farther out in the lake. Nothing of consequence. No human presence. He rode, and when nearing the boat, he half-turned the horse and halted it and sat surveying the scene with the Winchester balanced across his lap.

The gleaming black airboat was of the everglades-style: decked-over aluminum hull, an oversized grass-rake angling up from the bow, 0540 Lycoming aircraft engine, front and rear pedestal seats with an empty rifle scabbard rising next to each. A black hardhat sporting an aircraft landing light lay stowed beneath the front seat. Several spent beer cans floated in the sump hole below the engine.

After studying the boat, the boy leaned in the saddle to examine the muddy ground: several boot prints heading due east, the prints of one man heading straight into Rawlerson property. He righted himself, looking again at the boat, at the tracks. Then he dismounted and dropped the reins and walked forward cradling the rifle in his left arm. He circled the expensive craft slowly, admiring its every detail. Upon reaching the stern, he stopped to puzzle over strange words painted in large white script on each of the two rudders, the words *Lusus Naturae*. As he pondered the words' meaning, a shot rang-out in the palm hammock to the east.

The boy flinched at the sudden report, his head swiveling to the sound. He scanned the distant hammock's edge for movement. Nothing. He walked to his horse and swung into the saddle. He spun the animal northward and set off at an easy canter, riding up shore a short distance to an isolated clump of wax myrtle. There, he reined the horse around behind the squatty trees and halted it, the horse standing agreeably still as if knowing instinctively what was expected of it. The boy waited, watching the distant tree line through his leafy concealment. He did not have to wait long.

In a scant few seconds something moved at the hammock's edge, something dark emerging from the trees, something nebulous, a shadow come to life. Then, upon reaching direct sunlight, the shadow instantly morphed into a man dressed in full camouflage, a tall man shouldering a long gun and strolling casually toward the airboat, his hooded parka and wraparound sunglasses promoting an insect-like appearance at a distance.

His heart drumming audibly in his ears, the boy watched the man walk for a moment. Then he stepped the horse from behind the screening myrtles and rode forward at a fast walk, setting a course to intercept the stranger at the boat. He rode with his eyes fixed on the walking man, with the Winchester's brass butt-plate pressed to his thigh, its muzzle poling skyward.

Upon seeing the approaching rider, the man scarcely reacted, offered but a casual turn of the head, a brief glance, no sudden movement of any sort. The man merely continued his leisurely pace toward the airboat. And when reaching the craft, though the mounted boy was a scant sixty yards away, the man did not look at him. He stepped over the gunwale and climbed up to the front seat and turned and sat down. He sat watching the boy come, pump shotgun bridging his legs, gloved hands drooped over the weapon in a relaxed manner, his great insect eyes giving away nothing, his mouth a thin line of ambiguity.

When but a few yards from boat's bow, the boy thumbed the old Winchester's hammer back and stopped the horse. He sat watching the man watch him. He could see himself sitting his horse in each of the darkly tinted lenses. "Mornin," he said.

The man initially offered no reply. He turned his head first left then right before focusing again on the boy. "Yes," he said. "And a fine one at that."

The horse blew and stepped nervously. "In case you didn't know, this is private property," the boy said. "We don't allow no huntin—no trespassin of any kind."

The man turned and looked up and down the shore. He looked at the boy. "I arrived before daylight. I didn't see the signs." He reached and removed the sunglasses, perched them atop his hooded head. Blue eyes. Pleasant countenance. "Please accept my apology. My transgression certainly was not intentional."

The boy looked at the nearest no-trespassing sign, one tacked to a post a few yards down shore and just barely visible amid the tall switchgrass. He looked at the man. "I reckon they are gettin kind of hard to see."

The man nodded. "Especially in the dark."

"What was you shootin at?"

The man smiled sheepishly. "At—is correct," he said. "I missed an enormous wild boar."

"You missed."

The man nodded. "Didn't cut a hair. Suppose I'm lucky to be alive—some of the horror stories I've read about boar."

"You ain't from around here, are you?"

"No. No I'm not."

The boy leaned and spat. "Well just so you know. Takin hogs off another man's land is considered rustlin in Florida. It's a felony offense."

The man's eyes widened. "No kidding. Well my poor marksmanship was a fortunate thing, I suppose."

The boy nodded. "Well, no harm done, I reckon. But you best be movin on. Somebody else ketches you, they might not go so easy. Armed trespass is a third degree felony by itself. Even if you don't kill nothin."

The man stood and turned the pumpgun and slid it into the scabbard standing next to his seat. He smiled at the boy. "Consider me gone," he said. He sat down and reached and flipped a couple of toggle switches on the panel next to his right arm. He looked at the boy. "Say," he said. "You mind if I ask you a question?"

The boy looked.

"Your Winchester. It's a *One of one thousand,* is it not?"

The boy glanced at the rifle. "It's got that engraved on top of the breech."

"Yes, I know it does. I'm a collector of sorts. I have an eye for old firearms."

"Yessir. I reckon you do."

"How much will you take for it? I want to buy it."

"It ain't mine to sell."

"I'll pay top dollar. Maybe as high as ten thousand."

"It ain't for sale."

The man reached for the sunglasses atop his head. He slipped them on, touching them back on his nose with a finger. "Not for sale," he said. He sat very still for a long moment. Then he reached with his right hand and pressed a pushbutton switch on the control panel. The starter motor whirred and the boat's wooden prop began to turn slowly.

The boy began backing his horse. By the time the boat's engine fired, he was far enough away that the horse scarcely stiffened. When he spoke to it, the horse settled and continued to back until the boy halted it to watch the noisy proceedings at the water's edge: the man gunning the engine and sawing the control stick to and fro, the boat beginning to sway and the roar of the engine deafening and the man suddenly hauling back on the stick and the boat spinning leftward and shooting forward and onto the surface of the lake. As the craft roared away, a blast of wind and spray hit boy and horse, and the man threw up a hand and gave a little wave.

Easing the hammer down on the rifle, the boy swung the weapon back and slid it into its scabbard. He removed his Stetson and turned it in his hands while watching the airboat drag an ever widening V far across the lake. He looked at the hat and then set it on his head. "Seemed like a all right feller," he said. He leaned and spat and turned the horse and rode toward the hammock, toward the point where the man had emerged from the shadows.

Upon entering the trees, he paused momentarily to let his eyes adjust to the deep shade. Then he stepped the horse slowly forward, his eyes panning right and left. He found the dead hog after traveling only a few yards. Stopping the horse, he leaned forward, his arms crossed over the pommel horn, his eyes fixed on the carcass below. He shook his head and said: "I done been played for a fool, Limpkin."

The black feral animal was not large, the boy judging it to be about fifty pounds, a young sow that had never given birth, the left side of its head a bloody mess, mangled by a full load of buckshot administered at very close range.

Stepping down from his horse, he rolled up his sleeves and fingered his Case pocket knife from a pant pocket. He opened the knife's three inch blade and knelt down and quickly gutted the shoat with the horse standing and watching. After rolling the carcass onto its belly to allow the cavity to drain, he stepped to the horse and fetched a short length of pigging string from his saddle bag. Returning to the hog, he cut incisions behind each of its four knees, a slit between tendon and bone through which he threaded the string. He then drew the cord tight and tied it off, teepeeing the pig's four legs together. Next, slipping a hand between the front

7

and back legs, he lifted the animal like a crude satchel. He turned to the horse, the Appaloosa eyeing him suspiciously, flaring its nostrils and blowing but standing its ground. "It's just a little old pig," the boy said, "nothin to get all boogered over."

After hoisting the pig and hooking its bound legs over the pommel horn, he led the horse back out of the hammock, back to the lakeshore. At the water's edge, he dropped the reins and hunkered down to wash his hands and arms while the horse stood resignedly behind him, both the lake and the boy mirrored in one of its great chestnut eyes.

When the boy again mounted up, he glanced at the sun and then reined the horse around and urged it to a lope. He rode southeast, angling toward the same hammock where he'd gutted the pig, the palms and oaks above which the sun now hung suspended in its full glory, the sun and, just to the right of it, a wispy spire of pale smoke. Seeing the smoke, the boy abruptly halted the horse and sat studying the rising column in puzzlement. The horse tossed its head and stepped nervously, as if wanting to continue, as if knowing instinctively the smoke was a thing to be ignored.

"Now what?" the boy sighed.

He stepped the horse forward, shifting his course slightly to align with the smoke before entering the trees, before losing sight of it altogether. Inside the hammock, deep shadow once again hindered his sight and prompted him to advance cautiously. The ground strewn with storm debris: twisted and torn oak branches and fallen bromeliads; dry cabbage fans announcing loudly virtually every step the horse took. He rode slowly, weaving through the trees and the solemn stillness holding beneath them. And shortly the trees parted to encircle a small clearing in whose center stood a solitary and ancient orange tree, a tree whose lineage was said by his grandfather to date back to a time when Spain had thought to possess the sandy soil from which it grew. The boy had seen the tree before, had visited it on occasion to enjoy its sweet offerings. He also was familiar with the three elongated mounds to the right of the tree, had been told by his father at an early age that the mounds were Indian graves and never to be molested. But he had never seen the person who now sat cross-legged next to the mounds. A person that, from the back, appeared to be a woman, an elderly woman with long gray hair flowing about rounded shoulders, a woman whose strange and colorful dress was mindful of a rainbow, one having been captured and tailored in the long ago but now faded and tattered, fallen to ruin. The flames of a small oak fire licked directly beyond the woman, its smoke rising skyward like a product of her like-colored hair. As he watched, the woman did not move. She was still as the three mounds beside her.

Seeing the person, the boy briefly halted the horse and sat transfixed. Then he turned the horse right and walked it around the clearing's edge, slowly, so as not to unduly frighten the stranger. The ground littered with palm fronds, the horse raised a clatter but the woman gave no indication she heard. She merely continued to sit, gray-brown hands resting on bared calves of the same color, head slightly bowed as if sleeping, or possibly praying. Her attitude did not change as the boy maneuvered the horse directly before her and stopped it and sat peering down displaying a look of surprise.

His woman was a man, a very old Indian whose strange demeanor seemed to render the boy temporarily mute. For a long moment he sat the horse in silence, watching the old man and trying to decide what to do, the gutted pig pressing against his knee, the horse standing stock-still, head high, ears pricked forward. And when finally finding his voice, the boy said: "You know you're on private property, mister?"

The old man did not move.

The horse bowed its neck against the reins and tried to turn, but the boy would not allow it.

"You're trespassing on Rawlerson land," he said. "You're gonna have to leave."

At this, the man slowly raised his face to the boy. But he did not open his eyes. He opened but one eye, for where his left one should have been existed only an empty socket, a fleshy crater scarred so darkly as to resemble a cavern of infinite depth.

"But where would you have me go?" the man said.

When the one-eyed man moved and spoke, the horse rolled its two eyes and shied wildly. The boy instinctively hauled back on the reins and pulled its head down. But the man's appearance also unnerved the boy. Several seconds passed before he could calm the horse and muster a reply.

"Back to wherever you come from, I reckon," he said, not looking at the man's face, but rather at the plethora of jewelry and trinkets hanging from the man's neck: hammered coins cascading down his chest like crescent-shaped rungs of a silver ladder; a crucifix, a Star of David, a jade Buddha figurine, some strung sea-

9

shells, the claws of some animal. The boy looked and cocked his head in puzzlement and looked again, his thoughts wandering and then realigning. "Long as you
get off our property, I don't much care where you go."

The old man replied by reaching out a misshapen hand, by using it to scoop
some of the sandy earth upon which he rested. Then, his singular gaze fixed on the
boy, he extended the hand, palm up, as if making an offering of the soil. "Ah," he
said, "but this *is* where I come from." He slowly turned the cupped hand, allowing
the sand to drain to the ground. "How can I return to a place I never left?" He then
withdrew the hand, returned it to rest on his calf. "I go nowhere, young Rawlerson, for I am already there."

The old man's riddle-speak perplexed the boy. He looked up and swiveled his
head trying to locate the sun. Then he simply looked around, as if a solution to his
problem might lurk in the surrounding hammock. "If you're still here when I
come back, you'll go somewhere. You'll go to jail."

The man nodded. "Bring me some food when you return, some of the tobacco
you smoke. Do this for me, and maybe I will tell you things you do not want to
know." He again nodded and then bowed his head and became very still, the
smoke from the small fire lifting before him, accentuating just how still he'd
become.

The boy watched the man a few seconds longer, then turned the horse eastward
and rode from the hammock. In the open flatwoods he set a course for home, alter-
nately cantering and walking the horse for most of the three-odd miles. Upon
reaching the barn, he quickly hung the pig in the shade of the open bay then
looked to his horse.

He was rubbing the Appaloosa down when his father appeared, his father wearing an accusatory look and scolding him for not allowing time to properly care for
his horse. And as they hurried to his grandfather's meeting, he excitedly tried to
relate the unusual events of his morning to his father, tried to impress upon him
what an extraordinary morning it had been. But his father offered no comment.
His father walked in silence, striding quickly, eyes fixed straight ahead, seemingly
not surprised by anything the boy said, seemingly indifferent until they reached
July Rawlerson's office door. At the office door Seth stopped and turned to look
his son in the eyes. "What part of come-get-help did you not understand?" he said.

The boy dipped his head and looked at his boots. He looked at his father. Then,
exhaling audibly through his nose, he said: "Yessir."

**When the airboater** reached the far side of the lake, a middle-aged woman stood waiting between his truck and hitched trailer, a petite woman wearing jeans, a gray flannel shirt and an obvious scowl. Watching him come. Standing very still, and remaining so even as the airboat roared onto the trailer and to within inches of her person. But the instant he switched off the engine, breaking into a maniacal dance and unleashing a scathing diatribe: "Just what the hell do you think you're doin, mister? This is private property. That was a twenty damn dollar lock you murdered up there on my gate. I just bought the damn thing."

Paying the woman but a glance, the man climbed from his perch and commenced to strap the airboat down for travel. "I'll give you fifty dollars for your trouble," he said without pausing from his work.

"Fifty!" The woman exclaimed, brushing back a wild tangle of hair trying to claim her face. "I don't want no fifty. I want your sorry ass arrested. What's your name?"

The boat secured, the man reached and captured his jacket, pulled the pumpgun from its scabbard and turned to fix his cerulean gaze on the woman. "You don't want to know my name," he said.

The woman looked. She took a step back. "I ain't scared of you."

"You should be."

She waved a hand toward his truck. "I don't need to know your damn name, anyway," she said, turning to go. "I got your plate memorized."

To this the man replied "not for long" as he nonchalantly swung the pumpgun up one-handed and shot her in the back of the head. He then stepped forward and knelt beside her convulsing body. He lay his jacket aside and reached and slipped a cameo ring from a still twitching hand. "Very nice," he said, holding the prize up to the light and turning it right and left, "very nice indeed."

**2**

**July Rawlerson** needed neither words nor gavel to call the meeting to order. The patriarch of the family had only to fix his piercing gaze on the five people gathered in his small office, the hush following being palpable testimony of the power still residing in his dimmed and faded eyes. Yet no such look was necessary to quiet his eighteen-year-old grandson, John Garbodie Rawlerson. Bodie, as he was called, had not uttered a word since entering the room and seating himself next to his father. Amongst his elders, Bodie spoke only when spoken to.

The old man, a toothpick protruding from his mouth, sat with his elbows resting on an even older desk, a polished mahogany escritoire trimmed in brass-riveted leather. He cradled a manila folder in hands scarred and speckled by too many suns to remember, Florida suns and no other. When his audience was quiet, he cleared his throat, glanced at the folder and asked: "Fore I get started with this, there any urgent ranch business needs discussin?"

Seth Rawlerson looked at his foreman Pete Stalvey and, when Pete responded with a little wag of his head, shifted his gaze back to his father. "Nothin cept a little problem with a trespasser," he said. "Bodie caught a feller up in the northwest corner this mornin—an air boater that had killed a hog."

The old man's eyes narrowed. "Ain't no such thing as a *little* trespassin problem," he said. He looked at his grandson. "How'd you handle it, boy?"

The boy glanced at the hat in his lap. He turned the Stetson with his hands and looked at his grandfather. "Well sir," he said, "I reckon I didn't handle it too

13

good."

The old man was silent, continuing to stare at the boy.

"When I found his boat, I figured the best thing to do was back off—wait for him to come to it. I'd done heard him shoot, so I had a pretty good idea where he was."

"And?"

"He came to it. Didn't have to wait but a minute or so. He didn't try to run or nothin."

"So what was his excuse? They always got an excuse."

"Said he didn't know the land was posted—didn't see the signs when he come in fore daylight. Promised not to ever do it again. Said the shot I heard was him shootin at a wild boar. Said he clean missed."

"A wild boar?"

The boy nodded. "Yessir. He wasn't from around here. That was pretty obvious."

"And you believed him—his story about not knowin he was trespassin and all?"

"Yessir. I did. I swallowed it hook, line and sinker. But after he left, I found the hog he shot. Findin that shoat told me he was probably lying about everything."

The old man reached and plucked the toothpick from his mouth and looked at it and put it back. "So what you reckon you taught this feller—ketchin him like you done?"

The boy shrugged his shoulders. "Nothin, I reckon."

The old man was shaking his head even as the boy answered. "No. You taught him plenty. You taught him there ain't no consequences for poachin Rawlerson property."

"Yessir."

"Pain's the only thing will make a lastin impression on a poacher. You ketch him and don't hurt him, you're givin him an open invitation to steal you blind." The old man paused briefly and chewed his toothpick. He stared at the boy. "A poacher's weak point is his pocketbook, you know. You stomp on his pocketbook, and he ain't apt to come on your place again."

The boy fidgeted in his chair. He turned and looked at Pete Stalvey, but the foreman refused his appeal. Pete Stalvey's eyes remained focused straight ahead.

"You understand what I'm sayin?" the old man said.

"No sir," the boy said. "I mean, I'm not sure."

14

July leaned forward a bit. "Well looky here," he said. "That feller had a airboat, right?"

"Yessir. A real nice one."

The old man tapped the desk top with an index finger. "Well next time—and there likely will be a next time for him—don't go tryin to actually ketch the bastard. Confrontin armed poachers alone ain't the smart thing to do. You find his boat like you done, you use it to get the point across. You make sure he ain't got a boat to come back to. Burn it. Knock holes in the hull and sink the blame thing. Either one works damn well. I know, cause I've done both—done it more than a few times."

The boy was silent.

"Now I know what you're thinkin, boy. You're thinkin destroyin another man's property is just plain wrong. And I sure cain't fault you for thinkin that away. But when it comes to protectin your property, you got to take drastic measures. If you ain't willin to get down and dirty, there's plenty out there more than willin to take advantage of you." July paused and scratched the top of his head. "And callin the law ain't no solution. Leastwise, not for us Rawlersons. Us Rawlersons handle matters our own selves. Always have." The old man cut his eyes to Seth.

Seth nodded. "Yessir, always have."

July looked at the boy. "I don't mean to sound like I'm scoldin you, boy. I just want to be sure you know how to take care of yourself. Messin with trespassers is dangerous business, but it's somethin that's got to be done if you make your livin the way we do."

"Yessir. I understand."

"All right," July said. "There anything else?"

Seth smiled and nodded. "Yes, sir," he said. "I'm afraid there is. Bodie had himself some more excitement up there in Orange Hammock. He caught another fellow—an old friend of yours, I believe."

The old man looked puzzled. He mouthed the words: "Orange Hammock?" A look of recognition came into his eyes. He smiled. He looked at his grandson. "You ketch that old one-eyed Solomon, boy?"

The boy swallowed and glanced at his father, his father who had not bothered to mention that he knew who the Indian was. "No sir," he said. "Can't hardly say I caught him. I just seen his smoke and rode up on him."

July looked at Seth and looked at the foreman. He wagged a finger at the two men. "I told you that old Indian wasn't no figment of my magination, now didn't I."

Seth and Pete Stalvey, both grinning prodigiously, nodded in unison. "Yessir, you surely did," said Pete.

July returned his gaze to the boy. "You really seen him, didn't ya?"

The boy squirmed uncomfortably. "Yessir. I wouldn't make somethin like that up."

July nodded his head. He slapped the desk top. "Somebody else seen my old Indian," he said to no one in particular, "after all these years." He leaned forward and stared at the boy. "You try and run him off?"

"Yessir. I tried. He didn't pay me much mind, though."

The old man emitted a choking sound and slapped the desktop again. "Well don't feel too bad. I tried to run that scamp off several times fore I figured out what he was up to. You probably noticed he ain't the easiest feller in the world to figure."

The boy smiled. "Yessir. I noticed."

"Once I come to understand him better, I got to where I looked forward to his visits. Me and him spun a many a yarn, settin round that little old fire of his."

"You say his name's Solomon?"

"It's just a nickname I give him, on account of how he's always quotin from Ecclesiastes. I don't know his real name, or even if he has one."

"He come here cause of those graves in the hammock?"

The old man nodded. "Just payin respects. That, and makin sure ain't nobody messin with 'em. He's some kind of spiritual leader. Lookin after the dead is somethin he's obligated to do."

The boy nodded that he understood.

"You see him again, tell him I said howdy."

"Yessir."

"Ask him how he come to lose his eye. It'll give you an idea of what he's all about." The old man arched his eyebrows. "It's also apt to scare hell out of you."

The boy nodded but said nothing, his eyes shifting between his grandfather and the two men to his right, his father and Pete Stalvey, both grinning as if having shared a joke.

The old man shifted his gaze from the boy. He studied in turn the faces of the two others seated before him, the man and woman whose presence he'd thus far not acknowledged in any way: his youngest son Billy and his only daughter, Jo Beth. He looked and then he lowered his gaze to the manila folder clasped in his hands, the toothpick in the corner of his mouth seesawing. When he looked up, his eyes again shifted between Billy and Jo Beth.

Billy Rawlerson squirmed beneath his father's gaze, fidgeted in a manner belying his age. His younger sister, conversely, showed no emotion of any sort. The realtor/animal rights activist boldly returned the old man's gaze like a mirror fashioned from his own flesh and blood.

"Welcome to Curlew," July said, his demeanor detached as if greeting strangers. "Glad y'all could make it."

His daughter rolled the dark eyes given to her by him. "Just tickled senseless to be here," she said.

The old man's cheeks reddened a bit. He chewed his toothpick.

Obviously amused by his sister's audacity, Billy's mouth briefly hinted at a smile. But that flower never bloomed for it was his turn to address the old man. The used-car peddler shifted a little in his chair, coughed and said: "Thank you, Daddy. Thanks for having us."

After listening to the replies the old man briefly popped his jaws, leaving his toothpick mangled and splintered. He leaned and spat the woody remains on the linoleum floor. When he straightened, he looked at the manila folder and said: "Reckon there's no point dancing round the fire with this. I called you all here to tell you I'm fixin to die—to make a few things perfectly clear while I still can."

The room was silent. Then came the muted sounds of nervous shuffling and clearing of throats. The daughter Jo Beth was the first to speak.

"Why would you say such a thing?" she said. Then she repeated her question, the second rendition sounding like an echo.

The old man did not immediately reply. He turned his head slowly and looked at the many photographs of family and old friends lining his office walls, pictures that were yellowed with age and whose covering glass was no longer clear in its entirety but frosted and hazed where glass and wood came together. Pictures of champion bulls, favorite horses and dogs. He looked, and the room remained silent. Then he sighed and turned back to face his daughter. "Cause it's the truth," he said. "Doc Hutchinson and two specialists done told me so." He raised his hand and tapped the right side of his head above the ear. "Got a malignant tumor in my head the size of a guava, a glioblastoma they called it. Said it's fast-growin, inop-

17

erable."

The room was silent.

"How long have you known?" Jo Beth said.

"Got the second opinion last Friday. But I've suspected somethin was bad wrong for some time."

"The being sleepy all the time," Seth Rawlerson said, speaking to no one in particular, thinking out loud. "And the falls. No wonder you been losin your balance."

The old man nodded. "Splains a lot of things, don't it?"

Rising from her chair, Jo Beth stepped to her father's side. She reached out a hand as if to touch him but did not touch him. "Daddy," she said.

The old man recoiled a little, leaned back in his chair. "Now don't go gettin all motional. You didn't expect me to live forever, did ya?"

Withdrawing her hand, Jo Beth briefly stood looking at him, she, herself, looking like someone having just missed her bus. Then, she merely turned and shuffled back to her chair. She turned and sat and crossed her legs. "How long do you have?"

"Couple weeks, maybe long as six months. That's the best they could tell me."

Seth Rawlerson leaned forward in his chair. "We'll get another opinion. Just cause Doc Hutchinson and his specialists say somethin don't make it gospel."

The old man shook his head. "I seen the pictures. They ain't wrong. Besides, I knew somethin was up. That's why I come to get checked out."

The daughter clucked her tongue. "If you'd gone for a regular physical like normal people, they might could've done something."

"Might could've," the old man agreed.

Seth leaned forward even more. "Did they give you some idea what to expect? I mean, do we need to line up a nurse or somethin?"

The old man tapped the folder before him. "They give me a number to call, one of them hospice deals. But I ain't gonna call it. You do what you want if I go to havin seizures or somethin. They said there might be seizures."

Jo Beth cut her eyes to her brother. "You call that number today, Seth. God knows what kind of red-tape something like that involves."

Seth Rawlerson ignored his sister. "They give you any prescriptions or anything?"

"One, some kind of stuff supposed to calm me down—as if I need calmin down." He paused to snort and roll his eyes. "Main problem I got is stayin awake. Anyway, Pete's already picked it up for me. So if I go to throwin fits, you got my permission to give it to me."

Seth turned quickly to Pete. "You knew about this?"

Curlew's foreman nodded. "I was made to take an oath."

The old man opened the manila folder and began thumbing through the papers within. He studied for a bit then cleared his throat in the manner of one about to give a speech. He peered over his glasses at his audience, made a fist with his right hand and with it pounded the desk top a single time. "Curlew is to remain a workin ranch," he said. "I've said this before, but I'm sayin it now so there won't be no misunderstandin after I'm gone." He paused and looked squarely at his oldest son. "What say you, Seth?"

"Yessir. Never planned no different."

The old man shifted his gaze. "And you, Billy?"

Billy Rawlerson shot a quick glance at his sister, then: "No disrespect intended, Daddy, but why are you asking me? I've had nothing to do with Curlew for almost twenty years."

"Cause your name's on the deed. You want it to stay there, you best promise me you'll abide by my wishes."

Billy fidgeted. "You don't expect me to move back out here, I hope. I've got a business to run."

"Business," the old man said, the word sounding like he'd spat it to the floor. Shaking his head, he stared at Billy. "I only expect you to stay out of Seth's way, let him run this ranch as he sees fit."

"Got no problem with that. He's the expert." Billy paused and improved his position in his chair. "But what do I get out of having my name on the deed? I mean, if I can't do anything with it, what good is that?"

"Same good it's always been. You'll keep gettin them checks I been sendin you the past nineteen years."

The room was silent.

The old man continued to watch Billy for a moment, then shifted his attention to his daughter. He didn't have to say anything.

"And just how long is this to continue?" she said. "Curlew is only marginally profitable *now*. You have to know that raising cattle around here will soon be a losing proposition. What then? Do Billy and I just sit by and let Seth squander our inheritance?"

His daughter's words painted the old man's cheeks with color. "Your brother will find a way," he said. "We always have." He paused and reached and plucked a fresh toothpick from a shot glass on the desk. "This land has been cattle land for almost a hundred and fifty years, daughter. Ain't no Rawlerson ever gonna willingly turn it into somethin else. You agree with me now, or I'll be in Bud Townsend's office fore the sun sets on this sorry day."

The room was silent.

After a long minute, his daughter barked her answer. "Agreed," she said.

With Jo Beth's single word reply, the all-hands meeting was over, signaled by the old man slowly rising from his chair and standing with his hands braced against the desk-top for support. He offered no valediction of any sort. He merely stood and looked until the others also stood and began milling about uncertainly, as if bound by blood not to leave until the old man himself had left. Then he simply turned and shuffled stiffly from the office, taking with him whatever force it was that had so constrained the others. The five immediately turned in unison and began filing to the back of the office, to exit the old man's home. Jo Beth led the way. The boy Bodie brought up the rear, holding his sweat-stained Stetson and mincing his steps as not to clip his father's heels.

Outside, the early November sun stood high in a cloudless sky, a gentle breeze wafted from the west. The boy bummed a cigarette from Pete Stalvey and the two of them lit up and stood smoking beneath a great liveoak, the sole remaining tree in the old man's yard after the hurricanes. They watched Seth bid farewell to his brother and sister and then watched the sleek black Mercedes pull silently away on the marl ranch road, the luxury auto rocking and weaving as it negotiated the many potholes and washouts wrought by the storms. They watched the sedan grow smaller and smaller and ultimately vanish behind a gray haze of cypress almost a mile distant. Then they quit watching, and the foreman dropped his cigarette and snuffed it with his boot.

"Good thing we had us a dry October," he said, "That low-slung German Caddy couldn't of made it out here a month ago."

The boy flicked his cigarette into the drive. "That's a fact," he said.

The foreman cast a sideways glance at the boy. "So you seen the Indian, did ya?"

The boy looked. "Yessir. I did."

Pete Stalvey smiled and shook his head and scuffed the ground with his boot. "Well I'll be doggone."

"I take it you and Daddy ain't never seen him."

"Ain't nobody but July ever seen him. Leastwise, until now."

The boy kicked at the ground. "Well I sure as hell seen him."

Pete looked at the boy. "I reckon you did," he said. He stood silent for a moment, then: "The old man don't realize how much things have changed, you know."

The boy cocked his head slightly. "Changed how?"

"You go to burnin boats these days, you liable to get yourself shot."

The boy was silent.

The foreman studied something in the distance, a caracara sitting perched in a pine east of the old man's house, a Mexican eagle, a creature now common but one nonexistent to him a scant few decades prior. "You best go with your gut feelin out there. Your poachers ain't likely to be your granddaddy's."

The boy leaned and spat. "Yessir."

The foreman looked at the boy. "What you fixin to do, now?"

"I'm fixin to go butcher me a pig."

"That shoat's gonna be some fine eatin."

Bodie smiled and dipped his head. "You got that right."

\*

Though well past noon, Angela Rawlerson wore a pink cotton bathrobe as she sat rocking on her front porch. She watched Seth and her son approaching, watched them walking side by side and crossing the narrow corridor of pasture between her home and July's. She wore a pained expression, for though Bodie was now taller than Seth, he still shadowed his father and, she felt certain, would never cast one of his own. A cigarette was lodged between the fingers of her right hand and she drew on it then flicked it to the ground below the porch. She then reached with the same hand to capture a glass from the floor below her rocker, seemingly timing the move so her husband could not possibly miss seeing her down the last swallow of Bloody Mary.

Both man and boy stopped at the foot of the steps to stomp their feet on the concrete slab there for that purpose. They sat and removed their boots and stood them to the side before ascending to the porch in their stocking feet.

21

Angela watched all of this, but did not speak until her husband stepped next to her. "Well?" she said.

Seth Rawlerson stopped suddenly, as if noticing his wife for the first time. "Well what?"

"Afternoon, Mama," the boy said

"What was the big meeting all about?"

Seth did not look at his wife. He chose instead to study something even more distant, something beyond the sparse pine and palmetto flatwoods north of his home, something or nothing near the cypress ringing the edge of his world like a gray barrier to change of any sort.

"Daddy's dyin," he said.

"Lord God," said Angela. She reached quickly into the pocket of her robe and withdrew a single cigarette, a Bic lighter. She lit up, inhaling deeply. "You wanna elaborate on that?" she said, exhaling the words on a cloud of smoke.

"He's got a brain tumor. Doctors don't give him too long."

Bodie quietly stepped around his father and entered the house, a clandestine move seemingly unnoticed by either parent.

Angela drew on her cigarette, staring blankly in the direction of her father-in-law's house. "At least he's had a good long life doing what he loved."

"Yeah. I reckon."

"How'd Jo Beth take it?"

"All right, I reckon. Hard to tell with her."

Angela smiled. "I like Jo Beth."

"I know you do."

"I suppose she and Billy'll want to sell the ranch right away."

Seth looked at his wife. He shook his head. "Curlew's gonna stay a ranch long as I'm willin to work it. Daddy made 'em promise."

Angela blew smoke. "He made them promise?" ·

"Yeah, he did."

"And you think they'll honor it."

"Got no reason to believe otherwise."

"Well then you're an even bigger fool than your father."

Seth looked away. He stood a few seconds and then stepped into the house, passing through a threshold at once both familiar and foreign.

**3**

**In the late afternoon** he caught up his horse and saddled the gelded Appaloosa. He rode west toward Lake Kissimmee, following a cattle trail etched deep in the sandy soil, an ancient track winding erratically as though having been coined by thirsting cattle drawn to the lake by a shifting breeze. He rode through native pasture, a mixture of carpet and wire grass dotted with palmettos, gallberry, scrub oak and huckleberry, all low growing and stunted by regular burning. An occasional stand of yellow pine. Bands of hollow-eyed range cattle reacted to his passing with indifference. On several occasions he rode deer from their beds, flagging and high-bounding does and yearlings, an exceptional buck offering scarcely a glimpse as it low-crawled to effect its escape. The appaloosa instinctively tried to run the buck, but the boy held him to the trail and admonished him. "Not today," he said. "He'll leave the country if we run him today. Saturday week, you can pester that old buck till you drop."

He rode without deviation for a mile more, then forsook the cattle trail to follow a pair of parallel ruts overgrown with waist-high broom-sage, the remnant of road snaking southward toward distant trees. As he neared the hammock, deep shadow fostered by its trees began to thin, revealing a house beneath the oaks and palms. Upon seeing the structure, the gelding quickened its step and whinnied and shook its head, prompting the boy to reach and stroke its neck. "May as well settle down," he said. "We're not here to hunt. I just need to see the old place is all."

He rode beneath the hammock's outer fringe of trees and halted the horse and sat looking and listening. Quiet, the silence of a time long passed. The unpainted house was a clapboard cypress cracker home in complete harmony with the liveoaks and cabbage palms fronting it, with the pair of ancient cedars standing shoulder to shoulder with the tin-roofed building. The sprawling yard was free of grass, merely sand and leaves. A short distance to the left of the house, and obviously not nearly as old, stood a rambling pole barn housing a dozen horse stalls, a large concrete-floored dog pen.

Nudging the horse forward, Bodie advanced into the yard, riding past a firepit and on to an old porcelain bathtub, a makeshift water trough fed by a rusty pitcher pump. He halted the horse and dismounted, the Appaloosa stepping forward and sniffing at water in the tub while Bodie stood gazing at the house where his grandfather was born. He stood deep in thought for some time and then turned and spoke words to his horse that he had never said to a human: "I don't hardly know who I am, Limpkin. Now ain't that a sorry thing to suddenly figure out?"

The horse nickered softly and stepped forward and pressed its head against the boy's chest.

The boy smiled and combed the horse's matted mane with his fingers. "I know all about you, though. I took the trouble to learn about you."

A barred owl called deep in the hammock. An acorn struck the house's roof and tumbled noisily down the steeply pitched tin before falling again in silence. The owl called again, confirming to the boy that the sun was indeed setting. He reached and caught up the horse's reins and swung into the saddle. Then, with hat in hand, he spun the horse and pushed it to a lope. At the hammock's edge he turned sharply left, striking due west at a full gallop through low palmettos and wiregrass, the horse's ground-eating stride not wavering for almost a minute, until a once far strand of cypress loomed close and the boy gently tightened the reins. The horse ramped down quickly and entered the gray assemblage of trees at a fast walk, blowing and shaking its head spiritedly, sloshing through shallow water holding in the cypress and on into wax-myrtle and switch grass, beyond which there seemed to be nothing, a treeless horizon, the end of something, or perhaps a beginning.

Emerging from the myrtles, Bodie stood in the stirrups and looked and the lake unfurled before him, a shimmering mirror stretching westward to the edge of the earth, to a half-set tangerine sun he could admire without squinting. To the south a line of fence posts marched from the cypress he'd crossed and on out into the lake.

And beyond the fence, the lakeshore was treeless save for a solitary oak. Beneath the lone oak a saddled bay horse stood cropping grass. The boy smiled and settled back in the saddle and reached and patted his horse's neck. "Your gal's here," he said. But his horse needed no such declaration; it had already begun the arc that would take them to the oak.

He rode to the fence, to a point where the four strands of barbed wire had been cut and reattached to a spindly post not planted in the ground but secured to one that was by loops of stout wire. The bay filly beneath the tree watched their approach. She whinnied loudly as Bodie dismounted and lifted the top loop from the post, and again when he swung the makeshift gate to one side and let it drop. She emitted a low whicker when he and his horse passed through the gap and parted company, Bodie angling toward the lake, the appaloosa walking directly to the bay.

The girl stood waist-deep in water not far from shore but far enough that she bore no resemblance to a girl. She looked like a young man in her faded blue denim shirt and green ball cap, her blond hair only slightly longer than Bodie's. She was fishing, casting a top-water plug with flawless precision, working a Devil's Horse slowly through pickerel weed and lily pads, a stringer tied around her waist and sawing to and fro through the water behind her. She fished methodically, and never once looked back toward shore as the boy approached.

Stopping at the water's edge, Bodie bumped back his hat and hunkered down. He draped his arms across his knees and rested his chin on them as if settling in for a long vigil. He did not speak or gesture to the girl. He simply watched. Across the lake the sun was now gone, the western sky a crimson and gold memorial to its passing. And against this brilliance the girl slowly waded, a silhouette, a shadow of a girl stalking the shallows with the patience and stealth of an egret.

He watched the girl fish for several minutes, until movement in the lillypads to her left caught his eye. Then he slowly pressed to a standing position and spoke to her.

"You're fixin to get gator-caught," he said.

The girl did not respond, gave no indication she had heard him. She merely executed another cast and began patiently retrieving the lure. Then, with the plug almost home, she suddenly acknowledged his existence.

"I'm not worried," she said. "I know a cowboy that'll save me."

In the next instant, as the lure reached her rod tip, she abruptly turned left and threw up her arms. "Go on, git!" she said, brandishing the rod like a scepter.

Twenty feet away the water erupted as something large made a hasty retreat beneath the lake's surface, violently jerking pickerel weed mapping the creature's escape route in the growing darkness. The girl briefly tried to track the subtle movement with her eyes, then turned eastward and began wading toward the boy who was much easier to see, a virtual glowing presence on the shore before her.

The girl herself was beaming, but Bodie, possibly blinded by his position, seemed not to notice.

"You beat everything, Abby," he said. "Ain't you cold?"

The girl slogged to shore, the lake draining from her jeans, bare feet flashing starkly white with each step. Just prior to exiting the water, she paused briefly to hoist the stringer she trailed, the pair of flopping largemouth bass she had been towing.

"Gotcha some supper," she said.

"Already ate."

She continued on past the boy, fishing rod in one hand and strung fish swinging in the other, making for the oak where their horses stood cross-necked. "Liar," she said over her shoulder. "You Rawlersons never set down to supper before dark. You just don't want to clean 'em."

The boy followed, shaking his head. "Cain't believe you're wade-fishin in November. And barefooted! What's up with that? You Thompsons can't afford a pair of runnin shoes, or what?"

As she neared the bay horse, Abby laid the fish and her rod in the grass then straightened and reached into a tote bag dangling from the saddle's pommel. She withdrew a rolled pair of jeans and a towel and laid them on the ground. She was shaking, her teeth chattering uncontrollably as she struggled to unbutton her wet jeans. "Better turn your head," she said, but dropping her wet pants before the boy could possibly react. "If you see me naked, you'll have to marry me."

"For Pete's sake," Bodie said, turning to face the oak's massive trunk.

"Why Bodie Rawlerson, I believe you're blushing."

"Just get your pants on, girl. Fore you ketch your death."

Using the towel to pat the lake from her legs, Abby laughed. "I don't remember you blushing when we used to skinny dip."

The boy scuffed the grass with his boot. "I was too young to know I was supposed to."

Abby laughed again and then dropped the towel and stepped into the dry pants. She pulled them up and zipped them and stepped next to Bodie. "You can look now," she said. A pair of low-cut work boots were at the base of the tree, and she sat next to them and began pulling on the socks they held. "Course, I wouldn't mind if you never turned your head."

The boy looked down at her but did not comment. He waited until she finished tying her boots, then said: "Granddaddy's dyin, Abby."

The girl looked up, stared at the featureless oval the boy's face had become in the thickening darkness. An airboat droned far across the lake. The horses stepped and stood and blew. Leather creaked. A mosquito whined.

"He's got a brain tumor."

Abby looked away. She probed at something in the grass. "I don't know what to say."

"Nothin *to* say. I just thought you ought to know."

When she next spoke, Abby was standing. "I'm so sorry," she said, reaching out to embrace Bodie.

The boy stiffened. He hugged her in return, but only half-heartedly.

Abby released him and stepped back. "You must feel horrible," she said.

"I'm all right."

"How long? I mean—I saw him last week. He seemed fine."

"Doctors told him two weeks to six months. I reckon they just don't know for sure."

"You think it'd be all right if I stop by?"

"Don't see why not. He thinks the world of you."

The airboat droned. A brace of woodducks whistled overhead, the forlorn cry of the female rising and then trailing far to the north, fading until no longer distinguishable. One of the bass flopped briefly in the grass next to the horses.

The girl circled the oak's trunk and then sat at its base. Several dim lights winked at various points far across the lake. She counted them and was not surprised when there were more than she remembered. "It just don't seem possible he could die," she said.

The boy sat next to her, drawing up his knees and embracing them with his arms. "It sure don't."

"Does this change things for you? You still gonna start college in January?"

"Don't change a thing. I wasn't never goin to college."

27

"What?"

"Don't see the point. Ranchin's all I care about."

The girl was silent. A screech owl cried out to the east, a single drawn-out note too subtle to warrant attention from any save its own kind. The horses swished their tails and stood.

"You're just like him," she said.

"Who?"

"July."

The boy shifted uneasily. "You mean that as a compliment, I hope."

"I mean you're both too stubborn for you own good."

"Stubborn?"

"Yeah, stubborn." She reached and touched his arm. "Look, I love your grand-daddy, but you can't deny he's made some bad decisions. It's no secret the Curlew Cattle Company is just barely getting by. And why is that?"

"It ain't his fault. The market was bad for a long time. He did good just to hang on. Darn good."

"Oh, I agree. Considering that cattle is your sole source of income, it's a small miracle y'all didn't go under. But just think how good you could have done if July wasn't so stubborn, if he'd been willing to diversify."

Bodie abruptly sat upright, and the oak bark behind him raked his hat from his head. When the Stetson lodged between the tree and his shoulders, he briefly flailed with his arms to recapture it. "Diversify!" he said, setting the hat back on his head. "Where the hell did you hear a word like that? Diversify my butt."

"From my daddy. He *did* go to college, you know. That's why Thompson Farms is doin just fine. All those years cattle was down, our sod and citrus operations more than made up for it."

"Y'all are doin fine cause you got three times the land we do, three times the cattle."

"Yeah, and three times the expenses."

"Let's change the subject. You're wearin me out."

Abby sighed and shook her head. "Stubborn," she muttered. She leaned closer to him, until their arms were touching.

Bodie shifted uneasily. "I caught some feller poachin this mornin," he said.

"What?

He gestured north with his arm. "He killed a shoat up in the edge of Orange Hammock. Come in by airboat."

"Who was he?"

He looked at her sideways. "If I knew who he was, I wouldn't of said some feller."

Abby was silent. The airboat droned. She studied the lake for a moment then looked at him. "You're in a shitty mood," she said.

"I know it."

They sat without talking for several minutes, then Abby broke the silence. "Y'all still gonna hunt, Saturday week?"

"I don't know. Reckon it'll depend on how Granddaddy's doin. If he's up to it, we'll hunt. We ain't never missed an openin day. At least, not since I been around. You're comin, ain't you?"

"I will if I'm invited."

"When have you ever *not* been invited?"

"You know what I mean—if July's up to it and all."

"If he's up for anything, it'll be that."

The girl suddenly stood. She dusted leaves and sand from the seat of her jeans. "I've got to go, Bodie. Got a Communications paper due tomorrow—one I haven't even started. You want those bass, or not?"

The boy stood and also brushed his pants. "Yeah, I'll take 'em. Too late to throw 'em back. You got anything I can put 'em in? Limpkin's not too fond of fish."

"Course I do," she said, producing a folded garbage bag from her hip pocket. "I come prepared."

"You beat everything," he said.

When they walked to the horses the just-past-full moon hung suspended over the cypress to the east. A misshapen amber globe. A lesser sun rising and revealing a world colorless save for infinite shades of silvery-gray. The horses milled nervously, tossing their heads and blowing as boy and girl moved among them like foraging shadows in gathering their things and stowing them for the ride home. And when their masters mounted them they stomped and stood and turned in tight circles, as that part of them still wild briefly threatened revolt, a revolt that never materialized and never would.

"You be careful," said Bodie.

Abby suddenly leaned in the saddle to bridge the gap between them. She kissed his cheek. "*You* be careful," she said.

And with that they parted, riding from beneath the oak and into the moonlit stillness like apparitions born of nightshade, like mounted specters alike in every way save for their destinations.

4

**When Bodie reached the barn,** he unsaddled his horse and rubbed it down with a sheet of sackcloth. He brushed it and fed it oats and turned it loose in the trap adjacent to the barn. He skinned and filleted the two bass on a scrap of plywood, tossing the carcasses to an audience of cats whose existence in the barn was a thing rarely acknowledged. After washing the meat, he carried it to the house, noting along the way that his mother's Explorer was absent from the circle drive.

When he entered the house his father sat smoking at the kitchen table and did not speak to him. Seth Rawlerson greeted his son with his eyes, a complex look, convivial, but also tired, dejected. The house was very quiet.

Bodie placed the fillets in the stainless steel sink and washed them a second time, inspecting them for bones he might have missed. "You feel like havin some fish?" he said.

"You been fishin?"

"Abby caught 'em. I rode out to the lake to tell her about Granddaddy."

"She out there fishin all by her lonesome?"

"Yessir."

Seth Rawlerson smiled and shook his head. "You better latch onto that girl, boy." He smoked and then tapped the cigarette's ash in the coffee cup on the table before him. "How'd she take the news about Daddy?"

The boy shrugged. "All right, I reckon. It saddened her some, but not so you'd notice. She's not the type to carry on much."

His father pulled on the cigarette, smoked it down to the filter then doused it in the cup. "She's got more sand than most men, that girl. Awful cute, too. Don't you think?"

"Heck, I don't know. We're just buds is all."

Seth's eyebrows arched. "Well maybe I need to be makin you an appointment with the eye doctor."

Bodie was quiet. He floured and fried the fish in canola oil, then made a salad of fresh spinach, tomatoes and carrots. His father made coffee but mostly just watched his only child, an unmistakably prideful look imprinted on his face.

"You gonna make somebody a good wife one day."

"Yeah, right."

He brought the food to the table, along with plates and forks and two paper towels. He got blue cheese dressing from the refrigerator and then sat at the table but did not help his plate until his father was already eating. There were two fillets remaining, but he forked only one onto his plate.

"Boy," said his father, "if there's a better eatin fish than Lake Kissimmee bass, I've not had it." He ate, eyeing the lone piece of fish his son had selected. "You ain't hungry?"

"Not especially."

Seth ate. He gestured with his fork at the fillet between them. "You saved that for your mama, didn't ya?"

"Reckon I did."

"Well I hope she appreciates your thoughtfulness."

The boy stared at his food. "She's bored, ain't she?"

"What?"

"Mama's bored with us. That's why she's always runnin off to town."

Seth swallowed then reached for his coffee. He cupped the mug in his hands and eyed his son over its rim. "I'd like to say you're wrong, but I'll not lie to you. You're only half right, though. She ain't bored with you. She loves you." He sipped coffee and lowered the cup and again looked at his son. "It's Curlew more than anything."

"She's bored with the ranch?"

Seth nodded. "Has been for a long time."

The boy herded a piece of fish with his fork. "I don't get it. I'm never bored out here."

"That's cause it's all you've known. Your mama was born and raised in Miami, you know. Reckon you'd be happy in Miami?"

"I'd sooner be in prison."

"I reckon that's pretty much how your mama has come to feel about Curlew."

"She didn't used to feel that way. What happened?"

"You went and grew up on her."

The boy stopped chewing and looked at his father. He swallowed. "But I'm still here."

"Yeah, but it ain't the same. You got a mistress now, the same one I been preoccupied with for the last twenty years."

"You mean Curlew."

"Yeah, I do. In your mama's eyes you've become me, and that's the last thing she wanted to happen."

"I don't understand it."

"I know you don't."

They sipped coffee.

Seth pushed his plate away and lit a cigarette. He blew smoke straight up and then watched intently as it crawled along the ceiling.

"Why don't you just tell Mama to stay home?"

He looked at his son. "This is the twenty-first century, boy. Stayin home has got to be her idea."

"That ain't no answer."

Seth's eyes narrowed. "It's the only one I got to offer."

"Yessir."

The boy stood and gathered in his plate and fork. He placed them in the sink along with a squirt of dish detergent and turned on the water. "How come we don't have any orange groves?" he said without turning. "Or sod. Why don't we grow sod like everybody else?"

Seth smoked. He stared at his son's back through a thickening haze. "You best sit on them questions till tomorrow. Ask Daddy when you take him for a ride."

The boy turned off the water and half-turned to look at his father. "Take him for a ride? I thought we were cuttin out replacement heifers tomorrow."

"I got Pete and Onnie on that. Daddy wants you to drive him around some. Think he mainly wants to talk."

33

Bodie was silent. He walked to the table and took his father's plate and fork. "He gonna talk about his cancer?"

"I doubt it. Think he wants to talk about you."

Bodie returned to the sink and began washing the dishes. He was lost in thought and did not notice when his father rose from the table and left the kitchen. When he turned to find him gone, he poured a cup of coffee and sat in the chair that was still warm and smoked a cigarette belonging to the one who had warmed it.

\*

A little past nine a vague light briefly wandered the walls of the kitchen. A car door closed. The boy looked at the cigarette wedged between his fingers and then quickly dropped it in his coffee cup, in the cold coffee where two other butts already floated. He fanned the air with his hand and was still fanning when the screen door creaked its warning. When his mother stepped into the kitchen, he sat posed in innocence, slouched with his left arm lying snake-like along the chair's high back.

"Well, hey," Angela said upon seeing him.

"Hey, Mama."

She held a Gucci purse in one hand and a handled Burdine's bag in the other. She set the purse on the counter and opened the mouth of the bag, showing the contents as she came to him. "Gotcha something," she said.

Bodie looked.

"Three pair of slacks and a new belt. And socks. You really needed dress socks."

He sequentially handled the articles, admiring them and smiling appropriately.

"It's a start," she said. "When I'm done, you'll be ready for the cover of GQ." She reached and stroked the back of his head. "Those little UCF girls won't know what hit them."

He put the clothing back in the bag and stood and hugged his mother. "Thanks, Mama," he said. "But you don't need to be spoilin me. I got plenty of clothes."

"A college man can never have too many clothes."

He walked past his mother to the stove. He opened the oven door and reached and got the plate of leftover fish. "You had supper?" he said.

"No, I haven't. What's that you've got there?"

"Fish. And there's salad in the fridge."

Angela smiled. "It was awfully nice of you to think of me."

34

Bodie stepped and stood. "Daddy put me up to it. He figured you might be hungry."

"Oh?"

He set the plate on the table and dragged out a chair. "Go on and set yourself down. I'll get the salad. You want coffee?"

Angela's forehead wrinkled. She studied her son and continued to track his every move, even as she settled in the chair. "Water will be fine. It's too late for coffee."

The boy brought the salad, Italian dressing and a tumbler of water. He placed them on the table along with a knife and a fork. Then he deftly snagged his fouled coffee cup by covering its top with his hand. He carried it to the sink and dumped the evidence of his weakness before returning to the table and sitting across from his mother. He rested his elbows on the table, his chin in his hands. He watched her watch him.

Angela poured dressing on her salad. "What are you up to, Bodie?"

"Up to?"

"You never wait up for me. Something bothering you?"

The boy dropped his gaze to her plate. "I'm all right."

"You worried about starting college?"

"No."

"Well, what is it then? Is it July? You worried about your grandfather?"

The boy nodded. "Yeah, reckon I am."

Angela carved a piece of the fish with her fork. "Nothing lasts forever, Bodie. Nothing." She tasted the fish, chewed and then swallowed. "This is really good. I didn't know you were such a good cook."

"I've had a lot of practice, lately."

She laid the fork on the table. "So that's it. You're upset with me for not being here to heed your beck and call."

"I'm upset cause you're not happy."

Angela rose from her chair. She picked up the plate and fork and carried them to the sink. She set them on the counter top and then turned and crossed her arms and leaned against the counter. "And just why do you suppose I'm not happy?"

"I don't know. Cause ranchin ain't your thing, I reckon."

"Well you *reckoned* right. I'm sick of being left alone while you and your deliriously happy father play nursemaid to a bunch of dumb cows."

The boy could not look at her. "Nobody said you had to be alone. You could pitch in and join us."

35

Angela unfolded her arms, let them fall to her sides. "Look. I expected that you'd take your father's side in this. How could you not? You're as obsessed with cowboying as he is. He's made sure of that."

"I ain't takin nobody's side. I just want you to be happy."

She walked to him and touched him, cupped the nape of his neck with her hand and drew him to her. "It's too late for that I'm afraid. He can't change who he is, anymore than I can change who I am." She stroked his hair. "You're the only happiness Curlew has afforded me. If not for you, I probably would have left long ago."

Bodie was silent, his eyes closed tightly.

"Well I'm going to bed. You staying up for a while?"

He opened his eyes and looked at her plate. "You ain't gonna eat?"

"You can have it. I've lost my appetite."

When she had left the kitchen, he rose from the chair and carried the plate to the refrigerator. After putting the food inside, he shut the door and turned but did not move any farther. He simply stood staring blankly across the room. A moment later he dipped his head and said: "shit."

\*

He lay awake for a long time. Sometime after midnight he rose from his bed and pulled on his jeans and left the house barefoot and shirtless. Outside the moon was nearing its zenith, its cold light bathing the landscape and revealing it in great detail. A colorless day born of a subordinate sun and seemingly free of imperfection. He walked to the board fence encircling the yard and climbed it and sat perched on top of it like some pale being gone to roost. To the northeast, the reflected light of St. Cloud wrought a starless sky, several tower beacons flashed, evenly spaced and monotonous in their red winking presence. The smell of cattle and wood smoke hung in the air. It was center-of-the-earth quiet, the only sound an incessantly singing mockingbird in his granddaddy's oak, a daybird roused from sleep by the false promise of a full moon. He sat thinking, the cruel edge of the fence-board numbing his legs. After a while he bowed his head and cupped his face in his hands. He suffered soundlessly for a good while. Then he suddenly straightened and wiped his eyes with the back of a hand and hopped from the fence. He strode purposefully to the house.

Inside, he found his room sans the aid of light. He quietly gathered a shirt and his boots and socks and carried them into the kitchen. He wrapped his mother's uneaten fish in aluminum foil and placed it in a plastic Walmart bag, along with slices of white bread, an apple and a banana. He removed four cigarettes from his father's pack on the table and then hesitated briefly before putting one back. Then, slipping the smokes in his shirt pocket, he snared the bag and his clothes and exited the house. He sat the stoop and dressed his feet. Then he stood, donned his shirt, snatched up the bag and set out for the barn, his horse in the trap sensing his coming and calling to him softly.

After saddling the horse, he rode into the night's stillness, setting a northwest heading related to him by Polaris, confirmed by his own instincts. Crossing the flatwoods, he held the horse to a fast walk out of respect for it and his own mortality. The air cool and damp, the palmettos already glistening with dew. The horse's head turning side to side, the darkened world's fixtures sliding soundlessly by, indistinct, incognito.

He rode through bedded cattle scarcely seen, dark blotches in the night-grayed wiregrass, shadows abandoned by their makers. He saw the flashing lights of an airliner pass far overhead, and later, heard the faint roar of its engines. And when nearing Orange Hammock, he heard barred owls announcing the moon's zenith, wildspeak that was music to his ears, a sound as natural to him as his own thoughts. But then out of the dimmed and distant east rolled a sound still alien to him, the sound of coyotes lauding a fresh kill, a cacophony every bit as wild as the owls but only recently come to haunt the nights of his world. Beneath his breath, he cursed the newcomers, and as he did, the tail of his eye caught a glimpse of light in the rising darkness ahead, in the trees of Orange Hammock.

The tiny point of light came and went as he rode forward, but a residual glow always there, a weak point in the darkness where actual trees were visible. He moved toward the light, sawing the horse through the trees until the Indian's small fire loomed directly before him, licking steadily, silently. The old man sat cross-legged and slumped as before, as if scarcely having drawn a breath during the boy's absence.

Bodie halted the horse and sat watching the old man. The horse also watched, stepping and standing and bobbing its head, and then craning its neck to one-eye Bodie beseechingly.

"I brought you some food," Bodie said.

The Indian came to life. His head lifted. A brown hand rose like a separate entity from its resting place on his calf. The hand beckoned to the boy.

"Bring it to me," the old man said, a replica of the fire dancing in his lone dark eye.

The boy dismounted and turned the horse. He led it to the clearing edge and cinched the reins to a palm trunk. He touched the horse's neck reassuringly and then reached and lifted the Walmart bag from the pommel horn and turned and walked to the fire. When he stood across from the seated man, he leaned forward, bent at the waist as if offering the bag over some invisible barrier between them, as if wanting to keep his distance.

His singular gaze riveted on the boy, the Indian's hand flashed out and took the bag like a heron taking fish from a puddle. He set the bag in his lap.

"Sit," he said.

Bodie crossed his legs and slowly sagged to the ground directly across from the Indian. He waited.

The Indian watched the boy sit and then reached with his left hand and plucked a handful of oak limbs from a pile next to his hip. He fed the wood to the fire then opened the bag and reached within it. He withdrew the slices of bread, pairing them one beside the other on the inside of his thigh. Then he captured the foil package and peeled back its folded ends, his eye panning the fried fish within and then panning again. With the fingers of both hands, he cradled the exposed fillet, lifted it to his face. His nostrils flared. He nodded and then carefully lowered the fish, laid it on one slice of bread and then covered it with the other. Then, the sandwich lying on his leg, he slowly sucked in turn the fingers and thumb of each hand.

"That's bass from the lake," said Bodie.

The Indian looked. "I know. I saw the girl ketch it."

With his two hands he raised the sandwich to his mouth and, exposing teeth yellowed and severely worn, bit a large crescent from it. He chewed methodically, his eye closed but the crater seeming to maintain an incessant vigil of the boy.

"You walk all the way down there?" said Bodie.

"Down where?"

"To where that fish was caught."

The Indian swallowed. "No," he said.

He bit off more of the sandwich, two bites in rapid succession. He chewed.

"How'd you see her ketch it, then?"

The Indian opened his eye. He chewed and then swallowed.

"You will one day wish to marry that girl," he said.

"What?"

"When all is lost to you—you will see her for the first time. You will see that she alone offers salvation for someone like you."

38

The Indian ate the last of the sandwich and chewed it. After swallowing, he again sucked his fingers and wiped them on the wretched material covering his lap.

"No offense, mister, but I don't know what you're talkin about."

"I know you don't."

"You do?"

The Indian gestured with his arms, parted them in a wide sweeping movement. "This land was lost to me even before I was born," he said. "So I could not truly understand the great sadness my father carried in his eyes. And likewise, he could not understand the even greater sadness living in *his* father's." He paused and fed the fire more wood. "But you will understand. Your eyes will one day carry the sadness of my grandfather's."

The boy cocked his head slightly. "You tryin to tell me I'm gonna lose this land?"

"You can not lose what was never yours. But you will suffer greatly when it happens."

Bodie shook his head. He bumped back his hat and stared incredulously at the Indian.

The Indian did not look at the boy. He fingered the Walmart bag, opened it and studied its contents. "Fruit," he said, setting the bag on the ground beside him. "Give me the tobacco you brought. We will smoke, and maybe I will tell you more."

"I can hardly wait."

Ignoring the boy's sarcasm, the Indian extended a hand over the fire, palm up, opening and closing its fingers in the manner of a begging child.

The boy rolled his eyes and begrudgingly fished two cigarettes from his breast pocket. He reached and dropped one into the pleading hand.

The Indian quickly transferred the cigarette to his mouth and lit it using a flaming twig he plucked from the fire. He inhaled deeply from the cigarette, holding the smoke in his lungs for a good many seconds before exhaling it skyward. He watched the boy watching him. Then he raised a hand and pointed overhead. "The quickening moon has risen," he said. "There are many signs of this."

The boy exhaled smoke. "The quickening moon."

The Indian gestured with the hand holding his cigarette, shook it at the boy. "This land has always known change," he said. "Change is not new. But today it comes like a strong wind. This land will not survive such change. And neither will men like you and me, men whose blood is of this land. Men like you and me are finished, young Rawlerson." He paused to draw on the cigarette, his eye closing and not opening again until he exhaled. "It is a bad thing," he continued, "when a man's world passes before he does. A very bad thing."

The boy smoked. He thumped the ash from his cigarette and spat in the fire. He looked at the Indian. "Granddaddy says howdy. He said I should ask you how you lost your eye." He looked at the cigarette between his fingers. "But I understand if you don't want to tell me. It really ain't none of my business."

The Indian's eye flashed. He studied the boy, sucking his teeth and then drawing on his cigarette. "I did it," he said.

"You did it?"

"A long time ago. I meant to take them both but was too weak. I had only half the courage needed for such a task."

Bodie was silent.

The Indian waved his cigarette back and forth, up and down, as if conducting an orchestra seated in his mind, one performing for him and him alone. "As a young man," he said, "I witnessed what was happing to the people and this land, and what I saw caused me great suffering. I gave it much thought, how to save the people and this land, but the answer did not lie in my thoughts. So I came here, seeking the wisdom of the ancient ones, and they told me what must be done. They told me to kill my eyes for they were the source of such misery. They said only the blind are immune to such suffering as mine, that if blind, my world would always be as I needed it, that one must be blind to find happiness in a dying world." He paused and smoked his cigarette down to the filter. He exhaled. "They told me this, and they did not lie."

Bodie snuffed his cigarette in the sand and tossed the filter in the fire. "Damn," he said.

"Yes," said the Indian. "The thousands flocking to this land each week may have eyes, but they surely are blind. There is no other answer."

Bodie rocked forward and spat in the fire. He looked at the old man. "I got to go," he said.

The Indian nodded. "I will see you again, young Rawlerson."

Bodie stood and dusted his breeches. He took the remaining cigarette from his shirt pocket and gave it to the old man and then touched his hat brim goodbye.

As the boy mounted his horse, the Indian raised a hand and said: "Tell the old Rawlerson I said howdy, too."

"Yessir. I'll tell him."

**5**

**The following morning** Angela Rawlerson rose before dawn and prepared breakfast for her family: eggs over easy and grits and bacon and toast. It had been almost a year since she last cooked breakfast, but the boy and his father made no mention of such. They ate in virtual silence. Angela herself did not eat. She sat across the table, sipping coffee and smoking and watching intently.

When finished eating, Seth stood and stretched and patted his belly. "That was one fine breakfast," he said.

"Well thank you, Seth. Glad you enjoyed it."

Bodie watched in measured disbelief. And when his father strode outside he made no move to follow, though knowing it was expected he would.

Angela flashed him a questioning look. "You okay?"

He stared at his plate, tapping its edge with a finger. "I'm all right. Just tired is all." He stood and patted his jean pockets as if suddenly overtaken with the urge to inventory his possessions. Then he quickly circled the table, his eyes fixed on the door as though intending to catch up with his father. But when even with his mother, he stopped and reached and grasped her shoulder. "Thanks," he said.

Angela captured his hand. She smiled up at him. "Thank *you*, Bodie."

Outside he sat the steps and pulled on his boots while his father stood patiently waiting. And when freshly shod, he stood and together they walked shoulder to shoulder into a brisk morning, into a morning not yet confirmed by the sun, a windless morning, the pastures cloaked in fog.

"We'll take my truck," Seth said. "Don't think it'd be too smart you takin Daddy off in that wreck of yours."

"Yessir. I reckon not."

"You're right agreeable this morning."

"No reason not to be."

"No reason at all."

When they approached the barn, the crew cab's headlights painted two pickups, a Dodge and a Chevy, and the ranch's one-ton work truck. Three saddled horses in the marl turnaround, milling cautiously as not to trample their trailing reins. Pete Stalvey and Onnie Osteen sat perched on the work truck's flatbed, swinging legs and shielding eyes against the oncoming lights.

Seth pulled next to the Chevy and switched off the lights and motor. As he and Bodie exited the crewcab, a low growl emanated from the bed of the Chevy.

"Hush that noise, Buster," said Pete Stalvey.

The growling stopped.

Seth sidestepped toward the Chevy, craning his neck and peering into the bed. "Got a new dog, Pete?"

"Yessir. Cur and pit mix. Helluva ketch dog, but a little short on manners."

"Look at them shorty legs," said Onnie Osteen. "You ever seen a ketch dog with stubs like that?"

Pete leaned and spat. "Looks is deceivin."

Bodie joined his father next to the truck. The dog sat on its haunches amid a veritable truckload of empty Budwiser cans, its brindle coloring rendering it almost invisible in the predawn light. As his eyes adjusted, Bodie voiced his agreement with Onnie. "Darned if he *ain't* a low rider." He slid a hand over the rim of the truck bed, snaking it slowly toward the dog.

"Now don't go tryin to pet him," Seth warned. "Don't you see them pinned ears and raised hackles. He'll have you for breakfast, you give him half a chance."

Pete hopped from the flatbed. "Yeah, don't, Bodie. I'd hate to have to kill a dog I ain't worked yet."

Seth's eyes swam between the dog and his son until Bodie withdrew the offering. He then shook his head and turned and walked to his truck. He leaned inside the cab and fetched a denim jacket and a full pack of cigarettes. He turned to his son. "You run into any trouble today, call me on the mobile."

"Yessir." Bodie stepped and stood. He glanced at the horses, at Onnie sitting on the flatbed.

"Well," Seth addressed him, "you best get movin. Daddy's expectin you fore sunrise."

Bodie kicked at the ground with his boot. "All right," he said. He climbed behind the wheel of the truck and started the motor and would have pulled away had Onnie Osteen not suddenly hopped from the work truck and run to stop him. Double Ought, as he was sometimes called, came to the driver-side window and stopped. He stood staring at Bodie from beneath a hat brim soiled and faded and frayed. He was smiling but Bodie surely did not notice. Smiling was the norm for Double Ought, his most distinguishing trait.

"You gonna be there tonight?" Onnie said.

Bodie, his sleeved left arm relaxing on the truck's window ledge, one-eyed his friend. "Am I gonna be where tonight?"

Onnie cocked his head. "The pits, you knothead. Where else is there to go on a Tuesday night?"

Bodie tapped the accelerator, gunning the truck's engine. "I don't know. Maybe."

Onnie winked. "I hear that tattooed New Jersey gal's liable to be there."

"So?"

"So you best be there to keep the rest of us dogs at bay."

"I ain't worried."

"Yeah, right."

The boy again gunned the engine. "I gotta go."

Onnie took a step back. He stuffed his thumbs in his jean pockets. "I'll come by and pick ya up bout nine."

Bodie was silent. He eased the clutch out and backed away from his perpetually smiling friend. He backed the truck in a slow arc, engaging the clutch and shifting to first gear without coming to a complete halt. He then shot forward, driving east toward his grandfather's house, the sky beyond July Rawlerson's home beginning to lighten, the sun to come still but a footlight below the horizon.

As he rolled to a stop in July's yard, a fox flashed in front of the truck, a gray streaking to the yard fence but pausing to look back before ducking under and loping into the pasture, into the fog where it instantly disappeared, vanishing not like a fox but like a thing born of mist and mystery, like an offspring of the fog returning to the womb. After switching off the lights and motor, Bodie sat for a moment studying the fog, trying to pick out a pointed muzzle, a bushy tail. That he could discern only fog caused him to shake his head in amazement. Then, the fox forgotten, he turned and looked at his grandfather's house.

A light shone from the kitchen window, a sure sign that someone was up. He climbed from the truck and clicked the door shut and walked to the office entrance. He knocked softly. Shortly, the door opened outward, and he was bathed in amber light. Miss Ella Preston stood peering down, a dark silhouette save for teeth and eyes and harshly white apron. She smiled. "Good mornin, master Bodie. Come on in. Mistah July's waitin in the parlor."

While Bodie wiped his boots, Miss Ella turned and traversed the small office quickly, her rocking gate soundless, effortless. A jasmine-like scent trailed in her wake, a smell uniquely her own and one Bodie had long associated with comfort and kindness.

July was in the living room. Though fully dressed in kahki pants and work shirt, brown Wellington boots, he sat slumped in his favorite high-backed rocker, head askew, mouth agape, soundly sleeping. Miss Ella walked directly to him and gently shook his shoulder. "Mistah, July," she said. "Bodie's here. You needs to wake up, now. He done come to take you sightseein."

The old man slept.

Ella shook him again. "You got to wake up, now." she virtually shouted. She looked at the boy. "He'll come out of it directly. It just takes a while."

Bodie stood with hat in hand, watching and waiting as the old man slowly came around, drifting in and out of consciousness, eyes opening but only briefly. Glassy, unseeing eyes. Some sort of connection not being made within his brain. But the open cycle gradually won out and July eventually stared blankly at his grandson before saying: "Hey, boy. What's shakin?"

Bodie stepped and stood. He shifted his hat from one hand to the other. "Mornin, Granddaddy. I hear you want to go for a drive?"

July swallowed and smacked his lips. He blinked several times. "Yeah, I do. I want you to drive me out to visit Miss Ruby."

"Yessir, I'd be happy to. It's been a while since I been to the graveyard."

"You ain't the only one."

"I ain't?"

July wagged his head from side to side. "To my knowledge, ain't none of us been there in years. At least, been there to pay a proper visit and all." He frowned.

"I should've took you out there long before now, took you out there and told you the family history." He paused and again shook his head. "Fact is, I ought to be horse whipped for neglectin you the way I have."

Bodie turned his hat. "You ain't neglected me." He looked at Miss Ella but she turned away, refusing to meet his glance.

"Yeah. Well, seems to me I have." July gripped the arms of his chair and scooted forward. Pressing mightily with arms and legs, he rose to a standing position, teetering precariously until Miss Ella stepped in to steady him.

"Member your balance, now," she said. "You fall and break a hip, you won't be goin nowhere but the hospital."

"To hell with the hospital. I break a hip, you fetch my revolver and put me down for keeps."

"You hush with that cursing, now. Bodie don't need to hear the likes of that."

July looked at the boy. "Would you listen to her? Reckon I need to be hirin me a help-maid what knows she ain't sposed to scold them that pays her."

Miss Ella flashed Bodie a wink. "You just go right ahead. *See* can you find somebody'll put up with nonsense like I done put up with for eighteen years."

"Dime a dozen," July said. He began shuffling toward the office, his first steps cautious, tentatively taken as though fearing the floor may suddenly collapse beneath him.

Miss Ella did not rush to follow. Rather, she stepped close to Bodie, whispering: "You best stick close to him. He been shaky as a fresh born calf since right after yesterday's meetin."

Nodding to Miss Ella, Bodie hurried to catch up with his grandfather. He shadowed him through the office and opened the door to the outside and stepped clear to let the old man exit first. But July balked at the door. He stood in the threshold clutching the door jams and staring at the two meager steps below.

"Don't know if I can do it," he said.

Bodie looked at him. "Do what?"

July waved a hand at the steps. "I been up and down them things a million times, I reckon. But right now it seems impossible."

Bodie stepped and stood, his eyes shifting between the steps and his grandfather.

"I got no strength in my legs," July said. "None at all."

"Maybe if you hold on to me. Let me squeeze by you. You can hold on to my

45

shoulders. We'll go down 'em together."

July's eyes shifted between his grandson and the steps. "That might work," he said. He sidestepped to allow the boy to pass, but refused to release his grip on the left door jam. "You reckon you can catch me if I start to fall?"

"Yessir. I won't let you fall." Bodie eased past July and stood on the top step, his back to the old man. "Grab a hold," he said.

July obeyed, and together they slowly descended the steps in tandem, the simple act leaving July winded, his face flushed. He stood for a moment to compose himself, shaking his head and looking thoroughly disgusted.

Bodie waited patiently beside him. "You could've done it by yourself," he said. "There just wasn't no point in takin a chance is all."

July turned his head and spat. "If you wasn't here, I'd still be up there shakin in my boots. Have to tell ya, I was terrified of them two little steps." He motioned toward the truck. "But you got me down 'em, so let's get on. I got a lot to discuss with you."

Getting July in the truck proved to be another minor crisis, one the boy over-came by sheer strength, by ducking low and cradling his grandfather and lifting him into the truck seat. Once situated, the old man looked at him forlornly and said: "Sorry to put you to all this trouble." To which the boy replied: "Trouble?"

In the growing light they drove the main ranch road, the one marled and graded and leading to the paved highway, to Canoe Creek Road. July, usually a man of few words, talked incessantly, beginning even before they left his yard. He began by gesturing vaguely toward the weed-choked improved pasture surrounding his home, the pangola grass now thriving thanks to moisture provided by the hurri-canes of August and September.

"Pasture's in bad need of a mowin," he said, "Generate some new growth that'll do a cow some good, discourage them blamed thistles and dog fennels."

"Yessir. I think Daddy's got it planned for next week."

"Next week?"

"Yessir."

The boy drove slowly. Though intently listening to his grandfather, he rarely looked at him, his eyes shifting instead between the road ahead and the terrain through which they moved.

July plucked a toothpick from the ready supply in his shirt pocket and placed it in the corner of his mouth. He gazed out his side window. "They's just too many people nowadays," he said. "Time was, you'd get one little old hurricane and the cypress heads and ditches would stay slap full of water for months. Now, they's so many drawin on the aquifer that three big storms can't keep 'em full but a week or two." He shook his head. "Don't know what's gonna happen if they keep comin like they are. I surely don't."

"The hurricanes?"

"The blame people."

"You sound like your friend Solomon, Granddaddy."

July's head swiveled to look at the boy. "Solomon?"

"That old one-eyed Indian. I took him some supper last night. He like to of talked my ear off about how things are changin round here."

July's eyes narrowed a bit. "Well I hope you listened. That old man's got more sense than most."

"Yessir. I listened. He scared hell out of me, too—just like you said he would."

"Good."

Bodie was silent for a moment, then added: "He said to tell you howdy."

July nodded. He stared blankly at the windshield.

A quarter-mile from the old man's house, the truck rattled across a cattle-gap fashioned of railroad rails and crossties. Improved pasture gave way to native growth at that point: palmettos, longleaf pines, scrub oaks. To the west a strand of cypress rose from the fog like a procession of the old, gray and somber save for the crowns being tinted gold by the coming sun.

"Stop," July commanded.

Bodie touched the brake pedal, and the creeping truck halted. He looked expect- antly at his grandfather. "You see somethin?"

July shook his head. "Switch the motor off. I want to set here a bit."

When Bodie had done as told, July raised a hand and pointed at the windshield. "Curlews," he said.

Bodie looked, seeing several flights of the curved-beaked ibis, several ivory col- ored and offset V's moving slowly across the blue-black dome of dawn. "They're headed to the mudflats," he said. "I see 'em there pretty regular."

"Probin for worms. That's mainly what they eat." July reached and touched his grandson's arm. "You know why one leg of that V-pattern they fly is always longer than the other'n?"

"No Sir. I reckon I don't."

47

"Got more birds in it."

A chuckle was slow in coming from Bodie, but come it did when realizing his grandfather had told a joke. He had never known the old man to joke about anything.

The old man kept a straight face. He looked at the boy. "You ain't ever ate one, have you?"

"A curlew?"

"Yeah."

"No, sir. Didn't know they were edible."

"Poor man's chicken. That's what your great granddaddy called 'em. We ate a many a one durin the depression, cause they were easy to get. They wasn't hardly no deer back then, you know. This was all open range back then. When mandatory fencin got passed after the war, it helped the deer. And—around nineteen and sixty, I think it was—when the government eradicated the screwworm fly, they really took off. Deer got plumb plentiful."

Bodie looked, his head cocked in puzzlement. "How'd fencin cattle help deer? Deer don't pay no attention to a fence."

July smiled. "Yeah, but people do—honest people, anyway. Before fencin, property lines were a mystery. People hunted anywhere they damn well pleased. They wasn't no way to protect the game on your property, to see that it didn't get overhunted." Bodie nodded his head. "I never would've figured there's more deer now than when you were a boy."

"Well it's a fact."

A moment of silence, then Bodie asked: "About the Curlews, that why you named the ranch Curlew? Cause you used to eat 'em?"

"I didn't name the place. John Morgan named it. He gave it a name that would never let him forget how hard life can get."

"John Morgan?"

"My daddy—your great granddaddy: John Morgan Rawlerson. Everybody called him John Morgan, cludin me. I never once in my life called him daddy—not even when he lay dying of the pneumonia."

"JMR," Bodie said. "Them initials carved on the stock of your rifle."

"That's right. He carved them before I was born."

Bodie was silent, his eyes not on his grandfather but panning the woods. "Why didn't you call him daddy?" he finally asked.

July shook his head. "Nobody told me I was supposed to. My mama died givin birth to me. I was raised an only child by a father too busy for such things as man-

48

ners and proper upbringin. Course, when I started school I noticed real quick that none of the other kids called their folks by name. It was troublesome to learn I was different that away, but not so much that it cured me of the habit. I went right on callin him John Morgan, even though it eventually become a source of guilt for me. It's somethin I've always regretted, somethin that makes me sad to this day."

"I reckon he must not of minded. Seems like he would've straightened you out if it bothered him."

July smiled. "Not my daddy. John Morgan was all business. I doubt he ever noticed *what* I called him."

The boy fidgeted with the steering wheel then turned and stared into the thinning fog. Deer were moving among the cypress, two mature does and several yearlings, their winter coats so closely matching the fog and trees as to render them invisible when they stopped to gaze at the truck. "There's some deer, now," he whispered, raising his hand and pointing.

July looked, his dark eyes coming to bear on the animals like radar locking onto a target. "All butt-headed," he said. "Old buck done seen the truck and snuck off."

A few seconds later the animals bolted, their flags erect and waving side to side, but, oddly, running almost directly at the intruding truck.

"What the?" Bodie said.

"Somethin spooked 'em. Somethin other'n us."

The deer came on, mere flashes of white and shadowy gray as they darted and weaved through scrub oak and palmettos, quartering toward the truck and eventually crossing the ranch road less than fifty yards away, two does and three yearlings, all flat out in a run surely fueled by panic, a flight the likes of which the pickup's presence would not produce.

When the fleeing deer vanished from sight, both old man and boy instinctively maintained an unblinking vigil of the point where they had crossed the grade. In seconds their instincts were proven correct when the driving force behind the deer leaped into view, a deer-colored blur, only lower slung and flowing across the ground in a manner no deer ever fawned could emulate. Obviously feline, the creature stopped suddenly when reaching the crown of the grade, settled to its haunches and directed its ancient binocular stare directly at the truck, its too-long tail tipped in black and curling about the stock-still body like a separate entity, like a servant of serpentine nature whose sole purpose was to transfix any and all daring to gaze upon its master.

"Damn," breathed Bodie.

"Painter," said July. "A big'un. A big male."

49

**6**

**The panther watched the truck** for almost a minute, sitting on its haunches in the middle of the grade, its posture erect, truly regal. Then without warning the big cat rocked forward and turned and left the road in a ground-hugging crawl, moving snake-like, fluidly, an animated portrait of both stealth and power.

Neither Bodie nor July spoke for some time. They stared at the now empty grade, the scene they had just witnessed replaying in their minds. Bodie broke the spell. "He had a white patch on his shoulder," he said, his voice restrained, sounding almost reverent.

"Probably an old wound of some sort. Scars tend to hair-over white for some reason."

"Reckon he'll mess with the cattle?"

"Good chance. Cat like that takes the easiest meal. And ain't nothing easier'n a calf."

The boy shifted his eyes from the road to his grandfather. "We gonna hunt him?"

July watched the grade, the toothpick in his mouth rocking up and down. "Time was, I'd have broke my neck gettin the dogs and puttin 'em on that feller. But that time is gone. We ain't gonna do anything, cept maybe enjoy his company."

"But you said he'd take calves. We just gonna let him?"

"He probably won't be around long enough to do any real damage. A calf or two

51

won't break us."

"But what if he stays?"

"He won't. Big males like him will ramble a far piece huntin a female. That's the only explanation for him being here. He likely follered the river up from Okeechobee. He'll keep movin till he cuts a female's trail—or dies tryin. Scarce as painters is, it'll likely be the latter."

"You ever seen one before?"

"I seen one when I was about your age. But I never figured on seein another."

"I never figured to see the first one."

"Well, I hope I'm wrong sayin it, but you probably just seen your last. Safe to say I did."

The boy reached and gripped the steering wheel. "I'd kind of like to see him again. You reckon I will?"

"Not likely. Painters that make a  habit of showin themselves don't live too long. That old feller just made a mistake, but he's not apt to repeat it. He's been around enough to know better."

The boy gazed out his side window. "Granddaddy," he said.

"Yeah."

"Just curious. You not wantin to hunt that cat—is that because it's against the law—cause they're an endangered species and all?"

July deftly tongued the toothpick to the opposite corner of his mouth. "Law got nothin to do with it. It'd be a sin for me to harm that cat. Forty years ago I would've, but things have changed. Nowadays, me and him got too much in common. Be like killin my brother or somethin."

The boy cocked his head, squinted his eyes. "Your brother?"

July's gnarled and arthritic hands lay in his lap. He looked at them, turning them this way and that as if the explanation he wanted to voice was written in their wrecked and diminished existence. "I've had a long life," he said, "maybe too long. Seems like all I do anymore is set by and watch another thing I love cease to be."

"You feelin all right, Granddaddy?"

"I'm all right. Why?"

"I just never thought I'd hear you admit to lovin somethin that kills cows."

July looked at his grandson. "Me neither. I reckon gettin old done mellowed me out some. I don't know. All I can tell you is, a lot of things that used to aggravate me, critters like that painter, don't anymore. Anymore, if I get to see a big rattler or an old bull gator, things I used to kill on sight, I feel good. Seein things like that pleasures me now, I guess is what I'm tryin to say." He paused momentarily. "But I'll make no apologies for what I done in the past. I was like everybody else. All us crackers was just protectin our interests, tryin to survive is all."

"You don't need to apologize. We still got all them things"

July smiled dimly. "That's only cause you cain't hunt most critters to extinction, no matter how hard you try. Most critters'll figure a way around you, long as they got the room to maneuver." He paused and plucked the toothpick from his mouth, tossed it out the window. "Course, that's the problem, ain't it? There soon won't be no room to maneuver. What with the way this country's bein built up and paved over, all Florida critters, from coons to crackers, is in big trouble. And there's not a thing can be done about it. It's inevitable."

Bodie frowned. He studied his grandfather, as if hoping to see some overt sign that the old man's tumor was responsible for such pessimistic talk. But July appeared to be lucid, sitting there in profile, silhouetted against a fog-dimmed yellow orb that was the fully risen sun.

"Curlew ain't in trouble," he said. "Seems to me it ain't changed hardly at all."

"Compared to most, Curlew ain't changed a lick. But you have to know that's no accident. I done everything in my power to keep it from changin. I tried to keep it wild and natural, the way it was when I was a young'un like you." July patted his breast pocket, then withdrew from it another toothpick. Holding the sliver of blond wood between his thumb and index finger, he seemed to examine it, saying: "And I done it cause John Morgan told me to. 'Curlew is Rawlerson land,' he told me, 'and I expect you to keep it that way. Do whatever it takes to keep it like it is.'"

"So *that's* why you never diversified."

"Diversified?

"Yessir. You know. Citrus, sod farmin, leasin huntin rights…"

"I know what it means. I'm just surprised to hear you use a word like that. You been studyin, have you? Figurin how to make the place more profitable?"

The boy shifted uncomfortably in his seat, stretched his legs until his boots pressed against the firewall. "No sir. Not exactly. Just wonderin is all."

"Well, don't be ashamed to admit it if you have. It tells me you really care about the place."

The boy gazed out his window. "I care, all right. Ranchin is all I ever want to do."

July smiled and nodded his head. "I thought as much." He reached with his hand and touched the dash before him, touched it gingerly as though it were an object he had always wanted to touch but never before had the courage. "You ever wonder why I ain't been much of a granddaddy to you?"

Bodie turned and looked at him, but did not answer.

"You bein my only grandson, there's no excuse for the way I've neglected you. But I want you to know it wasn't done out of malice. It's just the way I'm wired up is all. I'm no good at rearing people. John Morgan was the same way, so reckon I come by it honest." July let his hand fall to his lap. "What I'm tryin to say is, I admire you. Though I've never once said it, I've always been proud to have you for a grandson."

Bodie looked away. A pair of whitewing doves had landed in the grade ahead of the truck. He watched the birds gather grit for their craw, short-legged and moving in compact circles, their smooth and rounded heads jerking nervously, tiny black-pearl eyes always watching. "Yessir," he said.

July watched his grandson. "It's good we seen that panther together," he said.

The boy looked at him.

"Seein him fits right in with what I got to tell you."

"Sir?"

"You know why painters cain't make it in this world?"

"Cause people won't let 'em, I reckon."

July nodded. "That's only part of it, though. The main trouble with panthers is they cain't change. With the whole world changin round him, a panther got no choice but to go on bein a panther. He cain't reason like you and me, cain't decide to go about earnin his livin a little differently." July reached and touched the boy's shoulder. "I got to act like a panther my whole life, but you ain't gonna have that luxury." He withdrew his hand but continued to study his grandson intently. "You understand what I'm gettin at?"

"Yessir, I reckon. You're sayin I have to be willin to change."

July nodded his head. "And you got my blessings on it. When I'm gone, you do whatever it takes to keep Curlew a workin cattle ranch, keep it a Rawlerson interest. Grow sod. Lease the huntin rights. Do whatever you think'll work."

The boy returned his gaze to the doves. "Daddy in agreement on this?"

"I ain't run it by him yet."

He looked at his grandfather. "Why? I ain't in charge of anything."

"Wanted to know your view first. Your daddy's been doin things one way for a lot of years. He's apt to put off makin changes till it's too late."

"And that's where I come in? You want me to stay on him about it?"

"You got to. There's no other way. Eight thousand acres of woods pasture won't cut it anymore. There's got to be some serious changes made if Curlew is to survive."

Bodie thought for a moment. "I don't know if I can bear to lease the huntin rights. The thought of a bunch of strangers traipsing all over Curlew is plumb depressin."

July nodded his agreement. "That, it is. But not nearly as depressin as losin the place altogether. You'll get top dollar for the huntin on Curlew, more'n enough to pay the taxes each year. And that's if you don't lease out the whole of it. You can set aside a couple thousand acres for family. Sort of have your cake and eat it too, so to speak."

"Still won't be the same."

July dipped his head. "No, it won't. A feller used to havin the whole pie ain't never gonna be satisfied with just a slice." He looked at the boy. "We've had some shining times on this old place, ain't we?"

Bodie smiled. "Yessir. We sure have." His eyes sparkled. "I seen that old crooked-horned buck, yesterday. Rode him up on my way out to the lake."

"Well I reckon he ain't died of old age, then—like we figured last season. Maybe you'll see him come openin day?"

"I was hopin to try. Are we huntin for sure?"

The old man's eyebrows arched. "Does a bull waller in the dirt? Course the Rawlersons is huntin next weekend. Even if it turns out I ain't up to it, I want you and your daddy to put on the hunt. And I expect you to keep puttin it on for years to come. Reckon you can handle that?"

"Yessir."

"Good Lord willin," July said, "I'll handle the doins this time." He turned his head and gazed out his side window. "And I sure hope He is willin, cause I'd like to say some goodbyes to the best bunch of friends a feller ever had."

The boy was silent.

The old man stared out the window. "Crank up the truck and let's get on to the cemetery. The mornin's about to get away from us."

\*

They drove the main ranch road a half-mile farther. When almost to Canoe Creek Road, the paved highway leading to St. Cloud, Bodie slowed and steered the truck into a deep-rutted woods road angling southwest. The road rough and sandy, Bodie drove slowly, his attention fixed on the keeping the truck in the winding ruts. When next he looked at his grandfather, July appeared to be sleeping, his head bowed and swaying to the undulating road. He slept to the end of the road and continued to sleep even after Bodie had stopped the truck and gotten out. As Miss Ella had done earlier, he shook his grandfather awake, shaking him and calling to him until July finally opened his eyes. The old man seemed thoroughly lost until seeing the four headstones standing directly in front of the truck. "The graveyard," he said, and then immediately set about trying to exit the truck. And with Bodie's help he succeeded, and together they walked slowly toward the small patch of ground where the old man himself would soon be laid to rest. A cool breeze stirred from the west, carrying the dank smell of lake, of life and death aquatic.

The cemetery was located on a pine island, on a slight knoll between two cypress heads, and consisted only of four quarried granite markers and the hog-wire fence encircling them. An enormous liveoak stood at the enclosure's south end, outside the fence yet its far wandering and moss draped limbs shading the entire affair. The ground around the markers was virtually barren of life, only a few sprigs of greenbriar sprouting amid sand and decaying leaves, a foil-wrapped pot holding the skeletal remains of an azalea bush, a small American flag faded and tattered.

July led Bodie to the marker second from the right, the grave of Miss Ruby Ann Combee-Rawlerson, born 1926, died 1984. The old man looked longingly at the marker and then looked at the boy. "I sure do wish my Ruby could've knowed you. She would've had herself a time tryin to spoil you."

Bodie removed his hat, turned it in his hands. "Yessir. Wish I could've known her."

July raised a hand and gestured westward. "She come from over in Polk County, you know. Her people were cattle people like us, owned a big chunk of land northeast of Lakeland." He looked at the marker. "Course it's all gone now, turned into a couple of developments and a big industrial park of some sort. Her daddy was a good man, a good Christian." He looked at the boy. "You a Christian, ain't you?"

Bodie shifted his weight, looked at the sandy loam beneath his boots. "Reckon I am. Mama had me get baptized a while back. When I was twelve or so."

"But are you a believer?"

Bodie shrugged. "I say I am, but sometimes I don't know. When I'm out in the woods some place it's easy to believe in God. But around people... Well, sometimes it's hard to believe in anything, I guess is what I'm tryin to say."

July nodded his head. "That's pretty much been my experience, too," he said. He looked sideways at Bodie. "You read the Bible?"

Bodie looked in the bowl of his hat. "No sir."

"Well you ever take the notion to start, read Ecclesiastes. It ain't but just a few pages. Old King Solomon wrote it, and he didn't dance around the fire. He flat told it how it is."

"Yessir," the boy said. He looked at his grandfather. "Told how what is?"

"Life."

July gestured to the headstone last in line, the one adjacent to Ruby's and inscribed: July Rawlerson, Born, 10 March 1918. "No explanation needed for this one, I reckon."

Bodie was silent. A cursory glance was all he could offer the symbol of misery yet to come. Seeing his grandfather's name chiseled in stone was for him like watching rumor morph into reality, something he was not ready to see. To effect an escape, he quickly sidestepped left and focused on a stone slab whose mildewed and pitted face held a message less distressing, one that simply piqued his curiosity: Sarah Overstreet-Rawlerson, Born 1900, Died 1918.

July followed his grandson's gaze. "That stone's the only picture I got of my mama," he said. "She died givin birth to me, you know, right out there in the old homeplace, in Rawlerson Hammock."

"Yessir."

"John Morgan told me what she looked like, said she was dark-headed and had eyes like mine, only more gentle. After he told me, I tried my darnedest to fix his description in my head. But wasn't no use. When I think of her, this stone is all I can see. Been that way all my life."

"She was the same age as me?"

57

"Yep. Forever eighteen."

"She related to the Overstreets around here?"

July shook his head and reached and scratched the back of his neck. "Don't think so. She was born in Missouri, so it's a stretch to think she was."

The boy looked at the old man but did not speak.

"He married her out there, in Joplin, Missouri. Brought her and that Winchester rifle your so fond of back with him, when he finished whatever it was he went out there to do." July paused to capture a toothpick in his breast pocket. He put it in his mouth. "He was born in Fort Pierce, you know."

"Yessir. Daddy told me."

"Actually, it was a little west of Fort Pierce. His daddy, James Arthur, a lifelong cowman hisself, ran cattle on several hundred acres off the Okeechobee Road, right on Five Mile Creek. He didn't own the land. He rented it from a yankee feller livin in Palm Beach."

July looked at the boy.

Bodie turned the hat in his hands, nodded his head.

"Anyway, John Morgan was the oldest of four kids. Had a brother named Archie, and two sisters whose names I cain't never remember." July waved a hand at the left-most marker—John Morgan's grave, born 1898, died 1970. "You got to understand that John Morgan was not one to carry on about his folks. About all I can remember him tellin me was..."

Pausing suddenly, July's eyes widened, his hands pawed the air as if seeking a railing to hold.

Bodie instinctively dropped his hat and reached and grabbed the old man by the shoulders. "You all right?" he said.

In the boy's grasp, July slowly relaxed. He looked around.

"I don't know what the hell happened," he said. "Just all of a sudden I got to feelin dizzier'n a swung cat. Reckon I need to set down a bit."

Bodie stretched and picked up his hat and then walked his grandfather to the truck. He cradled him and lifted him into the passenger seat. He thought the old man seemed exhausted but made no mention of what he thought. He simply circled the truck and got in and waited for the old man to dictate their next move.

The old man sat very still until the boy was behind the wheel. Then he began to talk: "His sisters both died of the influenza in 1912."

"Sir?"

"John Morgan's sisters. They died one after the other, in 1912."

"Yessir."

"Archie lived well into his thirties. Died up in South Carolina, in 1934. Some feller put a bullet in his head for stealin dogs."

"Stealin dogs?"

July nodded. "Back then, a good huntin dog fetched upwards of a thousand dollars. Shiftless characters like Uncle Archie made a business out of stealin 'em in one state and sellin 'em in another."

Bodie was silent, but the look on his face said volumes.

July snorted and shook his head. "I know," he said. "But you need to hear about all of your kin, even the sorry ones."

"Did John Morgan know what his brother was up to? Before he got caught, I mean?"

"He knew he was worthless. He tried to put Archie to work here on the ranch—when he first bought the place. But old Archie didn't last a week. They just wasn't no work in the man, John Morgan used to say. Said the smartest thing he ever done was to run Archie's tail off before he could sorry up the place permanent."

As the old man finished his statement, a slack-sided heifer emerged from the scrub beyond the grave stones, a Brahman-Angus cross, its head carried low and its drooping ears rocking to and fro. Upon seeing the truck, the cow halted and raised its head to stare incredulously.

Bodie watched the cow. "Was Curlew seeded with cows from the Fort Pierce herd?"

July shook his head. "Wasn't no Fort Pierce herd time John Morgan got up this way. Wasn't nothin left down there wearin a Rawlerson brand." He paused and smiled demurely. He reached and bumped the boy's arm with the back of his closed hand. "Course you had no way of knowin that, cause I ain't told you yet. I kinda got ahead of myself talkin bout old Archie."

Bodie grinned. "That's all right. It's all interesting to me."

"My granddaddy, James Arthur, got hisself killed in 1914. Horse stepped in a gopher hole one night when he was fox huntin. John Morgan said his daddy truely loved to fox hunt, loved to set around the fire, drink whiskey and listen to the dogs run. This particular night, he must've done more drinkin than settin and listenin, cause he up and decided to try and catch the fox fore the dogs did. He was gallopin full out across the flatwoods when the horse went down. Stead of a fox, he

59

caught himself a broke neck."

"I ain't never run a horse across the woods in the dark."

"Then I reckon you ain't been drunk yet."

"Not drunk enough to do somethin like that."

The old man chuckled. "You got a lot of experiencin ahead of you, boy. So much it makes me tired just thinkin about it." He looked through the windshield at the cow now standing in the shade of the great oak. "The first cows on this place come from right here in Osceola County," he said.

Bodie cut his eyes to the old man then back to the cow. "Yessir," he said.

"John Morgan bought the original heifers from some local feller, but I never knew who. He got his first herd bull from the Dudas, over in Brevard County. We bought Brahmans from old man Duda several times over the years, Every time we'd go to pick one up, John Morgan made mention of that first one, the one he got way back when."

July suddenly fell silent.

When Bodie looked, the old man's eyes were closed. "You all right, Grand-daddy?"

The old man's entire body jerked. He looked at the boy, his eyes glassy with fatigue. "I don't know," he said.

"I think I better get you to the house."

The old man stared. "Yeah," he said. "I reckon you better."

July was asleep before Bodie could turn the truck around, head tipped against the side window, open mouth welling a fine rivulet of drool. His color not good. Not good at all.

Bodie drove the rough cemetery road faster than he should have, twice almost losing control of the truck when it fishtailed wildly in sugar sand. Upon reaching the ranch road, he accelerated hard, steering with his left hand, trying with his right to reach his father on the mobile, his father not answering. After several attempts with the phone, he slammed it back in its cradle and focused only on getting his grandfather home. He drove, glancing repeatedly at the body sagged like so much dead weight beside him, his grandfather not reacting at all to the sudden jolts imparted to him by the uneven road.

When July's house loomed ahead, Bodie glanced across the pasture to the barn. No work truck. No salvation there. He drove on and slid the truck to a halt in the old man's yard. He flung the door open and leaped out and started for the house, only to stop and dart back inside the truck's cab to feel his grandfather's neck: the leathery skin warm; a faint but steady pulse.

He shook the old man. "Granddaddy," he said

Getting no response, Bodie slid from the truck and ran to the office door. He entered the house, calling for Miss Ella. And when she came to him, he hurriedly led her outside, speaking to her rapidly, telling her what awaited in the truck.

Miss Ella made no attempt to wake July. She took one look at the old man and turned to the boy. "You call your daddy?"

"I tried, but he don't answer. He must be away from the truck."

"Well try him again," Miss Ella said, turning and starting for the house. "I'll use the house phone to call Doc Hutchinson, to get a ambulance out here. If I ain't mistaken, Mistah July done caught hisself a stroke."

Bodie watched Miss Ella go and then reached for the mobile and dialed his father. He stepped and stood while the phone tolled incessantly in his ear, his eyes riveted on his grandfather. When there was no answer, he muttered "damn", then began the whole process anew.

***The man** cocked his head back to mark the midday sun. He shifted his position in the airboat's seat and resumed his vigil of the distant treeline, the switchgrass swaying gracefully in the wind. A pair of grackles, male and female, worked the muddy lakeshore to his left, the male's dark plumage a shifting kaleidoscope of color as the showy bird passed through light and shadow. He watched the industrious birds, and then he shifted his gaze to read the nearest posted sign for the umpteenth time. "Curlew Cattle Company," he said. "Just what is a curlew, I wonder?" He looked again at the sun, sighed deeply, then picked up the shotgun from his lap and turned it and stowed it in its scabbard. "Well, my young friend," he said, reaching to start the motor, "Looks like you win the second round, too." As the engine fired, he added: "Too bad you'll never know it."*

**7**

**The boy sat** next to his sleeping grandfather, hat in lap, patiently waiting. Over an hour had passed since he followed the ambulance crew through the emergency entrance and into a room scarcely larger than the bed in which the old man now lay—since he'd stood with his back to the wall and watched a stout, middle-aged woman undress the old man and wire him to a bank of equipment which she studied before jotting notes on a chart and turning and saying that vital signs were good and that a doctor would be in soon. After the woman had left, he'd settled in the room's only chair and had become lost in thought as he watched the old man inhale and exhale. And he remained lost until now, when a voice suddenly brought him back to the diminutive room and the grim reality within.

"How's he doing?" the voice said.

Bodie's head jerked to the sound. He stood, his hands capturing his hat and clinging to it. "Hey, Doc," he said.

The man stepping into the room was tall and thin, elderly, a thin crop of white hair girding his otherwise bald head, a stethoscope dangling from his neck, a chart clasped in his hand. "No offense, Bodie, but I would rather have seen you on opening day," he said, not looking at the boy but gazing at the electronic monitors beyond July's bed. He walked directly to the old man's side.

"Yessir. I hear that. The deerwoods is one place I don't mind seein a doctor."

Doctor Hutchinson looked at the boy. He chuckled and nodded his head and then turned back to his patient. Placing the chart on the edge of the bed, he pulled a slender light from his breast pocket and leaned forward. He pried open the old man's right eye and shined a tightly focused beam into it and, after repeating the process with the left, straightened and returned the light to his pocket. He donned the stethoscope and hop-scotched its receiver over the old man's bared chest, pausing and listening a good many seconds at each landing point.

"Miss Ella figured he had a stroke," said Bodie.

The doctor shed the stethoscope and looked at the boy. He shook his head. "Don't think so," he said. "He's simply in a deep sleep, put there by his tumor's progression."

The boy turned his hat in his hands. "Yessir," he said.

"I've seen it before." The doctor half turned and reached and pulled the old man's top sheet up, covered the starkly white chest and its crop of snaking electronic leads. He returned his gaze to the boy. "And I have to tell you, he may never wake up. Then again, he may be wide awake five minutes from now. A tumor in the right frontal lobe is like that. The symptoms are almost impossible to predict. No two cases are exactly alike."

The boy stood.

The doctor nodded. He lifted the chart from the bed and wrote something on it and then looked at the boy. "Seth on his way here?"

The boy shifted his weight from one foot to the other. "Yessir, he should be. I couldn't reach him before the ambulance came, but Miss Ella was gonna keep tryin."

The doctor nodded. How about your aunt and uncle? They been notified?"

The boy shrugged. "I don't know."

"Well, they need to know, too. There's some decisions that need to be made concerning your grandfather.

"Decisions?"

"Yes. We're going to move him upstairs in a few minutes—get him settled in a room. When your daddy gets here, tell him to have me paged. I'll explain to him all that needs to be done."

"Yessir. I'll tell him."

Tucking the chart under his left arm, the doctor extended his right toward Bodie. "It's always good to see you, Bodie."

He reached and shook the doctor's hand. "Thanks, Doc. It's good to see you, too."

\*

Seth and Angela arrived not long after a pair of orderlies transferred the old man to a semi-private room on the second floor. Bodie told what the doctor had said and then sat with his parents by the old man's side until his father handed him his truck keys and told him to go home.

"How will y'all get home?"

Seth Rawlerson waved a hand. "We brought both vehicles, just so you wouldn't have to stay."

"I reckon I'd like to stay."

"You need to get something to eat," his mother injected.

"I ain't all that hungry."

"I left chili on the stove. You just have to heat it up."

"Go on, son," his father said. "We'll call if anything happens."

The boy left his parents and found his father's truck in the parking lot. It was getting dark. The streetlights decorating St. Cloud shone like postscripts of the recently departed sun. In the false-twilight he drove west on Main Street, then turned south on Canoe Creek Road where at the edge of town the truck's headlights seemed to brighten substantially, where the true face of night revealed itself in full. He drove, and shortly a new twilight was born as the moon's leading edge crested the eastern horizon. He watched the moon come as he drove and, upon reaching his house, parked the truck and continued watching until its conquest of the horizon was complete. Then he opened the truck door and slid from the seat, feeling strangely drained—more so, he thought, than if he'd worked cows the day long.

He sat the stoop to remove his boots and then went inside. In the kitchen he lifted the lid from his mother's chili and smelled it and switched on the burner beneath it. Then he hurried to the bathroom, his bladder about to burst. When the chili was hot he ladled a bowl full and took it to the porch. He sat and ate in the moonlight, in the near silence of the Curlew night. And when the bowl was empty he lowered it and the spoon to the floor and leaned back and rocked his chair ever so slowly. He sat and rocked for a long time.

Around nine o'clock a set of headlights suddenly sprang from the invisible cypress far to the north. Bodie stopped rocking and watched the twin lights approach, bobbing and weaving and soundless, the glowing eyes of some furtive creature loping into his night. His parents, he first thought, but then heard the low rumble of a failed muffler. "Onnie," he said.

When the Dodge Dakota stopped in the circle, its lights extinguished but the motor continued to lope. The dome light flashed on and then winked out concurrent with a tinny click. Onnie Osteen ghosted toward the house, invisible save for a harshly-white shirt and like-colored Stetson. At the stoop, the portly cowman paused and stomped the concrete slab with first one boot then the other.

Bodie, who had remained still as the porch floor during his friend's approach, abruptly said: "You crack that slab, daddy's liable to fire you."

"Damn! I didn't see you settin there. You like to made me ruin my new breeches."

Onnie climbed the steps and clomped to the rocker next to the boy's. He turned and reached back and felt for the wooden arms and found them and flopped heavily into the chair's whickered seat. "I knew you'd forget," he said.

"I ain't forgot. Just don't feel like partyin is all."

The Dakota's motor loped. Onnie rocked.

"How's he doin?"

"The same, I reckon. He was still out of it when I left the hospital."

"Your folks up there with him?"

"Yeah," Bodie said, reaching his arm over the back of his chair, switching on the overhead light. He squinted at his friend. "New breeches, you say. Looks like new everything to me. Why, you even combed your hair. You must mean business, tonight."

"Sure as hell do. I been horny as a three-peckered billygoat lately."

"Lately? You were born horny."

"Yessir. I done decided there ain't no such thing as an ugly girl tonight. Anything nine to ninety and breathin tonight."

"Daddy ain't workin you hard enough."

Onnie rocked. "Well," he said, "you comin, or not?"

"Not. I'm just gonna set here and listen for the phone."

"All right."

Onnie pitched forward and, grunting loudly, pressed to a standing position. "Reckon I'll see you in the mornin, then." He started to walk but hesitated and half-turned to the boy. "Less I get lucky. I get lucky, I might just call in happy."

The boy smiled and rolled his eyes. "See ya in the mornin," he said.

8

**His parents** got home just before eleven. They found him sprawled on his back in the family room's leather recliner, sleeping in the confused light of a muted TV, a wireless phone bedded on his chest. They woke him and told him his grandfather's condition was unchanged and that he should not worry but should simply go to bed.

In the morning he was the first one awake. He primed the coffee maker in the moonlit kitchen and then captured the first cup-full it dripped. Then he captured a cigarette from his father's pack on the table and strode in his bare feet to the front porch. Outside, it was not as cool as the previous morning, the air heavy with humidity, stars to the north and overhead, but to the south, a raft of dark clouds sliding leisurely northward. Rain was coming; he could feel it.

He sat sipping coffee and smoking until seeing Pete Stalvey arrive at the barn. Then he set his cup on the floor and got up and moved to the stoop where he pulled on his socks and boots. He stood and walked toward the barn, grass in the pasture soaked with dew, a sulfury glow in the eastern sky, the moon half-submerged in the western horizon.

The foreman sat astride a hay bale just inside the barn bay, leaning forward, elbows bridged on knees, hands palmed together and supporting his chin in a prayerful manner. He stared blankly into the thinning darkness, seemingly lost in thought until the boy scaled the gate directly in his line of sight. Upon seeing Bodie, Pete dropped his hands to his thighs and sat upright. "Mornin, Bodie" he said. "Any word?"

The boy shook his head while crossing the marl turnaround. "Nothin since last night."

"He ever wake up?"

"No sir."

Pete stood and swung his left leg over the bale. He shook his head. "Damn," he said.

The boy stopped in the doorway and removed his hat. He looked in its bowl and set it back atop his head. "You ready to feed?"

"Been ready. Just waitin on Double Ought." The foreman folded his arms and craned his neck to look beyond the boy. "Reckon his old truck's actin up agin."

The boy was silent. He leaned and spat.

The foreman unfolded his arms, waved an index finger at Bodie. "But looky here," he said. "I'm done waitin. Let's you and me get it done fore the rain hits."

"Feels like rain, all right."

"Sposed to set in shortly, cordin to the Weather Channel feller."

The boy turned and walked toward the feed room, a raised block addition to the main barn, sliding metal doors, a loading dock married to its front. "I'll drag out the bags," he said.

Pete Stalvey turned the opposite direction. "I'll fetch the truck."

After the foreman backed the flatbed to the loading dock, the pair made quick work of stacking the eight bags needed. "Take 'em on out to the pasture box," the foreman said. "I'll feed up the horses and dogs."

Bodie nodded and hopped down from the truck bed. He opened the driverside door and started to climb in the cab, but hesitated when movement to the northeast caught his eye. He stood frozen with his left boot planted on the running board, seemingly mesmerized by what he saw.

Onnie Osteen's Dodge pickup was coming hard on the main grade, pulling a dust cloud stretching back to the distant cypress. Bodie shot a glance back at Pete Stalvey. "He'll never make the turn," he said, turning back quickly to see if his assertion was correct, looking just in time to witness the Dodge leaving the main grade, sliding sideways onto the barn road, its right side wheels momentarily lifting from the road and then slamming to the ground with force sufficient to cause the truck to rock violently, to fishtail wildly. A shower of cans and bottles rained to the ground from the sawing bed. Then, remarkably, the truck straightened and slowed and slid to a halt next to the foreman's parked Chevy.

After racing the engine a final time, Onnie switched it and the lights off and flung open the door. He exited the truck, his right hand cramming a Stetson on his head, his left stuffing shirttail into his jeans. He slammed the door and turned and walked briskly toward the flatbed and his gawking cohorts, grinning broadly and continuing to tuck in his shirt.

Bodie looked sideways at Pete.

The foreman leaned and spat and shook his head. "Crazy coot," he said.

Onnie stopped just short of the foreman. He grinned and stuffed his hands in his pant pockets. "Mornin, y'all," he said. "Sorry I'm late."

The boy stood trying to maintain a solemn look. "Mornin, bud."

The foreman crossed his arms. He stared at Onnie. "Truck trouble?"

Onnie, still smiling, shrugged. "No sir," he said. "Just didn't hear my alarm."

"Goin deaf, are you?"

Onnie cocked his head. "What's that, boss?"

The foreman's eyes sharpened. He waved a finger toward the flatbed. "Get your smart ass in the truck," he said. "That feed gits rained on, you'll sure as hell hear me."

Onnie jerked his hands out of his pockets. "Yessir," he said, turning and reaching for the truck's door latch.

The foreman turned on his heel and started up the loading dock steps.

Bodie climbed behind the flatbed's steering wheel and pulled his door closed. He started the engine and slipped the shift lever into drive and pulled away. He drove. He looked at his friend. "You better hope this rain ain't got lightnin with it."

"Why's that?"

"You're likely to get struck, tellin a whopper like that."

"What?"

"Didn't hear your alarm, my ass."

"That wasn't no lie." Onnie elbowed the boy's shoulder. "I didn't hear it. I wasn't home."

"What?"

"I spent the night over by Disney World."

The boy lifted his boot from the accelerator and braked the truck to a stop at a galvanized aluminum gate. "You finally got lucky, did ya?"

Onnie laughed. "Yep," he said. "Three times, that I remember."

The boy turned his head and spat out the window. "Open the damn gate," he said.

Nearly a hundred yearling calves—spread from one end of the eighty acre pasture to the other—simultaneously stopped grazing and raised their heads and stood glaring at the flatbed when it rolled through the gate and stopped. A few pointed their chins and bawled, but most stood stock still and watching. But when the truck began moving into the pasture, toward a long wooden feed trough standing in its center, all instantly moved as one, trotting to the vehicle, goggle-eyed and lowing continuously. The yearlings came to the flatbed like filings drawn to a magnet, and upon reaching it, swarmed behind it, followed it to the trough like a panic stricken mob. By the time Bodie and Onnie exited the truck, bovine chaos swirled about them. Yet the boys scarcely seemed to notice.

They stood between truck and trough, calves eddying about them like rising water, like schooling fish following an indecisive leader, the air thick with dust, incessant bawling. "I'll open and you dump," said Bodie. Then he turned and reached and dragged one of the double-layered paper bags from the truck bed. Grasping two corners, he shook the bag once, settling its contents, then stood it against his leg. He fished out his pocket knife and extended its blade and sliced a gaping hole in the bag's voided top.

Onnie snatched up the bag almost before Bodie's blade had completed its work. He turned quickly and pushed his way through milling calves, carrying the bag to the far end of the thirty-foot trough. He poured feed into the trough, stepping rapidly back toward Bodie, trying to avoid the chaotic scramble for position ensuing in his wake. In seconds he was back standing before Bodie, clutching the empty bag and gazing dejectedly at his own feet. "I wish you'd look at that," he said.

The boy looked.

"Them jugheads done stomped all the new out of my Justins."

The boy smiled. He reached and took the empty bag from Onnie's hand and indicated with his eyes that a full one stood ready against his leg.

Double Ought leaned and spat. He bent and hoisted the second bag, hugging it to his chest and turning and almost falling when a heifer was slow to move. "Git the hell out of the way," he said, kicking out at the calf and staggering forward in a comical dance, the feedbag hugged tightly to his chest like a legless partner.

In a scant few minutes all feed was in the trough and tranquility restored to the pasture. The boys stood with their backs against the high bed of the truck, legs crossed, arms folded against their chests. The calves were huddled around the feed box, tails swatting away flies, standing shoulder to shoulder and peacefully gorging themselves, the unmistakable look of ecstasy in their round and pupil dominated eyes. A light rain was beginning to fall.

"You got any smokes?" said Bodie.

Onnie snaked a hand to his hip pocket, producing a smashed-flat pouch of tobacco. "I got a chew."

Bodie took the pouch and opened it. He grouped a wad of the looseleaf with his fingers and loaded it into his mouth. He folded the pouch and handed it back and watched Onnie load his own chaw. He leaned and spat. "I ain't never been to Disney World."

Onnie cocked his head back and spat tobacco juice at the rump of a feeding calf some ten feet distant. He mopped his chin with his shirt sleeve. "I ain't either."

The boy looked at him. "You said you was there last night."

"No I didn't. I said I was by there. If you got to know, I was at the Hampton-freakin-Inn, the one next to the interstate."

The boy chewed. "Who was she?"

"Nobody you'd know."

"Try me."

Onnie uncrossed his legs and then crossed them back, reversing their order. "You don't know every girl around here."

"I know it."

"Anyway, this girl ain't from around here."

"She from Orlando?"

"No. Canada."

"A girl from Canada at the pits?"

"The pits is gittin to be a popular place."

The boy reached and plucked the tobacco from his mouth. He dropped the chaw to the ground and uncrossed his legs and raked dirt over the wad with his boot. "It's startin to rain," he said.

They drove to the barn in a steady drizzle. Pete Stalvey stood in the bay smoking a cigarette, just inside the drip-line, his brindle dog next to him, squatting on its haunches and tracking the arriving truck with its eyes. The dog growled when the boys exited the flatbed and came forward.

Pete Stalvey lifted a boot to the dog's muscular shoulder. "Hush," he said.
The dog hushed.

The boys stopped short of the barn door, stood in the rain eyeing the dog.

Pete looked at the boys. He exhaled smoke through his nose. "Come on in out of the weather. Buster ain't gonna bother you."

The boy circled the dog to stand beneath the barn's overhang.

Onnie did not move. He stood with his hands jammed in his pant pockets, watching the dog and grinning prodigiously.

"What the hell is so funny?" said Pete.

"I just cain't get over that dog's legs. Looks like somebody sawed a section outta each one, or somethin."

Pete smoked. He waved his cigarette at Onnie. "Well looky here," he said, "he may be short, but he's faster'n you might think."

Onnie ducked his head and scuffed the ground with his boot. "Shoot. Ain't no way that dog's fast."

Pete flicked his cigarette out into the rain. He pointed toward the feed room. "All right. Why don't we find out how quick he is. I got a six-pack says he can ketch you fore you get on that loadin dock."

Onnie looked at the dock and looked at Pete. "Budlight?"

"Any kind you want."

Onnie pulled his hands from his pockets. "You got to give me a head start."

"Well I don't know bout that," said Pete, reaching and adjusting his cap. "How much of a head start?"

"Half way."

"All right," Pete said without hesitation.

Bodie leaned and spat. He removed his hat and shook rain from it and put it back on.

Onnie pointed toward the dock. "I reckon that little puddle is bout half way. Don't turn him loose till I git to that little puddle."

Pete nodded. "All right. Git movin."

Onnie hitched up his jeans and turned and stepped toward the small pool of water ten yards away, walking with his head cocked to one side, keeping a wary eye on Pete and the dog.

At the completion of Onnie's first step, Pete simultaneously pointed a finger at him and spoke the dog's name. Seeing the hand, the dog's eyes locked onto Onnie, its entire body quivering. On Onnie's second stride, Pete calmly said "ketch", and the dog launched from the barn.

"Shit," said Onnie. He broke for the dock. He ran from under his hat, arms and legs pumping wildly, head jerking spasmodically as he repeatedly looked back at the fast closing dog.

"Don't look back," shouted Bodie.

But it was far too late for coaching. The dog reached Onnie before the boy's words, reached him and glommed onto his right pant leg just below the knee. Then the dog squatted and dug in with its hind feet, shaking and twisting its head until transforming Onnie's sprint into a backward one-legged jig, the dog snarling and pulling and shredding jeans. Onnie was hopping and grinning, saying nary a word.

The foreman whistled sharply. The dog released its hold and trotted back to Pete without a backward glance. Reaching the foreman's side, it turned and settled to its haunches and sat staring up at its master. Pete nodded and smiled thinly but did not touch the dog.

Onnie stood in the light rain for a couple of moments, legs spread wide, bent at the waist and grabbing his knees, gasping for breath. Then he straightened and walked toward the barn door with his torn pant leg flopping to and fro.

Pete watched him come. He dipped his head and wagged it from side to side. "Crazy coot's still smilin."

Onnie paused to pluck his Stetson from the small puddle that was to have been his starting line. He set the sopping wet hat on his head. He stood for a moment, his eyes panning from the puddle to the loading dock and back again. Then he turned to face Pete and Bodie, nodding his head and smiling more than ever. "I'd of made it," he said. "If that little son of a dachshund hadn't jumped the gun, I'd of made it sure as anything."

"Might would've," said Bodie. "But it wouldn't of been near as entertainin."

"I'll not argue the point," said Pete. He yanked a thumb over his shoulder. "Your beer's on ice in my truck."

Onnie's eyes widened. "You already got it?"

"Picked it up on the way in this morning."

"So your cheatin was premeditated."

Pete smiled.

Onnie cocked his head curiously and stepped inside the barn. He removed his waterlogged hat and briefly tried to shape it. He looked down at his boots and ruined pants and shook his head. "Danged if I ain't bout wrecked my new wardrobe."

Pete did not comment. He stood intently gazing across the pasture. "Yonder comes the boss," he said. "Somethin must be up, the way he's drivin."

Bodie stepped forward and watched his father's truck approach. He was silent, a strained look on his face.

*The man* paused before the frosted glass door to brush drops of water from his suit coat. He glanced back through the falling rain at his recently acquired Mercedes sport coupe then reached and rang the bell. A chorus of chimes within the posh Siesta Key home. A distorted figure arriving beyond the glass and the door opening outward and a stooped old woman peering around its edge. "I'm here about the lamp," said the man.

"Oh, yes," said the lady, "Mr. Lucious. Please come in."

The man smiled and nodded and muttered "close enough" beneath his breath as he stepped inside the home. A grand entryway then a spacious living room. Several lighted paintings gracing the walls.

"It's right here," said the lady, gesturing to a small Tiffany table lamp sitting on the white carpeted floor. "It was my grandmother's. We brought it here from New York, many years ago. It's in perfect condition, except for this small chip right here."

The man wasn't looking at the lamp. He stared instead at an impressionistic painting directly beyond the old woman. "That's an original Dali, isn't it?"

The lady looked. "Oh no," she said. "I'd never display an original. It's only a print."

The man stepped around her and leaned in for a closer inspection of the picture. "Ah yes," he said, then turned and focused his unblinking blue eyes on the woman. "I think you fibbed to me."

The lady's cheeks flushed with color. She began to wring her hands. "You didn't come here for the lamp, did you?"

"That's very astute of you."

"You're not going to hurt me, are you?"

"Certainly not. I promise you won't feel a thing."

**9**

**Seth Rawlerson** drove his truck directly to the barn bay, to his waiting cohorts. He did not get out. With engine idling and wipers slapping, he lowered his window and addressed his son. "Daddy's awake. He wants to see you."

"Yessir." Bodie circled the truck and climbed into the passenger seat.

Seth shifted his gaze from his son to the foreman. "Feed truck's supposed to be here around ten," he said. "Bodie and me should be back time he's done unloadin. If we're gonna be later, I'll call."

Pete nodded. "You want us to go ahead and move them calves to the loadin pen?"

Seth shook his head. "I'd just as soon not have to listen to 'em all night. Truck's not comin till noon tomorrow. We'll have plenty of time to move 'em in the mornin." Seth's eyes panned as he spoke and suddenly focused on Onnie. "What the hell happened to your breeches, Double Ought?"

Onnie grinned sheepishly. He motioned with his hand toward the sitting dog. "Caught 'em on them blame teeth of his," he said.

Seth's eyebrows arched. "You got dog bit?"

Pete Stalvey slapped the truck's hood. "We had us a little footrace," he said. "Bodie'll tell you bout it."

Though Seth briefly glanced at his son, his words were directed at the foreman. "All right," he said. "We'll see you in a little bit."

They drove toward St. Cloud, father and son, the gray-cast morning a fitting

75

backdrop for a journey such as was theirs. The rain intensified until standing water mapped every imperfection in Canoe Creek Road. A stiff southwesterly breeze slanted the rain and held sway over everything vertical. As they drove, the boy related how Onnie's pants came to be torn but said little else. His father said even less. At the hospital they paused before the main doors, water dripping from their person as they stomped boots and shook hats before entering. And what rain they could not shed, they carried with them to the elevator and on to the second floor room where the object of their shared melancholy lay waiting.

July's room being semi-private, Bodie and his father eased through the open door and past a man who was not there the night before, a skeleton-like figure sleeping with toothless mouth agape, cadaverous eyes half-open. The room was dimly lighted, quiet, the raspy breathing of the stranger and a barely perceptible high-pitched whine the only sounds. Beyond a curtain dividing the room sat Jo Beth, a smile of recognition leaping to her face. Her father lay next to her and looked as though he'd aged ten years overnight, propped up by pillows, eyes open but fixed on ceiling tiles overhead.

Seth and Bodie stopped at the foot of the bed and stood holding their hats. "Hey," said Seth.

Jo Beth stood. "You two look like drowned rats," she said. "It still raining?"

Seth stepped closer to the bed. He looked at his father. "Pourin," he said. "How you doin, Daddy?"

The old man's eyes swam to his son. "Not worth a damn," he breathed.

Seth turned his soggy cap in his hands. "You hurtin?"

"Naw. Just tired. My back hurts, but that ain't nothin." He looked at Bodie. "What's shakin, boy?"

Bodie stepped and stood. "Hey, Granddaddy."

"Reckon I give you quite a scare."

The boy bobbed his head. "Yessir. You did."

A call came over the PA system, a doctor being summoned. An orderly goaded a cart past the open door.

"We didn't finish our talk, did we?"

"No sir. I reckon we didn't."

"I fear we ain't never gonna finish it."

Bodie waved his hat in the air. "We'll finish it. You'll be comin home soon. We'll take us another ride."

The old man stared at the ceiling. The PA system blared again but no one in the room seemed to hear it.

July cut his eyes to his daughter. "I'm gonna have the boy's name put on the deed," he said.

Jo Beth straightened. She looked at Seth and looked at Bodie and then fixed her gaze on her father. "And my girls?"

"Your girls got no interest in the ranch. The boy's gonna run it one day."

Jo Beth stepped and stood. She crossed her arms and half-turned, and then she turned back. "That's just not fair, Daddy. You'd be cheating the rest of us, cutting our shares."

The old man focused his eyes on Seth. "Get Bud Townsend to draw it up pronto—bring it in here for me to sign."

Jo Beth uncrossed her arms. "Daddy!"

July looked at her. "My mind's made up."

Music suddenly erupted from Jo Beth's purse on the floor. Bethoven's Fifth. She reached and fished a cell phone from the purse and held it up and stared at it. "You've *lost* your mind," she said, shouldering past her brother and his son, the phone pressed to her ear. "Hello," she virtually shouted. She left the room speaking rapidly, the sound of her voice waning once she reached the hallway.

Bodie looked at his father, his grandfather. "My name don't need to be on no deed," he said. "Daddy's is on it. That's good enough for me."

July's eyelids sagged shut. "It needs to be on there," he said, his body visibly relaxing.

"Daddy?" Seth called.

The old man was silent.

Seth looked at his cap. He sighed.

Jo Beth suddenly reentered the room. She looked at the old man. She looked at Seth. "We aren't going to stand for this. You're not going to get away with this."

Seth cocked his head. "Me?"

"Yes, you. I know what your up to."

"I'm not up to nothin."

Jo Beth stooped and gathered in her purse. She stuffed the phone in it and turned and leaned over her father. "Daddy," she said. When there was no response, she briefly felt the old man's neck then turned to Seth. "You try and change that will, you'll hear from my lawyer." She started for the door but Seth stopped her.

77

He reached and captured her arm. "You need to settle down, Jo. There's no way I would ever cheat you and Billy. I don't know what got into Daddy. And that's the truth."

Jo Beth looked at Bodie and looked at Seth. Her expression softened. "Yeah," she said. "I guess you wouldn't." She looked at the old man and shook her head. "He's going, isn't he?"

Seth released his sister's arm. He inhaled deeply.

"I've got to go," Jo Beth said. "You'll call me if there's any change?"

Seth nodded. "I'll call you."

Jo Beth reached and touched the boy's hand. "Bye Bodie."

Bodie dipped his head goodbye.

Turning on her heel, Jo Beth hurried from the room, shouldering her purse as she went.

Bodie watched his aunt's departure then turned and sidestepped to the great window overlooking his grandfather's bed. He reached and with his fingers parted the closed Venetian blinds. He peered out. "What are we gonna do?"

Seth stared vacantly at the veneered nightstand rising beside the head of his father's bed, a tray supporting a pitcher and a pair of plastic cups wrapped in cellophane, his father's glasses, a small box of Kleenex. "We're gonna go home," he said. "No telling when he'll wake again. We'll stop by Bud Townsend's office on the way."

The boy lowered his arm and the blinds obligingly closed off the outside world. He turned his gaze to the old man in the bed. "I reckon we have to, don't we?"

"Yeah," his father said. "We do."

*

The lawyer's office was located in a small strip-center at the west end of town, sandwiched between a beauty parlor and a deceased video store. Seth parked the truck in the squatty, flat-roofed structure's potholed lot and, together with his son, got out and walked to a darkly tinted door bearing the inscription *Townsend & Associates*. They removed their hats before opening the door and stepping into a waiting room. The room was small, several leather armchairs backed against the leftmost wall, in front of them a coffee table topped with neatly cascaded magazines, to the right an attractive young woman sitting at a desk and looking up

78

expectantly from her computer screen.

"Can I help you?" the woman said. She had dark hair and eyes, olive skin, her words flavored by a faint Spanish accent.

Seth gave a quick nod. "Mornin, miss. Seth Rawlerson to see Mr. Townsend."

"Is he expecting you?" the girl said, her eyes fixed on Bodie.

"No ma'am. But he'll see me if he's here."

The girl got up and walked through the open doorway behind her. She disappeared briefly then reappeared and sat in her swivel chair and told Seth the lawyer would see him immediately.

Seth looked at Bodie. "You want to come?"

The boy shook his head. "I'll wait out here."

Seth looked at the girl and looked at Bodie. He smiled and nodded and walked through the open doorway.

Bodie watched his father depart then moved to one of the chairs and turned and sat in it. He looked at the girl. She looked at him.

The girl shuffled papers on her desk. "You don't remember me, do you?"

"You look familiar."

"Rosa Sanchez," she said. "I was a senior when you were a sophomore."

Bodie nodded. "You were a cheerleader."

Rosa Sanchez smiled. "Right. I was."

"I remember you."

The girl smiled again then swiveled her chair to look at the computer monitor. She typed a few keystrokes then turned and looked at Bodie. "Are you playing college ball?"

"I ain't in college."

The girl looked perplexed. "Thought I read where you got a scholarship to UCF."

Bodie set his hat in the chair next to him and leaned forward and plucked a magazine from the coffee table, a two month old issue of *Florida Wildlife,* a slinking panther gracing its cover. "It was just a partial," he said. "I didn't take it."

The girl watched him thumb through the magazine pages. When he settled back in his chair and began reading, she rolled her eyes and turned back to her work.

Bodie read the magazine's feature article on panthers, his father emerging from the back room just as he finished. Returning the magazine to the table, he picked up his hat and got up and followed his father to the door. Before exiting the building, he paused and turned and looked at the girl. "Nice to see you," he said.

The girl gave a little wave of her hand, but said nothing.

In the truck, Seth Rawlerson lit a cigarette and looked at his son. "You get a date with that gal?"

Bodie watched cars passing on main street. "No sir. Didn't try."

Seth exhaled smoke through his nose. He started the truck and put it in reverse and began backing up. "Damn, boy. The way she was lookin at you!"

They drove.

"Mr. Townsend gonna change the will?"

Seth nodded. "He's bound to do whatever Daddy wants. But it won't mean a thing if Daddy can't sign it."

They turned onto Canoe Creek Road. Seth smoked. Bodie gazed out his window, watching countless blue-tarped roofs pass by, countless homes still showing damage from the hurricanes. And when there were no more homes, he stared blankly at the passing woods. As they slowed to take the ranch road, he spoke. "She's married," he said.

"What?"

"Rosa Sanchez. She was wearin a weddin band."

Seth looked at his son then shifted his eyes back to the grade. After almost a minute, he said: "Well I'm damned relieved to hear it."

**10**

**Abby Thompson's** Ford pickup was parked at the barn when Seth and Bodie got back. The tractor-trailer from Lakeland Cash Feed also was there, backed up to the loading dock. The driver and Pete Stalvey stood in the turn-around discussing a bill of lading. Abby and Onnie sat on the flatbed, swinging legs and talking. A stiff wind gusted out of the west, the temperature falling.

Seth parked next to the flatbed. Upon exiting the truck, he said hello to Abby then walked to Pete and the driver. Bodie hopped up on the flatbed next to Abby. He thumbed back his hat. "Hey," he said. "Ain't you cold?"

Abby cast him a sideways glance, but said nothing.

Onnie grinned.

Bodie studied Abby's profile. "What's got you all pooch-lipped?"

Abby turned and looked him in the eyes. "You might've told me July was in the hospital."

Bodie leaned and spat. "I ain't seen you to tell you anything."

"You could've called."

Bodie rocked forward to look past Abby, to look at Onnie.

Onnie rolled his eyes and looked away.

"I should've called you," he said. "Reckon I just wasn't thinkin." He looked at her low-rider jeans and tank top, then glanced at his watch. "You already done with school?"

"It's Wednesday, dummy."

"I know what day it is. So?"

Abby looked at the ground. She swung her legs. "You never listen to me, do you?"

"What's that sposed to mean?"

"I've told you my schedule about a jillion times."

Onnie slapped his leg and laughed out loud. "Danged if ya'll don't sound married."

Abby looked at Onnie and smiled. Then she turned to see Bodie's reaction but he seemed not to have heard Onnie's remark. He was concentrating on something to the north, his eyes squinted and unblinking.

"That's a lot of buzzards," he said.

Onnie and Abby followed the boy's gaze and witnessed a column of circling black specks suspended above the distant horizon, the soaring vultures descending one after the other, spiraling downward and ultimately vanishing below treetops almost a mile away.

"Got to be somethin big," said Onnie, "to pull in a passel like that."

Bodie slid from the truck bed and walked to his father. Seth stood talking with Pete and the driver. When Seth acknowledged his son's presence, Bodie pointed out the buzzards. "I got time to go check it out?" he said.

Seth studied the circling birds. He looked at his watch. "Yeah," he said. "Might as well saddle your horse, go ahead and check on all them pregnant cows up there. Some of em's due to drop anytime now." He leaned and spat. "I hate to think it, but that many buzzards probably means one has already tried."

Bodie nodded and started to turn but then stopped and looked at his father. "All right if Abby comes along?"

Seth glanced toward the flatbed. He shrugged. "I reckon, if she wants to go. Not Onnie, though. I need him to get the tractor ready. I want to start the mowin tomorrow—first thing after we move them calves."

"Yessir. I'll tell him."

"And don't you and Miss Abby get lost out there. Me and your mama's goin back to the hospital to set with Daddy. I'd like you to come and spell us so we can get some supper."

"I'll be there."

Bodie walked to the flatbed. He looked up at Onnie. "Daddy wants you to prep the tractor for mowin tomorrow."

Onnie frowned and dipped his head. "Heard every word ya'll said. I get to work while you slip off to the woods with a beautiful gal."

After elbowing Onnie's ribs, Abby jumped down from the truck. She looked at Bodie. "And thank you for asking," she said.

Bodie looked away. He looked at Abby. "Well, you want to go with me, or not?"

"We ridin double?"

"We can, or you can ride Mama's mare. She could use some exercise."

"Double."

"All right."

Onnie slid from the truck bed, dusted his breeches and began waddling toward the tractor shed, his shredded pant leg whipping about his starkly white calf. "Oh lonesome me ..." he wailed.

Abby, watching him go, sighed: "Poor Onnie."

The boy rolled his eyes and shook his head.

They road out of the barn bay sight unseen. The feed truck was gone, along with Seth Rawlerson. The foreman and Onnie were beneath the equipment shed, bent over and connecting a six-foot bushhog to the tractor's PTO shaft. The wind had grown stronger, colder. Abby pulled close to Bodie, her arms encircling his waist, her cheek pressed against his back.

"You're freezin, ain't you?" he said.

"Just a little."

After negotiating the gates, Bodie guided the horse to the board fence outlining his yard. He dismounted and, leaving Abby sitting the horse, hopped the fence and went into the house. He reappeared a moment later carrying his rifle and two denim jackets. He propped the Winchester against the fence and tossed one of the jackets up to Abby. She slipped it on while he donned the other.

"This your mama's?"

He nodded. "She won't mind."

He hopped the fence and reached and got the rifle and turned and slid it into the boot scabbard. Then he caught up the reins and mounted up by standing in the stirrup and scissoring his right leg over the horse's neck. He touched the Appaloosa's flanks with his heels, and they rode north, the horse stepping lively as if unaware of the extra burden it carried.

"That jacket warm enough?" Bodie said.

Abby clung to him. "It is. I'm toasty now."

Only a few buzzards were still visible in the sky, but more than enough for Bodie to guide on. He first rode straight for the circling birds, covering nearly three quarters of a mile and crossing the twin sandy ruts of the cemetery road. Then he reined the horse more easterly.

"Where you going?" Abby questioned. "The buzzards are over there."

"Just gettin the wind right."

"Oh. I gotcha. You're gonna find whatever it is with your nose."

"You're pretty smart for a college gal."

Abby gave him a squeeze. She pressed her nose to his neck and took in his scent. "I could find you that way."

"What way?"

"With my nose."

"You're sayin I smell dead?"

"No, dummy. I'm saying you smell wonderful."

"Jesus, girl."

"Why are you blushing?"

"I ain't."

"Oh yes you are."

They rode, and the faint odor of carrion soon became evident on the wind. When Bodie turned the horse to the smell, the Appaloosa blew and tossed its head and he spoke to it and touched its neck reassuringly.

"You love him, don't you?"

"Who?"

"Limpkin."

"He's a horse."

"You still love him."

As they tracked the odor, the under growth thickened, tall palmettos and gallberry growing rank among towering pines. The smell soon ramped up to a stench. Then, when the horse pushed through a line of wax myrtles and into a small clearing, their search suddenly ended.

Amid a din of guttural croaking and flapping wings, vultures began launching from trampled broomsage in the clearing's center, from the dark carcass of an Angus heifer. Most of the buzzards were airborne in seconds, each beat of their great wings purchasing vast gains in elevation. Some peeled back right and left and glided and landed in nearby pines. Others climbed high, soaring in ever widening circles above the foul banquet they had abandoned. Two obstinate birds, a turkey buzzard and a common vulture, did neither. As Bodie turned the horse and circled upwind, the defiant pair displayed threateningly, their naked and wrinkled heads color-shifting, the both of them hissing and pacing about the heifer with a stiff, short-legged gate, their splayed and taloned toes lifting and planting and lifting again, a strange hypnotic dance continuing until Bodie stopped the horse and dismounted. Then, the pair flushed as one, their noisy departure raising a cloud of blow flies, a buzzing swarm that stayed aloft but briefly before settling back to the carcass.

Bodie let the reins drop and turned and offered a hand up to Abby. He supported her to the ground and then studied the dead yearling twenty feet away. "You might want to stay over here," he said. "She's likely pretty rank."

"I've seen rank before."

Bodie shrugged. "Suit yourself. Keep behind me, though. I need to try and figure out what happened to her." He stepped cautiously toward the carcass, his eyes panning the ground.

"You want to preserve the scene—like on CSI," Abby said.

Bodie glanced over his shoulder. "CSI?"

"The TV show. Don't tell me you've never watched it."

"All right. I won't."

A buzzard pitched from a nearby pine and glided away. Flies crawled the corpse in search of exposed flesh. The horse stretched its head forward and tested the air, its nostrils flaring and relaxing and flaring again.

Bodie stepped and looked. The ground around the heifer was trampled extensively, the broom sage bent and flattened as far as ten feet away. Close to the carcass, bare dirt was darkly stained with blood, sandy loam tracked and cross-tracked by countless buzzards. Bodie shifted his attention to the carcass itself, hunkering down near the hindquarters. The upside ham was practically gone, a great crescent-shaped chunk of muscle missing, the hip joint clearly visible. Blow flies rose from the ragged flesh, looping through the air in search of a new location on the carcass to make a deposit, to sow the tiny yellow pearls holding their species' future. He leaned and studied the rectal area and each of the hind legs. Then he stood and stepped right and leaned over the front shoulder, his eyes panning slowly from the slightly distended belly forward. Reaching the neck, he leaned even more and studied a good while and then straightened and turned to

85

Abby. "You ever seen a panther kill?"

Abby looked at him. She looked at the yearling. "A panther? You think a panther killed her?"

Bodie thumbed back his hat and nodded his head. "Yeah," he said. "I believe so."

"But there aren't any panthers around here."

"There's at least one. Granddaddy and me seen him yesterday morning."

Abby was silent, her eyes shifting between the calf and Bodie.

"We got a good look." He gestured east with his hand. "It practically posed for us in the middle of the grade, over by the cattle gap. Sat there eyeing us for almost a minute."

"But what makes you think it killed this heifer?"

"Process of elimination," said Bodie. "First off, she didn't just die on her own. Somethin killed her for sure. Caught her some time yesterday, I'd say. She's barely started to bloat, barely stinkin." He stepped left and pointed toward the animal's hind end. "Whatever tore into the paunch and fed on that ham, did it while she was still alive. Look how the blood pooled there. Her heart had to be beatin to produce that much blood."

Abby reached and touched Bodie's arm. "I'm impressed," she said. "But how do you know it wasn't coyotes, or even dogs? We've lost calves to both, at times."

He pointed at the calf's hind legs. "There's not a mark on her legs," he said. He dropped his left arm and raised his right to point at the cow's front end. "And look at her nose and ears; not a mark on 'em. Her tongue is pretty near gone, but that was done by buzzards. Buzzards always get the tongue and eyes first. No hide to get through. Coyotes and dogs attack the legs and nose to bring an animal her size down. It wasn't no canine done this. It was a feline."

The boy circled the eyeless head and leaned over and parted black hair on the back of the neck. "You see this?"

Abby moved close to him and bent at the waist and looked where he indicated. "Looks like a bullet hole," she said.

"Does, sort of," Bodie said, moving his hand a few inches to the right, where he again parted hair. "But so does this one." He marked the two holes with his thumb and index finger, measured the distance between them. "How wide you reckon a panther's bite is?"

"I'd say just about wide enough to make those two punctures."

He looked at Abby, nodding. "And look at this." He reached and brushed the hair where shoulder blended into neck, the hair just above the brisket. He pulled his hand back and turned it palm up for Abby to see.

"Blood," she said.

"It's done turned so black it's hard to see on her hair." He parted the hair with his fingers. "There's deep cuts here—made by the cat's claws, I reckon—as it held on to bite her spine. If we roll her over, I bet there's more on the other side."

Abby straightened and rested her hands on her hips. She smiled down at Bodie. "You're amazing," she said. "You're a regular Sherlock-freaking-Holmes."

Bodie rolled his eyes. "Yeah, right," he said. He stood and circled Abby, all the while looking at the ground. Shifting his gaze to the heifer, he said: "He tried to hide her, but didn't do a very good job." He gestured toward loose grass and dirt heaped against the cows belly. "See where he scratched the broom sage and dirt up here. It used to be on the carcass. Buzzards knocked it off."

"They cover their kills the way bobcats do."

Bodie nodded. "He's tryin to keep somethin from makin off with his future meals."

Abby's head swiveled right then left. "So he's probably still around here."

"He probably ain't far. But I doubt he'll come back for seconds." Bodie gestured vaguely in the air with a hand. "We've laid a lot of scent down."

"Then he'll have to kill again."

Bodie looked. "Well yeah," he said. "That's how he lives."

Abby's gaze sharpened. "I'm not stupid, you know."

"Never said you were."

"Your tone did."

Bodie reached and took off his hat and looked in its basin. "Sorry," he said. "That was just my frustration seepin out."

Abby studied his profile. The wind gusted and caused palmettos around the clearing to bend and sway. Vultures perched here and there in the pines, patiently waiting. "You frustrated over losing the heifer?"

Bodie set his hat back on his head. "No," he said. "She's dead and gone. It's knowin I'm likely to lose more, and there ain't a thing I can do about it. It just don't seem natural to stand by and let somethin slaughter your stock." He leaned and spat. "But on the other hand, it wouldn't seem natural killin that panther, either. I sort of like knowin the blame thing's around."

Abby reached and touched his arm. She smiled and shook her head. "Then I do too," she said.

Bodie fished his knife from his pocket and opened its blade. Stepping next to the cow's head, he knelt and deftly cut a tag from its left ear, a yellow wafer displaying the black numerals, 77. He stood and closed the knife and stuffed it and the tag in his pocket. He turned to Abby. "Reckon seven wasn't her lucky number."

Abby looked down at the heifer but said nothing.

"You want to go with me this evenin?"

"To the hospital?"

He nodded. "If Granddaddy's awake, it might cheer him to see you."

"I'll need to go home first—to change and get the horse off me."

"You don't have to on my account. Horse is one of my favorite smells."

"Mine, too. But I'm not a horse."

Bodie dipped his head and smiled. He scuffed the ground with his boot. "I reckon you got me there."

Abby smiled shamelessly. "Well now," she said. "That may be a first."

Bodie turned to her. He looked into her eyes but remained silent as the cow at his feet.

*

It was a little past five when they got to the hospital. When they reached the second floor Bodie's parents stood in the corridor outside July's room, arms folded about their chests, faces drawn and expressionless.

"Daddy's messed himself," Seth explained. "The aides are cleanin him up."

Bodie nodded. "He awake?"

Seth shook his head. "Doctor says he's in a coma."

"He could come out of it, though," Angela added, then shifting her gaze from Bodie to Abby. "Your folks doing okay?"

Abby smiled and nodded. She folded her arms and then unfolded them. She stuffed her hands into her pant pockets.

Seth gestured toward his son with a hand. "What did you find up there? Was it a cow?"

Bodie nodded. "One of the replacement heifers."

Seth looked puzzled. "One of the yearlins?"

"Yessir."

"Could you tell what happened?"

"Yessir. She was panther caught."

Seth stared at his son. He watched Abby nod her head. "Panther caught?" he said. "You see the panther?"

Bodie shifted his weight from one foot to the other. He looked at his hat and looked at his father. "Not right then, but granddaddy and me seen him yesterday. What with him gettin sick and all, I forgot to tell you."

Seth turned and glanced down the hallway. He looked at Angela and looked at Bodie. "I ain't never in my life seen a panther. You sure?"

"Yessir. And I'm sure he's what killed the heifer."

"I'm surprised July didn't shoot it on sight," Angela injected. "Ya'll must not of had a gun."

Bodie shook his head. "He said we're not to mess with him—said the old cat wouldn't stick around long enough to cause any serious damage."

Seth looked. "Daddy said that?"

"Yessir. He did."

Seth fashioned a tight-lipped smile while slowly wagging his head. He looked at Bodie and Abby. "Well, we're gonna get us some supper," he said. "Ya'll can go on in soon as those gals are done." He focused on the boy. "It's not likely he'll wake up, but if he does, call us. Bud Townsend's got the addendum to the will done. I'll have to get hold of him, get him down here no matter what the time."

"Yessir," said Bodie.

Shortly after Seth and Angela had gone, the aides finished their work and Bodie and Abby entered the room. They sat with the comatose July until almost ten. He never woke up, and he never got to see Abby. He never would see Abby again.

**11**

**The old man** remained in a coma for three days. He suffered periodic seizures, two occurring in the evening when Bodie was there to help the hospital staff restrain him, to witness an aspect of life that, once seen, is never forgotten, a revelation of suffering which he never could have imagined before now.

Meanwhile, life at Curlew proceeded in veiled normalcy. The sun rose and set. The stock watered and fed. On Thursday ninety-three yearlings were walked to the holding pen, a slow ballet of man and beast in which force played no role. By early afternoon the yearlings stood nose to tail and shoulder to shoulder onboard a cattle hauler bound for the Okeechobee Livestock Market. By sunset, two-thirds of the improved pasture had been mowed, the remainder mowed the morning following, along with the road shoulders to the highway and back. Also on Friday, nine horses' were vaccinated against equine encephalitis, their hooves cleaned and trimmed. After which, seventy-three replacement heifers were penned and inoculated against communicable diseases. Lastly, with the sun low on the horizon, Bodie released the six deer hounds from their pens and allowed them to hunt, to run a phantom buck until their pink tongues lolled, until their blood-borne desire to run more was sated, if only temporarily.

Saturday morning, Bodie rose before dawn and dressed and drove himself to the hospital. He found his grandfather's room eerily quiet. The stranger was gone, his bed stripped of its linens, its emptiness unsettling to Bodie. He eased to the chair by his comatose grandfather and quietly sat in it. He studied the old man's features: the hawked nose and unruly eyebrows, the paper thin and veined lids con-cealing eyes he'd always respected, power he'd once feared, the square shoulders and long gaunt arms, liver-spotted and loose-skinned, nearly hairless. He also studied the horrible bruises acquired during the seizures, the ones from being poked and prodded by people who were strangers and who never would be other-wise. He scrutinized every exposed inch of his grandfather's body, and then he spoke to him.

He told the old man Abby had come to see him, that she was sorry not to have come sooner. He told him about the slain heifer and, when done telling, asked the old man his opinion as to how long the cat would likely wait before killing again. He mentioned the one-eyed Indian, saying that he'd given a lot of thought to the things the man had said, that of all the things in the world that scared him, it was change that terrified him most. He talked incessantly, saying everything he could think to say, and was still speaking when Doctor Hutchinson suddenly appeared next to him.

Bodie leaped to his feet, stood holding his hat and smiling shamefacedly. "Hey, Doc," he said.

The doctor smiled and motioned with his hand for the boy to sit back down. "Hey, Bodie. You get any response from the old fellow?"

Bodie sat. "No sir. I reckon he ain't heard a word I said."

"Well, we don't know that for sure, do we? Could be that he hears everything—that he's just not able to let us know."

"Yessir."

"I personally think talking to a comatose loved-one is good therapy."

"You do?"

"I do—especially for the one doing the talking."

Bodie smiled. "Yessir." He raised a hand and gestured to his grandfather. "How you think he's doin?"

The doctor shook his head. "He doesn't have much longer. How much longer, I can't really say."

"Yessir."

The doctor peered over his glasses at the boy. "You going to be okay?"

"Yessir. I'll be all right."

The doctor turned and started for the door but stopped and looked back at Bodie. He nodded his head. "I know you will," he said. "You'll be just fine."

After the doctor left, Bodie sat a while longer then stood and donned his hat and reached and grasped his grandfather's hand with both of his own. "Goodbye, Granddaddy," he said. He turned and glanced at the doorway then turned back and leaned and kissed the old man's forehead lightly. "I love you." Then, releasing July's hand, he straightened and turned to leave…

"It was good to see ya." The words spoken scarcely in a whisper, barely audible, perhaps not audible at all.

Bodie stood frozen in place, staring at the old man's still and ashen lips. "Granddaddy," he said.

That there was no response did not shake the boy's conviction that his grandfather had spoke to him. He *did* speak to him. He was sure of it—absolutely certain of it. And nothing or no one would ever convince him otherwise.

*

It was almost noon when he drove home. A cloudless sky, pleasantly cool. He met his parents on the ranch road and pulled to the side and stopped and sat leaning out the truck's window to update them on July's condition, to tell them Doc Hutchinson's forecast. His father told him to stay close to the phone, that they would summon him if the old man's condition worsened. His mother repeated the same and then told him to be sure and eat something.

At the house he made a ham sandwich and carried it to the porch and sat eating it and gazing across the fresh-mowed pasture at his grandfather's home. He watched a pair of sandhill cranes striding long-legged and graceful in the midday sunlight, their tethered shadows bunched beneath them and mimicking perfectly the slow grace of their creators. To the north a half-dozen ironheads—wood storks—stood slump-shouldered and crook-necked, soundly sleeping on a ditch bank. A bull bellowed incessantly in the distance. From the east the dull roar of traffic coursing Florida's Turnpike came and went at the behest of a shifting breeze. He watched and listened and rocked, and then he rose from the chair and walked purposefully to the stoop where he sat and donned his boots.

He climbed the yard fence on the south side of the house and whistled sharply to his horse, his Appaloosa cropping grass in the pasture a few hundred yards west. The horse threw up its head, ears pricked forward, eyes searching for its master. And when Bodie moved toward the barn, the horse spotted him and came to him at a fast walk. The two of them, horse and boy, reached the gate to the barn trap simultaneously.

Minutes later he rode from the barn, turning the horse northward into a cool wind. Beyond the gates, he urged the horse to a lope. He held that pace across the open flatwoods and on beyond the cemetery road. Nearing the dead heifer, he slowed to a walk before proceeding through the myrtles and on into the grassy clearing. Buzzards again flushed from the carcass, but far fewer than before. He skirted the clearing's east edge until upwind of the remains and halted the horse and dismounted. He dropped the reins and stepped forward, looking for any sign signaling the panther had returned. But upon closer examination of the area, he lost all hope of finding such sign. The carcass had been reduced to mere hide and bones, the ground littered with black hair and feather's, rank with the smell of death. After surveying the scene but briefly, he turned and mounted his horse.

He continued north, riding through pine woods, an oak grove, a broad cypress strand. At the boundary fence, he turned the horse eastward, following the disked fire break at a walk, listing in the saddle and studying the turned ground intently. When almost to Canoe Creek Road, he cut the panther's track.

Bodie sat the horse studying the sign, leaning forward, his arms crossed at the wrists and resting on the saddle's pommel. The track was much larger than he had imagined, broader than a grown man's fist. The cat, having entered the firebreak from the south, had followed it briefly before stepping through the barbed wire and continuing northeast. Hair was on the wire, a brownish-gray tuft of it trapped in one of the barbs, the hairs black-tipped and less than an inch long. If not for the panther's tracks, he would have mistaken it for the hair of a deer.

Bodie studied the sign for several minutes, until his horse signaled it had had enough by dipping its head low, flaring its nostrils and blowing, its eyes rolling and whiting out. A shiver rippled through the animal, and after, its entire body stiffened. "All right," Bodie said. "I hear ya."

He stood in the stirrups and momentarily gazed at the woods beyond the fence. Then he settled in the saddle and turned the horse back west. He rode the fence several hundred yards but then quit it to follow a cattle trail angling southwest. When reaching the cemetery road, the horse put in to follow one of the sandy ruts, and Bodie made no move to stop it. He simply let the animal carry him where he himself had not yet formed the notion to go. And when the notion came to him, he leaned forward and stroked the horse's neck, thanking it for knowing what an animal such as it could not possibly have known.

At the cemetery's great live oak, he stood down from the horse and trailed the hogwire fence to the rickety gate, his left hand floating in the air and touching the top of each decaying post he passed. He opened the gate and stepped through and on to his grandfather's memorial, no conscious thought guiding his course, no reason or motive of which he was aware. At the stone marker he removed his hat and hunkered down and sat teetering on the balls of his feet. He read the stone's inscription, read it and reread it, reading until suddenly realizing the epitaph was complete, as if he himself had completed it, as if his own eyes had ordained that today's date be that of his grandfather's demise. He closed his eyes in horror. But his handiwork wrought by thought was ineffaceable. He reached and touched the granite and found the stone smooth and blameless, no date of death inscribed, his fingers disproving the lie his eyes had told, yet he still trembled. Suddenly, his eyes widened, and he sprang to his feet, saying: "The phone."

Sprinting to his horse, he caught the reins and leaped into the saddle. He spun the Appaloosa, cross-flogging its shoulders with the reins, whipping it to a gallop, pulling his hat down tight on his head and leaning forward, the wind rushing and the world blurring. He tested the horse, pushed it as he had never pushed it before, running it flat-out all the way home.

At the house, he left the horse lathered and blowing at the yard fence He raced up the walk to the porch, bounding up the steps but then stopping suddenly as if encountering an invisible wall. He stood before the front door, hand trembling above the brass knob. He turned and looked back at his horse. "You stupid bastard," he said to himself. And just like that, he stopped shaking. He reached and pushed the door open and stepped inside the house. He proceeded directly to the phone in the kitchen and, upon seeing the flashing message light, began to shake again, his hand now surely afflicted with palsy as he reached to press the play button.

"Hey, Bodie." His mother's voice. "We forgot to mention it earlier, but we'd like you to come and relieve us for supper. There's been no change, so we might as well plan on eating around the regular time. See you then."

Bodie exhaled a deep sigh. He glanced at his watch and then hurried outside. He led the Appaloosa to the barn where he unsaddled it and rubbed it dry. He rubbed its legs with liniment, all the while talking to the horse, or perhaps himself, trying to explain his odd behavior. He brushed the horse and combed the tangles from its mane and tail and fed it oats before turning it out in the trap. Then, hurrying back to the house, he rushed to clean himself before going to relieve his parents.

He reached the hospital at a little past five. A blood red sun was slowly descending into the southwestern horizon, the day's heat rapidly escaping. After parking his truck, he strolled inside and through the main lobby. The elevator occupied, he bounded up the switch-backed stairs. He entered his grandfather's room walking quickly, so quickly he almost plowed into his cousins, Margaret and Amy, who stood just inside the doorway. The room was packed with people. Besides his parents and Jo Beth's daughters, Jo Beth and Billy were there—Billy's wife, Claudia, and a man wearing a dark suit and holding a large Bible at his side. All in the room heard or sensed his entrance and turned as one to look at him, their common expression both strained and solemn. He felt paralyzed by their stares. He could but stand in the doorway and turn the hat in his hands, all the while knowing. Though not a word had been spoken, every face before him screamed it was so. July Rawlerson was dead.

**12**

**The stranger in black** strode boldly to Bodie, reaching out a sympathetic hand and trailing a celluloid aura revolting to the boy. The man—whom Bodie would later learn was the new pastor at Abby's church—spoke consoling words, uttered canned phrases the boy scarcely heard and quickly forgot. He would remember little else said in that room, in that modicum of minutes he stood gazing at a lifeless body only vaguely resembling his grandfather. What he would remember was the look on his father's face, a look so hollow, so lost, a new expression but one his father would employ often in the future. And oddly, he would also remember the men from Morgan Brothers' who came to collect the body, two immaculately dressed little fellows with bowed heads and clasped hands, men expertly solemn and speaking of the deceased in hushed tones as not to upset the living. He remembered them for the palpable relief their arrival swept into the room. Their presence on the scene allowing family members to leave, to go their separate ways packing somewhat clear consciences.

Bodie left with his parents. They walked together to the hospital's parking lot, his parents speaking to him for the first time since he arrived. The first time he was aware of, anyway. "He just stopped breathing," Angela said. "Less than an hour after I left you the first message."

Bodie pushed open the plate-glass door and stepped through and into the cool evening air. He stood holding the door open for his parents. "The first message? You left more than one?"

Angela stopped at the curb and turned to look at him. She nodded. "I called again once we knew for certain, once Doctor Hutchinson made the pronouncement."

Seth stood on the curb gazing up at the night sky. "How come you ain't heard the phone?"

Bodie looked at the sky. No stars visible. A town no place for stargazing. "I got antsy just settin around. Decided to go for a ride."

"You were ridin?"

"Yessir."

"Where were you the second time—when your mama called again?"

"Seein to Limpkin, I reckon."

Seth stepped from the curb and into the street. He stood with his arms folded and looking up at the boy. "So you come not knowin, then."

"Yessir. I never thought to check the messages again."

Angela was silent. She reached and touched Bodie's arm, her forehead wrinkling, her eyes compassionate.

Seth looked at the pavement and looked at his son. "Just as well, I reckon." He unfolded his arms and waved one at the parking lot. "Where you parked at?"

\*

That night, after his parents went to bed, he stood in the kitchen listening to the phone messages. He played them several times, and then he erased them. He walked to the porch and stood gazing into the outer dark, into a night whose moon had not yet risen and whose darkness was seamless save for the nightlights at the barn and July's house—his grandfather's house, a permanent fixture of his life, a guide-on, a pillar of life itself, a certainty now uncertain, empty, still and cold and lifeless as the man who built it. He stood and he watched, and he concluded his mother had been right: nothing is forever—forever existed only in the minds of children.

\*

The morning following he drove to Abby's church. He cruised the parking area, finding Abby's pickup parked beneath a tree, an ancient sycamore still holding its

98

brown leaves of the year almost spent. He parked next to the white Ford and sat waiting. On occasion an outsized leaf would fall from the tree and spiral down and come to rest on the truck's hood before him. The morning was windless and somewhat humid for November.

When the service let out, people filed from the church in a slow moving procession, the preacher standing on the steps, smiling and shaking hands, bidding his congregation goodbye. A few of the people were familiar to him, but the majority were strangers. And when Abby emerged from the double doors wearing a black dress and heels, he scarcely recognized her. He watched her shake the preacher's hand and smile and descend the steps and wind her way through the parked cars. And in watching, he had to admit Abby Thompson was a beautiful woman, strikingly so in her Sunday morning finest.

When she saw him waiting, Abby beamed and quickened her steps. "You're a little late," she said, leaning into his side window, her arms draped over his arm.

"Late?"

"For the services. Didn't you come to hear the new pastor preach?"

Bodie smiled and dipped his head. "Yeah, right."

"Then I guess you just came to see my new dress." She stepped back, executing a pirouette. "You like it?"

Bodie nodded. "I like it a lot."

Abby moved forward. She smiled seductively. "Well I'll be," she said. "A compliment from Bodie Rawlerson."

Bodie looked away and looked at her, his disposition shifting to serious. "Granddaddy's dead," he said.

Abby's smile dissolved. She studied his eyes. "I know," she said. "Pastor Roberts made an announcement. He asked the congregation to pray for all you Rawlersons."

"He did?"

Abby nodded.

Bodie was silent, his gaze fixed on the preacher who stood talking to people in the church doorway. "Where'd he come from, anyway?"

"Boston."

"Boston!"

"Yes, Boston. What's wrong with that?"

Bodie rolled his eyes. "Might as well be from a foreign country, or somethin."

Abby laid her hands on his arm. "Are you okay?"

Bodie looked at her. He smiled thinly. "Yeah, I'm all right. Just a little cranky is all."

Abby's eyebrows arched. "Just a little?"

"I'm tired is all. Didn't sleep too good."

"I can imagine." Her fingers kneaded the material of his shirt sleeve. "Do you know the schedule yet?"

"Schedule?"

"The funeral and all."

Bodie shook his head. "I reckon that's bein worked out right now. Daddy and Mama left for Morgan Brothers' when I left to come here." He reached and fiddled with the truck's gearshift. He looked at Abby. "What you fixin to do now?"

Abby shrugged. "I was just gonna go home. Why? Are you asking me out?"

"Why don't you meet me at the tree? I wanna talk to you about diversifyin."

"About what?"

"Just go saddle your horse and meet me."

Abby stepped back and threw up her hands, feigning fear. "Yes, master. Can I take the time to change?"

Bodie cast her a sideways glance. "You better do that. You come out there wearin that dress, I'm liable not to remember a thing you say."

"Hmmmm...," said Abby.

*

They sat with their backs pressed against the old oak's corrugated bark. Behind them the horses drifted peacefully, trailing their reins and cropping grass. A light breeze from the southwest. The air warm and heavy. On the lake a veritable armada of boats bobbed and glinted in the midday sun.

"Damned if it don't feel like summer's comin back," said Bodie.

Abby sat cross-legged with a long Bahia stalk protruding from her mouth, its Y'd end heavy with seeds. "Supposed to turn cold tomorrow," she said, speaking through clenched teeth as not to lose her crude pacifier. "It's Sunday, you know."

Bodie looked at her. "What's that got to do with anything?"

"You cursed. You shouldn't curse on Sunday."

He removed his hat and set it on the ground next to his extended and crossed

100

legs. He looked at the lake. "I don't believe you could fire a shot out there without hittin somebody."

Abby looked. "Specks must be biting."

Bodie's head sawed from side to side. "Specks can't be bitin. Ain't been cold enough yet." He uncrossed his legs and shifted his position and then leaned back against the tree. "How many acres y'all growin sod on?"

"*We* aren't growing any sod. We lease two hundred acres to Manny Del Gato. He does all the work."

"Really?"

"The upfront costs would be enormous if you tried to start a sod operation from scratch. It takes a lot of equipment, a lot of employees."

"So all I got to do is find some company like his wantin more land to farm?"

Abby pulled the grass stalk from her mouth. She eyed him quizzically. "You're serious, aren't you?"

Bodie nodded. "Me and Granddaddy talked about it. He told me to go ahead and do what ever it takes to keep Curlew profitable."

"You gonna lease out the huntin rights?"

"If I have to. But first I'm just gonna do some more fencin, put in more improved pasture, up the carryin capacity."

"*You're* going to do all that. Are you in charge now?"

"No."

"Well, sounds like you think you are."

Bodie plucked a piece of oak bark from the grass and tossed it toward the lake. "You know what I mean."

Behind them one of the horses shook and blew. A bassboat on the lake roared to a plane.

"It's sure going to be different around here," Abby said.

Bodie nodded and snorted. "Gonna be. It already is."

\*

When he got home his father sat at the kitchen table smoking a cigarette and perusing a sheaf of papers, the same documents July had brought to his meeting. "Where you been?" his father said, peering at him over wire-rimmed reading glasses.

"Out at the lake with Abby."

"She fishin again?"

"No sir. I asked her to meet me—to answer some questions I had."

Seth drew on his cigarette. "Questions?"

"I wanted to know how to go about settin up a sod operation."

Seth contemplated the long ash curving precariously at the end of his cigarette. "Sod," he said.

"Yessir." Bodie stepped and stood. He removed his hat and set it on the table. He dragged out a chair and sat in it. "I was thinkin maybe it was somethin you could do—not that you ain't already thought of it and all—somethin to sort of help out when the cattle prices take a dip."

Seth carefully reached his hand forward and tapped his cigarette over a porcelain ashtray, a hollow-backed alligator lounging next to the stack of papers. He fashioned a weak smile. "Bodie," he said.

"Yessir."

"You ain't got to tiptoe with me."

"No sir."

"I know you're just followin Daddy's instructions."

Bodie straightened in his chair. He drummed his fingers on the table. "He talked to you?"

Seth smiled and nodded. He tapped the papers before him. "He wrote it all out."

"He wrote it down?"

"He was a pretty smart feller, your granddaddy."

Bodie relaxed. He smiled and bobbed his head. "He sure did us a favor, didn't he?"

"Yeah, he did. He saved us from a whole lot of aggravation is what he done."

Seth snuffed his cigarette in the bowels of the gator and leaned back in his chair. He braced his hands against the table's edge and looked at his son, a serious calm flooding his face. "You're a man now, Bodie. You got somethin to say to me, you say it. I don't listen, you say it again."

Bodie reached and braced his own hands against the table. He returned his father's gaze. "Yessir. I'll try not to be shy."

Seth chuckled and got up and walked to the kitchen counter. He set to making a pot of coffee. "So," he said. "You know all about it now?"

"Sir?"

"Growin sod. Abby educate you on the subject?"

"Yessir. Enough to convince me it's something we ought to seriously consider."

"Well, we'll do just that. After the funeral, we'll give sod some serious consideration."

Bodie was silent for a moment. He sat watching his father measure out the coffee grounds. "It gonna be Wednesday, like we thought?"

"The funeral?"

"Yessir."

"Yeah, eleven o'clock Wednesday morning. The new preacher's gonna do the service in the chapel at Morgan Brothers'. Soon as he's done, the hearse will bring the casket to the main gate. Us pallbearers will switch it to the flatbed right there in the middle of the grade."

"The flatbed."

Seth turned to look at his son. "That's right. I ain't gonna risk havin to unstick a hearse. When your Grandma Ruby died, hers got stuck three times between the main road and the cemetery." He turned back to the counter to switch on the coffee maker. "Not the sort of thing you want to deal with during a funeral, I tell you. A regular fiasco is what it was."

"Can I drive the truck?."

Seth turned and stepped to the table. He bent at the waist and began organizing the stack of papers. "That's no job for family. Pete's gonna drive it. Him and Onnie are takin it out there in the mornin to dig the grave. If there's any problem with the road, will know before hand."

"The road's all right—a little sandy, but nothin serious."

Seth stood tall, the folder clasped in his hands. "That's right. Y'all drove out there only a few days ago." He stared blankly at the table top for a few seconds. "Darned if it don't seem like a year ago."

Bodie reached for his hat and rose from his chair. He stood looking at his father. "I'd like to dig the grave."

Seth looked at his son. "Well," he said. "I reckon Pete won't mind that a bit. Grave diggin's hard work." He nodded. "All right. You and Onnie take care of it in the mornin."

"I'd rather do it alone."

Seth shook his head. "No. You take Double Ought with you. He's gonna feel left out if he don't get to do somethin for Daddy."

"He's not a pallbearer?"

Seth shook his head. "Only need six, and I got eight—all of 'em with more seniority, so to speak."

"You, me, Pete and Uncle Billy I figure. Who else?"

"Bill Thompson, Charlie Costine, Jude Bronson and Ben Tucker."

Bodie nodded. "Granddaddy's buds."

"I'd wind up in a fistfight, if I was to bump one of them fellers for Onnie's sake."

Bodie smiled. "I reckon you would at that."

\*

The morning following the boys beat the sun to the cemetery. The day was slow in coming, streaks of high cirrus clouds feathering the heavens and prolonging the night. In the west, dark nimbus clouds were assembled along the horizon like an army of dark intentions awaiting orders. Warm and muggy, the whine of mosquitoes a monotonous undertone inescapable.

Bodie parked the flatbed beneath the great oak's far reaching limbs and switched off the lights and motor. He and Onnie sat, looking and listening. The tink of cooling metal. Barred owls called up and down the cypress strand to the north. Thrush birds flitted among palmettos beyond the headstones, indistinct, their movements hard to follow in the poor light, as if possibly not birds at all but the animated soul of dawn itself.

Onnie leaned and spat tobacco juice out his window. "Just listen to them owls tellin the news."

Bodie leaned out his own window and craned his neck to look overhead. "Their sayin the moon's straight up," he said, "but the old oak won't let me confirm it."

"No need to confirm anything. Owls don't lie."

Bodie pulled back into the cab and reached and opened his door. He slid off the seat and stepped clear and eased the door shut. "No, they don't. Owls speak only the truth."

Onnie opened his door and barreled out. He swung the door shut, producing a loud thunk. "You're full of it."

"I must be, agreein with you. Why you always got to slam the damn door like that?"

"What. You afraid I'm gonna wake the dead or somethin."

Bodie stepped to the rear of the truck and dragged an axe and a shovel from the bed. "You could wake the unborn, the way you fram around."

Onnie reached and grabbed a shovel and turned and began walking toward the cemetery's gate. "That proves you're full of it. If somebody ain't never been born, how the hell they gonna hear anything?"

Bodie, shaking his head, also began walking to the gate.

When Onnie reached July's headstone, he stopped and stood leaning on the shovel and staring at the ground. "You bring a tape measure?"

Bodie stopped to the left of the stone and stood gazing at its still incomplete inscription. "Why you need a tape?"

His right hand perched on the shovel handle's knob, Onnie gestured vaguely with his left. "How else we gonna know when it's six feet deep?"

Bodie laid the axe on the ground and waved his empty hand at Onnie. "You'll just have to stand in the hole every once in a while. When it's about a foot over your head, we'll quit diggin."

Onnie frowned. "Ha ha, you're so funny."

"Ain't no law says a grave hole's got to be exactly six feet deep. Hell, we're apt to hit water at four."

Onnie stood holding the shovel. He was silent a few seconds, then he chuckled out loud.

"What's so funny?"

"I just got a picture of the old man bobbin around in his coffin. He'll be mad-der'n hell if he's got to spend eternity seasick."

Bodie did not laugh. He stood in silence, measuring the ground before the stone with his eyes. He positioned the shovel and, with a deliberate stomp of his boot, drove its point deep into the sandy soil. He dug methodically, tossing dirt in a neat line north of the marker.

Onnie watched. "I didn't mean nothin by that. I was just horsin around." When Bodie did not respond, Onnie also began to dig, tossing his first shovel-full of soil south of the stone.

"All the dirt in one pile," Bodie said without missing a stroke.

Onnie slid his shovel beneath his small mistake and heaved it into Bodie's pile. "I loved your granddaddy, you know."

Bodie glanced up but said nothing. He continued to dig.

"Ain't no way I couldn't love him. He saved my life."

Bodie shoveled. "How'd he do that? He kill a shit-eatin dog?"

Onnie paused and leaned to one side and spat tobacco juice. "Go ahead and joke. I'm serious as a empty billfold. If he hadn't give me work when he did, I don't think I'd be here right now."

Bodie stopped shoveling and stood upright to stare at Onnie. "Would you listen to yourself. You ain't makin a damn bit of sense."

Onnie threw dirt on the growing pile. "You know what I mean. I would've died of the blues if I'd been forced to do somethin not envolvin horses and cows. July give me a home is what he done. I love it here, workin with you and Pete and your daddy. I reckon I'd just as soon stay on here forever."

Dropping his shovel, Bodie reached and picked up the axe. "Quit your ass-kissin and stand back a second." Then, taking a wide stance, he swung the axe in a sweeping arc, cutting through one of the great oak's feeder roots with a single stroke.

Onnie leaned against his shovel. "You better watch where you're steppin there. You almost walked on your grandma's grave. Walkin on kinfolk's graves is worse than breakin mirrors."

Bodie looked at the ground behind him and looked at Onnie and swung the axe to cut another root.

They worked and as they worked the sun rose and they began to sweat and cast shadows, shadows laying long across the land. And when those same shadows had pooled at their feet, Bodie climbed from the hole and looked and deemed their work complete. They stood for a moment, simply breathing and staring at what they'd done. It was a fine grave, they judged, the mound beside it rising like a monument to their effort. Then they gathered their tools and shed shirts and hats and slogged filthy and sweat-stained to sit in the shade of the great oak, to reflect on their labor.

Onnie sat with his back to the tree, his arms draped across his knees. A south-westerly breeze had developed, shuttling dark clouds overhead and causing the oak's outstretched limbs to dance and wave. "Man," he said, "I hope that rain that's comin has got cold behind it. I'm bout sick of the heat."

"Me too," said Bodie.

Onnie waved a hand at July's grave. "You reckon there's men makes a livin diggin graves?"

Bodie shrugged. "I reckon there's bound to be. Somebody's got to do it."

"If there is, they can't be white men."

Bodie gave Onnie a sideways glance. "That's racist thinkin."

Onnie wagged his head from side to side. "Oh no it ain't. That's logical thinkin." He turned and winked at Bodie. "Take a look at yourself. And you ain't dug but one grave."

Bodie rolled his eyes. "Jesus," he said. "Can't you ever be serious?"

Onnie watched the oak's limbs writhing in the breeze. "I was serious when I said July saved my life."

"I know it."

The wind blew. Clouds shuttled. A red-tailed hawk soared high above the oak.

"Why'd your folks sellout the way they did?" said Bodie. "Your daddy just tired of ranchin?"

Onnie snorted. "Money. Same reason behind every dumb move made in this world."

"They must've got a truckload of it—big as your place was."

Onnie nodded. "Yep, and two truckloads of misery, to hear Daddy tell it now."

"He come to regret it, then."

"Fore the ink was dry on the paper. He found out real quick just how much truth is in that sayin about not knowin what you got until it's gone."

"I reckon you did, too."

"I didn't find out nothin I didn't already know. But I was just a kid. Nobody listens to kids."

Rain drops large as marbles began striking the canopy overhead, raising a patter in the cemetery's sandy turnaround, the palmettos ringing it.

Bodie gathered in his hat and shirt. "We're fixin to get soaked with somethin other than sweat."

Onnie groaned and struggled to stand. "Be just our luck it come a flood and wash all the dirt back in that hole. It better not, I tell you, cause I'm too stove-up to dig it again."

"Well, quit your jawin and get in the truck. If we ain't here to see it, maybe it won't happen."

Onnie hobbled toward the truck's passenger door, his shoulders hunched up and turtling his neck. "Shoot," he said. "What kind of logic is that?"

Bodie hopped in the truck's cab and reached and started the engine. "The only kind I got to offer," he said.

**13**

**The viewing** was Tuesday evening from six to eight. Bodie arrived early dressed in his dark suit, his ill-fitting wingtips announcing his every step with annoying squeaks. He entered the small chapel alone, striding cautiously down the carpeted aisle toward a raised stage with a slender podium standing in its center. Anonymous organ music playing softly. At the foot of the stage, amid a forest of flowers, a polished wood casket sat balanced on a marble pedestal, the coffin's sectioned lid standing open at one end. The flowers—roses and lilies and tulips, some potted and some arranged on easels, all carded with the regards of those who'd sent them—fanned out from the casket in either direction. At the end of the aisle, Bodie stopped and stood rigidly, his gaze focused straight ahead initially, but then lowering slowly to the somber and gaudily painted visage within the coffin. His grandfather's face was that of a stranger, a picture never taken, a portrait never commissioned, so still and silent and lifeless, a burned-out sun destined never to rise again. He looked, and from that moment forward, he would hold no other memory of that day.

\*

Wednesday morning the Morgan Brothers' parking lot was filled to overflowing, a smattering of sedans and luxury automobiles, but mostly pickups and heavy duty haulers that were mud-caked and well used. Every seat in the small chapel was filled, the funeral home's lobby crowded with standing people, jam-packed, a stand of trees in need of thinning. The men sported business or western suits. There were many bolo ties clasped by turquoise set in silver, many seldom-worn Stetsons spotless and held delicately by strong and unadorned hands. The same anonymous organ music. The smell of perfume and cologne. There was much whispering and dipping of heads and thin-lipped smiling until Pastor Roberts appeared on the raised platform, until he took his place behind the lectern and called for quiet with his eyes.

He saw Abby come in with her parents, but was unable to speak to her save with a look, an appreciative gesture of his hand. He sat stolidly throughout the service, his eyes tearless and focused straight ahead, his thoughts in turmoil, mired in a swamp of sadness. And when the preacher was done speaking, he rose with all the others and stood waiting while the room emptied from the back forward, while the organist played *Just As I Am,* the notes coursing through his body and causing him to tremble but not waiver. And when all but the immediate family had filed out, he grouped with the other pallbearers and stood engaged in trivial conversation while the two little men of the home's employ moved about like suited drones in readying the casket for travel. Then he took his assigned place and lifted when told to lift and, together with his unpracticed team, carried the coffin that was to him impossibly light, a burden that could not possibly represent a man of his grandfather's stature. But he proffered no question as to why this was. He simply carried and walked with the others out of the building and into a day clear and cool and windless, to a black hearse with its red-velveted maw open wide and waiting. There, he briefly marveled at how smoothly his rosewood burden was accepted by the somber conveyance. Then he stepped aside feeling utterly lost until his father touched his shoulder and pulled his thoughts back to a place at least vaguely familiar.

He rode to the ranch with his parents, his father silent, driving with eyes fixed on the black hearse ahead, his mother in the Explorer's back seat, commenting on the service, on the attendees, on the absent. Behind them trailed Aunt Jo Beth's Mercedes, Uncle Billy's Expedition and a half dozen other vehicles transporting the preacher, Miss Ella and some of July Rawlerson's closest friends. They drove, and in what seemed only a moment to him, rolled to a halt on Curlew's main grade. The flatbed sat parked and waiting in the sandy mouth of the cemetery road. Pete Stalvey, dressed in a blue suit, stood rigid as a scarecrow beside the work truck.

When the pallbearers had transferred the casket to the flatbed, the procession continued on minus the hearse and Jo Beth's Mercedes, the hearse returning to St. Cloud and the sedan left parked on the grade. Pete drove the undulating road slowly and, upon reaching the cemetery's turnaround, cut a tight circle with the flatbed to allow room for all to park.

At graveside, a royal blue canopy now shaded a dozen folding chairs, a pair of brass guide rails in place to support the casket, green Astroturf laid down over the sandy ground and the mound of fill dirt and an enormous flower arrangement to be laid atop the casket. The men responsible for the setup—two raven-haired and olive-skinned men dressed in kaki—sat resting on the tailgate of a pickup. Nameless and faceless men that seemed oblivious to the procession's arrival, their dark eyes staring vacantly at the ground as the family and guests parked their vehicles and exited them and began moving their given ways, pallbearers shuffling to the flatbed, the others sauntering toward the cemetery's rickety gate.

Once the casket was positioned over the grave, Bodie shunned the chair designated for him and moved instead to the rear of the small gathering, to stand with Abby and Onnie. When the preacher began his graveside eulogy, Bodie felt Abby capture his hand, felt himself willingly accept the invitation. Glancing at her profile, he saw that she stared straight ahead, seemingly transfixed by the preacher's words. He himself heard scarcely a word until the Bostonian concluded his short service with the obligatory "ashes to ashes—dust to dust." He heard the final phrase and thought it fitting, thought it meshed perfectly with the scene playing in his own mind. But then, with the preacher's words still resonating in his mind, what he thought to be a far better benediction to July Rawlerson's life unfolded as if scripted by God Himself.

As Pastor Roberts closed his Bible and looked up, a brindled heifer ambled from the scrub oaks directly behind him, a stilt-legged calf close on the cow's heels, struggling to keep up with its mother. The newborn's burnt sienna hair was still glistening and whorled from its afterbirth bath, its eyes wide with the wonderment of one glimpsing the world for the first time.

With people filing to their vehicles, Bodie watched the cow and calf, a sense of great irony welling within him. And as he watched, he felt his hand being squeezed. He looked and saw Abby also staring at the calf, her free hand raised to cover her gaping mouth. And when he felt her tremble, heard her breathe "oh my God", he knew precisely what she was thinking: though July was gone, he had left a living legacy, one that would perpetuate itself for many years to come.

"I ain't never in my life wanted to name a cow," said Bodie, "but that little gal's timing has sure given me the urge."

111

Abby squeezed his hand again. "You've got to. She has *July* written all over her."

Bodie looked at her sideways. "July?" he said. "I was thinkin Funeral. I bet nobody's got a cow named Funeral."

Abby released his hand and seemed to shrink in stature. "Jesus, Bodie," she whispered. "Could you be any more irreverent? July's probably rolling over in his coffin."

Bodie, still eyeing the calf, smiled and shook his head. "No. I expect he's just chucklin a bit."

Then, turning to look at Abby, he noticed Onnie standing beyond her, Onnie, of whom he'd not fashioned a single thought throughout the ceremony. His stout friend stood with head bowed, the incessant smile gone, eyes closed and welling twin streams of tears. Bodie quickly averted his gaze. "I reckon I need to go," he said.

Abby studied his face, perplexed by his sudden shift of emotion. She reached and captured his hand. "All right. I'll see you in a little while. We've got to go by the house to get some things."

Bodie nodded, glancing again at Onnie before turning to locate his parents.

\*

When people began arriving at July's house, Bodie stood with Pete outside in the yard. He greeted the many guests, offering any direction or assistance needed. He escorted elderly women inside, carrying a plethora of covered dishes and food platters and coolers. And when there were no more arrivals, he stood with Pete beneath the old oak and smoked a cigarette before strolling inside to mingle and engage in trifling conversation, to answer incessant questions about his future. And shortly he felt numb. He felt abandoned, not only by his grandfather, but by tranquility as well. In close quarters with so many people, he felt miserable. But when the house began to empty, his misery slowly transformed into unexpected happiness when realizing he'd actually enjoyed the experience. And when only he, Miss Ella and his parents remained, he further realized the celebration of his grandfather's life had actually been medicinal. And in realizing this, he under-stood something always a mystery to him: why people troubled to keep such customs as wakes alive.

"Wakes ain't for the dead," Miss Ella told him. "Wakes are for those of us that's got to go on living."

**14**

**The sun was setting** when Bodie helped his father carry out the last of the garbage, four bulging plastic bags lugged to the side of July's house and added to those already there. Eight bags in all, along with two overflowing cans. "Can't forget to make the garbage run in the mornin," Seth commented while securing the can's lids with bungy cords.

"No, sir. I won't forget."

Seth stepped back and looked at the collection of refuse and looked at his son. "You'll likely have a mess to clean up. Daddy's cords will keep the coons out of the cans, but ain't nothin gonna keep 'em out of them bags."

"Yessir. I'll be cussin coons in the morning for sure."

When they walked back around to the stoop, Angela and Miss Ella stood talking at the foot of the steps, the two of them having just finished loading much of the leftover food into Angela's Explorer. Miss Ella eyed Seth plaintively. She shrugged. "Mr. Seth," she said. "I'm gonna need me a couple days to gather up all my belongings."

Seth dipped his head and looked at Miss Ella in the failing light. "No reason to hurry," he said. "The will's not bein read till Friday. I wouldn't do anything till we hear what Daddy had to say."

Miss Ella nodded and turned and started up the steps.

"Thanks for all your help, Ella," Angela said. "We would've been lost without you."

Miss Ella paused in the doorway. She half-turned and stood gazing out across the rapidly shrinking land. She nodded. "I sure am gonna miss you all." And then, not waiting for a reply, she stepped inside.

Neither Bodie nor his parents commented on their old friend's statement. They were silent, and remained silent during the short drive home. Once inside, their shared fatigue insured there would be no discussion of Miss Ella's plight nor any other painful memory of the day.

While Seth retired to the family room, Angela and Bodie sat at the kitchen table, sipping iced tea and staring blankly at the collection of casserole dishes they'd brought from July's house. Angela shook her head. "I'll never get these back to their rightful owners. I can't remember who brought what."

Bodie sipped his tea. With the hand holding his glass, he gestured to a dish of baked beans. "That one's Mrs. Thompson's. I seen Abby tote it in."

Angela reached and slid the dish indicated a few inches apart from the dozen or so others. She drank tea and set the glass on the table and looked at Bodie. "Speaking of Abby. Are you two an item, now?"

Bodie looked at his mother and looked at his glass. "An item?"

Angela smiled. "You know. A couple."

"We're good friends, if that's what you mean?"

"Good friends."

Bodie nodded.

"Well, you looked like a couple today, holding hands and all."

Bodie raised his glass and drank and set the glass back on the table. He looked at his mother. "You don't miss much, do ya?"

"Not much."

He smiled at her and scooted his chair back and stood. "I got to get out of these clothes," he said.

\*

The morning following Seth held an all-hands meeting in July's office. After Miss Ella had poured coffee for everyone, he sat behind the ancient desk and told his son and Pete and Onnie his plans for the Curlew Cattle Company. He told them it was his intention to cross-fence and to quadruple the present improved pasture acreage, to up the carrying capacity by at least one third. And he told them he had an appointment to see Manny Del Gato early the next week, a face to face meeting to discuss leasing several hundred acres for sod production. He talked, and as he talked his obvious fervor for the future infected everyone. And when finally he paused, the small room began to buzz with enthusiasm.

"I been waitin forty years to hear that kind of talk," said Pete, slapping his knee with his cap. He smiled and jerked a thumb at Onnie and Bodie, sitting to his left. "I can't hardly wait for these young fellers to get started."

Seth rose from his chair and stepped to the office's east wall, to a large aerial photograph of Curlew, a map of sorts shot in 1960 and affixed to the wall shortly thereafter. He gestured with his hand. "Startin next week, we'll take the tractor and begin choppin just north of the old homeplace. I reckon we can chop north as far as the cypress at Flag Ford. Then we'll work back east, all the way to the existing pasture around headquarters here. Time we're done, we'll have one big rectangle of about five hundred acres ready to disk and seed come spring."

Pete cocked his head to look at the map. He raised his hands in the air to frame the aerial photo, sighting through his palms like an artist gaining perspective. "We can cross fence here and here and here," he said, drawing lines in the air with a hand, "have us five separate pastures to rotate in and out of."

Seth let his arms fall limply to his sides. "You stole my thunder, Pete. That's exactly what I was fixin to say next."

Onnie leaned toward Bodie. "Just thinkin bout diggin all them post holes makes your back hurt, don't it?"

Bodie cast him a sideways glance. "My back feels fine."

Onnie looked at him and looked away and looked at him again, his eyes sparkling. "You're still jealous, ain't you?"

"Jealous? What the hell are you talkin about?"

"It's eatin you up that I got lucky and you didn't."

Bodie rolled his eyes. "Why should I be jealous. I knew you'd get lucky eventually. Even a blind hog finds an akern every once in a while."

Onnie cocked his head and gave Bodie a curious look, but Seth interrupted before he could comment.

"You boys got some idea I need to know about?"

Bodie looked at his father. "Sir?"

"Your private conversation. You don't agree with my ideas?"

"Oh, no sir. We like your plans. Onnie was just sayin how much he's lookin for-

115

ward to diggin all the post holes."

Seth eyed Onnie. "Well, you'll have your fill of it time we're done." He shifted his gaze to Bodie. "Land's got to be cleared fore we go to buildin fence."

Bodie turned his hat. "We startin today?"

Seth shook his head. "Not with the will bein read tomorrow. I aim to hit the ground runnin Monday mornin."

The boys nodded their heads.

"Today, I want y'all to ride out there and flag stumps. There's surveyor ribbon out at the huntin camp, several rolls in the top drawer of Daddy's night stand. Take it and mark anything likely to tear up equipment when we start the choppin."

"Yessir," the boys said in unison.

Bodie shifted in his chair and cleared his throat. "Speakin of huntin," he said, "you ain't forgot Saturday's opening day, have you?"

Seth shook his head. "I ain't forgot. We're not gonna host the hunt this year. It'd be too much to deal with, considerin all that's happened."

"But Granddaddy…"

"I know," Seth injected. "Next year we'll pick up right where we left off. I already spread the word at the funeral. Everybody understands."

Bodie was silent.

"But that don't mean you can't go. If you and Onnie want to take the dogs and have a race, have at it. Be good to establish a presence out there. It's openin day. There'll likely be a fool or two tryin to slip in on us."

Pete snorted and nodded his head. "Always is," he said. "And it's always the dumb ones on openin day, the ones suddenly taken with the urge to look for that greener grass."

Seth stepped to the desk and reached and picked up his cap and put it on his head. "If there's not any questions, this meetin's over."

The men looked at Seth and glanced at each other then stood and donned their own hats, their actions confirming that all were in agreement. The meeting was indeed over.

*

Within an hour they rode from the barn, heading west toward Lake Kissimmee. The morning sun beat warm on their backs, a gentle, southeasterly breeze sifting through the flatwoods, evaporating what little dew remained. They rode side by side, the horses stepping smartly as if pleased to be out and about.

"Why'd you want to name a horse after a bird?" said Onnie.

Bodie leaned and spat tobacco juice. "Why'd you want to name one after a dead singer?"

Onnie reached and thumbed back his hat. "Hell, that's a easy one. Elvis was the king. People are belonged to name stuff after a king."

"Yeah, well, Limpkin's colored up just like a limpkin, same chocolate brown with the same gray flecks speckled all through."

Onnie eyed the boy's horse. He nodded his head. "I reckon I'm gonna have to give you that one."

They traversed the flatwoods until intersecting the road leading to Rawlerson Hammock. The horses took up the fading trace without pause or command, each claiming a rut and pushing forward through tall grass, through belly-high broom sage that distinctly marked the dim trail's course, an amber stream flowing through a world otherwise green.

"I'll tell you somethin else," said Onnie. "A blind hog'll find just as many akerns as one with twenty-twenty eyes."

"How you figure?"

"Simple. Hogs hunt akerns with their noses. Everybody knows that. And sides, I ain't never seen a hog wasn't about half blind. Them little old beady eyes of theirs are about useless."

"Oh, I get what your sayin. You're sayin it wasn't her good looks that attracted you to that Canada girl—cause you were about half blind when you met her."

"What the hell are you talkin about?"

"Or you just sayin that you found her with your nose? Cause if that's what your sayin, I damn sure don't want to hear about it."

Onnie looked across the woods and looked at Bodie. "You're about a ornery cuss of a mornin, ain't you?"

When they reached the old home place, Bodie dismounted and strolled inside the house and came back out carrying three rolls of fluorescent pink ribbon. Tossing one of the rolls up to Onnie, he stuffed the other two in his pant pocket and swung into the saddle. They walked the horses north to the edge of the hammock and stopped and sat gazing at the extent of the task before them.

"Dang," said Onnie. "There's bound to be a lot of stumps out there. And even if there ain't a single one, it's gonna take forty forevers to prove it."

Bodie removed his hat and sat holding it while squinting his eyes and studying the haze of cypress far to the north. Then he put the hat back on his head and looked at Onnie. "It'll take longer than that, if we just set here talkin about it."

For the next three hours they crisscrossed the flatwoods, riding south to north and north to south again and again, their courses parallel, spaced a few yards apart, encountering few stumps but pausing to mark those few with a length of ribbon tied to a nearby gallberry or scrub oak. The stumps marked were all fat lighter, all hard as stone and of a height surely lethal to a tractor. And as they toiled the sun climbed in the sky, a goshawk skimmed low over the palmettos in search of prey, shadowing the riders and seeming to mimic their tedious repetition, though silently, effortlessly, a thing to be envied. They rode, and the sun climbed to its zenith and Onnie suddenly stopped his horse and slouched in the saddle, waiting for Bodie to notice. And when he did notice:

"Ain't it about lunchtime?"

Bodie glanced overhead and leaned and spat. "Close enough, I reckon."

Onnie raised a hand and with it gestured west. "Let's ease on over to the hammock there—see if your Injun friend's still around."

The boy looked. "He ain't there."

"You don't know that. Even if he ain't, we can pick us some oranges. Them's the best Parson Browns I ever eat."

Bodie looked at the hammock and looked at Onnie. "All right," he said. "I reckon it won't hurt to take a little break."

"Elvis says he damn sure needs one."

"Totin you, I don't doubt it."

They rode the half mile to Orange Hammock and threaded their way into its trees, the cool of the early morning still lingering beneath the palms and oaks, every bit as palpable as the deep shade preserving it. As they approached the small clearing, a drove of wild turkeys scattered before them, an old hen and her birds of the year, running low to the ground and evaporating like streaks of dark smoke in the hammock's undergrowth.

Onnie looked at Bodie sideways. He pointed at the fleeing birds, his mouth agape and his eyes wide. "Was that some of your Injuns runnin off?" he said.

Bodie cut him a glance but said nothing. He guided his horse into the clearing and stopped it and stepped down and stood in the whickered shadows holding the reins and studying the sandy soil. There was no trace of the one-eyed Indian or his small fire, not a footprint or charred coal. Not believing his eyes, Bodie dropped the reins and stepped toward the three burial mounds. He hunkered down where the fire surely had been and reached and dug into the soil with his fingers. Then he stood and wiped his hand on a pant leg and turned to look at Onnie who still sat his horse.

Onnie dismounted. "You look like you seen a ghost. What the hell you scratchin in the dirt for?"

Bodie waved a hand at his small excavation. "That's where his fire was. I'm sure of it. But there ain't so much as a cinder there now."

Onnie scarcely looked at the ground in question. He started for the orange tree. "Hell," he said, "everybody knows Injuns don't leave no sign. There could of been a hundred through here this mornin, for all we know."

Bodie glanced again at the ground. He turned and walked to join Onnie. "Well there was at least one here," he said. "I know I didn't imagine him."

Onnie stood gazing up into the ancient tree's branches. "Blame coons or some-thin done got all the low ones." He looked at Bodie sideways. "Somebody's gonna have to climb, I reckon."

"Somebody? Your arms don't look broke to me."

"Hell, I couldn't climb this tree if a bear was after me."

"Shoot," said Bodie. "Them was girls up there, you'd climb it like a squirrel." He reached and removed his hat and dropped it to the ground. He gathered himself and leaped and grabbed a stout limb and chinned himself sufficient to swing a boot into the first fork. After a brief struggle, he gained the fork and stood in it and reached and picked the nearest two oranges with one hand. He dropped the pair to Onnie and turned and picked two more. "Two enough, or you gonna make a pig out of yourself?"

"Oranges ain't fattenin. Pick me two more."

They ate the oranges in silence beneath the tree that produced them, sitting side by side, their backs pressed against the smooth bark, against the utterly hard wood. The horses each standing three-legged, heads hung, dozing peacefully.

A few minutes on Onnie waved an orange plug at Bodie. "Me and Pete figured the old man put you up to it."

"Put me up to what?"

Onnie chewed and spat out a seed and chewed some more. "Saying you seen his old one-eyed Injun."

"Well you figured wrong."

"He didn't?"

"No. He didn't."

"He never talked about him?"

"Not to me, he didn't. Leastwise, not until after I seen the man."

Onnie spat another seed then shook his head. "It just don't make sense, then."

"What don't?"

"Pete says it's been almost forty years since July seen him."

"So?"

"Says the feller was old way back then."

Bodie spat a seed. "Well I reckon he's been old a long damn time, then—cause I ain't lyin."

"You ain't no liar."

"I know I ain't."

Onnie's open Case knife lay in his lap. He captured it and began peeling the last of his oranges. "We gonna hunt, Saturday?"

Bodie swallowed and wiped his hands on his pants. "You want to?"

"Course I want to."

"Then I reckon *we're* gonna hunt."

"We gonna use the dogs, or just slip hunt?"

Bodie thumbed back his hat and turned to look Onnie in the eyes. He smiled knowingly. "I figured on usin just one dog. Old Joe's all we'll need to get that crooked-horn buck out of his bed."

"Crooked-horn buck? You seen him?"

Bodie nodded his head. "Last week. Jumped him up on my way out to the lake."

Onnie wiped his knife on his pant leg then folded it closed and slid it into a front pocket. He eyed the peeled orange in his hand. "How come you ain't told me?"

"I just did."

Onnie pried the orange in half with his fingers and divided each half and tossed one of the quarters in his mouth. He chewed. "Abby gonna hunt with us?"

"If she wants to."

"She'll want to," Onnie snorted. "I believe she'll do anything you ask her to."

"What are you gettin at?"

"Oh, nothin, really. I just been givin a lotta thought to why you ain't takin advantage of the situation."

"You been givin it a lot of thought."

"Yeah, I have."

"And now you're fixin to tell me what you come up with, I reckon."

Onnie grinned and nodded. "Abby's too much like you is the problem. She ain't erotic enough for ya."

Bodie visibly flinched. "Erotic?," he chuckled. "You mean exotic, don't you?"

Onnie leaned and spat an orange seed. "Whatever," he said. "You knew what the hell I meant." He wagged a finger at Bodie. "I think it's time you quit your whorin around and focus on the best darn woman any of us knows."

"So that's what you think, is it?"

"Yeah, it is."

Bodie rocked forward and pressed to a standing position. "Well," he said, "all right then."

Onnie looked up. "All right?"

Bodie was in motion by now, stepping toward the horses. "You heard me."

Onnie seemed in no hurry to go anywhere. He continued to sit until Bodie reached his horse. Then he frowned and shook his head and struggled to his feet. He bent at the waist and dusted sand from his breeches and straightened and started for his horse. He talked to himself. "All right," he said. "Shit. What the hell's that sposed to mean?"

*The redbone hound* *rose from its bed snarling and baring long white teeth at the man's approach. Yet the man came on, staring the dog down, causing it to ultimately cower and slink submissively to the far end of the porch. The dog shook and whimpered pitifully as the man ascended the steps and proceeded to knock at the door.*

*From inside the clapboard house: "Who's out there?"*

*"It's me," the man answered.*

*The door slowly opened inward revealing a sleepy-eyed fatman shirtless and barefoot, wearing dingy boxer shorts and several days growth of beard. One hand clutching the doorknob, his other spread-fingered and combing back greasy black hair. "What you want?" he said.*

The man slipped a hand into his pant pocket and fished out a thick envelope. He held it out. *"Why I've come to pay my rent, Mister Biggs."*

*"Oh,"* Biggs said, reaching to take the envelope. *"You're stayin another month then."*

*"Yes. It's all right, isn't it? You sound a bit disappointed."*

Biggs shifted his weight uneasily. His eyes darted about, looking everywhere but at the man. *"I can use the money,"* he said finally.

*"It's a lot of money."*

Biggs nodded his head.

*"So why did you come to my house yesterday?"*

Biggs eyes widened. *"I didn't. I ain't left this yard yesterday."*

*"Someone was at my house. If it wasn't you, who was it?"*

*"It was the meter-reader, feller from the power company."*

*"And you let him."*

Biggs let go of the door to plead with both hands. *"I cain't stop 'em from readin the meter. Only thing'll stop 'em is a bad dog. You got a bad dog they won't come in the yard."*

The man nodded his head. *"Okay,"* he said. *"You do that. You put a sign on my gate says: Warning—Bad Dog."* And with that, the man turned on his heel and walked away.

Biggs stood watching him go. Then he looked at the envelope in his hand and said: *"Lord help me."*

**15**

**The will was read** Friday morning as scheduled. It was a brief affair. With the holdings of Curlew Cattle Company already deeded to July's three children, the thin document brought to the ranch office by Bud Townsend contained only three paragraphs, three short sections addressing employees, family and the old man's goodbyes. But however simple, July's will was a touching valediction, its carefully composed words expressing emotions he rarely displayed in life.

Bud Townsend, dressed in his signature khaki pants, white shirt and crimson bowtie, started the proceeding at precisely ten o'clock. "If there are no objections," he began, "I will now read the last will and testament of my good friend July Rawlerson."

All in the room remained silent. The lawyer commenced to read.

July began by thanking Pete Stalvey, Miss Ella Preston and Onnie Osteen for their devoted service, by awarding them his personal savings, the amount to each proportional to length of service: Pete Stalvey, twenty thousand dollars; Onnie Osteen, a thousand; Miss Ella Preston, ten thousand dollars plus a life estate, the right to reside in his home for the remainder of her life. In closing, he told them that he loved them, that he was sorry he could not do more.

The second paragraph spoke to his children. "I've left you all that I was," he said, "the only thing of real value trusted to my care. Like each of you, this land was a part of me, surely my fourth child. It will always be a part of my soul, and I pray it will always be a part of yours. As for my other meaningless possessions, I leave their division to your discretion, the only exceptions I list as following:

To Seth Rawlerson—my *Billy Cook* show saddle

To William Morgan Rawlerson—my gold Rolex watch

To Jo Beth Rawlerson-Allen—Miss Ruby's wedding rings

To Angela Garbodie-Rawlerson—Miss Ruby's silver service

To Amy Elisabeth Allen—Miss Ruby's diamond broach (the one given to her by your daddy)

To Margaret Sue Allen—Miss Ruby's cameo ring

To John Garbodie Rawlerson—my 1873 Winchester rifle.

After reading the list, Bud Townsend paused briefly. His eyes scanned each face before him, twelve faces, of which, ten were largely expressionless. The other two, the faces of Miss Ella Preston and Onnie Osteen, were streaked with tears.

The room was silent. No one sought to speak.

Bud Townsend cleared his throat. He adjusted his glasses then proceeded to read the will's final paragraph, July's final words.

"And now, as you might have expected, I'll wind this thing up with a quote from Ecclesiastes, some words of wisdom that pretty well hit my life's nail smack on the head: *'I saw that there is nothing better for a man than to enjoy his work, because that is his lot. For who can bring him to see what will happen after him?'* That's how old Solomon saw it, and I reckon he was right. Regardless of what happens now, ranching was my lot, and I surely loved it. Thank you all for brightening up my life. I love you, and I bid you a fond farewell."

Mr. Townsend paused, then continued. "And then, written in his own hand, July added: *'Fear God and keep His commandments'*. He signed it: *'July nmi Rawlerson'*."

The lawyer straightened in his chair. He looked about the room. "That's it," he said, reaching and tapping the paper with an index finger. "A will of few words, just what you'd expect from July."

There was movement by members of the audience, a ripple of turning heads and clearing of throats. Onnie, sitting next to Bodie in the back of the room, used a shirtsleeve to mop his cheeks. Miss Ella got up and discreetly left the office, gliding quickly as if on a mission. Seth rose from his chair. He smiled at Bud Townsend. "Thanks, Bud. You gave it just the right touch."

The lawyer nodded his head and braced his hands on the desktop as if intending to rise. But he did not follow through with his intention. Billy Rawlerson's voice stopped him before he could.

"You must've skipped a name on that list, Bud. You didn't read what Daddy left to my Claudia."

Bud Townsend looked at Billy and looked at the will lying on the desk, the fingers of his left hand kneading his chin. "No," he said. "I didn't miss anything, Billy. Your wife's name isn't here."

The young woman seated next to Billy emitted an audible sigh. She crossed her arms and glared at Billy.

Billy, his lips pursed, evidently speechless, looked at his wife and looked at Bud.

Bud's mouth slowly opened, a yawn-like act that was not a yawn but the only expression left to one thinking ah ha. "I think I know what the problem is," he said. "You and Claudia married back in June, correct?"

Billy cocked his head slightly. "That's right."

Bud picked up the will and turned the printed side toward Billy. "Your daddy wrote and validated this in two thousand two—long before you and Claudia even met."

"Oh," said Billy, raising a hand to loosen the Windsor knot at his throat. He did not look at his wife.

Seth turned to his brother, waving a hand in the air. "I'm sure we can come up with something nice for Claudia. We all know Daddy would've wanted her to have somethin."

Bud Townsend rose from his chair. "Well I'm gonna let y'all work that out," he said. "I need to be getting on back to the office."

Jo Beth—who had scarcely uttered a word since arriving with her daughters and a man everyone took to be her new suitor—suddenly made her presence known. "You might want to stick around," she said, her gaze fixed on the lawyer. "I suspect Seth will be seeking your advice shortly."

The lawyer looked at Jo Beth and looked at Seth.

Seth turned to face his sister. He smiled but did not look happy. He looked puzzled. "I ain't needin no advice. What are you talkin about?"

Every eye swam to focus on Jo Beth. Miss Ella—who had just returned to the office carrying a tray of coffee and donuts—stopped in mid-stride when sensing the tension suddenly palpable within the room.

Jo Beth looked Seth in the eye. "Billy and I want you to buy our interest in Curlew."

Seth's thin smile quickly bled from his face. He looked at the floor and looked at the stranger seated next to Jo Beth. He shook his head as though annoyed by an insect.

Jo Beth continued: "We've checked the comparables and decided five thousand an acre is a fair price."

"Five thousand."

"Five thousand. And since our two-thirds interest represents roughly fifty-five hundred acres, you'll need to come up with around twenty-eight million, total."

"Shit," Onnie breathed. Barely a whisper, but sufficiently loud that everyone in the office heard him over their own suppressed gasps.

Seth's tan face and neck were now crimson. He glared at his seated brother, causing Billy to quickly look away. Shifting his eyes back to Jo Beth, Seth sighed, the strain evident in his face softening a bit. "What's this all about, Jo? I thought y'all were in agreement that nothin was gonna change. Why are you doin this?"

Jo Beth's face seemed to harden even more. "Why?" she said. "Because this property reached the switchpoint years ago. Because..."

"Switchpoint?" Seth injected.

Jo Beth flashed him a condescending look. "Yes, switchpoint—the point when the developmental value of land trumps any other use."

"I never heard of such a thing."

Jo Beth shot a glance at the man seated next to her. "Now there's a surprise," she said. She rose from her chair. Gesturing in the air with a hand, she said: "Look, it doesn't matter why. Our minds are made up. Will you buy us out, or not?"

Seth stepped and stood. He looked at Angela and Bodie and looked at Jo Beth. "You know damn well I can't come up with that kind of money. Even if I got somebody to float a loan—and I know that ain't gonna happen—there's no way I could make the payment."

Jo Beth folded her arms across her chest. She glanced down at her male friend then turned slowly back to face Seth. "Well," she said. "Then I guess Billy and I will have to buy *you* out."

Bodie suddenly stood. He waved his hat at Jo Beth. "Why don't you just *get* the hell out," he said.

"Bodie!" Seth exclaimed.

"Yessir."

"Set down!"

Bodie sat.

Seth was visibly shaking. "Jo Beth," he said. "I ain't for sale."

Jo Beth nodded slowly. She smiled. "Okay," she said, turning and reaching to gather in her purse. "Girls, Joe," she said to her daughters and male friend. She turned to look at Seth. "By the way," she said. "This is Joe Smith, my fiancée."

Amy and Margaret rose from their chairs, as did Joe Smith. Tall, silver-haired, immaculately dressed in a blue suit. He eyed Seth, dipping his head in greeting.

Seth looked at the man but did nothing to acknowledge his gesture.

Jo Beth walked to the office door and stepped aside, letting Joe Smith and her daughters exit first. She looked at Seth. "Now you know why I asked Bud to stick around. You need to ask him about partition suits. Billy and I will be filing one if you don't change your mind by Tuesday."

Seth's arms hung limp at his sides, a glazed look in his eyes. "I love you, too," he said.

As Jo Beth turned and descended the steps, Billy and his wife rose from their chairs. Claudia started for the door, but Billy hesitated. He looked at Seth. "I'm sorry about all this. But you need to accept our offer."

Seth was stone-faced.

"You don't want this going to court. This goes to court, you'll lose the ranch and a lot of money to boot."

Seth's expression did not change. "You best leave."

Billy slid a hand in his trouser pocket. He jingled some change, a set of keys. His eyes briefly panned the office. Then he turned and shuffled to the door. Descending the steps, he glanced back at his brother before gingerly swinging the door shut.

The room fell eerily quiet. Seth turned from the closed door and looked at Bud Townsend. He did not have to say anything.

Bud leaned and picked up his briefcase and set it on the desktop. He cleared his throat. "Well," he said. "I guess the rumor I heard is true."

Seth approached the desk. "Rumor?"

Bud nodded. "I heard Excalibur Homes was planning something big, one of those synthetic cities like Celebration—upscale homes, golf course, shopping mall."

Seth cocked his head. "Yeah."

"Yeah. I even heard a big cattle ranch bordering Lake Kissimmee was the proposed site. But I never dreamed it might be Curlew."

Seth stepped and stood, his eyes wandering the office walls. He looked at Bud. "You think Jo and Billy cooked somethin up with this Excalibur Homes?"

Bud looked at the desktop and looked at Seth. "I take it you don't know who Joe Smith is?"

Seth shook his head. "Today's the first I ever heard of him."

"He owns Excalibur."

Seth sighed and hung his head. He seemed to study something on the office floor. "How long ago did you hear this rumor?"

"Last week—Thursday, I think."

"Fore Daddy died," Seth breathed.

Bud nodded.

Seth reached and scratched the back of his neck. "Well what do you think? They can't make me do anything I don't want to, can they?"

Bud's eyes panned the people seated in the office, Angela, Pete, Bodie and Onnie. He turned and glanced at Miss Ella, Miss Ella still frozen in mid-stride and holding the tray of refreshments that would never be enjoyed. He returned his gaze to Seth. "You might want to hear what I think in private."

Pete and Onnie started to rise from there chairs, and Miss Ella turned to leave the office. But Seth stopped them with a look and a shake of his head. "There ain't nobody in this room not affected by this," he said. "Go ahead and tell us what you think. There ain't nothin you can say going to damage my feelins anymore than they already been damaged."

Bud nodded. He looked at Seth. "I think Jo and Billy never intended to sell you their interest in Curlew. They knew you couldn't buy them out. They just wanted you to say it in front of witnesses. They wanted the land all along. I suspect they're partnered up with Excalibur, that they intend to develop Curlew and make ten times the price they quoted you."

"So if I don't sell out, there's nothin they can do."

Bud shook his head. "I didn't say that. I wish that was the case. It's not. They will bring a partition suit against you, leave it to a judge to decide whether Curlew can be divided equitably." He paused and sat in the chair. "And I can tell you with some degree of certainty that it can't be. Jo and Billy will make sure it can't be divided. Nothing the judge proposes will suit them, because they don't want it divided. They want it all."

Seth looked perplexed. "Well, what happens if the judge decides it can't be divided? How's that work to their advantage?"

"The ranch will be auctioned on the courthouse steps, sold to the highest bidder, the proceeds divided amongst the three of you."

"Damn," Seth exhaled. "And Excalibur will be the highest bidder."

Bud nodded his head. "There's apt to be no other bidders, and certainly none with the resources of Excalibur. They could very well purchase *all* of Curlew for a fraction of what Jo offered you for your one-third interest. And worse yet, you'll get only a third of that fraction. Jo and Billy, on the other hand, being in cahoots with Excalibur, will get exactly what they wanted all along—eighty-three hundred acres of prime waterfront property."

Seth placed his hands on his hips and stepped and stood. He frowned. "Well, what do you think I should do?"

Before Bud could answer, Bodie stood and looked beseechingly at his father. "Tell him about the promise they made to Granddaddy. He made them promise, and we all witnessed it."

The lawyer was shaking his head before Bodie finished speaking. "Hearsay," he said. "If it's not in writing, witnessed and properly notarized, it never happened, so far as the court's concerned." He leaned back and swiveled slightly in the chair. "I told July what needed to be done, but he simply refused to do it. He said he'd not have his own children thinking he didn't trust them."

Bodie looked at the hat in his hands. He looked at the lawyer. "It ain't right," he said before settling back in his chair.

Looking at the boy, Bud shook his head. "No, it's not, son. But I doubt you'll ever convince your aunt and uncle of that. People infected with greed can fashion right from any wrong ever conceived."

Angela, who had been listening intently, suddenly spoke up. "So the only choice Seth has—is to take their offer?"

The lawyer reached and removed his glasses and rubbed an eye with the back of the hand holding the bifocals. Slipping them back on, he looked at Angela. "Be a whole lot smarter than letting it go to court," he said. He looked at Seth. "But there's another option you may want to consider, a way to greatly increase your income from this sorry mess."

Seth looked at the lawyer sideways. "Yeah," he said, "I'm listenin."

Bud rocked forward in his chair. Resting his elbows on the desktop, he brought his hands together and stared at Seth over his bridged finger tips. "Tell them you know what they're up to," he said, "that you want to be a full partner in the project. Once they get over the shock, they may just like the idea: no ugly court case, no family squabble." He paused and parted his hands, waved them in the air speculatively. "It's worth a try, I think."

Seth looked at the floor. He sighed deeply. "That ain't an option. I'd never be able to look myself in the mirror again."

Bud peered over his glasses. He nodded. "Cause of your promise to July."

"Yeah," said Seth.

"July is gone," Angela injected. "He's not going to know what you do."

Seth cut a glance at his wife. "Yeah, but I'd know."

Bud leaned back in his chair. "Then I have to advise you to take their offer," he said. "If you try to fight them, it'll wind up costing you dearly."

Seth was silent. He stared at the linoleum floor.

Bodie studied his father's hollow expression, the same look he'd first witnessed the night July died. As he watched, his anger transitioned to a feeling of utter hopelessness.

Seth raised his head to look at the lawyer. "I got to get me some air."

Bud Townsend nodded and rose from the chair. He reached and captured the handle of his briefcase and lifted it and began walking toward Seth and the door. "I need to go, but I'll be home all weekend. Don't hesitate to call."

Seth moved to the door and opened it and stepped aside to let Bud Townsend exit the office. "Thanks, Bud," he said as the lawyer descended the steps. "Thanks for everything."

Bud's only reply was to raise his free hand and give a little wave as he walked to his car.

Seth stood at the door and watched the lawyer's Chevy Blazer until it became but a tiny, black aberration in the gray horizon. Then he turned his gaze back into the office. "I'm gonna walk to the house," he said to no one in particular. He then stepped through the doorway, letting the door click shut behind him.

**When his mother** left the office to find his father, Bodie did not follow. He chose instead to leave with Onnie and Pete, to walk with them to the barn. The morning pleasantly warm. Little wind. The three strode the marl road in silence until Pete's brindle dog—out of sight in the bed of the Chevy—growled at their approach.

"It's me, dumbass," said Pete. "Shut the hell up."

The growling ceased.

Upon reaching the barn bay, the three of them stopped and stood between the open doorway and the parked flatbed. Pete removed his cap and stood looking into its bowl. "Now ain't this a fine mess we find ourselves in," he said.

Onnie leaned and spat. He looked at Bodie. "What the hell we gonna do, bud?"

Bodie bumped back his hat and shrugged his shoulders. He scuffed the ground with a boot. "I ain't got a clue. I still can't believe what just happened." He looked at Pete. "You reckon Mr. Townsend's right—there ain't nothin Daddy can do?"

Pete nodded. "He's bound to be right. It's his business to know this kind of stuff."

Onnie stuffed his hands in his jeans. "So we're out of a job, I reckon."

Pete put his cap back on his head. "Will be shortly—less some miracle happens tween now and Tuesday."

Bodie looked at Pete. "What kind of miracle? Thought there was no way out of this."

Pete bent at the waist and reached and picked up a small pebble. He straightened and threw the stone at nothing in particular. "There ain't," he said. "At least, no way that's likely to happen."

Bodie studied the foreman. "And what way is that?"

"Your aunt and uncle could have a change of heart—decide to drop the whole thing."

Bodie looked away. "That'd be a miracle, all right."

"Or, if somethin was to happen to both of 'em. Somethin happens to them and your daddy becomes sole owner of the place."

Bodie swung his head to look at the foreman. "What about Jo's daughters—Billy's wife? They'd probably go right ahead and deal with that Smith fellow."

Pete shook his head. "They'd have no say. Seth, Jo and Billy is tenants in common. Somethin happens to Jo and Billy, Curlew is Seth's. Period."

"You sure about that?"

"Sure as I can be."

Bodie turned and stood gazing out across the pasture.

Both Pete and Onnie watched him in silence for almost a minute, then Onnie said: "Now don't go gettin no ideas. You cain't run a ranch from prison."

Bodie turned. He looked at Pete and looked at Onnie. "No," he said, "*I* couldn't."

Onnie stepped and stood. He chuckled nervously. "Quit your foolin, bud. You'd never kill your own kin."

Bodie was silent. He again stared into space. Then he shook his head and said: "No I wouldn't. I'd like to think I couldn't kill any human being—no matter what they done to me."

Pete turned and stepped into the barn. He straddled a hay bale and sat on it leaning forward, his elbows resting on his knees. "Well what you reckon your daddy wants us doin right now? I hate to just set here pissin and moanin."

Bodie turned to look at him. "I reckon I could go ask him."

"You should do that. I expect he needs somebody to talk to anyways—somebody's got the same view of things and all."

Bodie nodded. "I'll be right back."

"Take your time. We ain't goin nowhere."

*

Angela found Seth sitting at the kitchen table. He seemed to be contemplating the cigarette in his right hand and did not look up when she pulled out a chair to sit across from him.

"You got another one of those?" she said.

Seth looked at her. He fished a pack of Winstons from his breast pocket and slid it and a green Bic lighter across the table. "I thought you'd quit."

Angela lit one of the cigarettes and drew on it and exhaled the words: "me too." She looked at him. "You feel like talking?"

"No. But I reckon we've got to, ain't we?"

Angela blew smoke. "I know you can't see it yet, but this may be a blessing. Fourteen million dollars is a lot of money. You'll never have to work another day of your life."

Seth's eyes widened. "A blessing! This ranch *is* my life. How can losin it be a blessing?"

"By you making the best of a bad situation. That's how."

Seth dropped his gaze to the table top. "I'd like to do that, but I don't know if it's possible."

"Sure it is. You just have to be willing to change is all."

"Change?"

"Yes. Change. Learn to relax and enjoy life. Travel, see how the rest of the world lives."

Seth rolled his eyes and sighed. "You just don't get it, do ya? After twenty years together we still don't speak the same language."

Angela stared at him but remained silent.

"My idea of makin the best of this situation is to find another place, buy enough land to start over. Ranchin makes me happy. It's all I know—all I want to know."

"In other words, you'd rather be miserable than change."

"I won't be miserable if I can put things back in order."

Angela shook her head. "You'll never be able to put things back *in order*. And you know it." She paused to drag on the cigarette. She blew smoke sideways, out of the corner of her mouth. "I know you didn't like hearing it, but Jo was right. The cost of land now makes it pure lunacy to even think about starting fresh in farming or ranching. And that switchpoint she mentioned, that's not just here. That's happened all over the state. There's no place where four or five million dollars will buy what you would need. You'd need ten times that to get back what you're losing."

Seth studied his wife, looking directly in her eyes. "Four or five million, you say. So whatever I do, I'll be doin it alone?"

"You will if you intend to stay in ranching."

Seth looked at her. He drew on his cigarette then reached and snuffed it in the bowels of the porcelain gator. He scooted his chair back from the table and stood. "So that's how it is?"

Angela dropped her gaze and stared blankly at the table. "Yes. That's how it is."

\*

Bodie was just climbing the yard fence when Seth exited the house. The boy stopped upon seeing his father. He settled atop the fence and watched him approach, his father who somehow seemed smaller in stature, older. When he spoke to him—"We was wondering what we should be doin"—Seth jerked to a halt and looked up as if having been startled from a deep sleep.

Seth looked at his son and then slowly panned his head, first one way and then the other. He looked down. "It's come to a head," he said. "I reckon there ain't no point in keepin it from you anymore."

"Sir?"

"Your mama and me. We ain't likely to be together when this mess sorts itself out."

Bodie was silent. His eyes darted about, as if searching for something worthy of study.

Seth stepped close to his son. He reached and briefly touched Bodie's hand that grasped the fence board. "It's been a long time comin. But I expect maybe you knew that."

"Yessir. I knew it."

"It's got nothin to do with you. It's differences between me and her—the same ones always been there."

Bodie tightened his grip on the fence board. He nodded his head. He looked at his shadow pooled beneath him.

Seth took a step back and looked away and looked again at his son. "I'm headed over to talk to Pete and Onnie—to tell 'em my plans. Why don't you go in and talk with your mama, let her know you ain't sidin against her."

"I don't know if I can do that."

"You need to. She ain't wrong in this. She's just doin what's best for her. Same as I'm doin."

Bodie swung his leg over the fence and hopped down on the pasture side. He brushed the seat of his jeans. "I'll talk to her. But I need some time to think on it first."

Seth dipped his head. "All right. Just don't let it go too long. That won't do nobody any good."

Seth climbed the fence and, with Bodie as his side, began walking to the barn. Neither he nor the boy looked back to see Angela come onto the porch and stand watching them go.

*

Pete and Onnie got up from their hay bales when they saw them coming. They stepped to the open barn bay and waited. The dog growled in the Chevy's bed as Seth and Bodie scaled the final gate and Pete told it to hush and the dog hushed.

Upon reaching the barn, Seth hopped up on the flatbed while Bodie moved to stand next to Onnie. It was just past noon and the sun warmed the boy's face as he gazed up at his father.

Seth gripped the edge of the truck's bed with his hands and cleared his throat. He looked at Pete and looked at Onnie. "I can't see no way out of this," he began. "Come Tuesday, I'm gonna accept Jo and Billy's offer. I'd like you both to stay on and help me handle the shutdown after I do."

"How long you reckon that'll take?" said Pete. "I mean, sellin off the stock and all."

Seth shrugged. "Got no idea right now. But I should know after I meet with 'em. I get the feelin they're in a big hurry to get started, so it probably won't be more than a few weeks, a couple months at the most." He paused, his eyes darting between Pete and Onnie. "You get a employment opportunity in the meantime, you go ahead and take it. I'll not begrudge you for it. I surely won't."

Both Onnie and Pete stepped and stood. Onnie said: "I'll stay as long as you need me, boss." Pete followed with "that goes for me too."

"I'll do everything I can to help you find work. There's bound to be somebody needin good hands. If there is, we'll find 'em."

Pete nodded his head. "If you don't mind my askin, what are you gonna do? You gonna find you a spot on the beach somewhere, drink beer and ketch up on your nappin?"

Seth smiled dimly and shook his head. "Naw," he said, "I intend to stay in the cattle business if I can find a place to do it. I can't make no promises, but if things work out, maybe y'all won't have to look for no job. Maybe you can still work for me."

Pete pointed a finger at his boss. "Well, looky here. You find a place and get it, I'll work damn cheap till we get it going."

"Me too," Onnie chimed in.

Bodie pushed back his hat. "And you'll have me for nothin, so there ain't no reason we can't do it."

Seth raised his hands. "Now don't get too excited. I've not found anything yet. And even if I do, it won't be no Curlew—not with the money I'll have to work with."

Listening to his father, Bodie gazed at the pasture to the north. The only world he'd ever known unfurling and running to the far horizon, to the distant cypress standing gray and comforting in its eternalness. There a swallow-tailed kite effortlessly plied its trade against an azure sky, knifing and soaring without visible means of support, without a single beat of wing. He watched the carefree bird with envy, certain it had no knowledge of the future.

"Well how bout this afternoon?" questioned Pete. "You got somethin we can do right now?"

Seth hopped from the truck's bed and stretched and looked around. He looked at Pete. "I can't think of a single thing seems logical. Y'all take the afternoon off— give me the weekend to sort my thoughts."

Pete nodded and turned toward his truck. "Well, the good Lord willin," he said, "I'll see y'all Monday then."

"Good Lord willin," said Seth. He turned to Bodie. "I'm headed to the house. You comin?"

The boy glanced at Onnie. "I'll be there directly. You go ahead."

When Seth turned to go, Onnie raised a hand. "See ya Monday, boss."

Seth walked. "See ya, Double Ought. Bright and early."

"Yessir. Bright and early." Onnie looked at Bodie and kicked the ground with his boot. "I reckon we ain't huntin tomorrow, are we?"

Bodie looked toward his granddaddy's house and looked at Onnie. He frowned. "I'm not. I never thought I'd say it, but I don't feel like huntin."

"I feel like gettin drunk is what I feel like. You wanna do that? Get us a bottle and say the hell with everything?"

Bodie feigned a smile. "Naw. Not now. Maybe tomorrow. Right now I'm gonna call Abby."

"Why you gonna call her?"

"Cause I feel like it. That's why."

"All right. But you ain't got to be so touchy, you know. I know your all tore up about this shit. I'm tore up, too. I'm tore up like a snake in a weedeater over this shit."

A smile spread over Bodie's face. He chuckled. "That's pretty tore up."

"You damn right it is, so don't go gettin snippy with me."

"I got to go."

"Well go ahead. I'll come by tomorrow. Maybe you'll be in a better mood tomorrow."

**It was past four** by the time he reached the lone oak on the lakeshore. Abby was not yet there. He dismounted and dropped the reins and walked to the water's edge and stood looking and listening, a light breeze wafting off the lake, cool, overhead a cloudless sky save for a pair of contrails forming a great mis-shapen X from horizon to horizon. The gleaming sun was nearing the horizon far across the water, less than an hour from setting. He hunkered down and pushed back his hat but continued watching the lake. A lone fisherman was flipping for bass along the south shore of Bird Island. A tri-colored heron stood still as a photo a few yards down shore. He watched, and in scarcely a moment, a single whicker from his horse announced Abby's arrival.

She approached from the south—her horse locked in an easy canter well suited to the shore's deep switchgrass—and was at the oak almost before he could rise and turn. She waved to him and slid from her horse and began walking rapidly to where he stood. "What's up?" she said. "You sounded a little weird on the phone. Something wrong?"

"Yeah," he said. And when she reached him he took her hand and led her up to the big oak and asked her sit with him.

Abby did as he asked, a bit awestruck that he did not release her hand even after they were seated. She looked into his eyes and, when he did not look away, knew for certain something had changed in her world. And the knowing caused her to tremble.

"We're losin the ranch," he said. "Curlew's done."

"What? How?"

He spent the next half hour recounting the day's events, telling her of his aunt and uncle's coup, of his parents imminent breakup. And when he was done telling the sun was gone, a gray haze settled over the land, twilight, thrush birds and owls summoning the night. Flights of mourning doves and ducks whistled overhead. A bull bellowed somewhere in the growing darkness. And amid it all, Abby gasping, "Oh my God. Oh my God."

She freed her hand from his that she might hold him close. And when she did, he did not pull away. He held her in return and they sat embracing each other for a long time. It was cave dark when he released her and stood and drew her up to him and told her that he loved her, that he wanted to marry her. Then he walked her to her horse and caught up its reins and asked her to follow him. And without hesitation she did as he asked, and she said that she always would.

She followed him through the inky night, riding beneath a billion stars strewn across the heavens like exploded mercury, through cool damp air that kissed the skin with the scent of pine and cypress and sweet wax myrtle, through rustling palmettos glistening with dew. She followed him, and he led her to the old home-place in Rawlerson Hammock.

They dismounted in the sandy yard and stood between the horses, embracing and kissing for a good while. Then he left her and went inside the old house where he found matches and used them to light a gas lantern. And when he brought the lantern glowing and swinging from his hand to the doorway, she came to him, and he led her trembling to the room where his grandfather was born. He placed the lantern on a trunk at the foot of the bed and turned to her. "You sure about this?"

Abby smiled. "Absolutely certain."

\*

The sun was already up when he woke the next morning. He showered and dressed and strolled to the kitchen where his mother sat sipping coffee at the table.

"Well good morning," she said.

"Mornin." He walked past her and went directly to the counter. He plucked his favorite mug from the cuptree and poured coffee and began sipping it without turning.

Angela watched him. "You were out late last night."

"Yeah, pretty late."

"You with Onnie?"

"No."

Angela reached and shook a cigarette from a pack on the table. She put it in her mouth and lit it with a slender chrome lighter and exhaled a cloud of smoke toward the ceiling. "Your daddy talked to you, didn't he?"

Bodie sipped his coffee. "Yeah, he did."

"He should've waited. We should have told you together."

Bodie was silent.

"Come over here and sit down—so I can look at you. I like looking at you."

He topped off his coffee and turned and stepped to the table and sat in the chair directly opposite his mother. He looked at her, but only fleetingly. He stared at the dark liquid in his mug.

"I've picked out an apartment in Kissimmee—north of town on four-forty-one. It's got two bedrooms."

"That's nice."

Angela smoked. "I'll not ask you come live with me. But I want you to know you will always be welcome. Always."

He glanced at her and saw her eyes swimming in tears. He knew what he wanted to say, but he could scarcely breathe. He could only nod his head.

"It's only because of you that I've waited this long."

He stood suddenly, like a man with urgent business. He hesitated, then circled the table and laid his hand on her shoulder. She reached and laid her hand on his. "I know," she said. Then he withdrew his hand and walked to the door and reached and got his hat from the wallpeg and stepped outside.

Angela sat. She scarcely turned her head to watch him go.

\*

After saddling his horse he rode from the barn and headed north at a fast walk. Storm clouds were building in the southwest. An erratic breeze carried the scent of change. He rode steadily northward until reaching the cemetery road. At that point the horse turned west and began following the sandy trail, and Bodie did not rebuke the horse but only spoke to it softly and told it he knew that it knew. Following the winding ruts at a brisk walk, the horse suddenly stopped short when encountering a huge indigo snake stretched across the road, a great specimen black as night and all of eight feet in length, a constrictor whose girth rivaled that of a man's leg. The horse eyed the snake's slow progress, stepping and standing and tossing its head while the boy stroked its neck and told it not to worry, told it that indigos were good snakes and something to be cherished, nothing to be feared. But the horse, holding firm to its convictions, refused to advance until the reptile's last black inch disappeared into the palmettos, until only a sinusoidal signature of its passing lay written in the sand. Even then the horse advanced fearfully, bolting past the snake's track and not settling to a walk until a good many yards down the road.

At the cemetery, Bodie dismounted and dropped the reins and briefly stood craning his neck to watch a passing crow, a forward scout calling incessantly to its brethren not yet visible but sure to follow. And when the crow had gone, he walked through the rickety gate and turned and stepped to his grandfather's grave. He read the inscription, the date of death now permanently etched in the granite. He hunkered down and removed his hat and told his grandfather all that had happened, told him even though certain himself the old man already knew. When done telling, he asked his grandfather what he should do. But when no reply was forthcoming, he quickly concluded that he'd asked the impossible, that the dead had no voice in such matters of the living.

From the cemetery, he rode west. He crossed a strand of cypress and then turned north and rode toward the boundary fence, taking in everything, seeing with great clarity the land of his forbears, his land. Reaching the fence, he turned back west and rode the firebreak listing in the saddle, reading what sign the plowed ground had to offer. When he cut the panther's track, his spirits lifted a little. He thought of the cat as he rode on, of how alone it must feel, how hopeless. And then he thought of Abby and knew he was not like the panther. He carried the thought, and his spirits threatened to soar. But upon reaching the lake, an emotion altogether different rose within him. At the lake, he was instantly filled with anger.

An airboat was parked on the shore, the same Glades-style craft parked there two weeks earlier, black and shiny and repugnant, the strange words *Lusus Naturae* mocking him from each of the boat's rudders.

He nudged the horse forward, eyes panning the grassy shore and the hammock's edge. Wading birds. An osprey soaring high overhead. Nothing. At the boat, he halted the horse and sat watching, reading sign. The same bootprints as before were etched clearly in the mud, several in a line headed for the hammock.

He leaned and spat. "Son of a bitch come back, just like Granddaddy said he would."

He stepped down from the horse and stood looking at the boat. He turned and looked at the hammock edge, studied it for some time. Then he turned back to the boat and reached to raise the lid of a small bow compartment. He leaned and looked inside: some rope, an anchor, a couple of lifejackets, a folded magazine. He leaned in farther and picked up the copy of *Guns and Ammo,* his eye settling on the address label. "Mr. Lathan Biggs, Box 9, Cowhouse Road, Lorida, Florida," he read aloud. He quickly peeled the label off and stuffed it in his pant pocket. Then, dropping the magazine back into the compartment, he lowered the lid and half-turned and grasped the grass rake protruding from the rectangular bow.

He pulled with all his might, leaning to the side, trying to spin the craft. But the boat did not move. He stepped to the horse and loosened his catch rope and uncoiled it and looped a half-hitch through the craft's bow eyelet. He pulled the rope tight, testing his work. Then he dropped the rope and walked to boat's stern where he stooped and removed the drain plugs, two plugs, port and starboard, brass with rubber seals. After tossing the plugs into the lake, he returned to the bow and reached and captured the rope and mounted his horse. He pulled slack from the rope and looped two turns around the pommel horn and began side stepping the horse toward the lake. When the rope came tight the boat immediately began to spin. Bodie continued to sidestep the horse in a slow arc until the bow pointed at the lake. Then he backed the horse until water lapped at its belly and the boat began to float. He then shook the rope loose from the pommel horn and, letting it trail through his hand, rode back to shore. There, he dismounted and, after briefly studying the hammock edge, sat in the grass and removed his boots and socks. He then stood and waded to boat's bow. He untied the rope and turned and, coiling the lariat as he came, slogged to dry ground, his eyes never on the rope but fixed on the distant treeline, searching for movement.

The boat sank as he donned his socks and boots, sinking stern first, the lake's surface reaching the engine's underside when the hull touched bottom. By the time he had secured his catch rope, the entire hull was submerged save for the bow tip, a beer can bobbing beneath the front seat, a petroleum slick expanding outwards from the stern area.

When he swung into the saddle, the horse stepped nervously and shook its head and blew. "The man was warned," he told the horse, reining it southward and urging it to a fast walk, a rising wind buffeting him and causing him to reach and press his hat down tightly on his head. Rain coming. He could smell it. He rode the shoreline several hundred yards and was about to turn east when something ahead in the shallows caught his eye, something red in color, a horizontal line too perfect for nature, a still aberration in the upright and swaying pickerel weed. He veered the horse toward the object, recognizing it almost immediately as a sun-faded fiberglass canoe. He rode directly to the craft and halted the horse and sat looking and listening. In the belly of the canoe lay a single wooden paddle, a shallow pool of water and a lidless coffee can turned on its side and rocking to the gusting wind. A few feet east of the bow was a lone footprint in mud, a smooth and seamless print, no tread design whatsoever. He studied the print and turned in the saddle to look eastward, to search the skyline over the hammock's trees. "No smoke," he said out loud. "Too windy. But it's got to be him."

When he rode into the hammock the world writhed about him, limbs dipping and rising and contorting in the wind, cabbage fans falling and tumbling, the temperature dropping. He rode steadily eastward, weaving the horse through the animated flora, the light waning and the wind giving voice to the eternally mute, raising song from leaf and limb. And when he reached the small clearing with its ancient orange tree, its anonymous graves, the old man was there, kneeling before the three mounds, very still, a statue had his wind-coaxed gray hair not been lifting and falling, lifting and falling.

Bodie circled the Indian and halted the horse. He stepped down and stood holding the reins with one hand and his hat on his head with the other. "Hey," he said.

The old man's head lifted. He looked at the boy. "I am glad you have come," he said. "Sit. I would speak with you."

The boy turned and led his horse a few paces to the closest palm and tied the reins to the tree and then walked back to the Indian. He sat and crossed his legs and removed his hat and stared into the old man's good eye. "I reckon you know what's happened," he said.

The old man nodded. "What has been will be again. What has been done will be done again; there is nothing new under the sun."

The boy looked at his hat and looked at the man. "Well, can you tell me what's gonna happen now? Can I save the ranch?"

The old man coughed a deep rattling cough and squinted his one eye, the wrinkles in his forehead deepening as he peered at the boy. "No man can know the future," he said. "Only God knows the future."

"But I thought ..."

"You thought I was something other than a man. But you were wrong." He paused to cough again, momentarily closing his eye. Then he opened it and fixed it on the boy. "And I was wrong to let you think it."

"But you knew we were gonna lose the ranch. You told me so."

The old man wagged his head slowly. "The sun rises and the sun sets, and then hurries back to where it rises."

"What?"

"What has happened to you is happening all over this land, happening to all who are like you. Your grandfather's sun, your father's sun, was already setting when you came into this world. But of course you did not know this. You came to love their sun, which is an unfortunate thing. Yes, very unfortunate for you, for their sun will not be your sun. That sun has set forever."

Bodie looked away. He watched the treetops waving overhead, the darkening sky. He felt a drop of rain strike his face.

The old man coughed and watched him and then continued to speak: "The grand feast this land offered our Grandfathers has surely ended. The table has been cleared. Only crumbs remain. But I ask you, are crumbs not better than nothing at all? A man can survive on crumbs. I have done it for many years."

"So your sayin that there ain't nothin I can do, that I should just make up my mind to get over it."

"Yes. And be thankful for the time you were permitted at the table. There are many less fortunate than you. A great many."

Bodie looked at the hat in his hands. He watched several drops of rain strike the leaves between himself and the Indian. "It's fixin to get wet out. You want me to take you somewhere? From the sound of that cough, you don't need to be gettin wet."

The Indian shook his head. "It does not matter."

"It don't matter?"

"No."

Bodie put his hat on his head and stood and dusted sand from his pants. He

145

looked at the old man. "Well I reckon I'll be seein you then."

"Perhaps," the old man said, "but I will not see you again."

Bodie momentarily stood pondering the Indian's statement. Then he touched the brim of his hat and turned and walked to his horse. As he swung into the saddle, the Indian raised a hand and said: "Young Rawlerson."

"Yessir."

The Indian dragged his arm through the air, made a sweeping gesture. "What is to become of this land?"

The Appaloosa turned in a tight circle, shaking its head and blowing. The boy tracked the old man with his eyes. "I reckon I just assumed you knew."

"No. I do not know."

"It's sposed to be developed—one of them instant cities."

The Indian dropped his gaze and looked to his left, at the three mounds. He looked up at the boy. "People who would do such a thing will not respect the old ones. To people who would do such things, the old ones were but shadows passing through. They will not matter to such people."

"They matter to me."

"Yes. And you will watch over them."

"I'd like to help you out, but I don't know what I could do. They ain't gonna listen to me."

"You will know what to do."

"I will."

"Yes. When you see me again, you will know what to do."

Bodie touched his hat. "I'll do what I can."

The old man nodded, the wind feathering his hair. "Goodbye young Rawlerson. Remember to fear God and keep His commandments. All else is meaningless."

He looked at the old man and nodded his head and said that he would try. Then he reached back and loosened the thongs holding his yellow rain slicker. He tossed the rolled-up coat next to the Indian and spun the horse and rode away.

The old man looked down at the yellow slicker and looked up to catch a final glimpse of the departing boy. "That is a good start," he said.

146

***The man sat*** *Indian fashion among the limbs of a storm felled oak, a bull-barreled Ruger Number One resting in his lap, a flat shooting .270 equipped with a Leupold three to nine power variable scope. Having arrived long before daylight, he'd been sitting thusly for several hours, watching his beached airboat, tending his bait. When the mounted boy finally appeared, the man felt the rush of adrenaline all hunters seek. His heart raced as he brought the rifle to bear. Taking a deep breath, he pushed the rifle's safety off and sighted through the scope. He tracked the boy all the way to the boat, and continued to scope him as he sat the horse looking and listening. "Cautious," the man said. "Good boy, but it won't do you any good. I'm invisible. Go ahead and turn your horse so I can turn out your lights. Come on. Give me the green light." But then the boy suddenly dismounted. As he walked to the bow of the boat, his horse behind him began cropping grass, began a slow turn to its right.*

*Ignoring the boy, the man held the scope's crosshairs on the horse, and when the animal's off side swung into view, the man said: " No". He raised his head from the scope and looked with the naked eye. He again looked through the scope. "Unarmed," he said. "Why would you come unarmed?" Sighing deeply, he engaged the safety with his thumb and lowered the rifle. He scarcely watched as the boy set about sinking his boat. He suddenly seemed interested only in the storm clouds building over the lake.*

**18**

**The rain** came in earnest a little past noon, falling in wind driven sheets that caused the cattle to cease all activity, to stand facing the onslaught with heads hung in a somber fashion. Bodie sat on the front porch watching the deluge, watching and hoping it would soon let up. When by three o'clock it was still drizzling, he rose from his rocker and walked inside and picked up the phone to call Abby.

"It ain't gonna stop," he said.

"Not till tomorrow morning. Least that's what they're saying on the Weather Channel."

"You got any ideas?"

"Why don't you come over here for supper."

"Supper."

"Yeah, supper. You have to eat. Besides, Daddy wants to talk to you."

Silence. His fingers tapping the back of the wireless phone.

"You still there?"

"I'm here. I was just thinkin."

"Hope you're not mad. I just had to tell somebody."

"I ain't mad. But how bout him?"

"He seemed pleased."

"Pleased."

"Yeah. I knew he would be. He's always liked you."

149

"Good thing, I reckon."

"You sound kind of down. Is something wrong?"

"No. Nothin's wrong. I'm just a little surprised your daddy wasn't pissed about last night."

"Last night?"

"Yeah. I figured he'd want to whip my tail for sure."

"I didn't tell him about last night, you dope. I told him you asked me to marry you."

Bodie laughed. "I know it. I was just messin with you."

"Yeah? Well I liked the way you messed with me last night better. I liked it a lot."

"What time?"

"Every time."

"I mean what time do you want me there for supper?"

Now Abby laughed. "We'll eat around six, but you can come over now if you want."

"I'll be there around five-thirty."

"I don't know if I can wait that long."

"You'll wait."

"Yes. I will."

\*

He had just stepped out of the shower when Onnie arrived. He heard his friend stomping his boots on the slab outside, stomping and cursing the rain. He walked to the front door wearing only his jeans, a towel draped around his neck.

Onnie stood on the porch with his boots in his hand, casting a skeptical look at Bodie. "You done forgot, ain't you."

"Forgot what?"

"That we're gettin drunk tonight."

Bodie pulled the towel from around his neck. He looked at it. "Yeah. Reckon I did. A lot's happened since yesterday."

Onnie set his boots down and stepped through the door. He sat at the kitchen table. "I done spent a fortune on Wild Turkey. A whole quart."

"Wild Turkey."

"Yeah. What the hell's come up could be more important than Wild Turkey? Nothin, I'll bet. You just wanna set around here sulkin bout your predicament."

Bodie laid the towel on the table and dragged out a chair and sat in it. "I promised the Thompsons I'd be over there for supper."

"The Thompsons."

"Bill wants to talk to me."

Onnie gave him a sideways look. He reached and pulled a tobacco pouch from his hip pocket and opened it and loaded a chaw in his mouth. He closed the pouch and shook it at Bodie. "You done asked him for a job, ain't ya?"

Bodie dipped his head and sighed and looked up. "No," he said. "I asked Abby to marry me."

Onnie's mouth dropped open, spilling tobacco on his lap. He gawked at Bodie. "You gotta be shittin me! You ain't never even dated the girl." He shook his head. "You asked her to marry you?"

"I did."

Onnie studied him briefly and then dropped his gaze to the bits of tobacco on his fly. He reached and pinched them up with his fingers and kneaded them into a ball. After stuffing the ball into his mouth, he chewed, and he stared some more at Bodie. Then he stopped chewing and smiled. "You sly dog, you."

"What?"

"You figured out how to get the next best thing to Curlew without spendin a cent. That's what you done. You're goin to hell, Bodie Rawlerson. Straight to hell."

Bodie looked away. "You think what you want. I asked her because I love her. I've always loved her. It just took somethin like what's happened to make me realize it."

Onnie smiled and shook his head. Then the smile bled from his face. "No foolin?"

Bodie nodded his head. "No foolin."

Onnie first wagged his head from side to side and then straightened in his chair. He leaned forward, resting his elbows on the table. He smiled. "This is great," he said. "You and Abby runnin Thompson Farms. Hell, you get situated with old Bill, and you can hire me on. It'll be like old times."

Bodie grinned. "You never know."

"You *will* hire me, won't ya?"

151

"If it plays out like you said, course I will. But Mr. Thompson ain't agreed to nothin yet. He may not think along them lines. He may think like you did and tell me to go pound sand."

"He won't think like that. He knows Abby's crazy about you. He'll do what ever she wants."

"I hope so. Cause I'm marryin her, with or without his consent."

"You are?"

"I am."

"Well maybe you ain't goin to hell—leastwise, not for this offense."

Bodie glanced at the clock on the wall. "I got to get dressed and get over there."

Onnie straightened and scooted his chair back and stood. "Yeah, I reckon you do."

"Sorry bout you spendin all that money."

"I ain't. Wild Turkey's never a bad investment. The longer you hold it, the better it gets. We'll get to it eventually."

"I expect we will."

*

It seemed much later than five-thirty when he reached the Thompson headquarters. With the steady drizzle and cloud cover, night had fallen early. He climbed from his truck and stood for a moment in the rain admiring the layout of Abby's world. A hundred yards or so east of her house stood an enormous main barn, all steel construction and freshly painted, and east of that, an equipment barn with two late-model John Deere tractors, a D6 Catapillar. West of the Cracker-style home was an eighty acre orange grove, the trees neatly pruned and loaded with fruit, the rows between them weed free and freshly disked. Several prefab steel holding pens were just visible to the rear of the barn, and beyond, seemingly endless improved pasture dotted with prime Angus and at least two dozen working horses. He stood and took it all in as if seeing the place for the first time. And as he looked a yellow lab appeared at his side, its nose lifting and testing the air, tail wagging uncertainly.

Bodie reached down and offered the dog his hand. He patted its head and spoke to it. Then he strode up the concrete walk to the front porch, the dog following close on his heels . After stomping his boots on the slab at the foot of the steps, he ascended to the porch and reached and rang the bell. Chimes, faint but audible. The dog barked once, shook rain from its coat and sat on its haunches, staring fixedly at the door, its ears perking to the sound of running bare feet on wooden floors. And when the solid oak door swung inward, Abby's two younger sisters appeared, Anna and Allison, ages nine and eight. The blonde, blue-eyed girls stood one behind the other, peering around the door's edge, smiling up at Bodie while giggling and turtling their heads.

"Hey, Bodie," they said in unison.

He smiled. "Hey, you two."

Anna turned her head and shouted: "Abby. Bodie's here."

Bodie removed his hat and stood shifting it from hand to hand. He looked down at the two girls and smiled and looked at the dog sitting next to him. When he again looked up, Abby was there.

"Hey," he said.

Abby stepped around her giggling sisters and leaned and kissed him lightly on the lips. "Hey," she said. She beamed. Taking his hat with one hand, she captured his hand with the other and led him inside, the still giggling sisters and the dog following in their wake.

Martha Thompson was in the kitchen. She stood peeling potatoes at the counter next to the sink. She turned and smiled warmly when they came in. She laid down a paring knife and wiped her hands on her apron and stepped forward with her right hand extended. "Bodie," she said. She smelled good. She smelled of onions and a blend of spices and herbs, of baking bread, smells sensed more by the stomach than the nose. She shook his hand and patted it and told him to sit down. As he and Abby dragged out chairs and sat at the small kitchen table, she turned to her other daughters. She spoke to the two girls softly but sternly, telling them to take the dog and go elsewhere. Anna and Allison left the room without debate, hopping and skipping and talking incessantly, the dog trotting at their heels, its toenails ticking the wood floor. Then Martha Thompson selected a chair of her own and sat in it and looked at Abby and looked at Bodie, her eyes full of life, full of obvious joy. "Well, son," she said, "I hope you like roast beef."

"No ma'am," he said. "I love it."

They sat and talked. Small talk. And shortly Bill Thompson appeared in the kitchen, tall, well over six feet, hands capable of palming a basketball, thinning brown hair, bifocal glasses. Bill gave Abby and Bodie a cursory glance then looked directly at his wife. "How long till you're ready?"

Martha glanced toward the oven and looked at him. "Bout twenty minutes."

He looked at the boy and extended his right hand. "Bodie."

Bodie stood and reached across the table and shook his hand. "Hey, Mr. Thompson."

Bill Thompson then looked at his daughter. "Me and Bodie's gonna take us a little walk. We won't be long."

Abby looked at Bodie and looked at her father. "Okay." She smiled at Bodie, her eyebrows arching.

Bodie followed Bill Thompson to the front door, donning his hat when Bill handed it to him, and then following him outside into the darkness. A light drizzle. Very little wind. "Let's walk to the barn," Bill said. And they walked and, when they reached the barn bay, Abby's father stepped inside the drip line and turned to look at Bodie. "You sure about this?"

"Yessir. I'm sure."

Bill Thompson removed his glasses and squinted to inspect them. After wiping each lens in turn on his flannel shirt, he slipped the bifocals back on. "I talked to Manny Del Gato this morning. He told me your daddy called and cancelled the appointment they had to discuss y'all startin a sod operation. And then, though I didn't ask, mind you, he told me why. Told me Billy and Jo Beth's forcin y'all to sell out." He paused and looked out into the darkness. He looked at Bodie. "Is it true?"

"Yessir. They hit us with it yesterday, after Mr. Townsend finished readin Granddaddy's will."

Bill Thompson again looked away. He shook his head and scuffed the ground with his boot. He looked at Bodie. "And only a few hours later you meet up with Abby and ask her to marry you."

"Yessir. I did."

"Did you consider that people might think that a little odd, seein as how the two of you have never even dated? At least, to my knowledge you ain't dated. I know you two have always been good friends and all. But you sort of skipped the most important part, seems to me. I was brought up to believe you're supposed to court a girl before you up and ask her to spend the rest of her life with you. You see my point?"

"Yessir. I do."

"Well, what were you thinkin? What possessed you to do this?"

"It was losin the ranch. I couldn't bear the thought of losin Abby, too."

"You're sayin you intended to ask her all along."

"Yessir. That's been my intention for as long as I can remember."

"And you just kept this intention a big secret, even from her."

"Yessir."

Thompson cocked his head slightly. "Why?"

Bodie shrugged. "Reckon I figured there wasn't no hurry. But I don't figure that anymore, not after yesterday."

Bill smiled thinly. "You weren't done testin the waters, so to speak."

Bodie nodded again. "Yessir. I reckon that was it. But I'm done now. Abby is all I want."

Bill Thompson reached and removed his cap and immediately set it back on his head. "Well, she loves you. That's pretty obvious."

"I love her."

Thompson nodded. He looked away and looked at Bodie. "I have to tell you I don't enjoy grillin you like this. I've always thought highly of you."

Bodie nodded and smiled sheepishly. "I didn't expect no less."

"This just came on so sudden and all. You can't blame me for bein skeptical of your intentions."

"No sir. I don't blame nobody but myself. I never should've taken Abby for granted the way I did."

"It's a failin of my own, takin people for granted. So I know how it makes you feel—once it dawns on you that you've done it."

"Yessir."

"Anyhow, one reason I wanted to have this little talk was to ask you your plans. You intend to try and stay in the cattle business?"

"Yessir. I can't imagine doin anything else."

"I was hopin you felt that way. I've seen you work cows, so I know your good at it. And young as you are, you're still the best I ever seen on a horse."

"Thank you, sir. Hearin that means a lot to me, especially comin from you."

"I'm only speakin the truth. And I am when I say that nothing would please me more than to have you work here at Thompson Farms."

"Would you feel that way if I wasn't marryin Abby?"

"Absolutely. I'd hire you without hesitation, simply because I know you'd be a

155

valuable asset."

Bodie dipped his head and stuffed his hands in his jean pockets. "Well I appreciate it, and I'll sure give it some serious thought."

"What's there to think about? You're fixin to be out of a job, aren't you?"

"Yessir. But Daddy's lookin to find another place. If he does, I feel obligated to help him get it up and runnin."

"Well the offer stands—case things don't work out in that direction."

"Yessir. And it's a load off my mind knowin it."

Bill Thompson smiled. "Well all right, then. All this jawin's made me hungry. You ready to eat?"

"Yessir. I am now."

# 19

**Sunday** morning he awoke to an eerie silence. He found his father already entranced before the office computer, searching incessantly for affordable land—found his mother packing her possessions with single-minded determination, with a sense of urgency that both frightened and sickened him. He drank coffee and paced from one parent to the other, invisible, watching them each in turn, waiting for an opportune time to say what he had to say. But when no such time ever presented itself, he left the house and walked to his truck. He drove to Abby's church and parked and waited, feeling numb and lifeless until the services let out, until Abby appeared in the church's doorway like a kept promise, a sunrise, a next breath. She came to him, and they spent the remainder of the day riding and exploring the Thompson property, exploring each other.

The morning following his father woke him before daylight and brought him to the kitchen and asked him to sit with him. He sat, and Seth poured them coffee before sitting himself. A notepad and pen on the table. "I got some things to run by you," he said, "see if you got anything to add."

"What kind of things?"

"Demands."

"Demands?"

"Demands I'm gonna present to Jo Beth, here in a little bit when I call her. Things she's gonna have to agree to before I accept their offer."

Bodie looked at his father. He cocked his head, trying to read the writing on the notepad.

Seth picked up the pen and used it to point to the top of the page. "First thing is Daddy's house. They can't touch the house cause of Miss Ella's right to residency, cause it's spelled out in the will."

"Yessir. I remember."

Seth tapped the pad with the pen. "Now our house is in mine and your mama's name. The house and the acre it sets on. But I want at least twenty acres to go with it, including the barn and pasture up to Daddy's place. That'll give us room to keep a few horses while we're looking for another place."

"You find anything on the internet?"

Seth shook his head. "Nothin yet. Leastwise, nothin suitable."

"Suitable."

"Enough acres to be profitable. I found several that would've been perfect had the askin price not been way over our head."

"How many acres you reckon it'll take?

"All depends. Woods pasture, at least three thousand. And even that's cuttin it pretty close. We'd probably have to work it by our lonesome. Probably couldn't afford no help."

He watched his father study the notepad. He shifted in his chair and took a deep breath. "There's somethin I need to tell you."

Seth looked.

"I asked Abby to marry me."

His father's mouth opened slightly. Seth looked down at the notepad and looked at his coffee cup and reached and picked it up and drank from it and set it back on the table. He turned his head and coughed and turned back to look at him. "And what did she say?"

"She said yes."

"Abby's a fine girl. I expect she'll make you very happy."

"Yessir. She already has."

"You set a date?"

"We talked about sometime in June. But nothin's firmed up."

"June."

"Yessir."

Seth picked up the pen and began doodling on the pad.

"You don't look too happy."

"I don't?" He dropped the pen on the pad and looked at his son. "Well don't let it bother you. I ain't had occasion to look happy in a while. Reckon I'm out of practice." He looked away. When he turned back, he was smiling. "I reckon you and Abby will just have to do something about that. Sort of retrain me, so to speak."

Bodie smiled.

"You've told your mama, I reckon?"

"No sir. I ain't yet."

"Well you better get on that. She could use some good news." Seth paused and looked away and looked at him. "And don't tell her you done told me."

"No sir. I won't let that slip." He sipped his coffee and put the cup down and pointed to the notepad. "You got anything more on your list?"

Seth looked at the pad. "Yes, I do. The cemetery. I'm gonna insist that it be excluded from any development, it and at least five acres surrounding it."

"They can't mess with the graveyard, can they? Ain't there some kind of law against it?"

"I've seen it done before when property was sold. Come in and move all the coffins to some public cemetery. But it ain't gonna happen with ours. They'll have to kill me first."

"You and me both."

Seth nodded and looked back at the pad of paper. "And the old homeplace," he said, "I want it spared."

"Yessir. Me too."

Seth looked at the pad and looked at Bodie. "That's all I've got. Can you think of anything I might've missed?"

"Yessir. The graves in Orange Hammock. I promised old Solomon I'd try to protect them."

"The Indian graves."

"Yessir."

Seth took the pen and began writing on the pad. "I'll put it down. I know Daddy would want 'em protected. There may be some law we can use. Seems like there ought to be, anyway."

"I seen him yesterday mornin."

"Seen who?"

"Old Solomon."

"You did?"

"Yessir. And I also seen that airboat again."

"Airboat?"

"Same one as before. The feller that killed the hog."

"You see him?"

Bodie shook his head. "But I fixed it so he may be out there yet."

"What?"

"I did like Granddaddy said. I sank his boat."

Seth stood. He picked up the notepad and looked at Bodie. He frowned. "Damn, son. You hadn't ought to of done that. It practically ain't our land anymore."

"He didn't know that."

"Yeah, but you knew it." He gestured with the pad in his hand, waved it toward the front door. "Go on over to the barn. Tell Pete and Onnie I'll be there directly— soon as I git this call to Jo Beth over with."

"Yessir."

Bodie stood and carried his cup to the sink. He walked to the door and reached and got his hat and dungaree jacket. While donning them, he watched his father fetch the phone and began thumbing a sequence of numbers on its keypad. When his father raised the phone to his ear, he quit watching and stepped out the door.

*

Onnie was a few minutes late. His Dodge rolled to a halt a few feet from where Pete and Bodie stood warming their hands at a smudgepot, an old grove heater glowing red in the thinning darkness. The morning was cold, low forties, the coldest day of the season thus far, cloudless sky, no wind, black smoke from the burning diesel lofting straight up, standing like a dark and translucent post in the morning air. When Onnie stepped from the truck wearing only a T-shirt and boxer shorts, Pete shook his head and made a choking sound. "Would you look at that knothead."

Onnie reached back into the truck's cab and fished out jeans and shirt and boots and hugged them in a crumpled mass to his chest. He pirouetted and reached back with a starkly white leg and kicked the door closed and began walking forward, his spindly legs scissoring like glow sticks in the dim light.

Pete watched his approach. "Them your legs?" he said. "Or you ridin a chicken?"

Bodie chuckled.

Onnie snorted. "Your so funny." He dropped his pants and boots next to the heater and hurriedly pulled on the shirt. "Damned if it ain't cold."

"Runnin round half naked, what do you expect?" said Bodie.

"I expect y'all could be a little more civil to a feller human so early of a mornin. I was tryin not to be late is all."

Pete turned to warm his backside. "You're late anyway."

Onnie leaned and gathered up his pants and stepped into one leg and then the other. He pulled them up and looked around. "I ain't late. Bossman ain't here yet."

They fed the dogs and washed down the pen slabs and returned to the heater and stood talking for almost an hour before Pete peered across the pasture and announced: "Yonder he comes—and he don't look happy."

Seth wore a grim look striding up to the men. He stopped and stood before them, his eyes panning their faces. "It's done," he said. "I talked to Jo and told her I intended to accept their offer. I got to meet with them Friday mornin in Orlando, to finalize things."

Bodie stepped and stood. "She agree to everything?"

Seth leaned and spat. "No. She's gonna fight saving the old homeplace. Said it would break up *the continuity* of their plans. Said it's got to come down." He paused and made a sweeping gesture with his arm. "She seemed willin to go along with the rest, the houses here and the cemetery—long as I'm willin to forfeit the acreage involved, take it off my third of the ranch."

Bodie frowned and dipped his head. "And the Indian graves—she was okay with that?"

Seth looked at him. "She wouldn't even consider savin them mounds. Said there was no proof they were even graves, no reference to them on some archeological map the State's got on record. I just got off the phone with Bud Townsend. He thinks she's right, said there's not much can be done to protect undocumented graves like them."

Pete looked at Bodie. "Your granddaddy used to say 'there's no remembrance of men of old'. Reckon that goes double for old timey Injuns."

Bodie kicked at the ground. "Parently so."

Seth shoved his hands in his back pockets. "Anyhow," he said. "Like I figured, they're in a big hurry to get started with their *Prosperity*." He paused and frowned, his eyebrows arching. "*Prosperity*," he repeated. "That's what their callin it—this city they intend to throw up out here. They want to get rollin with it soon as the zonin change is approved."

"*Prosperity* my ass," said Onnie.

Pete gestured with his hand. "Zonin changes can take time. A development the size they got in mind, it may take months to get all their plans approved—maybe a year or more."

Seth smiled and shook his head. "Bud says depends on how much pull you got. Says Excalibur's got plenty." He looked at Pete and looked at Onnie. "Today I want y'all to just busy yourselves with stuff around the barn here. Fix anything needs fixin. Do some cleanin if nothing else. I'm gonna be on the phone with Chiefland—let Jimmy Jenks know what's happenin here so he can be linin up buyers." He paused and turned to Bodie. "Your mama needs you, today. She's ready to move her things. Shouldn't take too long."

Bodie dipped his head and looked at his father. "Yessir," he said. He turned and walked to the gate and climbed it and dropped to the ground on the far side and began walking toward the house.

"Shit," said Onnie.

"Yeah," said Pete.

*

Angela stood next to her Explorer when he climbed the yard fence. A sheaf of hangered clothes draped across her extended arms. "Could you get the door for me?" she called.

Bodie hurried to her and reached and opened the Explorer's back door. His mother leaned inside the SUV, laying the clothes over boxes already stacked on the lowered rear seat. She extracted herself from the vehicle and looked at him and smiled. "Thanks. You wouldn't think clothes could be so heavy." She reached and brushed something from his shoulder. "Have you come to help me?"

"Yes ma'am. Daddy said you needed a hand."

She glanced at the barn over his shoulder then looked at him. "I know this doesn't make sense to you. But it will. You'll understand it in time."

He looked at her and looked at her heavily loaded Explorer. "I better back my truck over here. Your car ain't gonna hold much more. You got more stuff inside,

162

don't ya?"

She smiled, though unmistakable sadness dominated her eyes. "I didn't mean to hurt you."

"I ain't hurt. I just don't understand why y'all can't get along."

"We do get along. We've rarely had a cross word, your daddy and me."

"Then it really don't make no sense. What you're doin. No sense at all."

"Listen. I love your father. I expect to always love him. He's one of the finest men I've ever known. But I can't live his version of life." Angela reached and smoothed the front of his shirt. "There was a time I thought I could. But I've been miserable way out here. I simply can't take the isolation anymore. If I don't get out now, we'll wind up hating each other. And I'll not have that happen. Does that make any sense to you?"

Bodie looked away and looked at her. He nodded. "Reckon it's startin to," he said.

"Well, good. That tells me you're at least trying to understand. And that makes me feel a lot better."

Bodie reached and removed his hat and set it back on his head. "Ah, I got a little news."

Angela's forehead wrinkled. "News. What kind of news?"

"Well, looks like me and Abby are gettin married."

Angela squealed and said "what?" and reached and grabbed his shoulders and pulled him to her, knocking his hat off and causing him to brace himself against falling. "That's wonderful."

"Jesus, Mama."

"You asked her?"

"Friday evenin."

She stepped back. "And she said yes."

"Well, yeah. She did."

She stepped forward and hugged him again and released him and stepped back. "When? You haven't set a date, have you?"

"Sometime in June, we figured."

"Oh my God. That's not much time. I've got to call Martha Thompson. She'll go batty trying to plan a wedding on such short notice. She knows, doesn't she? Abby's told her."

"Yes, ma'am. She knows."

Angela stooped and picked up his hat and handed it to him. "Well let's get busy." She turned and started up the walk to the house but stopped suddenly and came back to him. She grabbed his shoulders and shook him. "This is so exciting," she said.

And then she turned and actually skipped to the house.

Bodie stood watching her go. He shook his head and chuckled to himself. "Damn," he said.

**20**

**The conference room** was situated on the ninth floor, windowless, containing only a single lengthy table lined with leather upholstered chairs. When a perky receptionist swept Seth and Bud Townsend into the room, Jo Beth, Billy and Joe Smith, along with a man they didn't know, sat at the table, all wearing dark business suits and sitting shoulder to shoulder like birds on a wire. Joe Smith smiled up at them. He gestured to the seats directly across from him, saying: "Gentlemen, please be seated." And they each dragged out a chair and sat in it and scooted them up to the table. Townsend set his briefcase on the floor beside him, withdrawing from it a manila folder and placing the folder on the table. Seth removed his ballcap and set it in his lap.

Joe Smith cleared his throat. He looked at papers segregated before him in neatly arranged piles. He looked at Seth and Townsend. "Would you like something to drink—coffee, soft drinks—bottled water?"

Seth looked directly at his sister. "You get them boundaries put down in writing? I seen the surveyors, so I expect you did."

Jo Beth looked at him, her demeanor detached, unwavering. She reached and, selecting a legal-sized document from two of the piles, handed them down the table to her brother. "The two houses and barn laid out in one contiguous parcel consisting of twenty-two point five acres. The cemetery centered in a five acre rectangle."

Seth took the papers and handed one to Bud, and both men began reading. They read, and then they swapped papers and read some more. When finished, Seth looked at the lawyer. Bud nodded his head, and Seth paired the two quitclaims in his hands and stood them and tapped them on the tabletop and looked at his sister. "You ain't changed your mind about the homeplace?"

Jo Beth shook her head.

"It don't mean a thing to you, does it?"

"On the contrary," she said. "It means a lot to me. Why do you think I want it gone soon as possible?"

At Jo Beth's response, Billy shifted in his chair and dipped his head and looked at the table. The man seated beyond him sat motionless, blue eyes unblinking and directed down the table but seemingly focused on no one.

Jo Beth gestured toward the manila folder in front of Bud Townsend. "You want to pass me your quitclaim—so I can review it?"

Bud Townsend looked at Seth and Seth nodded and the lawyer opened the folder and removed the document and passed it across the table.

"I'd like to put off sellin the stock long as possible," Seth said. "I'm lookin to buy another place. I'd like to keep some of the herd to seed it."

Jo looked up from her reading. "You found a place?"

"Not yet."

She looked at the quitclaim. "Three weeks," she said.

"Three weeks."

"We want all the cattle off the property in three weeks."

Bud Townsend reached and pulled at his bowtie. "That's ridiculous. It'll be months before you can do anything with the property."

Joe Smith tapped the table with a finger. "First of the year," he said. "Barring any unforeseen snags, we'll start clearing the first week of January."

"Well, why not give Seth till then at least. It's in your best interest, seems to me—give him more time to get the best price for the stock."

Jo dropped the quitclaim and looked directly at Bud. "Cause I do not want to give him more time, that's why. I've lived with the stigma long enough."

Seth eyed his sister. "Stigma?"

She glared back at him. "Raising animals for slaughter. I've waited a long time to disassociate myself from such a barbaric practice. And I'll not wait any longer. You've got three weeks."

Seth looked at his sister and then shook his head and sighed. "Savin the animals," he said. "I might've known."

"And darn proud of it," Jo said.

"How many cows you reckon there'd be if they weren't raised for the table?"

"Three weeks."

Seth's neck flushed crimson. "How many animals you expect to save by developin Curlew?"

"I *reckon* plenty. As of today, there will be no more hunting—no more blood sport."

"Hell, woman, when your done there won't be nothin *to* hunt."

Joe Smith raised his hands. "Now let's be civil about this. We want to part company on good terms."

Seth looked at him and then looked at Bud.

The lawyer placed his hands palms down on the table. "You ready to get this over with?"

"No, I ain't," Seth replied. "But I reckon I got no choice, do I?"

Bud shook his head. "None that makes any sense."

*

After dropping Bud at his office, Seth stopped at a Seven Eleven and bought a quart bottle of beer. He drove to the ranch road and turned in and pulled to the shoulder and stopped and switched off the truck's ignition. He opened the beer and sat drinking it and gazing out across the land. Moss in the cypress along side of him waved gently to a southerly breeze. The smell of manure and pine. A buzzard soaring silently overhead, circling and rising and circling until a mere speck against the clouds. He drank, and when the bottle was empty, he laid it on the seat and sat a while longer. Then he got out of the truck and circled it and took a leak in the ditch and got back in and started the truck and pulled away.

He reached the barn a little past noon. By the time he'd climbed from the truck, his three employees stood in the barn bay, eyeing him expectantly. He walked to them and stopped and stood facing them with his hands stuffed in his hip pockets. "Well," he said. "It's done. The Curlew Cattle Company is dissolved."

None of the three responded immediately. They all stepped and stood uncertainly. Pete reached and removed his cap and put back on. He looked at Seth. "They try to break it off in you?"

"They didn't just try. I got three weeks to sell-off the cattle."

"Three weeks."

Seth nodded. "I got till the ninth."

Pete shrugged. "Well, now we know, I reckon."

"Now we know. I'd like y'all to start with the south pasture this afternoon, move them older steers up here to the bull pasture. You do that, I'll get on the phone with Jimmy—see if he's come up with any prospects. First thing Monday, we'll begin sortin and preppin for shippin. We'll start whether he's found any buyers or not."

"We'll get on it," Pete said.

Seth nodded and then turned and began walking to his truck. "I know y'all got more questions," he said. "Just hold on to 'em. I don't feel much like talkin right now."

"Yessir," said Pete. He turned and looked at Onnie and looked at Bodie. "Well, y'all ketch up your horses. I'll throw a couple bags of feed on the truck and meet you out back."

As Pete headed for the flatbed, the two boys stood for a moment watching Seth drive to the house. Then Bodie quit watching and turned to enter the barn. "You better put your ass in gear," he said. "It'll probably take you most of the afternoon to ketch Elvis."

Onnie turned and looked. He reached back and got his tobacco pouch from his hip pocket and opened it and loaded in a chaw. "Shoot," he said. "Elvis ain't hard to ketch. He's just hard to find sometimes."

\*

Saturday morning he drove into town and parked his truck in the Westside Shopping Plaza lot. He parked directly in front of Gordon's Jewelry and switched off the engine and sat watching the eastbound traffic on highway 192. It was a few minutes before ten, cool, a few wispy cirrus clouds but otherwise clear. In a few minutes he saw his mother's Explorer slow on the highway and turn into the lot. When she parked in the space adjacent to his truck, he smiled and raised a hand in greeting. He got out and circled the SUV and reached and opened her door.

Angela smiled as she gathered in her purse and stepped out onto the pavement. "I didn't know you were such a gentleman," she said.

Bodie rolled his eyes. "I ain't. I'm just tryin to show my gratitude for you helpin me out like this."

Angela gazed up at him. She studied his face and smiled and said: "You are your father's son."

They strolled side by side to Gordon's plate glass entry door. Bodie reached and pulled the door open for his mother and then, after pausing to glance up at a cluster of tinkling bells, followed her inside. Behind a long display case an attractive young woman looked up and smiled and glided toward them. A man appeared suddenly in a doorway at the rear of the store, a short, bald fellow peering at them briefly over wire-framed glasses, and then stepping back out of sight.

"Good morning," said the young woman.

Angela, her eyes fixed on the display case, said, "morning." She leaned in and reached and tapped on the glass with a finger. "We want to look at your engagement rings. Are these all you have?"

The woman looked at Bodie. "We have more. Did you have something particular in mind?"

Bodie removed his hat and turned it in his hands. He looked at the woman and looked down at his absorbed mother.

"Something unique," said Angela. "Something special." She pointed into the case. "I kind of like that marquise cut there. What do you think, Bodie? You think Abby would like that one?"

Bodie leaned in next to his mother, his left hand clutching the hat, his right tracing the glass. "That one? The yellow gold?"

"Yeah, the one in the center. Does Abby like yellow gold?"

The woman bent and unlocked the case and slid back the glass and reached and plucked the mentioned ring from its velvet slot. She straightened and offered it and Angela took it with her fingers and turned to Bodie. "If she likes yellow gold, I think it's perfect. I think it's spectacular."

Bodie eyed the ring. "It's pretty," he said. "I like the way it sparkles."

"It's a full carat," said the woman. "Excellent clarity."

Bodie looked at the woman. "A full carat. How much does somethin like that cost?"

The woman stooped and reached into the case and removed a small tag from the slot where the ring had been. She straightened and held the tag close, turning it in her fingers. "It's only sixty-three hundred," she said.

Bodie swallowed. "Only sixty-three hundred."

"That's right. But that's before the discount. We discount all our jewelry twenty percent." The woman leaned in close to Angela. "And I may be able to give you the Christmas discount," she said in a lowered voice. "Beginning next Friday, we'll discount everything forty percent for Christmas."

Angela looked at Bodie. "Do you like it?"

Bodie looked at the ring and looked at his mother. "Well, yeah. I like it, but ..."

Angela looked at the woman. "You give us the Christmas discount, and we'll take it today."

The woman smiled and reached and took the ring from Angela. "I'll just be a moment," she said. She then turned and walked to the rear of the store, disappearing through the open doorway.

"Jesus, Mama."

Angela looked. "You like it don't, you?"

"Likin it's got nothin to do with it. How am I gonna pay for it?"

Angela turned to him and reached and grasped his arm. "Bodie," she said. "We're millionaires now. You don't need to think like that anymore."

"I ain't no millionaire. I'm broke as always. And I'm fixin to be out of a job."

"Well you don't have to worry about this. This ring is a gift from your father and me."

The woman emerged from the doorway looking solemn. Bodie watched her approach, then glanced at his mother. "Daddy don't even know I'm here," he whispered.

"He knows."

Upon reaching them, the woman's glum expression suddenly transformed into broad smile. She held out the ring. "Forty percent," she said. "Mr. Stevens is in a good mood this morning."

"Super," said Angela.

When they left the store, Bodie carried a small flashy bag, its tiny cord handles gripped tightly by the fingers of his right hand. He walked his mother to her car and stood patiently by as she got in and closed the door and lowered the window. "You going to wait for Christmas?" she said.

Bodie combed the parking lot with his eyes. He shifted his gaze to his mother. "Christmas."

"The ring. When are you going to give it to her?"

He raised the bag and looked at it and looked at his mother. "Today, if I can track her down."

"You know it should be special—how you do it and all."

"It'll be special. At least, to me and her it will be."

Angela smiled and reached and touched his hand as she started the Explorer's engine. "Well you be sure and call me—let me know how it went. And I don't want your usual abbreviated version. I want to hear everything."

Bodie smiled and thumbed back his hat. "Yes, ma'am," he said.

**21**

**He reached the oak** a little past three o'clock. He dismounted in the shade of the old tree and dropped the reins and stood picking beggar lice from Limpkin's mane. "How'd you git so burred up," he said. A cool breeze drifted off the lake. Several boats were far out on the open water, their occupants drifting for speckled perch, black crappie. In a moment he looked up from his preening and gazed southward. Abby was directly down shore, scarcely a hundred yards and closing.

She walked her horse beneath the tree and dismounted and dropped the reins and came to him. They embraced and kissed and she stood back and looked at him quizzically. "There's nothing wrong, is there?"

"No. Not that I know of."

She cocked her head and continued to look at him. "You sure?"

"Reasonably certain. Why?"

"It's just that every time you ask me to come out here, lately, there's something wrong. You always seem to have bad news."

Bodie looked around. "No. No bad news. Just wanted to set with you and watch them fellers fish for specks—see if they're bitin yet."

Abby looked at him. "Yeah, right."

He gestured toward the oak's great trunk. "Well. Have a seat. No sense wastin time now that we're here." He circled the tree and sat at its base and patted the ground next to him with his hand. "Come on, girl. The show's done started."

Abby came to him and sat down and elbowed his arm sharply. "You're acting goofy as hell. What's got into you?"

Bodie suddenly rocked forward and twisted his torso to look behind him. "Well me myself," he said, "I'm wonderin what's got *under* me. Feels like I'm settin on a rock or somethin." He reached his hand behind him and brought it back forward in one smooth motion, a small box wedged between his fingers, a gold box with a length of red ribbon wrapped around it and tied in a bow. "Well look at that. How you reckon that got there."

Abby looked at the box in his hand. She reached a hand forward as if to touch it but stopped short, her hand hovering in the air, trembling in the air.

"Well go ahead. See what we've found."

She snatched the box from his hand and slipped the ribbon off and raised the lid. "Good Lord," she gasped.

He laughed. "Darned if it ain't a rock."

"A huge rock." She carefully removed the ring from the box and held it up to the light, the sparkle in her eyes rivaling that of the stone. Then she turned quickly to Bodie, reaching with her free hand and pulling him to her. She peppered his cheek with kisses. "I love you. I love you. I love you." she said.

"I reckon you like it, then?"

Abby released him and looked at the ring. "How could I not? Just look at it."

"Well try it on. The lady said I can bring it back if it don't fit. They'll size it for you."

She started to slip the ring on her right hand, but stopped and looked at Bodie. "You're supposed to do it. If you do it, it'll never come off."

"Never?"

Abby elbowed him. "You know what I mean."

He took the ring from her and reached and caught her hand. When she extended her fingers, he slid the ring on. "It's a little snug," he said.

"It fits perfectly. You don't want it too loose." She extended her arm fully to admire the ring. "Good God. I'll be afraid to wear it."

"Not much good if you can't wear it."

"Oh, I'll wear it, all right."

Bodie gazed out across the lake. "That feller just caught one."

"What?"

"Third boat from the left. A feller just caught a speck."

"Your impossible."

He looked at her and looked at the ring. "I'm glad you like it."

She leaned in and kissed him. "I love it."

"What time's your company comin?"

"They're coming for dinner. Around six, I imagine."

"You got time to ride to Rawlerson Hammock?"

Abby looked at him and smiled. "I'll always have time for that."

He stood and offered her his hand. "Not always," he said. "It won't always be there."

She took his hand and he pulled her up. "You're saying they wouldn't agree to save the old house."

He shook his head. "They ain't gonna save anything they don't have to." He reached and pulled a piece of bark from the oak and tossed it toward the lake. "I have to tell you I thought about killin 'em."

Abby looked into his eyes. "You thought about killing who?"

"Aunt Jo Beth and Uncle Billy. If I'd killed 'em fore Daddy signed the papers, Curlew would've been all his."

"Jesus, Bodie. Don't say things like that. You never thought anything of the sort. You wouldn't kill anybody."

He looked in her eyes and smiled. "Oh I thought about it all right, but you've got me pegged. I was just blowin off steam."

*

They ran the horses most of the way, not slowing until Bodie suddenly reined his horse in just shy of the old homeplace. Abby was past him before able to stop her mare. By the time she circled back, Bodie was standing in his stirrups, gazing north toward Orange Hammock. She rode beside him and stood herself and looked and saw a spiral of buzzards over the distant trees. They watched, the horses blowing and tossing their heads. "You think the panther's made another kill?" Abby said.

"I'd like to think it has. But my brain says otherwise. My brain says it's somethin much worse."

Abby settled back to her saddle. "Well what does your brain say it is?"

Bodie turned his head to look at her. "I ain't jokin. I need to go look."

"I don't have much time."

"I'll make it up to you. I'm afraid this is somethin can't wait."

Abby nudged her horse forward. "Well, let's get to looking then."

He quickly caught up to her and reached and caught one of her reins and stopped her horse. "It may be somethin you don't need to see."

Abby cast him a stern look. "If you're going, I'm going."

He looked at the buzzards and looked at her. "All right," he said, but if it's what I think it is, you'll be sorry."

They rode, covering a half-mile of flatwoods at a lope. Nearing the hammock, they slowed the horses to a walk and weaved their way into its trees, craning their necks and watching. Vultures began launching from limbs overhead as they approached the small clearing, a cacophony of breaking branches and popping feathers, great wings flying a gauntlet of limbs and leaves to reach the open sky. Bodie tested the breeze. "I don't smell nothin," he said.

"Me neither."

They rode and the trees parted and in the clearing lay the old man, the old Indian curled fetal-like on the sandy ground. A common vulture crouched by his head, another perched atop his upright shoulder.

"Shit," said Bodie, bailing out of the saddle and running and cursing at the scavengers, sending the two birds flailing and croaking in opposite directions. And when they were gone, he stopped and stood looking down at the frail and withered body, at the yellow rain slicker still rolled and lying where he himself had thrown it. "Damn," he said.

Abby sat her horse, a hand cupped over her mouth. "Oh my God," she said through her fingers.

Bodie walked back to her and stood looking up at her. "You all right?"

"No I'm not all right. That's a dead body, a human body."

"Yeah, it is. Died sometime last night, I expect."

"Who is it? I can't tell if it's a man or a woman. How did you know?"

"An Indian Granddaddy called Solomon. He was a spiritual leader. I figured it was him when I seen the buzzards. He practically told me he was dyin last time I seen him. Bout a week ago."

"Well what's he doing here?"

Bodie gestured toward the mounds. "He comes here to visit them graves."

"So you knew him."

"Yeah, sort of."

"Well how come I didn't know about him? You never mentioned him to me."

He looked at the body and looked up at Abby. "I don't know. Reckon I didn't quite know what to make of him. I don't know why I never told you." He cocked back his head and turned slowly, scanning the canopy above. Several buzzards were still perched and leering hopefully. He looked at the body and removed his hat and set it back on his head. "I got to figure out what to do."

Abby's bay stepped nervously and tried to turn. She reined it back and looked down at Bodie. "There's only one thing to do. We've got to tell somebody. We've got to report it to the authorities."

He looked at her and he looked at his horse which stood curiously eyeing the body. And then he walked to the body and, stopping just short of the rigidly paired feet, sidestepped and stooped and gathered in the rain slicker. Grasping the coat's exposed tail in each hand, he stood and let it unfurl. He shook it open and turned and shook it again, bending at the waist and letting the billowed garment settle gently over the corpse. Then he turned back to Abby. "We ain't tellin anybody."

Abby stared incredulously at him.

He walked to his horse and gathered in the reins and swung into the saddle. He rode to her side. "You better head on home. I'll take care of things out here."

"I'm not going anywhere without an explanation. What do you mean you're gonna take care of things?"

"I'm gonna do what he wanted me to do. I'm gonna give him a proper burial."

"He asked you to bury him?"

"Yeah, I think he did."

"You think?"

"I know he did."

"You can't just go around burying people. It's against the law."

"Maybe so. But I've got to do what I think is right." He looked at the ring on her finger. "I hope it don't change nothin between us."

She looked at him and looked at the body. She sighed. "God, I hope you know what you're doing."

He tried to smile. "Me too. Now you better get goin. I've got to ride to the barn for a shovel. "

"You better call me when you get done."

"I will. If it's not too late. If it's late, I'll call you tomorrow."

175

"All right." She turned her horse.

"Abby."

She looked back. "Yeah?"

"You can't tell anybody."

"I ain't stupid."

The sun was set by the time he returned to the hammock. A quarter moon stood high in the darkening sky, slightly past its zenith. With the shovel balanced across his lap, he slowly picked his way into the hammock; it was significantly darker beneath the trees than in the open flatwoods, difficult to see. Thrush birds called randomly, seemingly from every direction. He made out many buzzards silhouetted in the canopy above. But there were none on the ground when he reached the clearing. He halted the horse and pitched the shovel next to the body and then stepped down. He reached into the saddle bag and fished out a coil of pigging string. He spoke to the horse: "You behave. I got enough trouble as it is." He draped the string over the saddle horn and turned and knelt next to the corpse. Beginning to smell. He reached and pulled the slicker aside. No flies. Flies would have left with the sun. He noticed the old man's hands clutching the tangle of trinkets at his throat. He thought that perhaps it was a last grope for comfort, for eternity.

He did not want to touch the body but knew it was not a matter of what he wanted. He took off his hat and set it on the ground. "Lord help me," he said. And he reached and grabbed hold of the eternally arched figure, pulling against its back until it rolled and stood balanced on forehead and knees. He held the body balanced as such and set his feet and crouched and reached his right arm beneath the old man's belly. He lifted with all his strength, pressing with his legs and propelling the body upward. In a flash, he ducked low and caught the rigid midsection on his shoulder, his feet launching into a crazy dance as he balanced the weight. The old man was heavy, much heavier than he had imagined. Bodie's legs threatened to buckle as he began to walk.

When he approached the horse it began sidling away, blowing and rolling its eyes. He spoke to it sternly and the horse settled. It stood for him, and he eased next to it and half turned and wrestled the rigid load head first over the curve of the animal's back. The weight transferred, he squatted and wrenched himself free of the man's legs, the colorful dress. Then he stepped back and bent at the waist and grabbed his thighs. He gasped for breath. "Jesus," he said.

After lashing the corpse to the saddle with pigging string, he got the slicker and rolled it and wedged it between the saddle's comb and the body. He got his hat and the shovel and mounted up and walked the horse from the trees, from the insufferable darkness now enveloping the hammock. As he rode the moonlit flatwoods, he spoke to the old man, telling him of his plans and asking his approval. And though no word was audible save his own, he heard the old man give such approval, and saw a moon suddenly brighter, a path perfectly clear.

At the cemetery, he dismounted and strode through the rickety gate, the shovel balanced over one shoulder, a crescent moon suspended over the other. He walked until just beyond his grandfather's grave and then stopped and swung the shovel from his shoulder and began to dig. He worked without pause the better part of an hour. Then he climbed from his creation and stood the shovel in the ground. He looked up at the moon, his clothes drenched with sweat. He stood motionless for several minutes, simply listening and looking. The drone of a distant plane. His heartbeat. Next to his grandfather's headstone, the tongue-shaped foil leaves of an artificial plant captured the light of the moon and glowed like the licking flames of a fire, but no ordinary fire, a fire producing no smoke or heat. He stood resting and gazing at the faux fire for some time, and when he'd caught his breath, he turned and walked to his horse.

Setting his hat on the saddle's pommel horn, he untied the corpse and dipped low and wrestled it onto his shoulder, the dutiful horse standing stock still, the night eerily quiet. He stepped toward the gate reeling like a drunkard, his burden's long hair taunting his back. A strange sight, a grotesquely deformed creature cavorting in the moonlight. Nearing the hole, he caught a boot and tripped and fell, the corpse pinning him to the ground, suffocating him. He fought to free himself, and was near tears by the time he had. "I'm sorry," he said. "I'm so sorry."

He himself had to get in the grave to bury the man with dignity. He could think of no other way. He dropped into the hole and turned and took hold of the old man's shoulder's and pulled. He dragged the body in slowly, trying to be respectful. Then he climbed out and turned to see what he had done but there was nothing to see. To the eye the hole held only darkness. He reached and grabbed the shovel and loaded it with dirt from the pile. He hesitated, staring at the darkness below his boots. "I didn't hardly know you," he said. "But what I knew was all good. I hope I did right. I hope it's what you wanted. It's the only safe place I know of." He swung the shovel and pitched the dirt and heard a muffled thud in the darkness below. "Ashes to ashes," he said. "Dust to dust."

**22**

**He called Abby** early the next morning and told her what he'd done. She was just leaving for church, so their conversation was brief. When he returned to the kitchen his father stood gazing out the curtained window above the sink. Without turning, Seth said: "Jimmy's got us a couple of buyers."

Bodie dragged a chair out from the table and sat in it. "He does?"

"Pretty fair price, too. Specially the pregnant heifers. Feller in Alabama wants all of 'em. Says he'll go a dollar thirty-five, maybe."

"That's good."

"Yeah, it is." Seth turned and stepped to the coffee maker. He topped off the cup already in his hand. "You give Abby the ring?"

"Yessir. I did."

"I reckon she liked it."

"She liked it a lot."

Seth nodded his head and sipped his coffee. "You been seein many turkeys?"

Bodie looked. "Turkeys?"

"Thursday's Thanksgivin, you know."

"I reckon I hadn't even thought about it."

"Me neither. But your mama has. She's countin on you baggin her a turkey. She wants to fire up that old oven out at the homeplace one more time—fore it's too late."

"Mama? Lookin forward to cookin?"

179

"Says she is."

"Hmm," said Bodie. He looked around the kitchen and looked at his father. "She plannin on just the three of us?"

Seth reached and set his cup in the sink. "If you mean can Abby come, your mama's way ahead of you. She's done invited the whole Thompson clan. Talked to Martha last night. Gonna be Thanksgivin and engagement party all rolled into one."

Bodie nodded. He smiled. "Well Abby and me best get to huntin, then."

"And you best do it today. It's gonna be mighty busy round here 'tween now and Thursday."

Bodie rose from the chair as if to leave but stopped and stood looking at his father's back. "Daddy."

"Yeah."

"I really appreciate you and Mama buyin Abby's ring for me."

Seth turned and looked at him. He smiled and nodded his head. "Well I appreciate you sayin so."

\*

He met Abby at Rawlerson Hammock around two o'clock. They were each dressed in camouflage, identical Remington 870 Turkey Guns secured in their respective boot scabbards. After greeting, they circled the old homeplace and rode south, walking the horses a quarter-mile through the hammock and on into the pinewoods lying beyond. They rode without talk or pause until the pines gave way to low palmettos and broomsage. There, they stopped and sat the horses and gazed across the open flatwoods at a distant strand of trees, a line of cypress fronted by oaks and palms and stretching east and west for almost a mile, the slant of the afternoon sun highlighting the palm trunks, painting them starkly white against the dark blur of oaks.

Bodie raised a hand and made a sweeping gesture toward the hammock. "Most afternoons you can count on 'em bein along in there," he said. "They'll feed the edge till bout sunset then move on inside the hammock, fly up to roost back in the cypress. Early as it is, if we scatter 'em they'll try to regroup." He paused and glanced at Abby, shaking a finger in the air. "A turkey keen on gettin back with the flock is a easy turkey to call. Nothin dumber'n a lost turkey, you know."

Abby's eyes narrowed. She frowned and adjusted her cap and cast him a sideways look. "How many times have we done this?"

"I don't know. Quite a few, I reckon."

"Exactly. And every time you stop right here and give me that turkey huntin 101 stuff."

Bodie leaned and spat. "Hell, girl. We ain't married, yet."

"So."

"So you're supposed to humor me when I try and tell you how smart I am."

Abby stared at him. She wagged her head and smiled and reached and pulled the slack from her reins. "Let's go kill a turkey," she said. "We get back to the homeplace, you can *show* me how smart you are."

*

Beginning Monday they worked cows from dark to dark for three days running, the weather stagnant, warm for late November. They emptied the outlying pastures of every cow, calf, steer and bull, herding them to the small pastures surrounding the barn. They sorted, counted and weighed. They administered proconditioning shots to guard against disease during the stressful days ahead. And when the sun set Wednesday they quit working, bone-tired, filthy, numb from the din of constant lowing surrounding the ranch headquarters, drained by the inescapable sense of finality at the core of their labor.

Bodie and his parents spent Thanksgiving day with the Thompsons at the old homeplace, at Rawlerson Hammock. To Bodie the affair seemed more like a wake than the festive gatherings of years past, palpable tension between his parents, the Thompsons struggling to rejoice their daughter's engagement while tiptoeing around the problems besetting their soon-to-be inlaws. It was a thoroughly depressing day for him, one whose end left him convinced that, except for Abby, he had little for which to be thankful.

Monday following an eighteen wheeler arrived at Curlew, a transport out of Auburndale came for sixty-three steers purchased by a broker in Green Cove Springs. It was the first of many haulers to come and go during the ensuing week. By Friday afternoon, only two cows remained on the place, the heifer calf now called July, and its two year old mother. As the sun sagged below the horizon, the men of Curlew gathered next to the trap holding the Brangus pair. They stood

181

silently, watching the calf nurse, the calf's mother watching them. The four men leaned into the same chest-high fence board, elbows lounging along its rough-sawed edge, chins resting on paired hands. They stood as if mesmerized until Pete suddenly cocked his head first one way and then the other.

"Well I'll be damned," he said.

The others simultaneously turned their heads sufficient to look at the foreman.

"I been standin here tryin to figure what was wrong. And it just dawned on me. In forty years I ain't never heard a evenin so quiet out here."

The others looked away. They listened to the soft nuzzlings of the calf continuing to nurse, watched curlews passing silently to the north, flying very high, the offset Vs gilded by a sun now lost to all but them.

Seth's eyes tracked the laboring birds eastward. "Y'all got any promisin leads on a job yet?"

The three looked at Seth. Pete stepped back from the fence and reached his arms skyward. He stretched. "I ain't looked," he said.

"You ain't?"

Pete lowered his arms and shook his head. "I'm sixty-two. The way I see it, less you start up a new operation, I'm flat out of luck."

"Bull," said Seth. "You ain't too old. You got years of work left in you."

"Yeah, well, my body says otherwise. My body says I done mugged one too many cows."

"So my findin another place has got nothin to do with it. You're just ready to quit."

Pete looked at the ground and looked at Seth. He smiled thinly. "No. I'd work for you, boss. You're used to my frailties."

Seth frowned and shook his head. He shifted his gaze to Onnie. "How bout you, Double Ought? You been lookin, ain't ya?"

Onnie stood with his hands tucked in his jeans. He grinned and dipped his head. "No sir. Not really." He cut a glance at Bodie.

Bodie stepped and stood. He looked at his father. "I planned to get Onnie a job at Thompson Farms—if we don't get a new place and all."

Seth's eyes sharpened. "You planned?"

"Yessir."

"Well you best stop plannin and start doin."

He looked at his father. "You're still lookin for a place, ain't you?"

"I'm lookin, but I've bout give up on findin anything. All I'm findin is just how bad I got screwed."

Everyone looked. "What do you mean?" said Bodie.

"The prices I'm seein, I shoulda got twice what I did." Seth removed his cap and scratched his head. He put the cap back on and looked at Pete. "Anyway," he said. "I'm tryin to say y'all best plan on fendin for yourselves."

Pete nodded his head but said nothing.

Seth reached into his hip pocket and removed a pair of folded envelopes. He separated them and handed one to Pete and the other to Onnie. "There's two checks in there," he said. "This week's pay plus a severance check—a week's pay for every year you been with us." He reached and shook both men's hands in turn and then stepped back and nodded his head.

Onnie waved his envelope in the air. "Will it be all right if Elvis stays a day or two longer? I can't get my uncle's trailer till Monday. He's usin it to haul mulch or somethin this weekend."

Seth smiled. "For all I care, Elvis can stay forever. Maybe then we'll get to see you once in a while."

Onnie grinned and dipped his head. He turned quickly and began walking for his truck. "I got to go," he said. "I'll see y'all."

"Well what's your hurry?" Bodie called after him.

Onnie did not reply. He continued on to his old Dodge as if late for an appointment. As he drove away, Pete smiled and shook his head. "Crazy coot."

"What's the matter with him?" said Bodie.

"Ain't nothin the matter," said Pete. "He just don't want nobody seein him cry is all."

**23**

**The following morning** he strolled into the kitchen expecting a reprimand for sleeping till almost eight. But his father was not there to scold him. The coffee pot was cold, the maker still primed and ready. So he switched on the machine and waited. He captured the first cup dripped and carried it to the table. He dragged out a chair and sat in it. And when a half hour had passed, he eased back to the master bedroom. There, his father was but a still lump beneath the covers, a lump whose rhythmic breathing seemed too shallow and hushed for a man truly sleeping. Bodie stood uncertainly in the doorway for a while, then he turned and went back to the kitchen. He piddled, washing the few dishes in the sink and drying them and putting them away. He smoked one of his father's cigarettes on the porch. And when Seth still did not get up, he left the house and drove his truck to Abby's. He stayed with her most of the day. When he returned home his father, wearing boxer shorts and a T-shirt, sat slumped in his office chair, staring blankly at the computer's monitor. He was unshaven and smelled of bourbon and cigarette smoke, a stranger, a man Bodie surely did not know.

For two days he watched his father's plummet into despair. Then he quit watching. Early Tuesday, he fled to the barn where he occupied himself with mostly meaningless tasks. He pampered his horse as never before, grooming and exercising it in the trap, taking it out for a long ride with no destination, no purpose. A meaningless journey during which he not only spoke to the horse but for it as well. He visited Miss Ella and talked of his troubles and then listened skeptically as she

185

said they would pass. And in the late afternoon, he counted down the minutes till Abby's return from class, till the sun would set and he could go to her. Night was good, he decided. He looked forward to the night.

Wednesday morning he herded five of the six deer hounds from the pens and coaxed them into the bed of his truck. Five Bluetick and Walker crosses, a gyp and four males. He drove to the highway and turned south toward Kenansville, the dogs all standing tentatively, noses lifted and testing the wind, long ears trailing like streamers. He parked at the entrance to Lake Marion Marina and got out and stood waiting next to the truck's bed. And shortly a pale blue F250 arrived from the east and slowed and pulled onto the road shoulder. The old man driving eased the truck next to Bodie's Ford and braked and switched off its diesel motor. He lifted a hand and smiled, white hair showing beneath a brown and misshapen Stetson, bib overalls, dungaree jacket. He opened his door and stepped out and circled the bed of his truck, his eyes fixed on the dogs.

"Hey, Mr. Costine."

The old man was busy stroking the head of each dog in turn. "Hey, Bodie," he said. "I only count five. You keepin that old black and tan?"

"Yessir. Old Joe's not for sale."

The old man retracted his hand and turned to face Bodie. "Can't say as I blame ya. He's one of the best strike dogs I ever seen."

"Yessir."

Costine's demeanor clouded. "I'm damn sorry about you all's misfortune. Damn sorry."

"Yessir. Me too."

"Yeah. I reckon you are." He hooked the straps of his overalls with his thumbs. He leaned and spat. "You ain't by yourself, though. Same crap's happenin all over."

Bodie stepped and stood. "Yessir. I reckon it is."

"And I'll tell you what's the problem. The problem's all these damn foreigners flockin to Florida. This very mornin I was standin in the checkout line in Publix, and they wasn't a soul around me speakin English. Not a soul. Felt like I done landed in a third world country or somethin. Yessir. That's exactly what's happened. Old Florida's done gone and turned into a frappin third world country. It surely has."

Bodie fought to stifle a chuckle. "Maybe so. But wasn't foreigners caused us our problems."

The old man released his overalls' straps and briefly swung his arms, swung them as if preparing for some sort of competition. "No. No it wasn't. I got to give you that. But it's foreigners that'll buy them houses they plannin on throwin up out there. They'll swarm in here like gnats to a dog peter. You wait and see."

A tractor trailer roared by on the highway and the old man reached and grabbed his hat and turned to watch the departing rig.

Bodie watched the old man watch the truck. "You been doin any huntin?"

Costine looked. "Yeah. A little. Ain't killed nothin, though. Run several good bucks. Never could get in front of 'em."

"Maybe our dogs will change your luck."

The old man glanced at the dogs milling about the truck's bed. "Maybe," he said. He brought a hand to his chin and cupped it pensively. "How much was you figurin to get for the five of 'em?"

Bodie shrugged his shoulders. "I ain't out to rob you. How's five hundred sound?"

"For the lot?"

"Yessir."

"Sounds like you've lost your mind. Them hounds is worth four times that."

"I know it."

"Then what are you tryin to pull?"

"I ain't tryin to pull nothin. Knowin you'll hunt 'em is worth the difference to me."

"I'll hunt 'em all right."

Bodie nodded. "And you're one of only a few left round here that will."

The old man looked at the dogs and looked at Bodie. "Five hundred."

"Yessir."

Costine reached and plucked a stack of folded bills from his bib pocket. He unfolded them and counted out five and handed them to Bodie. "I hope your daddy don't come whip me when he hears about this."

"No sir. He won't. I doubt he'll even notice the dogs are gone."

"Well you'll have to come hunt with me sometime."

"Yessir. I'd like that."

"We got another month left in the season, so call me anytime."

"Yessir. I'll do that."

After helping the old man load the dogs, Bodie said goodbye and headed for home. As he reached the ranch road, Onnie's blue Dakota was about to exit it. Bodie pulled next to the Dodge and stopped. "You lookin for me?" he said.

Onnie grinned and reached and pushed back his hat. He looked up the road and looked at Bodie. "Sort of," he said. "I been to see your daddy."

"Oh." Bodie looked away. He watched an armadillo emerge from the palmettos and begin to root the shoulder of the grade, the truck engines idling, the serpentine belt on Bodie's chirping like a mindless bird.

Onnie's grin faded, bled into a look of concern. "You doin all right?"

"I'm all right."

"I got me a job."

Bodie looked. "You did?"

"Just something to tide me over. Had to do somethin. I didn't know what was up with the workin for Bill Thompson and all. You ain't called me."

"I ain't known what to do. I'm still waitin."

"On Bill?"

"On Daddy."

"Oh."

"But I'm bout done waitin."

Onnie nodded.

"Where'd you find a job?"

Onnie grinned sheepishly and dipped his head. "Well, that's the thing. I wasn't lookin. It just kind of happened."

"Yeah?"

"Yeah. Your aunt Jo called me."

"Aunt Jo."

"She wants me to work security for *Prosperity.*"

Bodie was silent. He stared straight ahead.

"You ain't mad, are ya?"

Bodie looked at him. "What do you think?"

"It's just temporary. I got bills to pay. Besides, I'll be ridin fence right here. You can understand me wantin to do that, can't ya?"

"I can't understand you *wantin* to do anything for Aunt Jo."

Onnie looked away. "Well. I done told her I would."

Bodie reached and slipped his gearshift into drive. "Well you have a nice life," he said. He stomped the accelerator. The truck squatted and slowly pulled away, the rear tires spinning and launching dust and pebbles past Onnie's Dodge.

Onnie sat watching his rearview mirror. "Shit," he said.

\*

Seth was sitting at the kitchen table when Bodie came into the house. He had shaved and was dressed, but the coffee mug cupped in his hands held a brown liquid that was not coffee. Without looking he said: "You see Double Ought?"

Bodie walked to the sink and stopped and stood looking out the window. "I seen him."

Seth sipped his drink. "He only done what he had to."

Bodie was silent.

"You need to do the same thing. Tell Bill you're ready to work."

Bodie half turned. He looked at his father. "What are you gonna do?"

Seth stared at the mug in his hands. "I ain't got to do nothin. I'm a rich man, you know."

\*

He found Bill Thompson in the orange grove, driving a squatty John Deere and spraying the trees with fungicide. The great wheeled sprayer behind him trailed a misty cloud through light and shadow, trees dripping in its wake, small rainbows forming and dissipating. Upon seeing Bodie, Bill simultaneously cut off the sprayer and stopped the tractor. He stood and climbed down, leaving the tractor's diesel motor ticking at idle. He came to Bodie taking long ground eating strides.

"Hey, Bodie," he said. He was smiling.

"Hey, Mr. Thompson."

"You're early today. Abby ain't home yet."

"I come ready to work—if you still want me."

Bill reached and adjusted his cap. He looked at Bodie. "Your daddy know you're here?"

"Yessir. He give me the go-ahead."

"First thing Monday mornin all right with you?"

"Yessir. Anytime. I'll start right now if you want."

189

Bill glanced at his watch. "The week's half over. I expect we better stick with Monday—make it easy on my bookkeeper."

"All right. I'll see you Monday, then"

Bill nodded, and Bodie started to turn. "Wait," Bill said.

Bodie turned back. "Yessir?"

"On second thought, how bout Friday? I got nothin special goin on. I can show you around, devote the whole day to gettin you orientated."

"Orientated?"

"Yeah. If that's even a word."

Bodie smiled. "Friday sounds good. But what about your bookkeeper?"

"Bookkeeper? Hell, don't worry about him. The money I pay him, he deserves a little challenge every now and then."

Bodie smiled and nodded his head. "All right. What time you want me?"

"Seven. We start at seven."

"Seven. Yessir. I won't be late."

**Thursday** dawned surprisingly cold. When Bodie stepped onto the porch he was greeted by a cloudless sky, the eastern horizon giving birth to a gleaming arc of sun. For the first time in months he could see his breath, and it was a sight that pleased him. He felt invigorated. For an instant, the splendid morning revived a feeling he'd not experienced for days, the feeling of contentment he'd grown up thinking was his for life. Then he turned and saw Onnie's truck at the barn, and the feeling evaporated. He stared at the blue Dodge for a long time. Then he turned and stepped back inside.

Around ten he strode out of the house and sat the stoop and pulled on his boots. He walked purposefully to the yard fence and climbed it and set out across the pasture, a windowed envelope protruding from his hip pocket. Teal-blue sky. Cool. In the shade, almost cold. At the barn, he paused briefly in the turnaround and stood eyeing Onnie's truck. Then he moved on to the flatbed work truck and sequentially opened its two doors. He went into the barn and got a box of garbage bags then returned to the truck and began emptying out the cab: a plastic poncho, two flashlights, an odd number of leather gloves riddled with holes and jagged tears. From beneath the seat he dragged styrofoam cups, empty cigarette packs, tobacco pouches, a box of .22 long rifle cartridges. He piled everything into one of the bags and carried the bag to the passenger side. He set the bag in the floor and flared its mouth and began raking out the contents of the glove box: flashlight batteries and fuses, an assortment of tools, crumpled paperwork rust-stained and faded. When finished, he gave the cab a cursory inspection and then lifted the bag and carried it into the barn. Returning, he cleared the truck's bed of three shovels, an axe, a come-along winch and a pair of posthole diggers. A galvanized bucket holding a hammer and rusted fence staples. A couple of short pressure treated four by fours. Lastly, he fished the key from his pocket and slipped it into the ignition switch and shut the doors. Then he hopped up on the bed to sit and wait.

Around eleven the buyers arrived driving an older model Toyota long-bed that was mostly black, a large crucifix swinging from the rearview mirror. When the truck came to a stop in the turnaround, both doors swung open and two men stepped out of the cab, two short, stocky Mexicans with closely cropped hair, with remarkably similar features. Maybe brothers. Maybe not. The driver smiled broadly as he approached the flatbed, his dark eyes flashing and combing the vehicle in a covetous manner. He circled. And when Bodie hopped from the truck the man came to him and stood facing him without speaking. He simply nodded and reached back and pulled a thick envelope from his pant pocket and held it out. Bodie took the envelope and slid a finger beneath its flap to open it. Inside the envelope was a thick stack of hundred dollar bank notes. With the men watching, he counted the notes and then counted them again. Then he slipped the money back into the envelope and tucked its flap. He reached back and pulled the title envelope from his pocket and handed it to the driver. The driver gave the envelope a perfunctory glance but did not open it. He smiled and nodded and turned and began walking to his truck while his partner climbed into the flatbed's cab and pulled the door closed. The engines of both trucks started as if connected to the same switch, and then both trucks backing and turning and momentarily halting before lurching forward and pulling away in tandem.

Bodie stood watching the departing vehicles until billowing dust of their own making erased them. "Sod throwers," he said. Then, stuffing the envelope inside his shirt, he turned and looked at Onnie's Dodge. He shook his head and said: "Shit." He walked into the barn.

After catching his horse and saddling it, he rode to the house and left the horse at the yard fence and went inside. His father was still sleeping, and he did not bother trying to wake him. He left the envelope on the nightstand by his father's bed and got his rifle and a handful of cartridges from his own room and returned to his horse. He slid the rifle into the boot scabbard and mounted up and reined the horse northward. He rode listing in the saddle, his left hand braced against his thigh, head cocked downward, eyes fixed on the ground. When finally cutting Onnie's trail, he settled in the saddle and began following Elvis's tracks—an easy trail to follow with no cattle on the place.

The hoof prints led to the cemetery road and crossed it and continued on. But Bodie stopped in the sandy ruts and sat his horse. He gazed up at the sun. "He's noonin somewheres, fella. Probably done ate his lunch and nappin by now." He sat thinking a while longer and then simply followed the road westward. He eased the horse to a lope and held it at that pace until the great oak's canopy rose above the scrub ahead. Then he ramped down to a walk, the road bending gently and the palmettos and scrub oaks swinging aside and the graveyard sliding slowly into view. Elvis stood reined to the rickety gate with his head up and watching. Onnie lay flat on his back at the base of the great oak, hands married together and resting on his belly, hat tenting his face, a balled-up paper sack and a camouflaged thermos on the ground by his side.

Bodie rode directly to Elvis and dismounted and stood looking at the sleeping Onnie, listening to him snore. He smiled and eased down the fence until only a few yards from Onnie's crossed legs. He hunkered down with his back resting against one of the fence's lighter posts. He watched. Then he reached down and picked an acorn from the ground and tossed it, hitting Onnie's battered Stayform hat dead center.

Onnie nap-jerked and snorted, but then resumed snoring.

Bodie threw another acorn, this time hitting a thick-fingered hand.

Onnie stopped snoring but didn't move. He lay very still. Then from beneath his hat: "That you, bud?"

Bodie remained silent. He bounced another acorn off the hat.

Onnie's entire body jerked. His hands slowly unmeshed, his right one creeping up to the hat brim and tipping the hat up. "I figured it was you. Ain't no squirrel got that good of a aim." He grabbed his hat and uncrossed his legs and sat up. "Reckon I was really out cold."

"You sounded like a straight-pipe Harley. Heard you all the way up at the house."

"Shoot. I don't snore." He got to his feet and dusted off his back and breeches. He rubbed his hands together. "Damned if I ain't caught me a chill."

"Day like today, you ought to do your nappin in the sun."

"I done that earlier." Onnie gestured north with a hand. "Went pretty well till

193

Elvis tried to rake me off on the fence up yonder." He half turned and pointed down to his leg. "Tore my breeches pretty good."

"Sounds like security's hard work. Hazardous, too."

Onnie grinned prodigiously. "It's real tuff." He bent down and snared the thermos and sack and straightened and began walking toward his horse. "C'mere," he said, "look at what they give me."

Bodie got to his feet and followed. Standing by while Onnie rummaged through his saddle bag, he noticed his empty boot scabbard. "Where's your rifle? Elvis rake it off, too?"

Onnie turned, holding a slender booklet of sorts. "I'm not allowed to tote no rifle. No guns allowed on *Prosperity* property. None period. They only want me armed with this here ticket book."

"Ticket book?"

"Yeah. Ain't that a pisser. I ketch somebody trespassin, I'm to write 'em a warnin ticket."

"That ought to scare hell out of 'em."

"Yeah. And if I ketch some feller a second time, then they turn his name over to the real law."

Bodie frowned and shook his head.

"I know. Like some guy carryin a gun's gonna give me his real name and all. I told 'em it was stupid. But they didn't want to hear it."

"Well maybe after tomorrow you won't have to worry about none of it. You can tell 'em where to stick their tickets."

Onnie cocked his head. "Tomorrow? What happens tomorrow?"

"I start workin for Thompson Farms."

"No kiddin. You ask Bill about me?"

"I ain't brought you up yet. But I will."

Onnie grinned and looked away and looked at Bodie. He took a deep breath. "Reckon I don't know what to say."

"Nothin to say. I ain't done anything yet."

Onnie was silent. He just continued to grin and nod his head. Then he suddenly stopped grinning and stepped around Bodie. He leaned into the cemetery's hogwire fence and pointed to the mound of dirt next to July's grave. "What's that look like to you over yonder, next to your granddaddy there?"

Bodie stepped forward. "Looks like a grave."

"Yeah. Exactly. But what the hell?"

"It's the old Indian, old Solomon."

"Sure it is."

"I ain't shittin you. That's who it is."

"And you buried him?"

"Yeah. I buried him."

"Did ya kill him, or was he already dead?"

"Course he was already dead."

"So he *was* a haint—just like Pete figured."

Bodie rolled his eyes. "Jesus, Onnie. He died a couple weeks ago. Me and Abby just happened to find him is all."

"Abby saw him?"

"Yeah."

Onnie shook his head slowly. "Well I'll be." He thought for a moment and again gestured to the mound. "Why'd you bury him here? He weren't no Rawlerson."

"I just did."

Onnie studied him for a moment, then cocked his head back and looked at the sun. He looked at Bodie. "All right. If you don't wanna talk about it, let's go. They ain't payin me to stand around here."

"Go where?"

"Patrollin. You ain't got nothin better to do. Abby don't get outta class for hours. And then she's got finals to study for." Onnie turned and slipped the ticket book in his saddle bag. He grabbed Elvis's cinch strap and quickly drew it tight before the horse could react and blow up.

Bodie stood watching by the fence. Then he reached and loosened Elvis's rein from the wire and flipped it to Onnie. "You're apt to get fired, Jo sees me ridin with you."

Onnie mounted his horse. He sat shortening his reins and looking down at Bodie. "I'll just tell her I caught you trespassin. She's liable to give me a raise."

They crossed the cypress to the north and headed toward the boundary fence, the horses stepping spiritedly. The sun a warm hand on their shoulders but the air still cool, a light and variable breeze, the woods quiet and peaceful. At the firebreak they turned west, intending to follow the fence to the lake. But they'd scarcely made the turn when Bodie suddenly halted his horse. He sat staring straight ahead until Onnie got Elvis stopped and looked to see what was wrong.

Then Bodie nonchalantly turned his head and looked north across the fence. Speaking barely above a whisper, he said: "You see that guy?"

Onnie looked at Bodie and then looked where Bodie was looking. "What guy? I don't see nothin."

"Not where I'm lookin. Behind me."

Onnie started to turn.

"Don't look at him. He's about fifty yards, settin at the foot of a big pine."

"You sure it's a man?"

"Sure I'm sure. He's wearin fluorescent orange."

"What's he doin?"

"I just told you. He's settin. Probably watchin us and figurin which way he's gonna run."

"What you reckon we ought to do?"

"*We*? I ain't no security man. This is your show."

"Shoot."

Bodie leaned and spat. He straightened and looked at Onnie. "I reckon we just need to turn and ride up to him. Fan out a little. Be easier to cut him off when he bolts."

"You think he'll run?"

"Wouldn't you? I reckon he's bound to run with the fence right here."

"Well I ain't even seen him yet."

"Well you're fixin to." He reached and pulled the Winchester from its scabbard and swung it upright and stood it on his thigh. "You ready?"

"I reckon."

"Well let's do it."

When they turned the horses, Onnie immediately whispered: "He's still there."

"No shit," said Bodie.

They walked the horses forward, Bodie angling slightly left of the man, Onnie slightly right. The man did not move. He simply sat watching them come, visible only from the waist up, bright orange cap and coat virtually screaming here-I-am, his pale face equally loud, in jarring contrast with the dull pine bark behind it. As they closed the distance, the man showed no alarm. Quite the opposite, his eyes seemed to be smiling. Definitely smiling. When they got a little closer his lower body came in to view, blue jeans, legs crossed indian-fashion, a short semi-automatic shotgun bridging his thighs, bare hands relaxed in his lap. They rode to within a few yards of the man and stopped the horses and sat looking down at him.

The man seemed not to notice Onnie. His blue eyes were riveted on Bodie. "Hello again," he said.

Bodie's entire body visibly stiffened.

"I thought you might be along today. It's such a fine day. Don't you think?"

"I'm gonna have to write you a ticket for trespassin," said Onnie, his eyes darting between the man and Bodie.

The man was silent. He continued to stare fixedly at Bodie.

Bodie's horse pawed the ground but neither he nor the man seemed to notice. "I ain't sorry I sunk your boat. You shouldn't of lied to me. You shouldn't of come back."

The man smiled and slowly nodded his head. "You had every right."

"Yeah. I did."

"I'm not angry with you."

"I'm relieved to hear it."

"Anger has nothing to do with it."

"To do with what?"

"My being here now."

Bodie looked at Onnie who was looking at him. He looked back at the man. "And why is that?" he said.

"Why am I here?"

"Yeah."

"I've come to purchase your rifle."

"I told you it ain't for sale."

"Yes. But now I'm willing to pay a very high price. Very high indeed."

"It don't matter."

"Yes. It does matter."

The man slowly shifted his gaze to Onnie. "This does not concern you," he said.

Onnie sat slouching forward, an arm draped across the saddle's horn. "The hell it don't. I'm the law on this place."

"All right," the man said. And in a series of movements executed so quickly as to be blurred into one, he snatched the shotgun from his legs and shouldered it and fired.

Both horse and rider dropped as if a single entity, as if falling through a trapdoor sprung without warning. Then, with the roar of the blast still reverberating across the pine woods, he swung the gun on Onnie, Onnie digging his heels into Elvis's flanks while jerking the horse's head sideways, Elvis squatting and whirling and uncoiling, in mid-leap when the shotgun roared again. And when Elvis landed the leap, Onnie impacted the ground. He came to rest on his back, eyes open and swimming from side to side. He groaned and raised a hand and then lowered it and lay still.

The man stood and cradled the shotgun in his left arm. He glanced at Onnie. "Have it your way," he said. He scanned the ground to his right and then bent and picked up two empty shell casings and straightened and slipped them into his pant pocket. He walked to the fallen Appaloosa and stood watching the final movement the horse would ever make, a foreleg bent and slowly unbending. He saw the gaped mouth, and in the great chestnut eye, he saw himself. Then he looked at the still-mounted rider, a flower of blood blooming near the collar of the boy's denim shirt, a small rivulet coursing from his hair and flowing down over the bridge of his nose, dripping and dripping, the boy's eyes closed as if only sleeping. "A very high price," the man said. He bent down and reached and gathered in the Winchester from where it had fallen in the wiregrass. He held the rifle up to inspect it. He blew sand from the magazine feed and the breech. Then he lowered it and turned and walked toward the fence, the rifle swinging next to his leg, his head panning slowly from side to side. "Yes," he said. "A fine day. A gorgeous day."

**The Indian** sat with his back to a small fire, a fire whose writhing flames produced a silvery glow but no smoke, no heat. No ordinary fire, but merely the cold light of the moon harnessed and grounded and set to motion. Next to the old man lay a magnificent panther, a large male with a hoary scar bisecting its muscled shoulder. The great cat's eyes glowed with the light of the fire, two diaphanous moons fixed on Bodie and in which the boy could see nothing save his own twined reflection. No hope. No future. Nothing. And then the Indian turned to face him but could not face him for he no longer possessed either mouth or nose, or even a single eye. Where the old man's face had been was now merely an oval of darkness girded by smoke-gray hair, the same darkness lurking beyond the tiny faux fire's glow, a darkness Bodie somehow knew had been woven from every shadow ever cast, every fear ever conjured by man. He knew, and the knowing terrified him. He trembled and began to sweat profusely. And then he woke up.

He awakened to a world out of focus, strangely tilted on its side, a sensation of being trapped. He blinked and recognized the wiregrass pressing against his face, his left arm beneath his cheek and ranging outward through the grass, the pale blue cotton sleeve blood soaked and bent in a way no arm could possibly bend. He felt nauseous. And when the brown haze beyond his arm suddenly materialized into his horse, he vomited. He wretched violently and, in doing so, realized his broken arm was not his only injury. His heaving awakened pain in several other parts of his body, but before he could take inventory, he heard a voice.

"Bodie?" Onnie's voice. Definitely him but very faint. As if a long way off.

"Yeah," he called. He vomited again.

"I thought you was dead."

"I might be if you don't come give me a hand. What the hell are you doin?"

"I'm layin here lookin at the sky."

"What?"

"That feller shot me, too."

"You're shot?"

"I don't hurt none. Not like you'd imagine, anyways. My legs won't work is the main thing. I can move my arms but my legs are plumb dead."

"Damn," Bodie said to himself, his head throbbing, his left shoulder aching terribly. Something was definitely wrong with his downside shoulder, something besides the broken arm connected to it. He cut his eyes right to see his other arm. He raised it, feeling no pain but in the process seeing blood high on his chest, a sizeable patch near his collar bone, and in his shirt a perfectly round hole centered in the blood. Beyond all this, his right leg arched upward with the rise of Limpkin's ribcage. His boot still lodged in the stirrup, the horse dead between his legs. His right leg seemed fine but his left giving him only a sense of pressure, the weight of the dead horse. "You just hold tight," he called "I'll be there in a minute."

And from beyond the wall of horse came: "take your time," followed by a few seconds of silence. Then: "He wanted your rifle, didn't he?"

"What?"

"That feller. He shot us for a darn gun."

Bodie tried to think, to remember. "Yeah. I reckon he did."

"And he was the one shot the pig."

"Yeah."

"You didn't tell me you sunk his boat."

"I don't tell you everything. Now quit talkin. I'm tryin to think."

Bodie kicked his right foot free of the stirrup and jacked his leg back and got his boot against the saddle's comb. He pushed, but stopped almost immediately. He lay on his side gasping for breath, his leg beneath the horse suddenly awake and wracking him with pain, the sky spinning above him. "Jesus," he breathed.

"Hey, bud?"

"Yeah."

"How bad ya hurt?"

"I'm all right. Quit talkin."

"I'm hurt bad."

"Then quit talkin."

Bodie again pushed with his right leg. He pushed until at the threshold of blacking out, his teeth gritted against the rising pain, his eyes shut and watching bright points of light flash and extinguish and flash again. He pushed and saddle leather creaked and his left leg moved perhaps a few inches. Then he stopped pushing and lay in glorious relief for several moments.

"Bud."

"What?"

"I'm real sorry bout Limpkin."

"Jesus, Onnie. You need to quit talkin."

"I got to talk."

"No you don't. Just relax till I can get to you. Conserve your energy."

"I'm real sleepy."

"Are you bleedin?"

"Yeah."

"Bad?"

"The back of my shirt feels pretty wet."

Bodie set his jaw and again pressed with his right leg. "Please, God," he whispered. He strained and wriggled against the ground and felt the trapped leg move ever so slightly. He felt something shift in the ankle, actually heard popping and crunching. Bone parting and coming back together? His foot coming off? Whatever it was, the pain accompanying it was surprisingly dull, as though his overloaded brain was shutting down, no longer processing reports of pain.

"You see that?"

Bodie stopped his struggle and lay back. He stretched his right leg out and let it rest against the curve of the horse. "What?"

"That eagle up there."

He opened his eyes and cocked his head and looked at the sky. An osprey circled high above, its shrill, incessant cry barely audible. "Fish eagle," he said.

"Long as it ain't a buzzard."

"It ain't no buzzard."

"What you doin over there? All that gruntin sounds kind of obscene."

"I'm tryin to get my leg out from under Limpkin."

Onnie snorted. "Well ain't we the pair."

"Hush and save your energy. You're gonna need it, once I get loose."

"Elvis is at the barn by now. Maybe your daddy seen him."

"I wouldn't hold my breath waitin for that to happen."

"Your daddy's a good man. He's just a little turned around is all. He'll get his bearins directly."

Bodie did not answer. He was pushing again, inching his leg from beneath the horse. He developed a system of sorts. He'd push and gain, and then stop pushing to wriggle his body farther from the saddle. His left shoulder and arm were useless, protesting his every effort with excruciating pain. Still, he pushed and writhed until his naked foot emerged from beneath the horse. Though the foot was skewed at right angles to its leg, swollen, the color of ripe plums, he was free, wonderfully free. He let his head fall back against the ground. He lay panting for a good while and then slowly raised his head and tried to roll to his right side. If he could get to his right side, to his strength, he might be able to stand. But he tried only briefly before realizing the futility of such a thought. The pain was simply too much to bear.

"Onnie," he called.

Silence.

"Onnie."

"Yeah."

"You got to stay awake. I'm comin to you."

"You know what I just thought of?"

"No tellin."

"We never drunk that Wild Turkey."

"We'll drink it."

"Promise?"

"Yeah. Now shut up and rest."

"I got a favor to ask."

"What?"

"I sure would like to buy a plot in your graveyard."

"Quit cuttin the fool. You ain't one bit funny."

"I'm serious as a empty billfold. My folks won't like it. But they'll knuckle under, if you tell 'em it was my last request."

"Stop it, Onnie. You ain't dyin."

"Bury me next to your old Injun. Me and him can shoot the shit and all. I ain't never got to shoot the shit with a Injun."

"Crazy coot," Bodie breathed. He jacked his right leg up and dug his boot heel into the sand and pushed off, his right hand clawing at the ground and his neck extending and contracting, inching his head along like some sort of hard and hairy foot. He moved a few inches, and then repeated the process to gain a few more. He was going, back-crawling, willing himself across the ground, a floundered fish willing itself to water. And when he cleared the horse's body, he was exhausted. He paused to rest, rising up on his good elbow and craning his neck to see the extent of the ordeal still ahead.

Onnie lay belly-up in a patch of sunlight not thirty feet away, arms relaxed at his side, the ground around his upper body stained red, a crimson cape flared neatly beneath him and extending nearly to his waist.

"Onnie."

Onnie's eyes opened. Or were they already open?

"Wake up, damn you. I'm almost there."

"I am awake. I was just restin my eyes."

"Well I'm comin."

Onnie cackled. "That's what she said."

Bodie was moving again. "What?"

"That old Canada girl. You sounded just like her."

"I can't understand a word you're sayin. Shut up and rest."

Onnie cackled even louder. "Hell, that's exactly what I said. You must've follered me out there?"

Bodie paused again to rest. He rolled to his side and looked at Onnie, to gauge his progress. About twenty more feet, he estimated. When settling again on his back, a sharp pain stabbed at his right temple. He lay catching his breath, waiting for the pain to subside. "So I take it she was one of them French Canadians?"

"I thought you couldn't hear me."

"Well, was she?"

"Yes, she was."

Bodie back crawled, inching himself along, and when next he paused, Onnie was within reach, only a few feet from his head.

"You're gettin pretty good at that."

Except for his labored breathing, Bodie made no sound.

"You all right?"

"Yeah. Cept for my head splittin open."

"Well, you look like crap."

Bodie inched on until he lay side by side with Onnie. He rocked his head to look at his friend. "I don't doubt that," he said.

Onnie looked at him sideways. "You're pretty tore up."

Bodie tried to moisten his lips with his tongue. "Like a snake in a weedeater," he said.

"You're hurtin, ain't ya?"

"My head's killin me."

"It ain't killin you. You're too tough to die."

"I don't feel tough."

"Tough as squirrel hide," Onnie said, punctuating the words with a series of rattling coughs.

Bodie watched him cough, and then watched him wipe blood from his mouth with the back of a hand. "I don't know what to do," he said.

Onnie looked. "Me neither. I ain't never done this before"

Bodie was silent.

Onnie suddenly reached with his right hand and captured Bodie's left.

"What the hell are you doin?" said Bodie.

"I'm makin sure you don't go nowhere—do I fall asleep."

"That arm's broke."

"I'll be careful."

"Where in the hell do you think I'd go?"

"I don't know. I don't know much about it."

"Bout what?"

"Hell."

"Jesus, Onnie."

They lay without moving or talking for several minutes. A crow flitted from limb to limb in a pine top overhead, pausing periodically to cock its head and one-eye the curious pair below.

As Onnie watched the bird, a devilish smile formed on his face. "You got nice hands," he said.

Bodie did not respond.

"How bout a smooch?"

Silence.

"Bodie?"

The crow cawed once and flew from the pine; with the bird gone, Onnie suddenly felt utterly alone. "Oh Lord," he said. "Oh Lord."

\*

A little past eight Abby took a break from her studies to call Bodie. When the answering machine picked up, she left a message. She didn't say much. She simply told him how much she missed him and that it wasn't necessary to return her call, that she would see him in the morning when he reported for work. She hung up the phone actually relieved he had not answered. With finals in both Communications and Agribusiness looming the next day, she had precious little time for talk.

After breakfast the next morning, she walked to the barn with her father, the ninth day of December about to dawn clear and cold, a sliver of moon lounging on its back about two hours high in the eastern sky. They went directly to the barn office where Bill Thompson switched on the lights and a Kenner space heater. They sat in the two swivel chairs and Abby took out a composition notebook and opened it on her lap. Bill turned his chair to his cluttered government surplus desk. He opened a daily planner. The plastic clock on the wall read six-forty-five.

"Hmm," said Abby.

"Hmm what?"

"I figured he would be way early."

Bill glanced at the clock. "He's still got fourteen minutes to be early. He's eighteen. I'll be tickled if he's just on time."

"Yeah, but Bodie's eighteen going on forty."

Bill Thompson smiled but continued to scan the planner before him. "Ain't nothin wrong with a boy bein a little mature for his age."

They sat. And when the clock ticked past seven, Abby stood and began pacing the concrete floor. "Something's wrong," she said.

Bill pushed back from the desk and swiveled to look at her. He removed his cap and scratched his head. He reached into his pant pocket and withdrew a ring of keys and held them out to her. "Give him a call on the mobile. Maybe he's got truck trouble or somethin."

Abby took the keys and walked out to her father's truck. She dialed and waited, and when the answering machine picked up, she said, "Bodie, you're late for work. Where are you?"

When she turned off the phone, her father stood by her side, a glimmer of concern on his face. "You've got to go, ain't you? It's twenty after."

Abby put the phone in its cradle and stepped back and closed the truck's door. She looked out into the growing day and looked at her father. "Something's got to be seriously wrong. And I should've known last night. He always calls me back."

"Well you get to class. I'll drive over and check on Bodie. It's probably nothin."

Abby smiled thinly. "Thanks, Daddy. And call me on my cellphone. I'll never be able to concentrate if you don't."

Bill reached and patted her shoulder. "If I know somethin before eight, I'll call you. Otherwise, if you don't hear from me, everything's fine. You can't be answerin no phone durin an exam."

Abby looked at the ground and looked at her father. She nodded. "All right," she said. She then frowned and shook her head. "I just don't understand him sometimes."

"Well you best get used to that. Those times don't never stop comin round. Ask your mama. She'll tell you."

\*

By the time Bill turned onto Curlew's ranch road, the sun sat lodged in the eastern treetops. He drove the grade at a high rate of speed, slowing only when the house loomed off to his right, both trucks parked before it, Bodie's and Seth's. He drove into the circle drive and switched off the truck and got out and walked to the front door. He rang the doorbell and waited, and then he knocked loudly several times. He turned and looked at barn, at Onnie's blue Dodge. In the pasture a saddled buckskin paced back and forth along the fence, trailing its reins and staring incessantly toward the barn.

Leaving the porch, he walked to the yard fence and climbed it and approached the anxious horse. When he spoke to it, the buckskin eyed him suspiciously, but stood its ground and let him come. Moving slowly, Bill stepped close and caught up the reins and calmed the horse by continuing to speak softly, by stroking its neck. He looked, and immediately noticed dried blood matted in the animals dark mane, a perfectly round hole through its right ear, more blood streaking its cheek. Then he found a tiny smear of what was likely more blood on top of its rump. He looked at the barn.

"Bodie," he hollered, and the horse jerking its head high. "Hello in the barn."

He stepped and stood and looked back at the house. "Come on, boy," he said. He led the buckskin to the yard fence and cinched the reins to the top board. Then he climbed the fence and hurried to the front door. He pounded the oak wood with his fist and then reached and tried the knob. When the door opened, he stepped inside and called out: "Bodie. Seth. Anybody home?"

Sound erupted in the depths of the house, someone coughing, scurrying around. Then: "Yeah."

"Seth. It's Bill Thompson."

"Yeah, Bill. Be right there."

A few seconds on Seth walked barefoot into the living room, wearing jeans and slipping on a shirt. He looked rough, eyes bloodshot and puffy, hair disheveled.

"I hate to barge in like this, but I think we've got trouble."

Seth buttoned his shirt. "Trouble?"

"Bodie didn't show up for work, and there's a horse outside that's been shot."

Seth's eyes widened. His mouth opened. He stepped forward and shot past Bill to look out the open door. "Elvis," he said. "That's Double Ought's horse." He stepped onto the porch and leaned out as far as he could to scan the pastures and traps at the barn. "I don't see Limpkin." He turned and looked at Bill and then stared blankly at the floor. "Damn," he said.

"You ain't seen Bodie this morning?"

"No. I ain't. Reckon I ain't seen him in a while."

Bill looked at him and looked at the horse standing tied to the fence. "Well what's your definition of a while?"

Seth's eyes narrowed. "I ain't been feelin too good. I don't think I seen him at all yesterday. But I know he was here. He sold the flatbed for me, left the money on my nightstand."

"What about Onnie? Did you see him?"

Seth shook his head. "He's ridin fence for Jo Beth now." He turned and looked at Elvis. "With Limpkin gone, Bodie must've rode out with him." He looked at Bill. "You sure Elvis has been shot?"

207

"Positive. He's got a clean hole through his ear. Get your boots on while I call the law. The blood on that horse's done dried black. Whatever's happened, happened some time ago. Maybe the farm and ranch deputies will put a chopper up, save us a lot of time."

Seth hurried down the porch steps and sat and began pulling on his socks. "I'm gonna take Elvis and try and pick up their trail."

"Maybe you better wait for the law."

"I ain't waitin."

Bill descended the steps and headed for his truck. "All right," he said over his shoulder. "You got your cell phone?"

Seth stood and followed behind him. "I don't have a cell phone."

Bill stopped and removed the phone he carried on his belt. He turned and held it up for Seth to see. "My mobile number's the first one here. Alls you got to do is select it like this and press send."

Seth took the phone and studied it momentarily. He slipped it into his pocket and looked at Bill and nodded.

Thompson turned and opened his truck door and reached in for his mobile phone.

Seth began walking. When almost to Elvis, he turned and looked back. "Bill," he called.

Bill had the phone pressed to his ear. He held it there while turning to look. "Yeah."

"Thank you."

Bill raised a hand and nodded, then turned away to speak into the phone.

Reaching Elvis, Seth spoke to the horse while untying the reins from the fence board. He stroked its neck and examined the wounded ear, the dried blood. Then he mounted up and turned the horse northward. In the first few yards he found horse tracks and began following them. "Limpkin," he said. He patted the horse's neck. "Come on, Elvis. Take me to 'em."

He rode slowly until Bodie's trail joined Onnie's. Then he urged Elvis to a lope. Reaching the cemetery road, he stopped and sawed the horse first one way then the other, studying the sign. He struck out following the road west, following Limpkin's solo trail. At the graveyard, he paused briefly to unravel the plethora of tracks, to sit in puzzlement when noticing the strange mound of dirt within the fenced enclosure. "Reckon I need to get up here more often," he said. Then he adjusted his cap and put Elvis forward at a fast walk, following the tracks leaving the graveyard and heading north toward a strand of cypress. He rode, and the sign led him through the cypress. In the pinewoods beyond, the first buzzard caught his eye.

When the vulture flushed from a pine near the boundary fence, Seth's heart rate doubled. He dug his heels into Elvis's flanks, and the horse carried him forward at a gallop. At the firebreak, he reined the horse in and stood in the stirrups, the horse blowing and stepping a crazy waltz in the plowed dirt. He scanned the surrounding woods and saw several more buzzards perched nearby, dark ornaments in the thinly spaced pines less than a hundred yards to his left. Then, as he stepped the horse toward the waiting birds, something yellow caught his eye, bright yellow and just visible above a vague mound brown and mottled. He advanced and the yellow became a rolled rain slicker, the mound a fallen horse, a dead Appaloosa. "Please, God," he breathed. Then he saw his son.

Bodie lay close to Onnie, each boy on his back, heads almost touching, Bodie's left hand wedged firmly in Onnie's right, every eye closed. Had there not been so much blood, Seth might have thought them only sleeping. But he had no such thought. He leaped from the saddle not bothering to halt the horse. He hit the ground running but stopped just short of his son and began moving like a figure in a dream. He sagged to his knees at the edge of the boys' red pallet and became very still, a statue, a father turned to stone by the one rumor capable of such sorcery. He knelt, the horse behind him walleyed and backing. Then he tentatively reached out and touched Bodie's arm.

When the boy opened his eyes, a tremor ran the length of Seth's body. He swallowed and opened his mouth as if to form a word but no word took shape. He could only smile and touch his son again.

Bodie gazed up at him, the thin line of his mouth working dryly. "Daddy," he said, his voice but a whisper, scarcely loud enough to be heard over the murmuring wind. "I'm so cold."

Seth frowned and nodded his head. He raised a finger to his lips and shushed his son. "Just lay still. You're gonna be all right."

He stood and reached into his pocket and fished out the phone. He flipped it open and held it out at arms length and reached with his other hand and selected "mobile." He pressed send and brought the phone to his ear. He waited, his eyes scrutinizing his son below, the bare foot twisted and blackened, the blood soaked shirt, the wrecked arm and the alluvial fan of dried blood and dirt stretching from temple to temple. He took inventory of all of these, and then he said: "Bill. I found 'em."

**26**

**When** he opened his eyes Abby stood gazing down at him. His right hand was sandwiched between both of hers and the only part of him not cold. She was smiling, but he knew that she had been crying, the blue of her eyes somewhat paler.

"Hey," he said.

Abby squeezed his hand. "Hey, you."

He rocked his head to the side and saw his father and his mother, Bill Thompson and Pete Stalvey also there, and seated in a chair across the room, a man he did not know. All save the man in the chair looked at him and smiled. And he returned their smiles and slipped back into unconsciousness.

When he next awoke the lights were dimmed and only his father and the stranger left in the room. He could see more clearly. He noticed his cast arm, starkly white and held vertical by a strap going up and up to some sort of framework above his bed, his left foot similarly cast and propped high atop stacked pillows, a bandage covering the left side of his head and another constricting his upper right chest.

"How you feelin?"

He looked and saw his father standing close. "I got a headache is all."

"You got a bad concussion. Doc said your head walloped the ground pretty good."

"Doc Hutchinson patch me up?"

211

Seth nodded. "Him and a few others."

"How's Onnie doin?"

Seth swallowed and looked down at the linoleum floor and looked at his son. "Onnie's gone, Bodie."

"Gone."

Seth nodded. "He was dead when I found y'all"

Bodie stared at the fluorescent light affixed to the ceiling, his face stolid, giving nothing away. "Where's Abby?"

"They went to get some supper. She'll be back directly."

His eyes still fixed on the light, Bodie said: "Onnie." Then he closed his eyes and turned his face away. He said "Onnie" again, and then he said "no."

Seth grimaced and reached and touched the top of his son's head, patted it in a way he'd not done for many years.

The stranger rose from his chair and came and stood next to Seth, dark slacks, white shirt and burgundy tie, a semiautomatic sidearm nylon holstered and velcroed to his belt, brown hair graying at the temples. He looked at Bodie and looked at Seth.

Seth eyed the man then turned back to his son. "You don't feel like answerin no questions yet, do ya?"

Bodie turned his head to look at them. "Yessir. I'd like to."

Seth stepped and stood. He looked at the man and looked at Bodie. "You sure?"

"Yessir. Absolutely sure."

Seth raised a hand and gestured to the stranger. "This here's Lee Futch. He's with the sheriff's department."

The deputy dipped his head. "Hey, Bodie." He reached and got a small notebook and a ballpoint pen from his breast pocket. He flipped the notebook open. "Sorry to bother you so soon, but it's important that you tell me everything you can remember now. Give us a direction to start looking and all."

"Yessir. I understand."

Futch nodded his head. "Well, I guess the first thing I need to know is did you see the truck that hit you."

Bodie's forlorn expression did not change. "Yessir. I seen him."

Futch smiled sheepishly and nodded his head. "Tell me about it."

Bodie began by telling the deputy about his first encounter with the man. He took his time, pausing often to sip water through a straw and to lay with his eyes

212

shut and catching his breath. When he'd related about finding the dead hog, Futch abruptly stopped him.

"You say this happened the first week of November?"

Bodie looked. "Yessir."

"You remember the date?"

"I remember it was a Monday. It was the day my granddaddy told us about his tumor."

Futch looked at Seth. "A woman was murdered out there about that same time—across the lake, over in Polk County."

Seth's eyes widened. "I didn't hear nothin about it."

"We didn't work the case, but I remember seeing a bulletin. The body was found on the lakeshore by fishermen. Someone used a shotgun to almost decapitate the woman." Futch paused and looked at Bodie. "Your mentioning the hog is what brought it to mind."

Bodie looked back. "It's the same guy. Knowin what I know now, I'd bet on it."

Futch wrote on his notepad. When finished writing, he said: "And I wouldn't take that bet. Go ahead, continue with your story."

Bodie next told how he'd found the man's airboat later in November, how he went about sinking it in the lake.

"Do you know if the boat is still there?"

"It ain't there. It was gone the next time I was out to the lake. About a week later, I reckon."

"Did you get the hull registration?"

Bodie frowned. "No sir. I didn't."

Futch also frowned. He nodded. "You say the boat appeared to be new. Anything else distinctive about it—besides it being black and all—any decals or logos? Most air boaters tend to gussy up their rigs, personalize them a bit."

"Yessir. It had what I figured was a name painted on the rudders. Two words. Big white letters."

Futch looked on expectantly, his pen poised above the pad.

Bodie sighed. "Some kind of foreign words I never seen before."

"Spanish? French?"

Bodie shook his head. "Maybe Spanish. I just don't know. The second word was sort of like nature, only spelled wrong."

"Nature."

"Yessir. That's what it reminded me of at the time."

"And the first word?"

Bodie shook his head. "I just don't remember. I reckon it didn't remind me of anything."

Bodie watched the detective write on the pad. "Reckon I ain't much of a witness," he said.

"You're doing fine." Futch studied his notes, flipping back through the pages. He looked at Bodie. "So you think he wanted you to see him this time?"

"Yessir. He wasn't tryin to hide. The florescent orange and all. Besides, he pretty much told me."

"He told you?"

"Yessir. More or less. When we rode up to him, he said what a fine day it was, that he thought I might be along."

The deputy wrote on the pad. He looked up. "Did he look different? I mean besides the orange clothing and all. Had he changed his appearance?"

Bodie thought for a moment. "No sir. I don't think so. It's just that the first time he had that hood and all. You couldn't see much of his face. But this time. As soon as he talked, I recognized them blue eyes. His eyes are sort of strange. You don't hardly notice much else about him after you see them eyes."

"Strange how?"

"Just strange. I reckon because he don't never blink."

"He never blinked?"

"Not that I recall."

Futch made notations on the pad. "Okay," he said. "What about his speech? He have an accent?"

"No sir. He didn't have no kind of accent at all. He sounded pretty educated is about all I can tell you."

"All right. So what happened next?"

Bodie looked at the ceiling. "When we rode up on him?"

"Right. After he commented on what a fine day it was."

"When I realized who he was, I figured he was pissed about me sinkin his airboat. I figured that's why he'd come back. But he said that wasn't it at all. Said he didn't care."

Futch cocked his head. He looked puzzled but didn't interrupt.

"Then he told me why he'd come back. He wanted my rifle."

214

"Your rifle?"

"Yessir. My old Winchester. He offered to buy it from me the first time, back in November."

"What kind of Winchester?"

"Forty-four-forty. Model eighteen-seventy-three. You know, the gun that won the west and all. It's got *one of one thousand* engraved on top of the receiver."

"So it's valuable?"

"It was to me. It was my granddaddy's—his daddy's before that. Granddaddy left it to me in his will."

"We didn't find any weapons."

"No sir. Onnie didn't have a gun. And that feller took mine. I know cause Onnie told me he did. He saw him walk off with it."

Futch was silent. He nodded his head "I don't suppose you have the serial number?"

"No sir. I don't know that I ever noticed it."

Seth raised a hand. "Daddy might've recorded it. I remember him sayin one time that he ought to do that—write down all the serial numbers of his guns in case they ever got stolen."

Futch looked at Seth. "You need to find it."

"My great granddaddy's initials are carved in the stock," Bodie injected, "if that's any help."

Futch looked at Bodie. "That's a big help. What are the initials?"

"J-M-R," Bodie said, "for John Morgan Rawlerson."

Futch made a note and then looked at Bodie. "So when he said he wanted your rifle what did you do?"

"I told him it still wasn't for sale."

"And…"

"He snatched up his gun and fired."

"Can you describe his gun?"

"Yessir. It was a Benelli twelve gauge auto-loader. Black. Short barrel. Composite stock."

Futch smiled as he wrote on the pad. "I take it you know a little about shotguns."

"Yessir. I've handled a few."

"So he snatched up the gun and fired. He shoot you first?"

"Yessir. Me and Limpkin."

"Limpkin."

Bodie frowned and looked away. "My horse."

Futch nodded his head. "The one shot hit you both—you and the horse."

Bodie looked at him. "I reckon. I don't know. The last thing I remember was seein the muzzle blast."

"So you don't know how many times he fired."

"No sir. Had to be at least twice, though. Me and Onnie were a good ways apart."

"You find any hulls?" Seth injected.

Futch shook his head. "Nothing. Just a depression in the grass where the guy had been sitting."

Seth shook his head. "Cold bastard took the time to pick 'em up."

Futch nodded and then looked at Bodie. "Since we can account for only seven double ought pellets, he probably fired just once at you. We recovered the one removed from your chest plus five more from your horse's head and neck. The seventh we don't have but we know it grazed the side of your head."

"So Limpkin saved my life."

Futch nodded. "He blocked most of the load. Must've jerked his head up when the man moved to shoot. He was killed instantly."

Bodie's eyes grew moist. He wiped them with the back of his wrist. He looked away.

Futch looked at Seth. "I'm about done," he said. He looked down at Bodie. "You said you talked to your friend afterward. Did he say anything about the man. Anything at all."

Bodie continued to stare at the wall. "Nothin I ain't already told you."

Futch flipped the notepad closed and put it in his breast pocket. He looked at Bodie and looked at Seth. "You have my card. If you recall anything more please let me know."

Seth nodded. "You don't have much to go on, do you?"

"Not much. This guy covered his tracks pretty well." Futch paused and turned and started for the door. He motioned with his hand for Seth to follow. Outside in the hall he continued: "I don't mean to alarm you, but there's no doubt in my mind your son was ambushed, deliberately shot and left for dead."

Seth's eyes widened. "You sayin he's apt to try again?"

Futch shook his head. "I don't know what to tell you. I just know the guy that did this is no amateur. He even went so far as to brush out his tracks where he crossed the firebreak. We know he crossed the fence, but there's no trace of him after that. Nothing. As if he just up and flew away."

"So you're sayin Bodie might be a loose end he hadn't counted on."

"It's just a gut feeling I've got. I certainly have no proof."

"And he knows Bodie can identify him."

Futch nodded. "And as far as he knows, Bodie got his hull numbers and knows exactly what is printed on the rudders of his boat."

Seth removed his cap and scratched his head. He shook the cap at the deputy. "And he has to know Bodie ain't dead. It's been all over the news."

"I'll tell the media there are no leads. If he's still around, it may convince this guy he's got nothing to worry about."

"And if it don't?"

"I'll stop by here as often as I can. It's all I can do. There's no way my superiors will authorize round the clock protection based solely on a hunch. We're simply too shorthanded."

Seth placed his cap back on his head. He looked down the corridor and looked at the detective. "All right," he said, his voice rising. "I won't count on help from nobody."

Futch gestured with both of his hands. "Look, Mr. Rawlerson. I didn't have to tell you any of this. There's a good chance I've got it wrong. This guy could be half way round the world by now. I just wanted you to know what I was feeling."

For a few seconds Seth stood silently staring at the detective. Then he visibly relaxed and nodded his head. "Reckon what they say bout wantin to kill the messenger's got a lot of truth to it."

Futch smiled. "A whole lot," he said.

"I owe you an apology."

"No you don't. Yours was a natural human response. I'm used to it. You have to be in my line of work."

Seth smiled thinly and nodded his head. He jerked a thumb over his shoulder, gesturing to the closed door behind him. "I need to get back in there. My son might be needin something."

"Okay. I'm going to step outside and call the office. But I won't leave without letting you know what's happening."

\*

His father sat slumped in a chair next to the door, soundly sleeping. Abby, also sleeping, stirred when Bodie stirred. She lifted her head from his stomach and rubbed her eyes and looked at him pensively. She smiled and said: "Well hey, again."

"What time is it?"

She cocked her head to look at a clock on the far wall. "Looks like two-forty-five to me."

Bodie looked at the clock. "I'll be darned. Didn't know I had me a clock." He looked at her. "Is that am or pm?"

"Morning."

"Why are you still here?"

"Cause I love you."

He smiled at her and then shifted his gaze to his father. "Y'all need to go home and get some real sleep. I'm all right."

"It's Saturday. I can sleep all day, if I want."

"Saturday?"

Abby nodded.

"I need to talk to Onnie's folks."

She looked at the bandage on his head and reached and touched it lightly. "I talked to his mama this afternoon. She's a wreck. She said it was all her fault."

"She won't feel that way after she's talked to me."

"What do you mean?"

"Onnie's dead because of me. If I hadn't been with him, he'd still be alive."

"You don't know that."

"Yeah. I do."

Abby withdrew her hand and used it to wipe her eyes. "It's nobody's fault but that man who shot you all."

Bodie reached and gently brushed her cheek with the back of his hand. "Have you got their number with you? I need to call 'em once it's a reasonable hour."

"Yeah. I've got it."

"Good. Crawl up here beside me. I need to hold you for a while. Maybe you can actually get some sleep."

As Abby positioned herself next to him, Bodie emitted a pitiful groan. She stiffened and said: "Did I hurt you?"

Bodie smiled thinly. He wagged his head slowly from side to side. "No. I just thought about Limpkin layin out there with the buzzards."

Abby relaxed. She reached and touched his chin with a finger. "Daddy buried Limpkin."

"He did?"

Abby nodded. "He got his front-loader and took care of it soon as the deputies were done. He got your saddle and all. He even got your hat."

Bodie's eyes began to swim. He closed them tightly, giving a little nod of his head but saying nothing more.

*

As Seth removed the breakfast tray, Bodie reached and snared the phone from the wheeled cart next to his bed. His eyes switching between the phone and the scrap of paper Abby had left with him, he dialed the number with his thumb. Then he placed the receiver to his ear.

"Who you callin?" Seth asked.

Bodie cut his eyes to his father but didn't answer him. "Mr. Osteen," he said.

"That you, Bodie?"

"Yessir. It's me."

"How you doin? You sound strong."

"I'm all right. A little sore is all."

"Well that's good. That's real good."

"Mr. Osteen, there ain't no way I can tell you how sorry I am about Onnie."

"I know it. You don't need to even try."

"Yessir. I do. He got shot cause of me. He tried to save me is what he did."

"Onnie did?"

"Yessir. He sure did."

"Well I… I thank you for callin and tellin me, Bodie."

"Sir."

"Yeah. I'm here."

"He wanted me to ask y'all somethin."

"Yeah."

"He wanted me to ask y'all to bury him in our cemetery."

Silence at the other end of the line, then: "I can't talk no more, Bodie. I'll have to get back with you."

"Yessir. All right."

As he switched off the phone and placed it on its cradle, Bodie saw the look on his father's face. "You don't mind, do ya? I mean, if they're willin to do it and all."

"Did Onnie really want that?"

"Yessir. He made me promise to ask 'em."

Seth turned and stepped to the window and stood gazing out through its open blinds. "Well I hope the Osteens aren't insulted by such a request."

"Insulted?"

"Yeah. Their only son askin to be buried in somebody else's cemetery. I'd take that as an insult, myself." He reached and parted the blinds with his fingers and seemed to study something in the parking lot below. "You should've run it by me first."

"Yessir. I should have."

Seth turned and looked at him. "And while we're on the subject, who or what is that next to Daddy?"

Bodie's eyes shifted from side to side. "Reckon I should've told you about that, too. It's old Solomon."

Seth's eyebrows arched. "What?"

"Abby and me found him dead up in the hammock."

"And you just took it on yourself to bury him in our cemetery."

"Yessir. Reckon I did. He sort of asked me to, though. The last time I seen him alive."

"Sort of?"

"It's kind of hard to explain."

"It's gonna be real hard, if the law finds out."

"Yessir. I know it."

Seth again stared out the window. "Reckon we need to put up some kind of marker. He was the kind of feller ought to be remembered, from what I hear."

Bodie's eyes swam to look at his father. He blinked several times. "Yessir," he said. "He surely was."

**27**

**Onnie** was laid to rest Tuesday-noon on a bluff overlooking the St. Johns River, a few miles south of Deland in a small church cemetery already home to many of his ancestors. A steady drizzle fell throughout the ceremony, it dim as dawn beneath the cloud blanketed oaks, even darker in the hearts and minds of all in attendance. When it was over, and the mourners began shuffling to their cars, Bodie alone remained seated in a wheelchair beneath the graveside awning. He sat for some time with the rain pattering and the river slipping silently by. Then he mopped his eyes with his one sleeved arm and looked up and raised that arm in a little wave. His waiting loved ones came to him and sheltered him with umbrellas and wheeled him away. And when they'd gone from that place of the dead, though the rain continued to fall, it raised no patter. With them gone, in that place of the dead lived only silence, and the coursing river below.

Fearing the Osteen's wake may be too taxing, Seth and Abby drove Bodie directly home. He rode quietly in the crew cab's front seat, gazing out the window, seemingly lost in thought until approaching the house and noticing Onnie's truck still parked at the barn. Then he sighed deeply and emitted what was surely an involuntary groan. Seth glanced over at him but said nothing. Abby reached forward and briefly massaged his neck. And when coming to a halt at the house, he refused the wheelchair, vowing never to use it again. He hopped one-legged up the walk and on up the steps, teetering precariously at the top before turning and virtually falling back into a rocker. He sat breathing heavily and gazing across the

221

pasture at the blue Dodge. His father briefly watched him and then stepped on into the house. Abby dragged another rocker close and settled in it, the expression on her face pained, undeniably critical.

"My gosh you're stubborn."

He looked at her, forging a faint smile.

"Didn't you hear anything Doc Hutchinson said?"

"I heard him."

"So you're just ignoring him."

Bodie glanced right and left, down at the floor as if suddenly having lost something. "I wonder where my hat is?"

Abby glared at him, pursing her lips and shaking her head.

When Seth abruptly returned to the porch, he had in his hands a Ruger Blackhawk revolver and a box of .44 magnum cartridges. Both Abby and Bodie looked at the pistol and looked up at Seth.

"You ain't gonna shoot me, are ya?" asked Bodie. "Alls I did was hop a little."

Seth seemed not to hear him. He stepped past Abby and turned and sat on the slatted bench positioned there against the wall. He laid the revolver in his lap and slid the cartridge box open and counted out five rounds. Then he closed the box and set it aside and began loading the pistol. "Till I tell you different," he said, "I want you to keep this close at all times. Don't even go to the bathroom without it."

Bodie leaned forward enough to look past Abby at his father. "He ain't gonna come back."

Seth shook the revolver's cylinder closed. "Yeah? Well you're probably right. But just in case you ain't, do as I say."

"I ain't that lucky."

"What?"

"I'll have to hunt *him* down."

Abby swiveled to look at Bodie, her eyes waxing wide.

Seth laid the pistol on the bench and pointed a finger at his son. "You listen here. This ain't no movie or somethin. You're not huntin nobody down. Futch said this guy's nobody to be messin with. Said if he's gone, we best say good riddance and get on with our lives."

Bodie was silent.

Abby turned to Seth. "Bodie can identify him!"

"Exactly. He's the only one that can."

She turned to Bodie and grasped his hand. "Oh my God, Bodie."

Bodie shook his head. "He's not gonna do anything. He'd of already done it if he was."

\*

That night, long after his father had gone to bed, he got the magazine address label from his wallet and hobbled into the office and switched on the computer. He logged on to the internet and typed the words *Lusus Naturae.* He scanned again and again, not to find the words' meaning—he already knew they were Latin, that they meant *freak of nature.* He searched now for some link to the man, anything which might explain who the man was. When finding nothing useful, he scanned the name on the address label, the name Lathan Biggs. After reading the short list of futile hits, he scanned Lorida, Florida, finding that there was not much there, just a dot on Highway Ninety Eight in Highlands County, a feminine sounding name near the northernmost tip of Lake Istokpoga. Lastly, he left the internet and opened his father's new Earth Viewer program, zooming in on Lorida, on Cowhouse road and what he thought might just be the very home of the man named Biggs. He studied a good while, dragging the mouse and zooming-out and zooming-in. Then, bleary-eyed and aching, he shut down the computer and went to bed.

\*

In a few days his shoulders healed sufficiently to withstand the pressure of crutches. Instantly more mobile, he finally was able to escape the house. For several days running he and Abby ventured to the barn, the journey arduous and time consuming, the big revolver tucked inside the arm sling, a plastic garbage bag covering his cast foot. Each trip almost a carbon copy of the previous one, they visited Elvis, brushing and pampering the buckskin, consoling him like an old friend. They fed the Brangus heifer, reaching through the fence boards and stroking both it and its now gentle calf. Then, with the lounging cats eyeing them suspiciously, they'd simply sit and talk, the conversation initially upbeat, focused on the future, but invariably ending mired in the depressing past. It was then that Abby sensed she should go, leave Bodie to sort things out for himself. And after she'd gone, he always did the same thing: rise zombie-like and crutch to Onnie's truck where he'd slide behind the wheel and simply sit, truly lost until his father would come and find him and take him home to begin the whole process anew. A vicious circle, he knew. A trap inescapable, he thought. But then, on a dreary cloud-filled day, he was reminded of the one true thing he'd learned about life: Nothing in it is forever. Nothing. Not even the bad.

It happened as he sat in the Dakota's cab with the driver's side door open, his bad leg trailing down and resting on the ground, his crutches propped against the leg. Movement in the rearview mirror caused him to look and see a shiny new Cadillac approaching the barn. The white sedan rolled to a stop directly behind his blue shrine. When the car's passenger door opened, Mr. Osteen emerged.

Bodie swiveled to exit the truck but stopped when Mr. Osteen reached him and stood looking down at him in a puzzled manner.

"Hey, Mr. Osteen."

"Hey, Bodie." Osteen raised a hand and pointed toward Bodie's slung broken arm. "What you doin with that hogleg?"

Bodie glanced down at the pistol. "Oh," he said. "Nothin. I thought maybe I'd shoot some rats is all."

"The old Dakota got rats has it?"

Bodie grinned sheepishly. "No sir. Not that I've noticed."

Mr. Osteen looked out across the pasture and looked at Bodie. "Your daddy called me, reminded me to come get the truck."

"He did?"

Osteen nodded. "I lied to him, told him I'd plumb forgot about it. Truth is, I just couldn't bear to see it."

"Yessir. I understand."

"I know you do. But do you understand how wrong-headed that is?"

"Sir?"

"Onnie don't want me moping around on account of him. He never let nothin get him down. It's what I admired most about him. He shed misery like a duck sheds water."

Bodie smiled. "Yessir. He did."

Osteen scuffed the ground with his shoe. "Anyhow. I'm glad your daddy called me. I needed somethin to shock me back to life." He reached into his pant pocket and withdrew a single key. "Here you go. See if she'll crank."

Bodie reached to take the key but stopped and withdrew his hand. "Don't reckon I can work the clutch," he said.

Osteen looked at his leg. "Didn't think of that. Slide on out, and I'll do the honors."

Bodie maneuvered his good foot to the ground and positioned his crutches and stood and sidled out of the way. Osteen ducked inside the cab and inserted the key

224

in the ignition switch. When he pushed in the clutch and turned the key, the starter groaned sluggishly then turned over. The engine roared to life, and he looked up at Bodie and smiled.

"Had me worried there for a second," he said, speaking loudly to be heard over the motor. He studied the gauges. "Got plenty of gas." He looked at Bodie. "Holler at my brother in law. Tell him to go on ahead."

Bodie pivoted and looked at the man still seated in the Cadillac. He raised his hand and signaled a thumbs-up, and the man waved and started the car and began backing and turning.

Osteen reached and pulled the door closed and slipped the transmission into reverse. He looked out at the boy. "Thanks, Bodie. You take care, now."

Bodie stooped as low as his crutches would allow to see in the cab. "Mr. Osteen."

"Yeah."

"There's a bottle of Wild Turkey under the seat there. I'd like to have it, if it's all right with you?"

Osteen looked at him and leaned to his right to study the floorboard. "Wild Turkey?" he said. He reached down and snared the quart bottle by the neck and dragged it from beneath the seat. He held the bottle up for inspection, then looked at Bodie. "It ain't never been opened."

"No sir."

Osteen frowned. "You ain't of legal age, are ya?"

"No sir."

Osteen looked at him and looked at the bottle. "Well I don't know. I don't want to be accused of contributin to the downfall of a minor."

"I promise you nobody'll know where I got it."

"I'll know. You get hammered on this stuff, no telling what you're apt to do."

Bodie shook his head. "No sir. It's not like that. It's just somethin between Onnie and me. Somethin sentimental and all."

"Sentimental."

"Yessir."

Osteen briefly studied the bottle then guided it through the truck's window. "All right," he said.

Bodie reached and took the bottle. He dipped his head. "Thank you, sir. I really appreciate it."

Osteen nodded. He reached and tested his gear selection and then turned to look behind him.

"Mr. Osteen."

Osteen looked. "Yeah."

"Did you forget about Elvis?"

"Mr. Osteen smiled broadly. "Naw. How could anybody forget Elvis?"

Bodie looked. "Sir?"

Osteen laughed. "I'm just messin with you. Elvis is yours if you want him."

Bodie was momentarily speechless. "I don't know what to say."

"Just say you want him. That's what Onnie'd want to hear."

Bodie managed a closed mouth smile. He nodded, his eyes beginning to swim.

Mr. Osteen also nodded. Then he smiled and eased out the clutch and backed away.

*

Two days before Christmas he and Miss Ella were sitting on his porch sipping coffee and talking when a blue Mercury Marquise appeared on the ranch road. They watched it come. When the car turned toward the house, Bodie reached and got the pistol from the floor and slid it into his sling. He smiled at Miss Ella, as she was watching him with a concerned look. "Just don't want to scare nobody. It's probably just a salesman or somethin." When Detective Futch emerged from the car he returned the Ruger to the floor. "Not a salesman," he said. "It's the law."

"I don't know which is worse," said Miss Ella.

They bid Futch sit down and he sat and Miss Ella brought him coffee.

"Your father's not here?"

Bodie shook his head. "He's runnin errands."

Futch nodded. He eyed the pistol. "You've not had any trouble, have you?"

"No, sir. Not a bit."

The detective sipped his coffee. "And I don't think you will, either. That guy seems to have vanished from the face of the earth."

"Nothin on the airboat?"

Futch shook his head. "I found a guy at Overstreet Landing thinks he might have seen it once. Whatever that's worth."

"And my rifle? Nobody's tried to pawn it, I reckon."

Futch sat up in his chair. "Pawn it? You obviously don't know the value of that rifle. I looked it up. A Winchester *one of one thousand* in good condition is worth a small fortune. Could be as much as two hundred thousand. Speaking of which, did your father find the serial number?"

226

Bodie shook his head. "I reckon Granddaddy never got around to writin 'em down."

"Well, in this case, it probably doesn't matter. Your rifle is very rare. If one is sold, regardless of the serial number, there's a good chance we'll find out about it. Honestly, though, him trying to sell it is about the only hope we've got. If he just sits on it… Well, if he does that, all bets are off, so to speak."

"Yessir."

Futch set the cup on the floor and rose from his chair. He stretched and looked at Miss Ella. "I thank you for the coffee, ma'am."

Miss Ella smiled and nodded.

He gazed at the flatwoods to the north. "It sure is pretty out here. Peaceful. Gloriously quiet." He turned suddenly to look at Bodie. He reached into his pant pocket and brought out a folded sheet of paper. "I almost forgot. This is for your father."

Bodie reached and took the paper. He didn't ask what it was. He didn't have to.

"He told me about your situation, and I said I'd see what could be done."

"Situation?"

"The burial mounds. He said you wanted to save them."

Bodie's eyes brightened. "The Indian graves?"

Futch nodded.

"Our lawyer said there was nothin could be done."

"Well your lawyer was mistaken. Give that to your father. It spells everything out."

\*

New Year's eve Abby drove him to the old homeplace. It was late afternoon and in the sky the clear promise of a cold night. They took the hound, Old Joe, and they built a roaring fire in the yard with the dog sitting its haunches and watching and waiting. And when the sun dipped from sight, they walked the hound to the edge of the hammock and stopped and stood gazing out over the land, three hearts beating, the evening suddenly and profoundly quiet, as if God Himself had shushed the world. "Hunt 'em up," Bodie commanded. The black-and-tan launched soundlessly forward into the thickening darkness, and they humans returned to the fire.

They sat close with the night descending and the flames writhing in their eyes. They waited and they uttered not a word, and when the night was full grown there came from the surrounding darkness a single mournful cry, a rolling bawl that prickled the skin and caused nape hairs to stand and dance, a cry touching a part of the soul long dead in most, a part surely doomed in us all, a wild petition that haunted the imagination even after dampening and tailing off to a deafening silence. And then there came another.

In the fire's vague light they looked knowingly at one another, and they rose and walked out to stand beneath Orion and a billion others. They stood very still and listening, Bodie leaning into his crutches, Abby into him, the hound opening again, farther away, excitement rising in its voice, then the dog reading scent as a musician reads sheet music, issuing bellow after bellow, a steady chop of song having lyrics old as time itself.

"God, I love that sound," said Bodie.

Abby pressed closer. She nuzzled his neck and kissed his cheek. "God, I love you."

He turned and they kissed.

With the hound's song fading northward, Abby said: "Happy New Year." And when Bodie did not reciprocate, she was not surprised. In his silence, she clearly heard him crying, and she understood completely.

\*

The last week of January a large sign appeared near the mouth of the ranch road. He first saw it when his mother drove him to have the casts removed from his arm and leg. Future site of *Prosperity,* the veritable billboard read. *A Planned Gated Community.* Below the words was a color-coded map of the world to come, an artist's rendition of the future paradise. And on the map, the cemetery and the area around the former ranch headquarters were crosshatched with lines, indicating they were not part of the development. Seeing this did not surprise Bodie. What surprised him was that a small portion of Orange Hammock—the exact location of the Indian graves—was similarly depicted.

"Look at that," he said, gesturing with a hand so that Angela might see.

"Look at what?"

"It shows the burial mounds as private property. It's not part of their stupid *Prosperity.*

Angela beamed. "That's cause it's not going to be. Your father forced them to set aside an acre—to preserve the graves."

Bodie looked at her and looked at the sign. "That statute Mr. Futch dug up?"

228

Angela nodded. "Florida Statute 827.05. The state archeologist confirmed they were graves. Excalibur gave up the acre to avoid a drawn-out eminent domain battle with the state."

Bodie looked at his mother. He chuckled and shook his head. "How'd you remember a number like that?"

Angela looked right and left and then eased her Explorer forward onto Canoe Creek Road. She looked at Bodie and smiled. "I helped draft the letter to the state archeologist."

"You helped Daddy?"

She nodded.

Bodie was silent for some time. He sat gazing out the passenger window until they reached Highway 192. Then he looked at his mother and said: "Thanks, Momma. I really appreciate what y'all did."

Angela simply smiled.

*

In the days following he began walking in the late-afternoon, exercising his newly liberated leg, limping noticeably at first, but gradually regaining his old athleticism. One day, when returning from one of these workouts, his father sat waiting for him on the front porch. A day with no wind. The sky a gray dome empty of all life. The threat of rain palpable in every breath of air Bodie tasted. When nearing the front stoop, he noticed his father's eyes were smiling.

"Feels like it's fixin to flood," Bodie said, turning and settling on the steps to remove his boots.

"Let it flood. You can use the rain. Your grass is lookin right parched."

Gingerly removing his left boot, Bodie paused to look over his shoulder. "*My* grass."

"It's yours now. I'm buyin me a piece of land."

Bodie half turned on the step. "You are? Where?"

"Just below Fort Drum. It's only a couple hundred acres but it's pretty. At least, the parts I've seen in pictures are pretty—appears to have a lot of palm hammock, and a stretch of creek runnin through it that's sposed to be chocked full of warmouth perch and stumpknockers."

"You mean you bought it without ever seein it?"

Seth nodded. "I put a deposit down."

Bodie shook his head. "But I don't understand. Two hundred acres ain't big enough."

"It's big enough for me. And plenty big for my grandkids to ramble when you and Abby come to visit."

"You're aimin to live down there."

Seth nodded. "It's got a nice frame house and a good barn. All the comforts I'll need."

Bodie turned from his father and sat staring blankly at his diminished left ankle. "What does Mama think about it?"

Seth stopped his rocker. He leaned forward a bit. "You reckon Abby will want to live here?"

"Sir?"

"After the weddin, I mean. I'm givin y'all the house and land here. You think she'll like the idea?"

Bodie looked at his father and turned and looked across the pasture at the barn. "I expect she will."

Seth studied his son. "You don't seem all that excited yourself. You don't like the idea?"

"No sir. It ain't that. You know I love this place. It's just that things been changin so fast lately. I reckon I'm scared to feel much one way or the other." He turned and looked at his father. "That make any sense?"

Seth sat back in his chair. He rocked. "All the sense in the world. You get to workin for Bill, things will settle down. You'll get back to normal."

He gazed at his grandfather's house, Miss Ella hanging clothes on the line in the side yard. Simply seeing her there was comforting. "You reckon it still exists?"

"Do I reckon *what* still exists?"

"Normal."

Seth did not reply. He could only rock the chair. He could not bring himself to mouth the only answer he himself believed to be true. Finally, he said: "Why don't you drive down there with me tomorrow—take a couple of days and walk the place out, see what I'm gettin into?"

Bodie looked. "You're goin tomorrow?"

"I planned on it."

Bodie shook his head. "I can't go tomorrow."

"What you got that can't wait?"

Bodie dipped his head. "Well, me and Abby…"

Seth smiled. "You don't have to say anymore," he said.

**28**

**When Seth left** for Fort Drum at dawn the next morning, Bodie hurried to his room and got a small canvas tote bag he'd packed the night before. He carried the bag to his truck and set it on the seat and got in and drove to the barn. There, he got Onnie's catchrope from the tackroom and got back in the truck and headed for the highway.

After gassing up in Kenansville, he drove highway four-forty-one south, crossing highway sixty at Yeehaw Junction a little past eight o'clock A few minutes later, fearful that he may encounter his father, he practically held his breath while zipping past tiny Fort Drum. Then he relaxed a little. Virtually no traffic. Mile after mile of pine and palmetto flatwoods. He reached and pulled a roadmap from his tote bag and stole glances at the route he'd highlighted weeks before. "West on sixty-eight," he said to himself, "then another hour and a half, maybe two."

It was nearly eleven o'clock when the turnoff for county road six-twenty-one loomed and then passed on his left. His heart raced as he slowed the truck and began looking for Cowhouse Road. When he saw its marker ahead, he began to sweat. It was happening. He was making it happen, morphing the hazy dream he'd conjured for weeks into startlingly clear reality.

When he made the turn onto the southbound road, nothing surprised him, the scene almost exactly as Earth Viewer had foretold. He drove a few hundred yards then pulled off the pavement onto the road shoulder. With the engine idling, he reached into the bag and withdrew his father's revolver. He checked the long straightaway ahead, the rearview mirror. No vehicles. He loaded the magnum with six cartridges, closed the cylinder and laid the weapon on the seat next to his leg. Then he took a deep breath and pulled back onto the road. He drove slowly, scanning ahead for mailboxes, row upon row of orange trees passing on his left, pasture land dotted with range cattle on his right. A cloudless sky. Warm for February. He drove, and soon it was there on his left: a pair of mailboxes, one of which bore the number 9, the name L. Biggs stenciled in black letters.

Stopping the truck, he sat and studied the dirt lane traversing an orange grove to a cluster of old oaks a few hundred yards east. A glint of tin escaping the oaks' dark green canopy. He glanced at the pistol on the seat. Then he eased the truck into the lane, driving forward at a crawl. Upon clearing the citrus trees, the sandy ruts of the lane began a gentle bend to the right and a clapboard house loomed ahead in the small cluster of oaks. A red Dodge pickup parked on the Bahia grass lawn, parallel to the home's raised porch. A trailered bassboat north of the truck, its metal- flake finish sparkling in the late-morning sun.

When Bodie rolled to a stop in the yard, a rangy redbone hound dropped from the porch and trotted to his door, the dog periodically pointing its nose skyward to howl his arrival. The instant he switched off the truck's engine, the hound fell silent and stood eyeing him with its head cocked and its tail whipping lazily from side to side. As Bodie swung his door open, a large man stepped from the house onto the porch, a barefoot man with thick black hair combed straight back, checked flannel shirt untucked and tenting a substantial belly, baggy jeans.

Stepping to the ground, Bodie clicked the door shut then removed his hat and dropped it back in the truck's cab, landing it directly atop the revolver. He spoke to the dog, and the hound sidled to him, its tail wagging, its nose lifting.

"He won't bite," called the man on the porch.

Bodie stroked the dog's head once then proceeded to the porch. He stopped at the foot of the steps and looked up at the man. "Mr. Biggs?" he said.

"Yes sir. You lookin for a guide?"

Bodie shook his head. "Nosir. I'm not here to fish. I'm lookin for a man. I was hopin you could tell me where to find him."

Biggs sidestepped until in front of a wooden rocker then sat in it and began to rock. "Well Red says you're all right, so come on up here and take a load off. You want somethin cold to drink? I got beer and soda."

Bodie stepped up to the porch. "No thank you, Mr. Biggs. I'm kind of in a hurry." Stepping closer, he extended a hand to the seated Biggs and Biggs offered his and they shook and then Bodie turned and sat in a straight-backed chair with a cowhide seat. He reached into his shirt pocket and withdrew a curled bit of paper. He briefly tried to straighten the address label then gave up and handed it across to Biggs. "I peeled this off a magazine I found in a airboat."

Upon reading the label, Biggs' expression changed. He suddenly looked ill. "Guns and Ammo," he said.

"Yessir. That was the magazine. You know where I can find the feller that owns that airboat?"

Biggs shifted his gaze from the label to the orange grove bordering his yard. "The airboat black?" he said.

"Yessir. All black, with *Lusus Naturae* painted on the rudders. That's Latin— means freak of nature."

"Freak is right," Biggs said below his breath. He studied Bodie. "This feller, he a friend of yours?"

Bodie shook his head. "No sir," he said. "He took somethin belongs to me. I'm tryin to get it back."

"And you don't know his name?"

"No sir. I was hopin you did."

Biggs stared again at the grove. "Well I don't either," he said.

Bodie was silent. Finally, he said: "You don't know how he come to have your magazine?"

Biggs waved a hand in the air. "Oh I know that all right. I watched him take it off my nightstand—right after I waked up in the middle of the night with him standin over me."

Bodie leaned forward in his chair, listening intently.

Biggs shook a finger at him. "You might want to think twice about confrontin that man—if that's what you aim to do."

"Yessir. I've done that."

"You done what?"

"I've thought about it a whole lot."

"Oh. Well good. What's he got of yours that's so important?"

"It ain't what he's got. It's how he went about gettin it."

"And how's that?"

"He killed my best friend."

Biggs leaned forward and spat on the ground below the porch. "That don't surprise me none. I figured he had it in him." He raised an arm and pointed at his dog, his hound now curled in a ball and dozing in shade afforded by Bodie's truck. "Old Red there's a good judge of character, and he's been terrified of that man since he showed up here last August."

"So you're sayin he's still around here?"

Biggs shifted his position in the rocker. He looked at the lane leading to his house and he looked at Bodie. "Now listen here … What did you say your name was?"

"I didn't say. I figured it best you not know it."

Biggs seemed to study the porch floor. He looked at Bodie. "Why don't we get the law out here? I'd hate to see a young feller like you get hurt and all."

Bodie leaned and spat in the Bahia grass. He looked Biggs in the eye. "No sir. I need to do this myself—so I know it's done right."

Biggs leaned forward and cupped his face in his hands. "Hell," he said. "You're liable to get us both killed." He straightened and looked at Bodie. "That man kills you, the next thing he's gonna do is come up here and kill me."

Bodie rose from his chair. "Well I thank you for your time, then." He turned and started down the steps.

"Where you goin?"

"I'm fixin to follow this drive on back behind your house," Bodie said over his shoulder, continuing to walk toward his truck. "There's two mailboxes out there on the hardroad."

Biggs pried himself from the rocker, throwing up a hand like a referee calling a foul. "Wait just a dang minute," he said.

Bodie stopped and turned to face the man.

"He ain't there. He left out of here early this mornin. But he's liable to come back anytime. You go drivin in that way, he's gonna know you're there."

Bodie shrugged. "Well, tell me how to go—so he won't know."

"Shit," said Biggs. He briefly stood mumbling to himself, then he pointed beyond Bodie. "Go back out to the damn pavement. A couple hundred yards south they's a grove road will take you back behind my rental." He paused and stepped and stood with his hands on his hips. "And don't holler for no help from me, cause I won't be here. I'm takin  Red and goin to Sebring for a couple of days. That feller thinks I wasn't here, maybe he won't want to kill me too."

Bodie smiled and raised a hand goodbye before turning and hurrying to his truck. Once he'd climbed behind the wheel and started the engine, the redbone hound slowly rocked to its feet and stretched and trotted for the house.

Biggs stood the porch until the orange grove erased Bodie's truck. Then he turned to go inside. "Cowmen," he said, shaking his head. "Never seen one yet wasn't hardheaded as hell."

\*

A cold front crept in during the night, rendering his return trip home a gauntlet of swirling wind and rain. He drove gripping the steering wheel with both hands, leaning forward and sighting through the ragged sweeps of his one functional wiper. Slow going, a full four hours just to reach Canoe Creek Road. By the time he turned onto the ranch road, the new gray day had formed, the grade a muddy mess and lined with rain-speckled pickups, their windows fogged opaque by frustrated workmen waiting out the rain. Bleary-eyed and exhausted, he drove past the worker's trucks, through the land already cleared and on into the woods yet untouched by the hungry machines, fighting to stay awake, to keep his truck in the center of the slick grade. He drove and his home was soon there, the house looming dreamlike far across the rain glistened flatwoods, a welcome sight indeed had his father's truck not been parked in front of it. No longer sleepy, he braked to a halt, his eyes darting between the distant crewcab and the rifle lying next to him, his old Winchester propped muzzle-down against the seat. He sat for a long moment, the mindless wiper keeping perfect time with the beat of his heart. Then he took a deep breath, exhaled an expletive and drove on.

He entered the house carrying both canvas bag and rifle in one hand, with a single hope swirling mantra-like in his mind. But that hope dashed instantly by his father's presence at the kitchen table.

Seth looked up, his eyes drawn immediately to the Winchester, as if the rest of his world had gone white and the rifle alone was left to see. Save for his jaw going slack, he briefly seemed incapable of movement. Then his eyes slowly panned upwards and focused on his son's.

"Hey," Bodie said. He shifted his weight from one leg to the other, then looked down at the wet boots he'd not remembered to remove.

Seth dropped his gaze to the table top, on it a large topographical map trying to curl at its edges but held in check by the gator ashtray, a steaming mug of coffee. A pack of cigarettes and a Zippo lighter to one side. He reached and pulled a cigarette from the pack and popped it in his mouth. He got the lighter and thumbed it open and struck a flame. After lighting the cigarette, he said: "Welcome home," his voice having an unmistakably dour ring to it.

"I wasn't expectin you to be here."

"Obviously," said Seth, waving his cigarette at the Winchester. "Were you figurin to keep that from me forever?"

"No sir. I didn't really figure much past the goin and gettin it part."

Seth smoked. "Thought we were gonna forget that man."

"I never said that."

Seth looked him up and down. "You all right?"

"Yessir. I'm fine."

"How bout that man? How's he doin?"

"He ain't dead, if that's what you're askin."

"I'm askin what happened. I want to know everything, beginning to end."

With his free hand Bodie removed his hat and hung it on a wall peg. He turned and stepped to the kitchen counter. After setting the bag on the floor, he reached and tore several paper towels from the roll mounted above the sink. He then turned back facing his father and began wiping the Winchester dry using the wadded-up towels. "About all I can tell you right now is I handled the situation. I'll tell you everything eventually, just not right now."

Seth stubbed his cigarette out in the gator. "You're beginnin to piss me off," he said, his face flushing with color.

"Well. I don't mean to. Just don't want you gettin in trouble over somethin I did. I expect the law will pay us a visit before too long. When they do, the less you know the better."

Seth reached and got another cigarette from the pack. After lighting up, he slammed the lighter to the table. "How am I to protect you, if I don't know anything?"

Bodie laid the rifle and towels on the counter. "I'm pretty sure I won't need protectin, if you'll just let me handle it."

"You're *pretty* sure?"

"Yessir, I am."

"How many laws did you break?"

236

"A few, I reckon. But I ain't done nothin I'm ashamed of—nothin at all."

Seth smoked. He stared blankly at the map before him. "How come you didn't ask for my help?" he said.

Bodie leaned against the counter, gripping its edge with his hands. "I figured you'd try and stop me." He watched his father, waiting for a response. When none came, he continued. "Besides, I didn't want no help. It was somethin I needed to do for me—for me and Onnie." He crossed his arms about his chest. "I needed to know I still *could* do somethin."

Seth looked at him. "Somethin to prove you wasn't paralyzed for life, you mean?"

Bodie's eyes widened. He nodded. "Yessir. Exactly."

Seth laid his cigarette in the gator and stood and walked to within a step of his son. "You couldn't save Granddaddy from dying, and you couldn't save the ranch. You couldn't even keep your mama and me from splittin up. But you sure as hell found that man and got your rifle back."

Bodie nodded, his eyes beginning to swim.

Seth reached out his hands and grasped his son by the shoulders, pulled him in and embraced him as though he may never let go, a gesture completely out of character, something he had no recollection of ever having done before. As he clung to Bodie, he briefly struggled to find the right words before concluding that none were needed, that holding his son was enough.

\*

The law finally came calling five weeks later. Just after sunset on the Ides of March. Detective Lee Futch and a younger deputy named Johnson, arrived just after Bodie got home from work at Thompson Farms. Seth and Bodie invited the men in and the four of them claimed chairs at the kitchen table while the night settled over all outside.

"Y'all like somethin to drink?" asked Seth.

Futch reached and loosened his tie. He looked left at the young deputy then looked at Seth. "No thank you. We're fine. We stopped and had supper on the way out." He then looked at Bodie and said: "Freak of nature."

Fashioning a puzzled look, Bodie said, "What?"

"Freak of nature—it's what the words on that guy's boat meant. They're Latin:

*Lusus Naturae*, freak of nature."

Seth leaned forward. "You found his boat?"

"Found him," Futch said. "At least, we're pretty sure it's him." He reached into his breast pocket and withdrew a stack of photographs and, after sorting through them, passed one across the table to Bodie. "This fellow look familiar?"

Bodie took the picture, turned it right side up and studied it. A photo of a corpse lying on a steel gurney. "Damn," he said. "He's dead. What happened to him?"

"Is it him?"

"Yessir. It's him."

"Are you certain?"

Bodie nodded. "Bad as he looks, it's him."

"He was dead when his landlord found him—died of dehydration according to the Highlands County Coroner."

Seth reached and took the photo from Bodie. "Jesus," he said upon viewing it. "How does a man go about dyin of dehydration in Florida?"

Deputy Johnson rocked back in his chair. "He gets somebody to tie him to his bed," he offered, "tie him up so good that no way in hell he's ever going to get loose without help."

Neither Seth nor Bodie said anything. They both continued to watch the deputy as though awaiting further explanation.

Futch slid another photo across to Bodie, saying: "This picture was taken before they cut him loose."

Bodie looked. "Looks like a catchrope," he said.

"It's a lariat," Johnson injected.

Futch frowned, flashed the deputy a why-don't-you-just-shut-the-hell-up look. He then looked at Bodie and nodded. "I guess you could say somebody caught him with it, all right."

Seth studied the picture. Then he looked at Futch. "Where's this at? You mentioned Highlands County. Where in Highlands?"

"In the middle of nowhere," said Futch. "A little place called Lorida."

Seth nodded. "I know Lorida—it's just north of Lake Istokpoga." He turned and looked at Bodie. "But you said this feller didn't sound like no local." He looked at Futch. "Who is he? Where'd he *really* come from?"

Futch leaned back in his chair. He scratched the back of his neck. "We don't know who he is. FDLE has exhausted all means of identifying him and come up empty. They know he came to Lorida last August, the landlord told them that, but they don't know for sure where he came from. The airboat was stolen from a dealer down in Homestead, early in August, the business owner murdered in the process."

Seth slid the photo back across the table. "So he'd definitely killed before?"

Futch nodded. "Many times, it seems. Besides the airboat, they found numerous valuables in that little house and yard. All sorts of stuff, luxury autos, paintings, jewelry, firearms, rare coins—even an antique gas pump supposedly worth a fortune. So far FDLE has connected him to nine murders by tracing different items, and I'm told there's sure to be more, maybe a lot more."

"What about Bodie's rifle?" asked Seth. "Will he get it back when they're done?"

Futch opened his mouth to answer, but Johnson was already talking. "Wasn't no Winchester one of one thousand," he said, blurting the words out as if having held them in far too long.

Futch briefly shut his eyes, an overt attempt to compose himself. Opening them, he looked squarely at the deputy and said: "There was considerable cash found in the house, so he likely sold some things. You live on a cash only basis, you have to sell something once in a while."

The muscles in Johnson's jaws visibly rippled. "What about the lariat?" he said.

"What about it?" replied Futch.

"The report said tests proved it was the real deal—that it had been used on cattle and horses."

"I know what the report said. What are you trying to say?"

"I'm saying that whoever killed that man probably brought the lariat with him."

Futch, looking at Bodie and Seth rather than the deputy, replied: "So you think it was likely somebody in the cattle business that did it?"

Johnson nodded. "I think it's a strong possibility." He looked at Bodie. "You've got a rope like that, don't you?"

Bodie looked at the man, then reached a hand forward and gestured to the photograph on the table. "Yeah, I do, but that ain't it."

Seth leaned forward, resting his elbows on the table and glaring at Johnson. "It ain't mine either," he said, "just in case you were gonna ask."

Before Johnson could respond, Futch suddenly stood and gathered in the two photos. "Well I guess we're done here," he said, standing the pictures on edge and rapping them once on the table before stuffing them into his shirt pocket. "The positive ID is what we came for, so we'll leave and let you get some supper. Sorry for the inconvenience."

Seth and Bodie stood. Seth extended his hand to Futch. "No problem, Lee," he said, shaking the detective's hand. "Thanks for the information. It's good to know that feller's no longer a threat."

Bodie also shook Futch's hand, saying, "Yessir. That goes for me too."

Deputy Johnson, who had remained seated, rose from his chair and turned toward the door. "I'll be in the car," he said over his shoulder.

Everyone stood silently looking at one another until a car door was heard to slam outside. Seth then said: "I take it he thinks we had somethin to do with that man's death."

Futch nodded. "Yeah, well, he's young. He doesn't quite understand what's important yet." He turned for the door. "But he will, if he sticks with this job long enough." He stepped through the doorway but then stopped and half-turned to look at Bodie. "Oh by the way, Bodie," he said.

"Yessir."

"You should know that I will no longer be looking for your rifle."

Bodie stepped and stood. "You won't?"

Futch turned and started down the steps. "No I won't. Got too many things more important to occupy my time."

Bodie looked at his father, and Seth simply shrugged. Then the two of them stood watching the Mercury go, watching until the waning lights were abruptly snuffed-out by the cypress head far to the north. Then Bodie said: "He knows."

Seth turned and stepped inside. He walked to the refrigerator and pulled open its door and stooped to stare inside. "I think strongly suspects is more like it. Did you intend to kill that man, leavin him tied up like that?"

Bodie sat at the table. "Reckon I did, but I told myself I was leavin it up to Providence."

Seth looked. "Providence?"

"Yessir. I figured whatever happened after I left was meant to be. If he had any friends, he'd probably survive. If he didn't, which is what I really believed to be the case, he was dead, cause no way was he gettin loose on his own."

"You tie a mean knot. I can vouch for that."

Bodie nodded.

"Well how did you do it? How did you get the drop on him. Did you have to fight him?"

"Nosir. Wasn't no fight. He wasn't home when I got down there, so I just slipped in through a back window and waited on him. He showed up a little after dark, and I cracked him over the head with your revolver soon as he stepped through the door—tied him up fore he came to."

"Damn," said Seth. "Well did you talk to him, try to find out who he was?"

"I tried, but he never said a thing other than somethin about time and chance happenin to us all. He just lay there lookin like he didn't have a care in the world, for the most part."

Seth shook his head. Then he turned and reached into the refrigerator, pulling out a large bowl covered with foil. "Some of this leftover chili all right with you?"

Bodie didn't answer. He stared blankly at the wall.

"Bodie."

Bodie looked.

"This chili all right with you?"

"Yessir. I reckon so."

"You all right."

"I can't get them pictures out of my head."

"You forget them pictures. That man got what he deserved. What you did's no different than shootin a rabid dog. No telling how many lives you saved, so you just put them pictures away for good."

# 29

**The day following,** after feeding the stock and the hound Old Joe, he fetched the quart of Wild Turkey from the tack room and carried it to his truck. He wrapped the bottle in an old towel and stashed it behind the seat and climbed in and started the truck. He drove north with the sun approaching its zenith. As he neared the paved road, a revolting sight unfolded before him.

Three big diesel rigs were parked one behind the other on the shoulder of the grade. Three front-loaders and a D-9 Caterpillar were perched atop the lowboy trailers, a half-dozen pickups parked here and there in the flatwoods west of the grade. Beyond the tractor-trailers was a television news van and, next to it, a gathering of suited men and a lone woman, the lot of them wearing hardhats and holding shovels. His Aunt Jo Beth scarcely paid him a glance as he eased his truck past the groundbreaking ceremony, nor him her. He merely drove on without looking back.

He parked beneath the ancient oaks south of the church and switched off the truck and stepped out into the small gravel lot. He got the bottle from behind the seat and shut the door and followed the shaded walkway leading to the cemetery. A stiff breeze from the west. Cool. The dank smell of the river was palpable in the air, the tea-colored water gliding soundlessly below the rim of the bluff. He walked, and when coming to the Osteen plot, he stopped and stood gazing at the freshly hewn granite stone now marking Onnie's grave. He removed his hat and surveyed with his eyes the length and breadth of the graveyard. Not a living soul.

He dropped his hat behind him and knelt down and stood the bottle in front of his knees. "Hey," he said. "You ready to have that drink?"

He listened. The wind sighed through the limbs overhead. In the distance, a bluejay mimicked a hawk. Silence.

Raising the bottle, he broke the seal with his thumbnail and twisted off the cap. He reached the bottle forward and tilted it, pouring a small umber pool in the sand before the stone. Then he righted himself and raised the bottle's mouth to his own. He drank, and a shiver coursed through his body. He shook his head and replaced the cap and set the bottle on the ground. He turned to his left and reached with his hands and began excavating the sandy loam, digging dog-like until fashioning a hole of some significance. Then he stopped digging and turned and fetched the bottle and stood it in the hole. He buried the bottle, raking in the dirt and then patting it down.

When he stood and gathered in his hat, the drone of an airboat far upriver captured his attention. Faint. He cupped an ear and listened until the sound bled to nothingness. Then he quit listening and focused his eyes on the grim ground before his feet. He said: "I found him, Onnie. I found him and I made sure he don't never hurt no one else. I ..." He sagged to his knees. His head bowed, he clutched his hat and began to sob uncontrollably. He wept for some time, then he wiped his eyes and said: "You'd think I'd feel better, with that man gone and all. But I don't." Bodie cut his eyes to the granite marker. He silently read the inscription then set his hat on his head and touched its brim and said, "I got to go, bud. But I'll be back, so save me a drink." He then started to turn but stopped short and looked back at the grave. "I almost forgot. I used your catchrope on that bastard. It worked real good."

\*

It was getting dark by the time he reached Angela's apartment. His mother had prepared for him a pork roast and all the trimmings, and he ate until he hurt. After supper they moved outside onto her small balcony. They sat in uncomfortable wrought-iron chairs and simply visited. They conversed a good long while, speaking mostly of Abby and the coming wedding, talking in raised voices to overcome traffic noise rising from the street below, a pleasant evening until Bodie suddenly redirected the flow of conversation.

"Daddy bought a place," he said.

Angela scarcely blinked at his announcement. "I know."

"You know?"

"He called to boast three days ago."

Bodie squirmed in his chair. "Well? What do you think?"

"I think it was nice of him to give you and Abby a first home—awfully nice."

"I mean about the new place. He said it's real pretty."

Angela stifled a laugh. "Pretty! It's in Fort Drum, for heaven's sake. Have you been to Fort Drum?"

Bodie frowned. "I been through there a bunch of times. Seems like a nice place to me."

Angela rose from her chair and stepped to the railing and stood looking down at the passing cars. "Look, Bodie," she said. "You might as well face it. People have different perceptions of good and bad."

Bodie turned his hat in his hands. He looked into its bowl. "Yeah, I reckon they do."

"It's just the way it is."

"Yes, ma'am."

He sensed her turning to look at him. He felt her gaze. That he should reciprocate occurred to him, but he could not coax his eyes from the hat. He could look any man in the eye—any woman for that matter. He always could. But his mother was somehow different. His mother was his mother.

He left for home a little after ten o'clock. A grand, snowy moon suspended in the heavens, full grown and justly lording over the night. Traffic was heavy initially, but tailed off dramatically once he turned onto Canoe Creek Road. He drove lost in thought, his mind flitting from one depressing notion to another. His headlights painted patches of low-hanging fog hovering about the road, mist that shape-shifted and swirled with his passing. He drove, and was almost to the ranch road when a fawn-colored form caught the tail of his eye, an elongated aberration in the roadside Bahia grass. A road-killed deer, he figured, but then realized there was something odd about what he had glimpsed. The lines, the dimensions didn't register. The object was by him so quickly. After hesitating briefly, he let off the gas and touched the brake.

When the truck came to a stop, he sat for a moment looking and thinking, the truck ticking at idle. No sign of another vehicle. The far-reaching cast of his headlights was the only artificial light, everywhere else the hoary glow of moonlight. He slipped the gearshift into reverse and began backing, gripping the seatback with his right hand and sighting through the rear window. And when the hemisphere of light guiding him revealed the object, he cut the wheel and backed onto the road's shoulder. He shut off the lights and the engine and again inspected the darkened roadway. No cars. He opened his door and got out and quietly clicked the door shut. He stood for a moment, letting his eyes adjust to the moonlight. He had no flashlight but it didn't matter. In just a few seconds he could see remarkably well. He walked north along the roadside, straining to make out the dim entity in the grass a few yards away. When within a few feet of it, he no longer had to strain. He stopped and stood with his hands on his hips, eyeing the corpse. A few seconds on he inhaled deeply. When he exhaled, it was to proclaim: "Son of a bitch."

The great cat lay on its left side, its legs positioned as though death had caught it in mid-stride, had ordained that it lope through eternity. Bodie hunkered down and reached and stroked the thickly thatched hair along its back, the animal still warmer than the air. He touched the whiskered muzzle. Sticky wet. When he withdrew the hand, a dark smear painted his fingers, a smear that was not red in the moonlit world but one that was most certainly blood. He could smell it was blood. He shifted his gaze to the muscled shoulder, to the slash of white that was an obvious flaw in an otherwise perfectly camouflaged creature. He ran his fingers over the area, a raised and jagged feel, a fault line, a keloid scar. Retracting his hand, he stood and looked up and down the highway. He removed his hat and set it back on his head. He stepped and stood, and then he turned and strode to his truck.

Backing the Ford to within a few feet of the panther, he left the engine idling and got out and stepped to the rear. When lowering the tailgate, he was startled by the sudden appearance of his shadow in the truck's bed. "Crap," he breathed. A pair of headlights approached from the north. He quickly ducked down and grabbed the cat by the scruff of its neck and the base of its tail, lifting and turning and swinging the dead animal onto the truck's tailgate, but a rear paw hitting the lip of the gate and stopping the hindquarters from loading. Grunting audibly, he braced a hip against the cat's back and grabbed the tail with both hands to finish the job. Then, his truck now fully illuminated, he shoved the carcass farther into the bed and raised the gate shut. He did not turn and look at the approaching lights. He simply stood with his arms draped over the tailgate, catching his breath and listening to a closing vehicle that was most certainly slowing, a diesel truck that was probably going to stop. "Damn," he said. "With my luck, it has to be the game warden."

When the truck pulled onto the shoulder and stopped, Bodie turned to face it. The headlights blinding but then winking-out and only amber parking lights left to glow the truck's position, the motor rattling at idle. "You got trouble, Bodie?" a voice called.

Bodie relaxed a little. "No sir. Nothin recent, Mr. Costine."

The old man stepped down from his truck and shut the door and came forward, the white shirt he wore rendering him easy to see. "I thought maybe you'd done tore up your truck on a deer."

"No sir. I ain't hit nothin."

"You didn't hit nothin?"

"No sir. What's got you out so late? You been to church?"

"Naw. I been to the picture show. A western called *Open Range*. You seen it?"

"No sir. I haven't."

"Old Robert Duval. Pretty good shoot-em-up."

"Yessir."

Costine leaned and spat. "I heard about y'all gettin shot out there. Looks like you healed up all right."

"Yessir. I'm doin pretty good."

"That's good." Costine rubbed his hands together briskly. He stomped his feet. "Well I'm bout to freeze standin here. Reckon if you ain't got no trouble I'll be goin."

"Well I sure appreciate you stoppin to check on me and all."

"I always stop, if it's somebody I know. Course these days that don't happen much. These days, seein somebody you know is a rare thing."

"Yessir, it surely is."

"Well I've got to go."

"Yessir. I'll be seein you."

The old man turned and began walking to his truck, lifting his knees inordinately high to avoid fowling his penny loafers in the tall grass. About halfway there, he suddenly stopped and turned around and stepped back to Bodie. He wagged a finger in the air. "Now listen here, Bodie Rawlerson. I'll not get a wink of sleep tonight if I leave here not knowin what you got in the bed of that truck."

Bodie stepped and stood. "I figured you seen me."

"I durn sure seen you loadin somethin. It's a deer, ain't it?"

"No sir. It's a panther."

"A what?"

"A panther."

The old man turned and looked out into the night. He looked at Bodie. "Well I don't know if I can believe that."

Bodie jerked a thumb over his shoulder. "I reckon he's still here. Why don't you see for yourself."

Costine immediately stepped to the truck. He placed his hands on the side rails and leaned to look in the bed. "I can't see..." He shaded his eyes with a hand. "That ain't no... Good God Almighty! It *is* a panther!"

"Yessir. A big male."

"Well what do you know about that? A sure enough panther. Did ya run him over?"

"No sir. Somebody else did. I just happened to see him layin here."

Costine stroked the cat's fur. "You got good eyes. Most people wouldn't know a panther from a petunia. He sure is handsome. You gonna skin him out?"

"No sir. I planned on buryin him."

Costine nodded. "You're better off doin that, I reckon. A panther skin liable to buy you a heap of trouble these days."

"Yessir."

"Well I sure am glad you showed him to me. It's somethin I never figured to see. Somethin truly special.

Bodie nodded his agreement.

"It's a shame he got hisself killed."

Nodding again, Bodie reached and scratched his neck. "Mr. Costine?"

"Yeah."

"They's probably a law against me buryin him, you know."

Costine spat in the grass. "Don't you worry. I ain't gonna tell nobody."

The old man stepped back from the truck and extended his hand. Bodie reached and they shook hands and the old man turned and high-stepped to his idling truck. He climbed behind the wheel. When he'd shut the door, he gave a little wave out the window and switched on the headlights and drove off into the night. Bodie stood watching him go until a distant bend in the road sequentially winked out the truck's tail lights. Then he himself got moving.

Once back on the highway, he almost missed the turnoff to the ranch road. Had it not been for all the heavy equipment parked there, he would have. The arched Curlew Cattle Company sign was gone, having been torn down and pushed into a pile of palmetto roots and small saplings. After making the turn, he stopped long enough to retrieve the sheet-metal sign and then drove on. The grade was now gouged and rutted, a barren void bordering the road for several hundred yards. The smell of wood smoke, diesel and turned ground. As he drove, a wind sprang up out of the west, a weak zephyr at first but building quickly to a near-gale. By the time he reached the cemetery, the natural world was in motion. The great oak's wandering limbs bowing and swaying in the moonlight, casting whickered shadows that writhed like ambiguous snakes over the sugar sand below.

He carried the panther from his truck draped over his shoulders, the shovel in his right hand, the long feline tail sawing stiffly in the wind, bobbing cadence to his wobbling stride. The cat was almost equal to his own weight, and every pound of it weighed heavily on his mending ankle. He walked, and when just beyond the Indian's grave, he stopped and settled to his knees. He bent forward in the manner of the truly humbled and let the great cat slide gently to the ground. When he rocked back upright, he became very still, sitting on the balls of his feet, looking and listening. There was no sound save for the steady thump of his heart, the wind soughing through the limbs of the oak. Next to his grandfather's headstone, the moon-lighted foil leaves of the artificial plant licked upward in the wind, danced in the wind. Cold flames. A fire, but no ordinary fire. And next to him, the round eyes of the magnificent panther gazing eternally, two diaphanous moons in which he could see nothing but his own twinned self. And when seeing himself in duplicate, he inhaled sharply and recoiled back on his heels. His eyes wide with wonder, he looked from the panther to the faux fire, to the old Indian's grave and the seamless dark beyond. He trembled and began to sweat profusely but, this time, he did not wake up.

\*

When just able to see the old oak, Abby exhaled a sigh of relief and halted her bay mare. She sat looking and listening, an exasperated look on her face. The buckskin Elvis stood cropping grass beneath the lone tree on the lakeshore, both horse and tree blackened to silhouette by the sun setting beyond. No wind. The lake a gleaming sheet of chromed metal, its far edge replicating the descending sun. From the northeast ebbed the sound of earthmovers, a din of growling and roaring incessant. She touched the bay's flanks with her heels and the horse sprang forward at a canter. Reaching the tree, she reined the horse in and dismounted and dropped the reins. The twin peaks of Bodie's knees were just visible beyond the oak's trunk, and she strode purposefully toward them.

"We need to talk," she said, clearing the oak's trunk in time to glimpse a pair of binoculars being quickly laid out of sight behind Bodie's leg.

Bodie, looking up and smiling awkwardly, subtly moved his arms sufficient to cover a Bible in his lap. "We do?"

Abby squatted and, bracing against the tree, settled at Bodie's side. "Yes. We do. I'm worried about you."

"I'm all right."

"You're not all right. You're mourning Onnie's death like it happened yesterday."

Bodie turned and gazed at the lake. "It ain't just him."

"Yeah. I'm listening."

"It's been everything. But I'm gonna be all right."

Abby gestured to the Bible in his lap. "You find something helpful in there?"

He followed her gesture and looked down. He shifted his back against the oak. "Oh, that. Thanks for not laughin."

"I would never laugh *at* you. But I have to admit, it does tickle me to know I'm not marrying a complete heathen."

"It was Granddaddy's. I brought it along to read Ecclesiastes. I sort of promised him I would."

"And?"

"I read it twice"

"You must've liked it."

"I did."

She admired his profile. She snaked an arm around his shoulders, the pulse of his presence instantly pumping comfort through her self entire. As the horizon claimed the last remnant of sun, the chromed lake reflected a riot of color. "Are your eyes going bad?"

"My eyes."

250

"I've never known you to use binoculars. Why now?"

He reached and shifted the binoculars' position on the ground and then returned his arm to rest on a knee. "They were granddaddy's, too. I was just tryin 'em out."

"Detective Futch told you that murderer is dead."

Bodie cut his eyes to look at her. "Yeah he did. He even showed me pictures."

"So why the binoculars?"

"I told you why."

Abby was silent. She watched the night slowly shrinking the lake, the world. "So that's what you've been doing all afternoon—reading the Bible and testing binoculars?"

Bodie pulled at some grass next to his leg. "They bulldozed the homeplace today."

Abby gave his shoulder a squeeze. "Bodie," she said.

"Yeah."

"You've got to start looking ahead. You can't change what's happened, so why dwell on it? It's a complete waste of time. It's like chasing the wind or something."

He looked at the pale oval her face had become. He smiled. "Now you sound like old King Solomon."

"Don't try to change the subject." She moved her hand to worry the hair on the back of his head, her fingers working delicately. "You aren't ever going to change, are you?"

"I hate change."

"I know that. But it doesn't answer my question."

"Reckon I can't change. I am what I am."

Abby was silent.

"Well. You asked me."

She leaned into him and gently kissed his cheek. "Yes I did," she said. "I just needed to hear you say it."

A pall of silence dropped suddenly over the land as the last earthmover switched off for the day. The subtle murmurings of existence returning instantly, emancipated by the same switch, a watery explosion down the shore, the whine of mosquitoes, an owl's call, and then another, the random and far off croaks of curlews passing high overhead, their white plumage gilded by a sun now lost to all save them.

251

Abby began counting lights across the water, her pointed finger bobbing white in the strengthening darkness.

Bodie watched her. "Don't that depress you?"

"What?"

"Countin them lights all the time."

"A little."

"Then why do it?"

"I don't know. I guess I just like to know what's coming."

"I know what's comin. Wish to hell I didn't."

"Why? Not knowing won't stop it."

Bodie reached and plucked his hat from the grass and set it on his head. He picked up the Bible and the binoculars and struggled to his feet.

Abby leaned her head back against the oak to look at him. "I take it we're leaving."

"I'm about to starve."

Abby stood. She reached and playfully jabbed his stomach with a finger. "Well praise the Lord." she said.

"Cause I'm hungry?"

"Cause you finally got a problem I can solve."

"You beat everything."

"Well I'm glad to hear it. Hope you still think so fifty years from now."

"I'll think it as long as I got a brain to think with."

"Forever, then?"

"I didn't say that. I can't say that. I ain't a kid no more."

"What?" Abby said. She grabbed hold of his arm and pulled him forward, like a mother might do her child. "Let's go," she said, "before I get too confused to cook."

When they went for the horses there was not yet a moon and the darkness loomed formidable, the horses moving like shadows of horses, tossing their heads and their bridles tinkling their whereabouts like bells rung for the blind. When they caught them up and mounted them, the horses stomped and stood and backed in tight circles as that part of them yet wild threatened revolt, a revolt that never materialized and never would. Then together they rode from beneath the old oak and into the just fell night, into their future, the days of trouble yet to come.

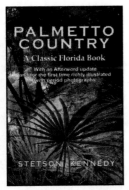